Turf and Surf

Who Owns Your Paradise

Bob Spearman

ISBN: 1495230414
ISBN 13: 9781495230417
Library of Congress Control Number: 2014901080
CreateSpace Independent Publishing Platform
North Charleston, South Carolina

To my lovely wife, Barb, who reveled with us as we lived through that time, and later conspired to write the story, typed my scribbles and endured endless edits.

To great friends, Billy & Steff, who lived the beach life and made it fun.

To Joanne Innes, Cindy Blackburn and Jane Bishop, all excellent authors, diligent editors and faithful friends who kept me in bounds and moving toward the goal.

Prologue

~

Paradise! At least to some, Myrtle Beach is their idea of paradise. This beach resort, also known as the Grand Strand, is fifty continuous miles of pristine beach.

Each Memorial Day weekend brings a tourist tidal wave to paradise, and life is full speed ahead. An exaggerated release of pent-up hormonal-driven desire spawns a unique beach-resort behavior, which transforms this otherwise-quiet beach town into a surreal, riotous setting for one hundred days each year, the summer season.

They get drunk, cruise Ocean Boulevard, build sand castles, play arcade games, and ride roller coasters and the Tilt-a-Whirl. They shop for beach souvenirs. They live incognito away from the small-town people who know them. They eat cotton candy and seafood and stay in hotels near the beach. The crowd does not watch in judgment here.

They all sing the praises of the unique regional sound known as "Carolina beach music." They know every word of every hit song. They dance a popular regional dance known as the Shag. They ride waves, swim, fight, meet summer loves, meet future spouses, and find seashells and sharks' teeth. Some drown, some spend a night in jail, and some never go home.

Every year they build more hotels, more roads, more restaurants, more golf courses, and more artificial Putt-Putt turf tactfully adorned with windmills and pirates. The greed that fuels the growth is blind to the erosion of the resort's appeal that brings the tourists, who bring the money. The undertow to control the turf is swift, powerful, and lethal.

Chapter 1

His terminal path was irreversible and had been certain from the moment he palmed the cash at the blackjack table. The greedy moment was his second chance. Once before, he had attempted to steal from them. It was only a small amount that would not be missed, or so he thought. But they caught him, and later in an isolated shed deep in the woods, he experienced what they called awareness training...and he suffered. He survived the test only to gain a renewed, but baseless, confidence.

Greed can blind the goodness of a soul. Its selfish nature ignores those things important to the rest of humanity, consumes more than its share, and discards its rubble. Greed cultivates only that which feeds its insatiable appetite.

As time passed, the fear and pain dissolved with the distance of the memory. He learned from the experience and now believed that he knew the unwritten rules crucial to his survival. He settled back into the routine of his job and yearned for acceptance into the family. His desire to be one of them was fueled by an internal fiery ambition, which caused him to forsake all who had loved him before, and this temptation for easy money made him a different man.

He had underestimated the pertinacious spirit and the tenacity of their stewardship regarding family money. The lesson they taught him that night in the shed had faded, giving way to the undeniable force of addictive greed, which romanced him and enticed him to take the short stack of hundreds left on the table by a distracted, inebriated gambler. He palmed it with a swift practiced motion; no one would know. The drunk was barely conscious and unaware, but the ever-watchful eyes had seen the quick hustle. They showed him the camera replay before his trip to this final place to endure their wrath.

Scars are etched and spoils discarded along greed's ugly trail. Greed is a cancer that tangles its suffocating tentacles to all it can reach and eats away the foundation of its subsistence. Greed devours and moves on to its next host. Greed teaches greed.

They tied him by his wrist to pilings under a dilapidated industrial dock on the Sampit River. The river branched and flowed in a deep channel previously used by ships that had served the Georgetown steel mill. The mill was closed and forgotten. Greed had converted this life-giving estuary into an abandoned, rust-colored wasteland. The murky channel was a frequent path for large bull sharks cruising upstream from the bay in search of schooling mullet and trout. Sharks would not overlook this tempting morsel for long.

Before the big predator arrived, the thief hung in the changing tides for two days with his mouth taped shut and his castrated loins slowly seeping his bodily fluids to mingle with the secretions of bloody chum bags secured about his waist. He was the anointed temptation and the warning. The water rose to his chin and receded to his waist in a slow, consistent, tidal cycle. He had guessed what might finally happen, but did not know how long before death would come. Anxious, but resigned to his fate, he wished the end to be now. He craved the satisfaction of relief, but there was no answer to his false prayer offered to a feigned religion.

The beast circled, moving faster as it sensed the source of the blood trail and tested the defenseless nature of the prey. It became more aggressive. He felt the first tearing punctures of the powerful, predatory attack as the hidden beast surged and ripped away the lower half of his body in one crushing bite. The attack was painful at first but ultimately delivered anticipated relief from his tortured trial. For a few short moments, he remained alive and conscious and watched as his life's blood drained away. He saw the mortal wound but did not dwell on the implication. The attack was fueled by hungry, gluttonous greed.

Greed is often without mercy.

He had lived a short, highly charged life on the edge, with all that a young single man could want, but he had wanted more. While seeking more than his due, he had crossed the avarice boundary patrolled by a greater greed, and then he paid. His termination was the justice dispensed by an unmerciful, pestilent force, a force he had once nourished, but never allied.

He no longer felt pain, released his apathetic grip on life, and floated, rising above the body that was once him, watching the shark attack again and again in a ravenous feeding frenzy that would not stop until the prey was consumed. His soul was already gone, maybe to his final paradise.

The setting sun illuminated the clouds in a peaceful orange-and-blue sky. His violent death did little to disturb nature's beauty at the end of this fine summer day.

Greed will prune the fresh buds of nature's spring
and sour the taste of its life's stream.

A young hitchhiker stood on a high bridge that crossed the Sampit River. He was tired and hungry, but he stopped to watch the sunset over the vast stretch of pine forest that swallowed the winding river to the west. Without concern he looked down the river channel to see thrashing water under an abandoned pier. The dim light and the distance to the pier conspired to obnubilate his view of the prey and the predator. The water settled to a calm, black surface. He quickly lost interest and looked back at the distant sunset, picked up his bag, and moved on. He was going to Myrtle Beach, and he was sure that life would be better.

Chapter 2

Battleship gray merged to powder blue as the eastern sky met the new day. Pelicans flying in a disciplined flight formation skimmed the glassy, rolling surf. Sandpipers raced along the seafoam cast to shore on the edge of each wave.

"I love this time of day. It's just so perfect." Edna sighed.

"Me too. I just wish it didn't come so early." Evelyn yawned and rubbed her eyes.

Each morning Edna and Evelyn walked a half block west from their apartment and crossed four lanes of asphalt, known as the Kings Highway, to purchase one of their little decadent pleasures: coffee and a warm Krispy Kreme doughnut. With the treats, they returned east two blocks, kicked off their flip-flops, and walked on the cool beach sand, to their favorite morning rendezvous off First Avenue South.

They enjoyed commanding views of the surf from this spot in front of the Swamp Fox Roller Coaster and Amusement Park. The two thirty-something friends relaxed on seats attached to either side of a lifeguard stand positioned near a high-tide beach drain know as the swash. While watching the calming turmoil of the surf, they savored each bite of the scrumptious, hot doughnuts. Both had a habit of dipping the sugared, caloric bombs into their coffee prior to each bite.

The early-morning salt air, the ocean's constant music, the sand creatures scampering for their morning meal, and the new beachcombers' bounty of shells left on the high tide were all things precious to these aging, but not old, former beach babes.

They had come to the beach during the most impressionable time of their young lives to experience the joy of the glitter and lights of Myrtle Beach in the summertime. At first, to stay or leave was an easy choice, but time rerouted the path to any other place. Each swore to the other she would never leave, and the promises had been kept, so far.

———————

As friends since elementary school, Edna and Evelyn had enjoyed the summer beach vacations of their youth. They had played all the Pavilion games, shared cotton-candy swirls, ridden go-carts and all the amusement park rides. Each had swooned over a beach romance, falling in love for a week with a guy they would never see again.

Edna and Evelyn lived in an affordable two-bedroom apartment over Eddie and Vera Rondell's garage. The girls had been renting this beach apartment from the Rondells for over ten years, and they had all grown to be like family.

Evelyn was Twiggy-cute, anorexic thin, and wore thick, black-rimmed glasses. She had straight black hair that she trimmed when the bangs hung over her eyes and had an uncanny ability to select unflattering fashion styles that hid her natural beauty. She was a prime candidate for a professional makeover.

With each of the many minimum-wage jobs on her Myrtle Beach resume, she left when the breaks were cut back, the boss was too bossy, or she just needed a change as a reminder that her dream was still possible. That new job would surely provide the bridge to greener grass and a path to her dream. She typically found the new patch of green grass to be maintained by similar gardeners.

For now Evelyn worked the two-to-ten shift at the Krispy Kreme doughnut shop. The shift was too late for breakfast and too early for the late-night pot-toker's feast. But someone was needed to tend the counter for that late-afternoon sugar urge and for those who craved the hot, sweet appetizer that Krispy Kreme had delivered in the South since 1937. While the Krispy Kreme was short on bridges, it provided rare opportunities to pick up extra cash tips to supplement her hourly minimum wage.

Evelyn lived for the coffee, her cigarette breaks, and the occasional big tipper, the guy who dropped by more for conversation and a break from loneliness than a doughnut. For a few minutes, they met each other's needs—a caffeine, sugary, afternoon high, mixed with a no-brain, incoherent conversation about the latest government-induced gripe, the sports report, or the weather. The tippers left thinking someone cared, and Evelyn left with a tip.

She held holy her ten-minute break allowed each hour by store management. The only smoke break location was out back on a concrete step, but in the heat or in the rain, Evelyn was there. For nine minutes and fifty-eight seconds, every hour, she sat on the back step thinking about her future and occasionally what her soul mate might be like when she finally found him. The available candidates were rare visitors at this job.

She wondered how long she would work the counter at this joint. Was she trapped in a life gradually morphing into someone she had never wanted to be? For now this beach resort was her place, her inescapable island of life.

She punched out at exactly ten every evening, a cigarette in her lips and a tired dream in her heart. When she left, she walked across Highway 17, the Kings Highway, to "her" happy hour at the Frisky Rabbit. She had a seat at the end of the bar that was always open for her. Each night Evelyn met her friend and soul mate, Edna, at the end of the bar, in the middle of life.

Edna still had the same curvaceous figure of her early twenties, with all the right parts in the perfect places. She dressed in a modest style but accentuated her positives and could still turn a few heads. Since her early teenage years, she had pampered her waist-length blond hair with expensive shampoos and one hundred brushes each and every night.

From the first week of her arrival at the beach, Edna had worked in a gift shop touted as the world-famous One-Eyed Flounder. She had worked her way up through the employment ranks of the Flounder, learning the retailing tricks required to succeed in the extremely competitive business of selling tourist trinkets in a coastal resort market.

She had toiled faithfully through the growth years to see each new addition to the One-Eyed Flounder as it slowly expanded upward and outward into a multilevel tourist bazaar. She was one of the few who could navigate the many aisles, rooms, and stairways without getting lost. She knew where every item in the store was supposed to be located.

On occasion and more often recently, she hinted to her supervisor, her supervisor's manager, and the storeowner that she felt capable and deserving of the opportunity to move into a management position or at least a floor supervisor position. Unfortunately, all of these growth opportunities were currently filled and were likely to remain that way, as the owner had overstocked the positions with relatives. Most were lazy, clueless, unmotivated, and overpaid. Edna continued to labor silently under the supervision of the owner's twenty-eight-year-old son, Darrell Jr.

———

All too quickly their morning routine was done, the sun was surprisingly hot in the early morning sky, the doughnuts were eaten, and the last sip of coffee emptied from their mugs.

"Ready to go?" Edna asked with an obvious reluctance to leave.

"No. But I guess it's time. You know I could sit here all day and play on the beach. The tourists aren't here yet, and the beach is so fresh and clean with all of the trash gone, but it won't be long. I see 'em coming already, one by one."

"Yep, the confused and thankless horde will be along directly. Look at that guy over there at the edge of the water already digging a hole in the sand, and for what? What is he thinking? The guy gets up at seven a.m., puts on a swimsuit, and starts diggin' a hole in the wet sand. Has that particular urge ever hit you—to go out and dig a hole in the sand before dawn? I mean...what the hell?"

"Well, now that you ask—like, ah, nope, haven't had that urge—but then I get to see this masterpiece of nature everyday, so I suppose I'm just spoiled. I've never been able to figure out what goes through the minds of most tourists anyway. They almost seem like an alien breed of some sort. It's freaky, 'cause they look like the rest of us, except with a sunburn."

"Hey, you know, you might be right. Maybe it's just a disguise or something to fake us out!"

"Oh, Edna, you're crazy, girl. Let's get our fat butts moving. We got things to do."

"Speak for yourself, fat butt. I'm gonna waltz my fine, tight, young stuff on back to the house. Maybe some redneck stud in a jacked-up pickup truck will whistle at me when I cross Ocean Boulevard! Woo-hoo! You know how I love that kind of intellectual love call," Edna teased with sarcasm.

"You will just never grow up, you silly thing."

They both laughed and trudged through the sand, flip-flopped over the hotel parking lot, and trotted across the asphalt of Ocean Boulevard. No studs of any type were out this early, but a large four-door Buick with Quebec licenses plates almost hit them.

The driver, with oblivious concentration, guided the car forward in the wrong lane, ignored the pedestrian crossing, turned sharply across four lanes without even a glance in his side mirror, clipped a stop sign, and continued weaving down a side street as if nothing had happened. Ahh, another day in paradise had begun. Summer was coming fast, and the Canadians were migrating back to their northern habitats.

The girls decided to reroute their path home, giving the main road and the unpredictable morning traffic a wide berth. They cut through the amusement park, taking a boardwalk trail that passed near the base of a large wooden and steel guy-wire structure, the world-famous Swamp Fox Roller Coaster.

"Edna, is that the kiddie train I hear running at this ungodly hour?"

"It sounds like it, but it's too early. They never run that noisy thing much before noon. If it's not against the city noise ordinance, it should be."

The kiddie train was a small-scale replica of a passenger train and served as an amusement-park ride, normally complete with a properly attired engineer to drive kids and their attentive parents on a twisted route through the amusement park. They could hear the signature whistle of the engine making its way along its railed path beneath the massive trusses. The park was closed, and the girls were curious.

The miniature engine rounded a curve from behind a manicured Ligustrum hedge.

"Oh my God! What the—" Edna and Evelyn stood paralyzed with shock, their mouths agape as they stared at a naked young man with hands and feet tied and lashed across the engine. His head and upper torso were positioned over the front of the train and appeared like a figurehead on a ship's bowsprit. A plastic bag filled with a small quantity of a greenish-brown substance was stuffed in his mouth and secured with duct tape. He seemed to be alive, but frozen in place.

"Call nine-one-one, call nine-one-one, call nine-one-one! Oh shit. Oh shit." Evelyn trotted around in a small circle, her arms tucked at her sides and her hands flapping up and down on her limp wrist. She was not sure what to do, so she vacillated in place.

"No, I have not been drinking, ma'am!" Edna barked with extreme irritation to the emergency operator. "You tell the emergency boys to get here and get here quick. This boy doesn't look so good."

Finally, after thirty minutes, the Myrtle Beach Police arrived in their normal, less-than-rapid response to strange tourist sightings. The miniature train with its naked patron made ten more trips around the track before the first police car rolled into the parking lot. The officer eased one leg out of the car, and the rest of him struggled to follow. He carefully cradled a hot Krispy Kreme between his thumb and index finger. He reached back in the car to retrieve his coffee before moving his attention to this early-morning emergency.

Thirty minutes later the park manager arrived to turn off the ride. Lights were flashing, and sporadic sirens broke what was left of the early-morning calm. A small command post had been set up to support all the rescue teams, including policemen, fire trucks, firemen, an ambulance, and three EMTs. Two-dozen Krispy Kreme doughnuts, a coffee thermos, and a small tarp were brought to the scene, while police gathered evidence.

The process was slow, and the mild enthusiasm decreased as the doughnuts disappeared. Sea gulls hovered, squawked, and looked for crumbs. Bored with the official disinterest and lack of progress, Edna went home to get ready for work. Evelyn went to take a nap before her weekly grocery-shopping duties.

The victimized young man, a first-year summer worker, was employed at the park. He had only been on the job for three weeks. He was confident, cocky, and considered a cool dude in his western Kentucky hometown. The teenager's prayers had been answered with a summer job at the beach and a chance to get out of his nothing town for the summer. He was in heaven with girls, the beach, girls, pot, and girls. He relished the nightly parties that were easier to find in this town than a hamburger. He loved the crowded bars.

His small beach pad was a room in the Hutches Apartments located behind his new favorite bar, the Frisky Rabbit. All of these things created his perfect domain. He had met a pot dealer staking out new turf and had negotiated the rights for a small franchise to supplement his meager, ride-operator income. It was all good.

The young man had a bag of pot stuffed in his mouth and a note written with indelible black marker ink across his chest and duplicated on his back, saying, "Go Home." The next day, he did.

The victim could not identify the assailant who perpetrated this weird crime of assault and harassment. The police report recorded the description of a thick, muscular man with a ski mask and gloves. The young man did not want to talk. He was scared, close-lipped, extremely anxious to go home, and of course, he did not claim the pot; it must have belonged to the attacker. At least, that was his story. He told the police he had no idea what the message was about, but he was not sticking around to help find the guy. His adventure in paradise was over.

Chapter 3

From his front porch, Eddie watched the morning activity at the Swamp Fox Amusement Part with mixed feelings of disdain, regret, and satisfaction. He was weary of the unrelenting surge of unruly summer workers and overwhelmed by the continuous, unabated onslaught of tourism.

Eddie and Vera Rondell were lifelong residents of Myrtle Beach. They lived in the same house where Vera had grown up. For many years they had lived in an apartment over the detached garage, but after her parents died, the couple moved into the main house. Sixty years ago the modest white two-story frame house with gingerbread trim had been built on a quiet street near an isolated stretch of beach. It had been a quaint beach cottage.

Eddie had worked for thirty years at the Georgetown paper mill. Five days a week, he had endured the thirty-mile drive each way, first to save on rent and later to care for Vera's parents. Moving from this paradise had never been an option. The resort town had grown up around them without their concurrence.

The vacationers were like an infected wound that healed during the winter months, only to have the scab scraped away each spring and the wound grow deeper. Tourists would blow into town, raise hell for a week, and then go home. The arrogance of each year's crop of summer workers was overwhelming and caustic. These punks thought they owned the place for the summer season. To Eddie, these unwanted trespassers were infuriating, and he weathered each year's crop with an increased anger and boiling anxiety.

The Frisky Rabbit bar was less than one hundred yards down the street from Eddie and Vera's house. Cottages rented exclusively to summer workers were nestled between the bar and Eddie's property. A scattered row of palmetto trees mixed with an eight-foot-high waxed-leaf Ligustrum hedge to visually isolate the co-ed cottages that were filled with loud, rambunctious, college-aged summer workers.

And if the bar and the cottages weren't enough, a fast-growing lifeguard business had built an office and lifeguard dormitory across the street. The guards raced to check in at the office each morning before eight o'clock and raced out again two minutes later to set up their stands, tires squealing on both entry and exit. The same loud chaotic process took place around six o'clock, but with music, drinking, and loud profanities added to the irritating mix. Some guards who lived in the guardhouse raised the noise level late into the night.

Eddie and Vera had a clear view of all of this activity as they attempted to enjoy the summer evenings on their porch. The loudest and most obnoxious, late-night party hounds of all summer workers surrounded the couple's quaint beach cottage.

Each summer developers discovered new space to squeeze more hotels on beachfront lots. Each new business required more workers. Eddie wished all workers could be handled like many hotel maids and maintenance workers, who were collected each morning from surrounding communities, transported into Myrtle Beach, and shuttled back to their homes at night.

Eddie saw the hotels, tourist trinket shops, fast-food restaurants, and arcades as an overgrown forest sorely in need of a vigorous thinning. He could relate to the words of a Joni Mitchell tune, "They paved paradise and put up a parking lot." But in his version, they put up another tourist trap. The last big hurricane to hit Myrtle Beach was Hazel in '58. Eddie thought it was time for another one. Too bad Hugo hit so far south; another fifty miles north, and he would have had his wish.

"Vera...honey...oh, Veeeerrraaa! I'm going fishing for a while down at the pier. You need anything before I go?" Eddie set two surf rods and a bait bucket in the back of his pickup truck.

"No, darlin'. What's all the noise over at the park? My goodness, there's police cars and everything. Was someone hurt? Do we need to help?" Vera stepped out from behind the screen door and onto the front porch.

"No, sweetie, if Myrtle Beach police officers, EMTs, and firemen with all their vehicles and gear can't help 'em, we sure as hell can't."

"Now, Eddie, no need for you to be swearing. You just go on and fish a spell, and forget about all that. Don't be gettin' all worked up. I love you. Now get along, or those fish are all going to be done with their breakfast."

Chapter 4

Vernon was a tall, lanky, chain-smoking, nearsighted, hip mountain man with a bad haircut. He was pissed. With this kiddie train catastrophe, he had lost three bags of pot and a new salesman who had been located in a prime sales location. It had taken two weeks to recruit the right guy to put on the job. The kid was new in town, young, and not extremely perceptive. The temptations of the promised reward of money and girls attracted more potential sales agents to build this marketing pyramid than a free recruitment breakfast at a Mary Kay Pink Cadillac Convention in South Florida.

Vernon was the new self-proclaimed pot sultan for the summer in south Myrtle Beach, a territory stretching from Central Avenue south to Garden City and twenty miles inland to the town of Conway. He had worked hard to establish this position, and he would not relinquish this claimed turf easily. And someone was messing in his business.

During the previous summer, Vernon halfheartedly stumbled through numerous jobs but had learned the ways of Myrtle Beach, the hot nightspots, the restaurants, the amusement parks, and the way of the summer worker. He was really not all that smart, but his subconscious was a keen observer of the facade.

Vernon had worked jobs in three amusement parks, the go-cart track, two restaurants, two bars, three hotels, a T-shirt shop, a gift shop, and a water park, and was typically fired from each job shortly after he was hired. He was lazy and a natural screw-up, showed up late, spent more time trying to pick up female customers than selling, took a little cash for himself, came to work stoned, and once got caught having sex with a questionably young girl while riding the Tilt-a-Whirl. Vernon was not what you would describe as a model employee, but during the summer, few employers checked resumes for work history or references. If you could walk and talk, not necessarily at the same time, you could get a low-wage job serving the tourist industry.

Vernon and his two undaunted thugs stood in front of the Frisky Rabbit waiting impatiently on Booney, the bar owner, to arrive. While the trio waited, they watched the emergency response team help Vernon's mentally tortured young dealer recover from his naked night ride on the small train.

"Son of a bitch! Harley, I thought I told you to keep an eye on that boy! What the hell, man?" Vernon barked, exasperated with his young thug.

"I was watching him, boss. I watched him almost all night, and I was getting bored, man, and then this bodacious hot girl with gigantic hooters sort of distracted me. It wasn't my fault, man."

"Did you get any?" Vernon asked sarcastically with obvious rhetorical intent.

"Naw, she ran when I tried to talk to her, started yelling for the cops or something, but then when I came back, the guy was gone, so like, you know, it wasn't really my fault or anything."

"You dumb ass, you just don't get it, do you? David, what about you? I mean, dammit, there was two of you idiots to watch one guy selling dope. How friggin' hard can that be?"

"Yeah, like, it wasn't me, man. I was on break, man. I tested some weed from one of the other new dudes we hired, you know, just checkin' to make sure he wasn't cuttin' the stuff too much, and then I sorta jumped a ride on the roller coaster 'cause a guy I knew was running the ticket booth, and—"

"Shut the hell up! You losers have got to be two of the biggest idiots ever. Jesus H. Christ! What were you thinking? Never mind, I don't want to know. All I know is you assholes owe me three bags of weed."

Vernon turned away from the rescue and pointed at a disheveled, troubled, young dude staring out through a small barred window on the front of the Frisky Rabbit bar.

"And this idiot, when we get his ass out of here, no more beer chug-gin' for him. Jesus, you turds are more trouble than you are worth."

With a disgusted look on his face, Booney pulled into a reserved parking spot next to the front door of the Frisky Rabbit. Last night Vernon had misplaced another one of his new lifeguard pot dealers; Shoots McCoy. At the time no one cared where he was.

Shoots' cell-phone alarm had roused him to an early-morning con-sciousness. He had opened his red eyes to find himself lying under a pool table next to a naked girl he didn't know but maybe should have remembered. It took him a few minutes to figure out where he was and more time to find his clothes and then finally to discover his dilemma of being locked in the bar.

The owners always bolted the doors of the Frisky Rabbit from the outside. Shoots had thirty minutes to be on the beach, or he would be fired. The guard had already been warned twice about late arrivals. He called Vernon for help.

Shoots now had five minutes to hit the beach, or Vernon would lose another well-placed dealer. Booney opened the four padlocks securing metal bars and unlocked the two dead bolts. The liberated lifeguard emerged on a run, heading back to the guardhouse to get his gear before making his way to the beach.

After a quick check for damage in the bar, Booney emerged from a back poolroom with a young girl who squinted at the bright light of day, buttoned her shirt, and staggered to her car. She opened the door and crashed down in the front seat. Booney pushed her feet in and shut the door. Complaining to himself, he locked the front door to the bar and walked over to Vernon.

"Hey, man, you and your boys are going to get busted, or somebody is going to get hurt. You might want to stifle the crazy shit for a while, dude, or it ain't gonna be cool around here, you know what I mean, man. And Murph, he's pissed too, man, so you need to chill."

"Sorry, Booney. I'll talk to the boys, see what I can do. Here, dude, take this for your trouble." Vernon slipped Booney a plastic bag with four fat joints, and then he looked down the street at the running guard, who caught his flip-flop on the curb and fell headlong into an eight-foot camellia bush in Eddie's front yard.

"Jeessuss H...get in the van, boys, he's never gonna make it in time. See ya, Booney. We gotta get that sorry asshole to the beach. Stay cool, man, stay cool."

Chapter 5

The Frisky Rabbit bar was frequented by local inhabitants who enjoyed the bargain beer at happy hour and by summer workers who came early and stayed late. An arbitrary collection of tourists mingled with this odd group. The tourists were pleased to have stumbled upon this "beach in-crowd" and their wild party nights.

Lifeguards from Leonard's Beach Service typically filled the bar early. Most guards worked ten hours on the beach each day, seven days a week. After dropping their umbrella and float rental money at Leonard's office, they migrated in small groups across the street to the Frisky Rabbit to quench their unquenchable thirst.

The guards were attracted by twenty-five-cent draft beer served at happy hour. To start their night, each guard bought three or four dollars worth of the cheap beer and went to one of the game rooms that were populated with pool tables and foosball tables. After chugging ten or fifteen foamy drinks, this sweaty, sandy, suntan lotion-covered crew served as the catalyst to ignite a rowdy crowd. Each night a friendly gathering morphed into a boisterous party riot.

Two former Leonard's Beach Service lifeguards owned and operated the Frisky Rabbit. After one particularly good summer, they decided to hang around a couple of months to play some golf. They never left. Murph and Booney had saved a little money from their summer toil, and with great enthusiasm over a few beers, they acquired the bar from a tired owner.

Murph and Booney saw the location, with an existing liquor license, as a recipe for riches. They first changed the name from The Kings Highway Lounge to The Frisky Rabbit. The name was selected to match the bar's motif and the attitude. They had added wall sections painted with eight-foot-high replicas of X-rated cartoons Murph found in an adult comic book. The cartoon characters were tall, skinny, upright, and reminiscent of Bugs Bunny. They brought in pool tables, foosball tables, pinball machines, a bodacious sound system, and a couple of neon beer signs. This outrageous environment, with its cheap beer and loud music, attracted young summer patrons like fish to chum.

The Frisky Rabbit had proved a successful formula and had flourished for ten years now. Relative to other beach bars, it was a foundation, an established turf, a rock of Gibraltar for the summer bar scene. The crop of summer workers cycled year after year, but the Frisky Rabbit remained.

Murph and Booney saved some money, another opportunity came along, and they purchased a small house on an adjacent lot. Exhausted by the crowd, the previous owner left town. He could no longer deal with the rampant growth, the tourists, and the noise that came with both. He sold for a low price and a quick sale to move to a quiet, remote beach far from this maddening crowd. The opportunistic young men added to their beach empire by building some cheap summer-rental facilities behind the house.

A tenant could rent a single room, but most summer workers were accustomed to college dormitory life and picked the cheaper rent of a shared room. The beds were army surplus, metal cots from an era so long ago that no one remembered the troops being treated so cruelly. The toilets and showers were common use, first come, first served. Tenants were expected to clean up after themselves, but that expectation was rarely met, so security deposits were forfeited.

This clientele provided Murph and Booney a fair income for their real-estate investment. The young landlords put up with the noise, minor damage, loud music, late payments, fighting, and all the other crap these kids dished out in a summer of fun. They knew the game; they had played it themselves.

This job was like running a college dorm without the constraints of administrative oversight. They, the owners, could set the rules. If you didn't like it, if you were too much trouble, you hit the road. One or two expulsions from this summer school of the real world, and the rest of the tenants knew the landlords meant business. This turf belonged to Murph and Booney.

Summer tenants were as predictable as the ocean tides that they worshiped. They came and went; they were sometimes calm, pristine, and alluring, but occasionally rough, noisy, and disastrous. With each tide perceivable change goes unnoticed, but change does occur with each cycle. Who, over time, could compare and remember the previous state with accuracy?

Each tide leaves its rejected bounty and takes away the poorly built sand castles. All the while, the surf churns with a constant, calm, soul-relaxing tune. A subtle change to the surf or turf requires a violent undertow. Swimmers caught by the force of an undertow survive by going with the flow, rising to the surface, and gradually easing their way out of the deadly fluid grip. Those who fight the hidden, underlying force head on will be consumed.

The Frisky Rabbit was a well-established sandbar with strong currents flowing on all sides. The bar had survived many storms. The sand shifted with the tide, and grains of sand moved on, only to be replaced by others, but the bar remained.

Chapter 6

During the summer, constant and unabated waves of humanity roll into Myrtle Beach. Most people come to the resort for a vacation, to enjoy the sun, surf, and sand, but some come seeking seasonal work. Others come to get away from their life and to live their dream. Bo Jr. washed in with that latter group, searching for better turf and a better existence.

He was a thick young man, both in body and mind. Every summer and every school break from the time he was ten years old, he had worked long hours on the family farm under the draconian supervision of his father. He had grown tired of 5:00 a.m. tractor rides to the field and sweaty, dusty afternoons spraying cotton and picking tobacco.

Finally he had yielded to a simmering desire to see other things in the world. Late one night Bo Jr. packed his bag and left home on foot. He put out his thumb and started down what he hoped would be his path to freedom, a new life at the beach. He had just turned nineteen.

At eight the next evening, after a series of short rides, Bo Jr. completed the seventy-mile trek to the beach. His last ride picked him up at the base of the Sampit River Bridge in Georgetown and left him at a Sinclair gas station across the highway from The Blue House Restaurant and Lounge, on the west side of Myrtle Beach.

The Blue House sign said, "Beer—Food—Open Nightly," but Bo Jr. was hungry, thirsty, and tempted by the gas station's fine menu, so he ponied up his last five bucks for an overcooked rotisserie hot dog and a cherry Coke. The young man quickly gobbled his gas-station culinary delight, licked the ketchup and mustard from his thick, callused fingers, and chugged the last swallow of sweet soda. He belched with pride to signal the end of his meal and wiped his mouth on his shirtsleeve.

Bo Jr. picked up a gym bag that held everything he owned and shuffled across the highway, dodging the continuous parade of cars and trucks that ferried vacationers and daily workers, like the tide, back and forth to the beach.

Bo Jr. had been named through a combination of historic family icons and aristocratic Southern leaders, allowing him to carry a title that framed his heritage as a true product of the South. His full given name was Beauregard Pinckney Calhoun the Fourth. The compilation of famous Southern and national leaders included Confederate General P.G.T. Beauregard; Charles Cotesworth Pinckney, a Revolutionary War general from South Carolina and a leader in the Constitutional Convention; and John Caldwell Calhoun, a quick-tempered South Carolina politician who once served as vice president of the United States.

Calhoun was the foundation of the family's claim to heritage and bloodline. He was a fiery orator, a strong supporter of slavery, and a passionate defender of the ways of the Old South. J.C. had achieved a bit of fame for a fistfight ending with the cane-clubbing of a rival fellow legislator. Bo Jr. and his relatives often demonstrated similar behavior.

Bo Jr.'s mother had added the fourth at the end of his name in an attempt to further validate his unconfirmed and dubious heritage. His name had been shortened quickly to Bo Jr. because he was a junior. His dad knew from personal experience that pronouncing ownership of either one of the first two names of Beauregard or Pinckney as your baptized title in the current, less-aristocratic, rural South would bring constant harassment and get you in a fight quicker than a Yankee spitting on the Confederate flag in Charleston.

Beau was acceptable as a nickname, but only if spelled B-o. Pink would not be used. The supplement of Junior was needed to avoid confusion around the house with his dad. So despite his mother's and his grandmother's objections, his dad called him Bo Jr., and it had stuck.

His vocabulary was more limited than that of his ancestry, especially after a few beers. He was a mean drunk who often engaged in his own shouting matches and physical battles. His size, strength, personality, and obviously limited future made him a dangerous person at an early age. He was more apt to use a baseball bat or tire iron than a cane like his arrogated ancestor, John C., and so modified the parallels of his heritage.

As the night was getting on and a crowd gathered at The Blue House, Bo Jr. decided to move there. Tired and restless, standing outside on the edge of the parking lot, he was anxious for action and money. A man checked his identification at the door, and Bo Jr. eased in beyond the foyer. As his eyes adjusted to the dark, he quickly surveyed the joint and went for a seat at the bar.

He planned to have his way, eat, drink, and slip out on his tab as the crowd grew. He was mean, unusually large, and strong for his age, and was confident he could handle the few bar bouncers he had seen. With this youthful bravado, he reckoned he could leave at his leisure.

He settled down on a barstool, ordered a Bud draft, and started a tab with a stolen credit card imprinted with the name of Thelma James. Bo Jr. had nowhere to go and nowhere to sleep, but he had the resolution of a young man exploring the world while oblivious to the dangers. He was neither troubled nor intimidated by his present condition.

Ignorance may be bliss—or not. Bo Jr.'s attitude was fortified partially by an arrogant confidence in his physical abilities and partially by stupidity, but more so by his ignorance of a world with more complexities than the one he knew. He was on unfamiliar turf.

As a restaurant and lounge, The Blue House at nine thirty in the evening didn't appear to be much of either to his young, untrained eye. The parking lot was half-full, but he saw only a few people in the joint. He wanted action, he wanted a party; he was at the beach.

After drinking four beers, nature called, and he went to the toilet. Activity in the lounge was still very slow, with a few well-dressed, dark-haired guys sitting casually watching the Atlanta Braves play the Cincinnati Reds on the bar TV.

When Bo Jr. entered the overly large men's room, he noticed a few people he had not seen in the restaurant or the lounge. One of the well-dressed guys from the bar stepped up to the wall urinal next to him. Bo

Jr. had noticed two of the gentlemen in the john go through a different door than the one he had used to enter. He heard busy noise, bells
ringing, and some hearty cheering, not common to the other parts of
The Blue House Restaurant and Lounge. As he went out, the large well-
dressed man, who had followed him from the bar, positioned himself
between Bo Jr. and the mysterious door, allowing only a passage back to
the lounge. He sat at the bar again, ordered another draft beer and some
nachos, and watched the rest of the Braves game.

Around ten thirty, Bo Jr. grew tired of sitting. This place seemed
dead, with no resurrection anticipated. He had a beer buzz coming on
and needed to pee again. With a bit of trouble, he got up and walked to
the toilet. He had been thinking a lot about the noise and laughter he
had heard on his last trip. When he entered, he went straight for the
curious doorway.

The moment he pushed it open, two big guys who had followed him
in grabbed him by both arms and vigorously pulled him in the direction
of the toilet. Bo Jr. caught a quick view of the festive crowd playing
cards behind a second open door.

He was not accustomed to being pushed around by anyone but his
dad, and he hated it. Bo Jr. turned on the two who had redirected his
path and got shoved again. Invoking his best decision of the night, he
backed off, at least for the moment. He was a good match for one of the
bouncers, but not both. He was not drunk enough yet to lose that more
sensible discretion.

With all things considered, Bo Jr. knew the time to leave the lounge
was fast approaching. He wanted to be cool and incognito, so he peace-
fully returned to the bar and another beer to let things settle down.
After eleven thirty p.m., a crowd started to build, composed mainly of
middle-aged locals who knew one another, many of who had recently
completed their evening's shift at other restaurants and tourist-related
occupations. This scene was not the wild party gang he wanted to join.
He decided it was time to hit the road. Bo Jr. knew he had been followed
on his trip to the toilet and must have been watched, so he developed a
plan, one contrived surprisingly on his own.

He sat down at the bar next to a newcomer who appeared lost.

"Hey, man, did you know there's a casino in here? That's where the real party is—all kinds of wild people in there. They got some pinhead bouncers guarding the door, trying to keep it secret or something."

"You don't say...where?"

"There's a door marked 'Private' next to the men's room. It may take two of us to get in there. Tell you what, I'll distract the guards, and you go for the door; don't stop for nuthin'."

"What about you?"

"Well, I'll come later, don't you worry 'bout that."

The fellow appeared inebriated and curious and agreed to the plan. Bo Jr. had his diversion with the unsuspecting new confidant. Before leaving the bar, he ordered another beer to serve as another cover to mask his departure. Who would suspect? Bo Jr. whispered to his new friend that he would take another route to draw the attention of the bouncers.

Two thugs were now settled near the men's room door, and one followed the new guy into the toilet. Bo Jr. had lost himself in the crowd; at least he thought he had. He cautiously maneuvered toward a side door he had previously discovered on the far side of the restaurant.

A noisy ruckus arose by the "Private" door as Bo Jr. looked back to make sure he had not been seen. He stepped out through the door, smelled the fresh night's smokeless air, and looked up at the stars, confident in his success. Bo Jr. never knew what hit him. His starry night turned to black.

Chapter 7

At five forty-five the next morning, a lifeguard was just returning to his room at the Hutches Apartments after another drunken, dancing, screwing binge-night on the town. Earlier that morning he had been kicked out of a hotel room for illicit and raucous behavior. The hotel security guard tried to ignore the ruckus, but finally had to act. Hotel guests had registered numerous complaints about the noisy room with reports of rhythmic pounding from a headboard, loud groans, and sexually charged screams. It just wasn't right. They were on vacation.

For this night's adventure, the lifeguard had smoked pot, snorted cocaine, popped two Viagra pills, and washed it all down with liberal amounts of Southern Comfort whiskey. He had met the three wild, young girls on the beach and had shared some of his mind-melting concoction with them, leading to this all-night reversed gangbang. The girls were taking turns in an ill-conceived contest to wear the young man down. They had been approaching success, but then the young man was evicted.

A middle-aged couple from Charlotte with four children in the room next door had registered the most frequent complaints. The complaining adults first met while vacationing at the beach. They had been teenagers in summer love and had enjoyed two wild summers together. Their children, two girls and two boys, lay silent and still in their beds with eyes wide open throughout the marathon, dreaming of the time they too would be old enough to go to the beach for the summer, without parents.

With the first and second complaint, the security guard assumed the guy would soon be finished and if left alone, the problem would go away. He was irritated by the interruption, but soon dozed off again. The complaint calls continued, and finally, after it was clear the issue would not resolve itself, he hiked up to the room. He evicted the young man, warned the three naked girls, who claimed to be eighteen, and then went back to what could be salvaged of his nap.

The young lifeguard was exhausted, drunk, stoned, sore, and had spent an hour driving aimlessly around the same two blocks, until by mistake he made a different turn and found his way home. The glaring white light of the Krispy Kreme shop with its familiar green-and-red sign had been his beacon, leading him home to the Hutches.

His car scraped a chain link fence and knocked over two trash cans on the way in. As he hoisted himself out of the car, he grabbed the horn, cutting the otherwise-quiet night with a blaring blast. The horn did not bother him. He slammed the car door, took two steps, wobbled, fell backward on the grass, and passed out staring at the sky, arms straight out with a smile on his face.

He was home. Someone from the Hutches would eventually check his pulse and urge him to go inside or cover him with a sheet. He was among friends and relatively safe. His lifeguard buddies would wake him within the next ninety minutes so he could begin another day guarding the beach, making it safe for swimmers to swim and surfers to surf.

"Jesus, what was that? Ahh, I was sleeping so good." Edna groaned and rolled over in bed to check the clock.

"Some idiot with a loud horn hit a trash can. Wow...crap, I had a great Kevin Costner dream going. I'm tired, pissed, and horny, but awake now, thank you very much!"

"Oh God, I'm tired."

"Better talk to someone who knows you."

"Oh hush up."

"Geez, what time is it?"

"Uhhh, I think it's almost six. My eyes are blurry. Hang on a sec. Yeah, it's almost six. Did you say Kevin Costner? Give me a break. How old is he?"

"I don't know. I had a crush on him when I was in middle school, and now I am old enough to have the Kevin I remembered, even if only in my dream."

"Evelyn, you are really weird...let's just get up and go to the beach early today. Doesn't make sense to sleep another ten minutes."

"It does to me. That's all I needed was another ten minutes with my Kevin dream. He was just about to—"

"OK, OK, I get the picture. Now get that lazy fat butt up out of that bed."

"Darlin', speak for yourself. I am one fine, tight piece of femininity."

"Have you been to the Pavilion arcade again looking at yourself in the distortion mirrors?"

"Oh, you hush; you're just jealous."

The girls laughed, dressed, and brushed their hair. After years of living by the Frisky Rabbit, the girls were accustomed to the noisy commotion and the behavior of summer workers. They had been a part of this unruly crew when they first came to the beach. Edna was having a bad hair day, so she wore a One-Eyed Flounder baseball cap. They walked past the lifeguard sleeping in the yard as they headed to the Krispy Kreme for coffee and doughnuts.

The sky was clear, promising the grand arrival of an orange glow on the eastern horizon. Although they grumbled about getting out of bed, they really did not mind the early morning, for this addiction gave them their greatest pleasure. They would take a nap later when the sky was more a more common blue. The girls held a religious allegiance to this morning ritual.

In this early dawn between dark and light, they crossed the four lanes of Kings Highway. Edna sensed something different in the dimly lit panorama of the strip-mall shopping center fifty yards west of the Krispy Kreme. The Western Sizzler Steakhouse's signature red neon bull sign was not glowing, and the brilliant icon was hard to overlook. The perpetually illuminated red gas tube molded in the shape of a longhorn steer had glared brightly since the restaurant had been constructed. That neon bull was an unmistakable guiding light to tourists in pursuit of affordable family dining. Its effulgent glare was irritating to those who called this turf paradise.

Edna stared at the dark void and could see some movement where the sign should have been. She grabbed Evelyn's arm and walked forward to the restaurant, away from the white brightness of the Krispy Kreme. As her eyes adjusted through the dim light, Edna made out the struggling form of a person hanging from the wall as if crucified on a cross. The arms were stretched and tied to the neon horns of the longhorn steer.

The girls cautiously hurried to inspect the odd sight. Strapped to the non-illuminated sign was a young girl, a summer worker, who lived in the Hutches and worked as a waitress at the Western Sizzler. She was naked except for a restaurant menu serving as a loincloth and a bag of pot taped in her mouth. A thick, black marker of some type had been used to scribe letters across her ample bare chest. "Go" was written on one breast, and "Home" was written on the other.

When Edna went to help, the girl's eyes grew wide with fear, and she shook her head no. Edna backed away and bumped into Evelyn, who was inexplicably jogging in a small circle. Her arms were tucked against her ribs, with her hands flapping up and down on limp wrists. With the bump Evelyn broke from her trauma dance and jogged to the Krispy Kreme to call her police friends. With the dispatcher's report of a naked woman tied up, the time required for the first officer to arrive on the scene seemed more rapid than the response two days earlier to help a naked man strapped to a train. Perhaps the department was making an attempt to improve on its performance.

The police arrived and took the required photographs for investigative evidence and a few for personal consumption prior to their attempt to release the girl from her cross. Her angry eyes grew narrow and dark as the delays to release her continued. Most of the on-duty and some off-duty officers in the area arrived to assist in the investigation. Several officers had been sitting in the Krispy Kreme shop, so naturally they too offered to help. Finally, the officer in charge of the crime scene began to inspect the girl's predicament. Being bound and gagged only represented a portion of her problem. She was standing on a box and her ankles were tied together. The box had a large red button that she held down with her feet. She was struggling to stand firmly on it. The officer carefully cut and pulled the tape from her face and removed the pot from her mouth.

"Is this yours, or a going-away gift from someone who apparently doesn't like you?" the officer asked suspiciously.

"I'm standing on a bomb!" she screamed.

The police immediately fell back behind the squad cars and called in the bomb squad. Curiously, some members of the squad were already on site. It wasn't as if Myrtle Beach needed a full-time dedicated bomb squad, but they did have some equipment and basic training in bomb recognition and diffusion techniques.

In thirty minutes they had the bomb squad truck, the fire department, and a healthy supply of EMT personnel on site, just in case. A crowd of protection and rescue personnel had formed in the parking lot. After all the support staff and equipment were in place, the officer in charge took the next important step; it was part of his training.

"How do you know it's a bomb?" he shouted from behind the police car.

"Because he told me it was! He said if I lifted my foot from this button, the bomb would go off!" She shouted in anger and frustration. "I've been here for hours. I need help, you son of a bitch!"

A suited-up bomb squad officer brought his full complement of sophisticated bomb-diffusing tools and was followed closely by the bomb transport wagon. The officer first cut the rope binding the girl's ankles. He then reached to his tool pouch, pulled out a fresh roll of gray duct tape, ripped off a piece, and moved closer. The officer reached down and put his finger on the red button, allowing the girl to gradually remove one foot and then the other. The officer maintained a constant pressure and placed the strip of duct tape on the red button and firmly anchored the tape on both sides. A second officer in full bomb diffusion attire placed another piece of tape over the button, forming a cross to ensure the bomb trigger did not move. With all the technology and training available, duct tape saved the day.

The girl was untied and released with only her Western Sizzler menu loincloth for cover. An EMT moved in to offer a blanket. Few members of the emergency service crowd could remember the color of her eyes, but they had all memorized the message written on her chest, "Go Home." Why her? Who wanted her gone? Why would someone want this gorgeous young lady to go away?

The bomb squad determined that a bomb was indeed contained within the box. The X-ray performed by the squad showed only a small amount of explosive device surrounded by some organic material. Forensics determined the bomb to be a cherry bomb with a fuse placed next to a Butane lighter. The organic mass around the cherry bomb was doggy poop. Firecrackers and a bag of crap—not deadly, but it could make a smelly mess. A prankster with time on his hands and a weird sense of humor had built this bomb, not a terrorist or professional hit man. Whoever the villain was here, he was not a killer, only someone attempting to send a frightening message, "Go Home."

Evelyn and Edna told what they had seen, were released and thanked for their help. The female victim was questioned for several hours before she was released. This abduction and assault was the second of its kind in three days. The police suspected either a copycat felon or a pissed-off, serial-assault maniac who wanted people to "Go Home." If this assault pattern continued, the local chamber of commerce might get involved, and the pressure to solve this crime would really get intense. This message was not the kind they would want conveyed to their precious tourist population.

The girl had been a bit sketchy on the description of her attacker. He was strong, thick, tall, and wearing a ski mask. She was scared. He had promised to come again if she didn't leave town now. She was packed and gone by noon. The Hutches had another open room. The Western Sizzler had one less employee and the beach one less summer worker. Vernon had one less lid of pot and one less dealer.

The waitress had been a valuable addition to Vernon's network. He had met her at the Frisky Rabbit one night. Shortly after, she became a willing dealer while working at the Sizzler. Every afternoon before she went to work, she rolled a number of different-sized bags of pot within white paper napkins, just the way silverware was wrapped for the restaurant. She kept a variety of weights in her serving smock. With the right request, from the right person, she delivered. While you were eating, you could pick up a joint, or more; just leave your payment with the tip. She had moved a lot of Vernon's inventory with her marginally discreet plan.

Beach lifeguards came to the Sizzler in droves, enticed by a marketing gimmick offered by the owner. Guards paid for their discounted steak, and all the extras were free. They left the waitress tips according to the size of their napkins. Summer workers who were friends of guards learned the methods for acquisition, and the Sizzler became an extremely busy place. The waitress made slave wages, however the pot business was a real winner. But someone had noticed, and now she was gone.

Some in the police department were getting curious. The events were weird, even for a summer at the beach. The first guy tied to the train could have been a prank, but the kid was terrified, so there must be something more. A new investigator, Detective McKenzie, began to look for similarities. Walking the area, he stood for a moment in front of the Hutches with his back to the apartments. He looked to his left and forward and saw Leonard's Beach Service Guard House and just beyond, the Swamp Fox Roller Coaster and Amusement Park. Farther to his left, he saw Eddie and Vera's house, and beyond their property was the wall of hotels blocking the ocean view. He looked to his right and across Kings Highway to the Krispy Kreme and a short distance behind that, the Western Sizzler restaurant. He turned more to his right to see the Frisky Rabbit.

Both victims had lived in the Hutches. Both were summer workers. Both had a bag of pot stuffed in their mouth. Both had the words "Go Home" written on them with a wide, black, indelible marker. Edna and Evelyn had discovered both. Both victims had been so frightened that they left town that day. Neither had been severely injured, humiliated and traumatized, yes—but not physically harmed. These kids were young, and they were scared. Detective McKenzie started asking questions at the Frisky Rabbit, with Murph and Booney first on his list.

Chapter 8

~

Bo Jr.'s unconscious dream gradually merged through a semiconscious haze to a head-throbbing nightmare of awareness. As the fog lifted, he slowly gained clarity and could feel the stiff, thin ropes cutting into his wrists and ankles. He lay spread-eagle on a table that started to move and tilt him upward and finally onto his feet. He was naked, with a bright light shining in his face. He looked down to see himself straddled above a long, razor-sharp blade mounted on a wooden support. The blade would have just touched his testicles if not for the cold room and his fear. As he tugged and struggled with the ropes tied to his wrist, he noticed that the blade moved upward. He stopped pulling.

A calm, stern voice from behind the light said, "That's right, kid, move your hands or your feet, and you'll cut yourself. Self-castration is not a pretty sight."

Bo Jr. looked more closely at the blade and noticed dark stains on its support that may have been the blood of some other poor slob who had found himself in this same compromising position. He stood on a concrete floor covered with a slick, green slime.

"Stand there, kid, until your legs get weak. Then cramps will take hold, you will lose your footing, and swish, he becomes a she." The voice laughed. "Oh, we've seen it before, plenty of times, especially after a long night of drinking. You're dehydrated; all that beer you stole from me is still inside you, and I'll bet you really need to take a leak. When you do, you'll slip on your own piss. If not, if you can hold it, sooner or later you will start to cramp up. I don't care. I'll just sit here and watch.

A big fellow like you should be a sight to see." The voice sounded so calm and stoic, it was scary.

"Help me!" cried Bo Jr.

"Help you?" he shouted. "Who the hell do you think you are? You tried to rob us! You were trying to be a wise ass! You want me to help you? Hell, I'm just here to clean up the mess when you're done. But first we will provide you with some awareness training, because you need to be aware of who you are dealing with, young man."

Bo Jr.'s mind was still foggy, with a throbbing head from the clubbing. He was beginning to understand the magnitude of his predicament. Bo Jr. was not a scholar, but he knew intimidation, and he understood that someone was trying to scare him. He considered they were doing a damn good job of it. If they had really wanted to kill him, they would have done so already.

Bo Jr. was tough, and despite his current, compromising situation, he stood strong. He had learned from his daddy that when being punished, don't cry or show weakness, because that will only bring more punishment. He stood strong and defiant on the outside, but scared and helpless on the inside. He gathered himself, firmed his jaw, and raised his chin.

"Yeah, yeah, I see ya, kid, you're tough. We'll see how long you can stand there before you cut yourself," the man behind the light taunted. The tormentor walked out, and the door closed.

The test was on. Bo Jr. stood strong, but wondered what the hell he had gotten into. Didn't make sense for people to go to all this effort to recover a few bucks on a bar bill; something else was going on here. They had let him stand over the sharp blade, for what? Maybe this torture was a test. Bo Jr. let his mind consider that perplexing issue for a moment. He began to sweat under the bright light. The room temperature was growing hotter by the minute. To Bo Jr. the torture test lasted forever, but only an hour had trudged by when his captors returned.

Tony, the Blue House owner, was always looking for local muscle that could blend into his team. He had a recently vacated position to fill. Bo Jr. seemed a potential prospect to bring into the fold. They had checked his ID and confirmed that no one had reported this young man as missing. They had also discovered that he had a long record of minor arrests. It would be done slowly, nothing bold or outright—a debt was owed, the leverage was present, and in Tony's favor.

"Bubba, you wanna get a break here?" Tony hissed. "You wanna way *not* to die?"

"Yeah, I mean, yes sir," Bo Jr. answered, with some effort to maintain his cool.

"That's right, son—sir—a little respect, I like that. Maybe we gotta way for you to survive. It's a slim one, but maybe, just maybe, we can find it in our hearts to give you one chance to earn a little more time on this earth. What do ya think about that, punk?"

"Yes sir!" Bo Jr. had learned long ago how to get past the moment, how to survive a beating to live another day. He knew his situation would only get worse if he wasn't released soon. He was hot and dripping sweat. The floor was wet and slippery, and in a short time, the cramps would come.

"What do ya mean, 'yes sir,' boy? I asked you what ya thought about a chance, dumb ass."

"Yes sir, I'd like a chance, sir, please give me a chance," Bo Jr. responded in a sincere level tone.

"Hey, hey, hey, I like it. The kid's tough, he's got respect, and he knows a good deal when he hears one. OK, kid; let me lay out your particular situation. We're gonna cut you down, but here's what's gonna happen. You owe me five hundred bucks for the beer, because that's how much I'm chargin' for it, that and the other perks like this little character-building session. The Blue House is a private club, at least some parts, and I can charge what I want. I'm cuttin' you a break, punk, and discounting your bill to five hundred dollars plus a promise. Most people who tried what you did would be dead by now and rotting in the swamp, so count your blessings. I'm sensing some potential with you, so here's the rest of the deal. Until you pay off your debt, the balance is earning points, and you get to pay this debt by working for me. We got a door for you to guard and some other miscellaneous support work, errands to run, shit like that. We'll see how you do. If you cross me, punk, we'll feed you to the sharks, after we hurt you. This little exercise here tonight will seem like child's play. You understand me, punk?"

"Yes sir, I'll pay you back, and the work is no problem, sir, I came here looking for work. I'd be proud to work for you, sir."

"Yeah, we'll see about that. Guido, show him his job. We'll see, punk. You do not want to cross me again."

Bo Jr. thought, how lucky can a guy get, a little hassle, and I'm in with some tough guys at a bar in Myrtle Beach. I couldn't pick a better job. I'll have everything I came for. The fiery excitement of his dream job was about to be doused with a bucket of cold reality.

Guido cut the ropes and carefully removed the reverse guillotine platform and its razor-sharp blade from between Bo Jr.'s legs. Guido had seen other potential recruits who had failed to pass this endurance test to make the team. The gauntlet trial was not always like this one; the mob had invented numerous methods to slowly taunt a person before they were killed or released with a painful and harsh warning.

Often it proved more profitable to scare the shit out of some poor slob to ensure future collections were fully paid on time. If you had some guy paying his tax every week, let him keep paying. So Bo Jr. was now one of those poor slobs. It did not matter whether he was paying his tax, some protection money, his union dues, or working for the family, he had to understand the potential consequences for failure to comply with the directions Tony handed down.

Guido had previously been ordered to carry out the penalty action on some of his co-workers, and he had no doubts about Bo Jr.'s future should he have a weak moment or lapse in judgment. Guido saw the fear and anxiety in Bo Jr., behind his eyes, where others might not notice. He could tell that the kid had been roughed up before and knew how to respond to reduce the pain and then continue to act tough. They would need to further test his heart and loyalty before he was allowed the secrets of their business.

"What's your name, boy?" asked Guido in a rough tone.

"Bo Jr., sir."

"Bo Jr., eh. That's one fucked-up name, kid, but I guess they had to call ya something. Let's go. Put your clothes on and wipe your face."

They walked out of a farm shed that was hidden from a rough dirt road by a thick stand of small pines. Both climbed into a black Crown Victoria and started the drive back to The Blue House Restaurant and Lounge, but not before Guido made Bo Jr. put a burlap sack over his head and lie down in the backseat under a blanket. The location of this house would remain a family secret for now.

"Kid, you're on the payroll, but we don't trust your ass yet. Keep your yap shut. I'll tell ya when you can get up. You're not smelling like roses, so I'm gonna leave the windows down until we get back into town, so stay down."

Bo Jr. lay in the backseat, still sweating and worried. He thought he was OK, but now as he lay with a bag over his head, he was not sure. The car had been parked on a white sandy road, in a pine thicket, in the swamp. Bo Jr. had grown up in an area much like this one. The ride on the dirt road seemed to last a very long time, but he convinced himself to adjust for the anxiety, and he figured the rough, washboard ride was closer to fifteen minutes before Guido stopped and then pulled onto a paved road.

He heard no other cars passing for another fifteen minutes. Bo Jr. caught a hint of a familiar unpleasant odor. The car slowed, now obviously negotiating traffic, and the air became redolent with Georgetown's trademark paper-mill odor. In a few minutes, the smell would be dissolved and replaced with fresh salt air blowing from the coast, westward from Winyah Bay up the Waccamaw River. Bo Jr. knew where he was just by the familiar smells in the air.

For Bo Jr., the eerie part of this journey was the shed hidden in the woods. The mob had a place to handle their unruly partners and clients in great isolation, in their own time, without interruption. His worry began to subside as the ride continued north. Bo Jr. knew the four-lane highway led back to Myrtle Beach. If they were going to take him away from this remote, wooded place, with its clear potential for easy body elimination without a trace, he hoped he was on his way up.

Chapter 9

After unlocking the doors to the One-Eyed Flounder, Darrell Jr. moved aside and let the gift shop workers stream in. He turned the sign hanging in the front door from Closed to Open and jumped back into the store's electric golf cart. He drove the cart two blocks south on an uncrowded Ocean Boulevard and two blocks west to the Krispy Kreme shop in search of his morning coffee and doughnut.

It was early, and as he cruised the boulevard, he casually gazed at the open but empty arcades, lunch counters, beachwear shops, and a wax museum. He passed the Ghost House of Scary Horrors, a new attraction opened this summer. The spooky, three-story-high facade had replaced a ladies dress shop that time had passed by. He rode between a sleeping amusement park and a block of two-story, dated, look-alike hotels showing "No Vacancy" signs.

Darrell Jr. crossed Kings Highway and parked in front of the Krispy Kreme as the last of the police and rescue vehicles were packing up and driving away from the Western Sizzler Restaurant. For a moment he cared and wondered what might have happened, but then his mind returned to his desire for coffee and a hot doughnut.

He was the twenty-eight-year-old son of the owner of the One-Eyed Flounder, and his ambitions did not center on education or business, as his father would have liked. He had barely completed high school. After years of a pampered life living at home and having his fun in the sun, he had only recently felt the urge to get a job. For most of his young life, Darrell Jr. frequented the beach during the summer and played golf in the spring and fall. During the winter off-season, the gift shop closed like most other businesses along the Grand Strand.

When Darrell Jr. was old enough to care, he no longer cared. Dad had enough money, and Darrell Jr. was confident he would get his later. It was only under the threat of being disowned and removed from "Dad's will" that Darrell Jr. finally came to work.

In a short time, he had begun to actually like the store. Darrell Jr. quickly understood that he did not need to work, as plenty of low-paid hourly workers were available to perform the labor. Darrell Jr. developed a talent of making flirting appear like work, like he was serving customers. If young, single girls were not easily found in the store, he would look for the signature bored, young, vacation wife whose husband was off drinking somewhere with friends or playing golf or both. Hell, this gig was easier than picking up girls on the beach or in a bar. Darrell Jr. had been working on his technique to meet women since he had achieved puberty.

One year, while acting as a beach lifeguard, Darrell Jr. had developed a successful method with women based on one "law of large numbers." With the help of some friends, Darrell Jr. was able to land an assignment at the worst lifeguard money spot on the beach, the First Avenue swash.

The swash was a high-tide creek that connected a large pond to the ocean for only an hour of each tide. The swash was more of a drainage ditch than a creek and presented dangerous, swift currents when the pond emptied with the falling tide. No hotels with cash-flush tourists were located behind the swash area. A different, lower-income clientele was somehow attracted to this unappealing and unsafe swash beach, and it was always crowded on weekends.

Lifeguards received the majority of their pay from sales commissions on floats, chairs, and umbrellas, and the more profitable locations were held by the senior guards. Since no one with money to spend on such luxuries went to the swash beach, and because it presented the real possibility for a lot of hard, dangerous work for a lifeguard, the spot was assigned to the lowest-ranking rookie on the beach.

Darrell Jr. quickly found that in this swash location, he was surrounded by drunks, nonswimmers, and locals looking to grab some free umbrella time. Despite his lack of awareness, Darrell Jr. did notice the enormous volume of walking beach traffic passing his stand. He was witness to the great humanity parade as it "cruised" the beach.

Darrell Jr. was immune to the unique human emotional elements and couldn't care less about what was going on in the minds of the individuals or the dynamics of the groups that passed. He was unaware that in the mix, he watched loneliness pondering the next move, a lover forlorn, a couple planning the future, children playing, and joggers jogging. He watched an unending drift to and fro, testing the water's edge, aimless searching for a shark's tooth or some other prize offered up by the sea.

To Darrell Jr. the most exciting part of this simultaneous north-south migration was the number of scantily clad female participants. There were short ones, tall ones, skinny ones, fat ones, flat ones, well-endowed ones, blondes, redheads, brunettes, young, old, together in groups, in couples, singles, two-piece suits, one-piece suits, low-cut bikinis, and more. The overwhelming quantities of the female herd walking, swimming, or sunning on the beach mesmerized Darrell Jr. As he was never busy renting umbrellas, and as it was a sure thing that any swimmer who got in trouble on his beach would be washed south by the swash current to the next guard, Darrell focused all his time on the women passing.

As a descendant of generations of gift-store retailers, Darrell Jr. had been taught from an early age about success based on high traffic count. Over the years Darrell Sr. had studied the traffic that passed his stores and that of his competitors. Carefully collected data showed that at the beach resort, one could hope to attract between 2 and 5 percent of all the potential passing customers. Even the worst storefront advertising should yield at the lower end of at least 1 percent. His conclusion was to put your store in a high-traffic area, and if you could just sell to 2 percent, your business would be successful.

Although his personal storefront advertised a dubious appeal factor, Darrell Jr. put this knowledge to work with the women walking the beach. He was not a bronzed, muscular blond-haired sun-god like some of his fellow guards, but he was not ugly either. He was a bit pudgy, but he covered the imperfection with an oversized lifeguard T-shirt. The stenciled T-shirt did more than cover the acne on his back; he used it as his calling card to help establish contact.

He had tried a number of different lines in an attempt to develop some short-term, week-long vacation relationships, but he was too impatient. Darrell Jr. had never been that diligent; he just wanted to get laid, like many other eighteen-to twenty-year-old males at the beach, and no emotional bonding was required.

After a couple of weeks, he decided to dispense with the courtship ritual and use the known successful formulas of the retail business. Darrell Jr.'s new line to every single female who walked past his beach was, "Do you want to fuck?"

The message was not complex, sophisticated, or filled with innuendo. Darrell Jr. just got to the bottom line. He had to deal with some rejection while using this strategy. But with between fifteen hundred and two thousand women per day passing his location, Darrell Jr. was able to validate the retail model that he had been taught: seeking a customer capture rate between 2 and 5 percent. He actually achieved a rate far below the low end of the model, but the numbers proved sufficient to satisfy his needs.

Incredibly one, sometimes two, women per day would say, "Hell yeah!" He developed many strategies to deal with the actual fulfillment of his offer. Some women took him to sea for some brief underwater action powered by the constant rolling waves, letting them experience all the thrills of public sex without being arrested. Sometimes he would take them to the seldom-used elevator on the north side of the hotel behind his lifeguard stand. Of course, if the girl du jour or du moment had a nearby hotel room, then he opted for the luxury of a bed. He was more inclined not to get that personal; he just wanted that brief moment of conquest, passion, and relief. That was Darrell Jr. He was one of those guys who, when he had it all, wanted something more and was too dumb to realize when he had enough.

As a lifeguard he had been surrounded by the less privileged, within sight of those more successful and next to nature's flush. His life had developed a similar pattern; he had all he could enjoy, he could see success, but he did not feel he was in it. He lived and worked where life flushed by in a polluted current and a dangerous undertow, and still he was unaware.

Chapter 10

Yielding to exhaustion, Bo Jr. fell asleep during the ride back to what he hoped would be a good job at The Blue House Restaurant and Lounge. Even though his torturous ordeal had lasted only a few hours, he felt like he had been straddled over that sharp blade for a week. Before that harrowing experience, he had traveled for twenty-four hours, mostly on foot, covering the seventy miles from his home in rural Williamsburg County, and then he had his short time drinking beer at The Blue House. He was exhausted and starved.

As instructed, Bo Jr. was stretched out on the plush-leather rear seat of the sleek Crown Victoria, his head still covered with a sack. He was snoring. The sack was rising and falling with each exhaled breath. As the snoring reached its crescendo, Guido had to turn up the volume on his music. Bo Jr.'s nasalized drone had interrupted Guido's "happy place."

Riding in the luxurious, company car and listening to his favorite Italian opera stars was his solitude. Guido turned the amplifier volume to a level marked thirty-two on the dial, boosting the eleven Bose stereo speakers to the body-vibration mode. The operatic finale blasted its closing notes as Guido turned into a concealed drive beside a small blue cottage behind The Blue House Restaurant and Lounge. The Crown Victoria rolled to a smooth stop under the recently enclosed parking shed. A thin line of cedar trees and a clump of green, leafy shrubs formed a border between the cottage and the parking lot.

Guido lived in the cottage and viewed the organic buffer as his portal curtain. When he crossed from the cottage dimension of real life to the Blue House property, it was show time, and he was on stage. His stage required an intimidating presence with a certain custom and persona. When he passed back from the parking lot to the cottage, he was more at ease, in his world, with less need to be fully alert, less need to project force or determent. When he was home, he was more like the true inner Guido. Guido lived two lives. He survived the tough-guy life, but he desired the family homelife. Right now all he had was this world of hired muscle, and that train had a one-way ticket.

"Wake up, kid," Guido barked. He shut off the engine and pressed his remote control device, closing the garage door to conceal their presence.

Bo Jr. rustled, gave a few snorts, and began to come around. He jerked upward, grabbing and swinging his huge fists, not sure of his surroundings, feeling trapped under the hood. He woke up, not from the music or Guido's bark, but because the car stopped and silence followed. The fuzz in Bo Jr.'s head began to clear. Instinct motivated him to yank the bag off his head, but he quickly remembered the reason for it and stopped.

"May I remove the bag now, sir?" He regained his composure and yawned under the hood.

"Yeah, you can take it off, kid," Guido answered, shaking his head in mild amazement at how unflappable this kid seemed to be. He had the basic internal structure for the makings of a good muscle sidekick, but much work was required. Bo Jr. pulled the bag off his head, looked around, and climbed out the back door. Guido led the way to the side door of the cottage that opened directly into a small but sufficiently sized kitchen.

"Have a seat, son," Guido directed. "You're one lucky little fuck, ya know that, kid?" he said with a half smile, not expecting a reply. "We like what we see here with you and your potential, but we're gonna make a few changes, and you're gonna like em! You give me any shit, and you'll find your ass staked out in the swamp, hoping to die before the vultures start eating on you. We'll make sure you look really tempting to the birds. Can you imagine lying there, all alone, can't move, and the vultures circling above, waiting for you to ripen up before they drop down to pick you apart? They start with your soft parts. I'll promise you, it won't be a good thing."

Guido practiced his art of creating intimidating, visual imagery. His talent served him well in his chosen profession. If you put vivid images in the mind of the mark, then violence was rarely required. Occasionally, he had to deal with the dumb thug who either couldn't mentally process his proposed vision, or just didn't believe he meant it. In these rare cases, Guido would have to follow through, precisely as promised. Those who knew him were aware that Guido wasted no time with false threats. They knew that if he promised a vision, and he always added the threatening promise, Guido would deliver exactly as described. One of his favorite disposal methods involved sharks. Those beasts left no evidence.

Bo Jr. got the picture. He was not as dumb as he looked on such matters. He had seen the results of bad drug deals; they were rarely pretty, and the muscle always won. Bo Jr. wanted to be with the muscle.

"Sir, you don't need to worry 'bout me. I want to work at your business. I want to be in your organization."

"Bo Jr., you ain't never gonna be part of this organization. You don't have the right bloodline. You may work here, but you'll never be a part of what's here, so just get that shit outta your head right now. It will never happen. Never!"

Bo Jr. remember how his mother and grandmother had talked about their family heritage and a right to be counted as worthy, part of the society *in* crowd with traceable, noble bloodlines. All he had to show for their desires and efforts was his name, which had been gradually eroded and reduced from its former self, just as his family fortunes had vanished through the years.

"By the way, kid, what's up with this Bo Jr. name thing? Isn't that name redundant or an oxymoron or what?"

Bo Jr. felt the need to explain. "Well, sir, I'm named after my dad. They call him Bo. Actually, my whole name is Beauregard Pinckney

Calhoun the Fourth, but that's worse than Bo the Fourth, and that don't go over so well where I'm from. My dad said that neither Beauregard nor Pinckney allowed a fellow a fightin' chance. He used Bo to get along when he was growin' up, being he was Bo the First, so he changed my name to Bo Jr."

"Well, boy, that's quite a label, but I can't see how any one of those combinations makes sense anywhere. How did you get named the Fourth when your dad was the First, and now they call you Junior? Hey, just...just never mind. But given you obviously got this name heritage and everything, I'll give you your due. I've got a family name myself, but they call me Guido. You can call me that or Mr. G, take your pick." Guido grabbed a bottle of water from his fridge.

"I got to tell you, though—I can't be going around here calling you Bo Jr. The Blue House is a class joint, and we got our reputation to consider. I'll tell you what; I'll call you Bo J for short. It has a ring to it, a little more class. It almost sounds French, and French is considered sophisticated whether we like 'em or not." Guido folded his arms and looked content with his decision on Bo Jr.'s new name.

"OK, sir, whatever. Long as I can make some money, meet some girls, it's all the same to me what y'all call me," Bo Jr.—or should that be Bo J—replied. He was resigned to the fact that people call you what they want, what they think you are to them. One more letter gone, one more step down. One less letter, and he would be his father, and that was not the direction Bo J wanted to go.

"Welcome to my home, Bo J. For now you stay in the small bedroom off the hallway. I've got rules here. This house will stay the way you see it, clean! If you eat or use something, you clean it up, when you use it—not later, but immediately. If you bring a date in here, I don't want to know it. If I have a date in here, you don't interrupt, you sit outside, sleep in the car, I don't care. My point here is, I'm sharing my home with you, and you are gonna live by my rules," Guido instructed without a hint of compromise in his voice.

"Yes sir, I'm familiar with that drill," Bo J replied.

"We are on call twenty-four/seven. If Tony calls, we drop what we're doing and run to see what he needs. We start our day at 6 p.m., and we work until the place closes, which is often around dawn. Come on, I'll show you."

With Bo J in tow, Guido passed through the cedar tree boundary, crossed the parking lot, and opened the side door to the Blue House. Bo J felt the scene a bit surreal as they entered the lounge he had tried to stiff just the night before. The place looked different in daylight. Dim bar lights at night had successfully concealed a lot of bad.

"After 10 p.m. we start charging five bucks to get in the place. After midnight we only allow members to enter, and that rule stands seven days a week."

"I thought bars closed at twelve on Saturday night," Bo J said.

"That's the law. Bars open to the public in this state are required to close at twelve on Saturday night, at 2 a.m. Monday through Friday, and must be closed all day on Sunday. We comply with those laws for the public bar; anyone here outside of those hours must be a member. We have annual memberships, monthly, weekly, and even one-night memberships. We get a lot of one-nighters." Guido showed Bo J the membership booth, member ID badges, and the process for stamping those allowed in the game room.

"Local residents, summer workers, traveling salesmen, and loyal customers for one hundred miles in all directions are all part of our membership. We are *the* place for all the poor slobs around here who work nights. By the time our patrons get through taking care of tourists at their own businesses, most bars are closed. They can come here and party on their clock. We pay the right people so we aren't hassled, and we follow the rules for membership. Remember that, 'cause part of your job someday will be to check membership cards."

Guido had walked to a large, heavy, steel door in the hallway just past the toilets. "Women" marked the entry hall on the left, and "Men" marked the portal on the right. The heavy center door was marked "Private." Inside the passageway to the men's room was a table with towels, aftershave, mouthwash, mints, and a small wicker basket. Guido continued the lecture.

"One-nighters must be with a member or someone we know, some-one famous for something. For a one-night membership, we charge ten bucks. Most pay it, 'cause they don't want to be embarrassed in front of their friends. It's a great profit maker for the club. We comp some of the guys in the well-known bands like the Tams, the Embers, or the Swinging Medallions; they party with their friends and help keep the mystique of the place alive."

Guido stopped and stared at Bo J to emphasize his point. "Mystique is important to people, 'cause they all wanna be part of something famous. You're gonna find that out, son. Hell, that's why you showed up; you wanted to be part of something! The mystique about a place that's spread by word of mouth is a secret for success. So here's your job."

Bo J moved closer to the suspicious private door, the entrance he had seen on his previous visit. He wanted to know what was so damn secret that it required such vigilance.

"Tonight, after nine, you will stand or sit here by this table. You will offer the bar patrons a towel after they wash their hands, or give them any of these toiletries they might need. The wicker basket is for tips. Prime the basket with a couple of ones and some quarters to let people know what it's for. Your most important job is to keep anyone from going through this door, unless I bring them through. Your ass depends on how well you guard this door. You got that, Bo J?"

"What's behind the door?"

Guido opened the door to what appeared to be a bingo parlor with large card tables, a bar, and five taller tables draped with custom green-canvas covers.

"Protecting this room for members only and keeping out some snooping authorities who ain't on the payroll is your job, and your life depends on it."

They moved into the room and stood between the tables. "We have bingo seven nights a week. We have blackjack, poker, roulette, craps, and slot machines, all for our members. This room is not a casino. It is a game room for our members. Should they decide to bet against one another, which may include the dealers, who are members, that is their decision. We only facilitate their enjoyment of board games, cards, or dice. If any heat that don't belong or some drunk attempts to come through that door, you flip this wall switch next to your towel table, and that will lock the door and turn on the alarm our other bouncers can hear in their earpiece."

Guido walked to Bo J's post and demonstrated how the switch worked.

"But that's the emergency mode. Most people should just be redirected back to the lounge. We have others who help herd the crowd. You are responsible for this door." Guido pounded the door with the back of his meaty fist and looked at Bo J to see if he got the message.

"So you want me to be your bathroom attendant?" Bo J asked somewhat in disbelief. "After all the crap you put me through today, y'all want me to be a damn bathroom attendant?"

"Yeah, that's right, kid, and you're gonna like it! This is where you start in our business. You may see this work as demeaning, but if you fuck up, you're gonna wish you had just done your job with a smile. Now trust me, this job is important. At this table you'll receive some major tips. You might meet a lady or two while they wait in line. Give it a try, prove yourself, and you could move up." Guido tried to calm Bo J's obvious dissatisfaction. "Besides, you got no choice. You owe the boss."

He paused for a moment to let Bo J realize his plight and settle down. "It'll be easy, you'll see. Now come on, let's get you cleaned up and get you a suit or two. We need to show a little class around here, create the mystique. You can't be no slob in this business. Tony don't allow it!"

They locked up and walked side-by-side back to the cottage. Tony watched from his office through mirrored glass, thinking this kid might actually be a good unpaid addition to his team. Tough love was required, and Guido was just the guy to deal it out.

As they walked, Bo J asked, "You guys got any good weed for sale here? If not, I know a great source; it'll make your toes curl and make you crave a KK dozen sugar high."

"What the hell is a KK dozen sugar high?" Guido was curious.

"It's what you do after you get an outrageous case of the munchies. You go to Krispy Kreme, order a dozen fresh glazed, and you eat all those hot fresh doughnuts straight from the glazing pot. The sugar high is what comes next. It makes the high from the pot better and last longer, but with more calories." Bo J announced this formula with the confidence of experience.

Guido shook his head and chuckled at this young man. "I tell you what, first we'll get you a couple of new suits, which will go on your bill. Then we'll drop by the Krispy Kreme, one of my favorite spots, before we start our workday. After that we'll talk about where you get your weed." Guido was beginning to like Bo J's spirit. And to think, just hours before, they had been mentally torturing this man-boy. This quick reversal of fortunes and the forgiving nature of Bo J gave Guido reason for caution. He didn't understand yet what made this young man tick.

Chapter 11

Guido and Bo J drove to Santorre's Men's Store located on the perimeter of the Grand Strand Mall. The store was purposely positioned on the Bypass at the intersection of Highway 501, a direct route connecting to Interstates 95 and 20. Santorre enjoyed the fruits of a well-established chain of stores strategically located at primary distribution points along Interstate Highway 95 from Miami to Boston. In recent years new strip-mall outlets had been opened along Interstate Highways I-75, I-85, I-26, I-10, I-40, and I-20. Growth followed the highways.

Locations for Santorre's stores were carefully selected to form a network that allowed the movement of inventory between stores. When Santorre found a solid growth area near one of his strip-mall stores, he would also open a classic neighborhood Italian restaurant. His wine inventory was unmatched.

Santorre's growth, sales, and cash deposits were amazing when compared with other merchants in the neighborhood. The banks welcomed the business he brought to town. The fine Italian suits and select vintage wines were a very expensive inventory to maintain, but his business ventures achieved highly profitable returns, driven by customers who demonstrated an unusual proclivity to purchase his suits, ties, pasta, and wine with cash.

The apparent profitability of the neighborhood Santorre storefronts provided a camouflaging veil for the fuel that propelled his growth. The drug business needed distribution and money management like any other business. Santorre's suits, pasta, and drug shipments were well managed.

From whatever location the drugs came to the mob, domestic or as an import, Santorre had the distribution network on the East Coast.

When the cash was collected and eventually brought to each store to pay for a suit or to his restaurant for a signature meal, or a bottle or two of expensive wine, Santorre took the deposit. If he had too much cash from a bulk sale at one store, he moved the cash with other inventory to another store that expected lower deposits that week. Santorre was a good bookkeeper; the business and his life depended on it.

Guido walked confidently into Santorre's with Bo J a short two steps behind. Alonzo, the local store manager, was waiting for them just inside the front door. Alonzo and Guido were of equal size and strength. You wouldn't want to tangle with these two men in a dark alley or in the middle of Main Street at noon, for that matter. After the appropriate cheek-touching and back-slapping greetings were exchanged, Guido turned to introduce Bo J, who was wiping his runny nose with the back of his right hand. Guido slapped the back of Bo J's head.

"Whatsa matta, you dumb shit! I bring you here to meet this man, my friend, my brother, to shake his hand, and you stand there wiping your sloppy nose. You trying to embarrass me and insult my friend? Go to the toilet, wash those hands good, and get your ass back here quick!"

Bo J didn't do it on purpose. He thought to himself, what else would he wipe his nose with? He meant no insult. He worried as he washed his hands and prepared his best apology. Bo J knew he had a lot to learn, but he was willing.

"I'm really sorry, sir. If I caused you any grief or insult or anything, I didn't mean nuthin' by it. My hands are really clean, I washed them twice." Bo J blurted out his untimely apology as he quickly walked out of the toilet and up to Guido and Alonzo. Unfortunately, Guido and Alonzo were talking, and his earnest, youthful exuberance interrupted their conversation. Bo J received another whack on the back of his head and had a painful recollection of home. How long would he have to endure such humiliating treatment?

Finally, Guido said, "Alonzo my friend, I want you to meet Bo J. This boy has a few debts to pay the boss, and he'll be helping out for a while at the Blue House. If he didn't owe the boss, we probably woulda killed him and left his body to the crabs in the Waccamaw River already, but that would just waste my time and pollute the river, so here he is. We need to suit him up and start to teach him some manners."

Alonzo reached out his hand to shake Bo J's recently cleaned right hand. Bo J felt a firm killer grip and gave his best back. It was always important to trade firm handshakes with tough guys.

"You must be something special," Alonzo said with a grin and a laser-beam stare into Bo J's eyes, searching for a hint of deceit. "Tony usually don't give punks like you a chance to pay their debts, and I've never seen Guido speak so highly of anyone." He was making Bo J nervous, and although Bo J understood this technique was only another attempt to intimidate him, to test his savvy, he still looked away. He blinked, which brought more curses and head pops from Guido.

"Don't ever let anyone stare you down, boy, except me. Your job depends on your ability to be mentally and physically tough. The eyes are a mighty tool that can be used to control weaker men. Damn, I've gotta lotta work here!" Guido shouted in frustration.

"Let's get this boy dressed," Guido said in a more composed tone, suddenly shifting the focus and direction of the conversation. Alonzo was ahead of the game; he had already selected four suits, eight shirts, a dozen ties, belts, shoes, socks, and underwear—an entire wardrobe, all the right sizes. Alonzo was good at sizing up his customers and his enemies.

"But I can't afford all these clothes, sir. I can't pay for all this!"

"Yes, you can, and you will," said Guido as if Bo J had no choice. He didn't.

Chapter 12

~

After Bo J was dressed and the remaining wardrobe items were put away neatly in the cottage closet, Guido drove to another favorite spot closer to the beach and prominently located on Kings Highway. The Krispy Kreme doughnut shop was something they both agreed on.

"Try not to get any doughnut crumbs or coffee on your new clothes. Use the napkin to wipe your mouth while you eat, and don't slurp your coffee." Guido was starting to sound like Bo J's father again, but he didn't care. They were at the KK, and he had no plans to order coffee.

Evelyn saw the well-dressed, middle-aged Italian hunk walk in the front door; at least, that's how she would describe him to Edna. She had seen him before, maybe twice, once while she was out back on a smoke break, and another time he was leaving as she arrived for her shift. Now she would have an opportunity to serve him and maybe discover his name.

"Afternoon, fellas, what can I get you?" Evelyn asked with a smile. In front of each man, she laid down napkins that displayed the green-and-red Krispy Kreme logo.

"Afternoon, doll. I'll have a coffee and four hot glazed," Guido offered up without much thought.

"I'll have a Co' Cola and six hot glazed," added Bo J.

The doughnut-cooking production was primarily automated and available for viewing by customers through windows located behind the counter. As customers awaited their delectable treats, they could watch the doughnuts being covered with melted sugar glazing as they moved along a stainless-steel wire conveyor belt. Shortly thereafter the warm pastries were delivered onto their plates.

Hot-glazed were only served at Krispy Kreme counters at the point of production and only if the customer requested it. This treat was a culinary delight held as a secret in the South "since 1937," until tourists and long-distance truckers predictably leaked the news to other regions of the country after fortunate encounters at a Southern-based KK. Each *hot-glazed* provided the customer with a bucket of calories and twice the sugar intake that should be legally allowed in most states, but the melted sugar coating on each doughnut was oh so good, and no one complained.

The average human could reasonably consume two *hot-glazed* without blood-sugar escalations that might affect his ability to drive. Guido and Bo J were, of course, not average humans, and neither worried about blood sugar.

The tantalizing smell of fresh cooked doughnuts followed Evelyn from the kitchen to these two thrill-seeking customers. An invisible redolent temptation drifted in the air as she passed customers sitting at the counter, causing them to consider the prospect of just one more hit. More orders were placed along this aromatic path.

Bo J and Guido each bit into the first hot one before the plates touched the counter. They each consumed half of one pastry treat in one bite and ceremoniously licked the warm, moist glaze from their fingers. Conversation would not interrupt their culinary craving.

Bo J's combination of "a Co' Cola and six hot-glazed" would yield a sugar rush with the stimulation thrust of an adrenaline shot to the heart. His normally aggressive, youthful behavior, combined with the effects of this snack, could morph his current calm demeanor into that of a hyper-manic fidgety bull of a boy or induce a coma.

Evelyn's experience in this business whispered a caution to her brain. With a sly grin on her face, she watched and waited for the sugar drug to take effect.

"You boys hungry, or just in need of a quick fix?" Evelyn asked as she removed two empty plates from the counter.

"No ma'am...we just love hot Krispy Kremes," Bo J mumbled between gulps. "I could eat these...even after a full meal."

"No, beautiful, we just needed a break and a little pick-me-up before work," Guido responded smoothly with a smile and a wink. "Thanks for bringing these so fresh."

Beautiful! Doll! Who was this debonair Yankee gentleman? Evelyn had met damn few gentlemen, North or South. But the Southern smooth movers normally said *darlin', sweetie,* or *honey.* The less-smooth suitors, those more on the redneck side, used other less-flattering descriptors. She had heard them all and understood the words as preludes to their same desired end. Her typical answer was, "In your dreams," the most neutral thing she could say without causing her customer to become angry and to reduce her typically insignificant tip to zero.

The friendly banter kept her loyal customers coming back. She made them feel like they had a friend, a temporary confidant, and a place where someone cared to know their name. She was someone with whom they could share their troubles and joys, someone to listen, someone for those who had little else in their world; Evelyn was their girl.

For an endless cup of coffee and a couple of doughnuts, most orders totaled less than two bucks. With this purchase customers expected service, conversation, a clean ashtray, and a place at the counter for an hour or two. A 15 percent tip on this bill was unacceptable, and she rightly challenged inadequate offerings. The daily "counter leaner" knew the drill and paid a fair share for service with a caring smile.

"What's your name, doll?" the big man asked in a low, sultry voice.

"My name's Evelyn, what's yours?" she asked in her most sincere, caring manner. Evelyn felt a positive click here, a woman's intuitive moment. She wanted the man to see her for herself, not a waitress behind a doughnut counter whom he might try to maneuver into a one-night stand.

When she was asked this most personal question from an obvious "one doughnut and gone" client, she would make up a name. Evelyn and Edna played this name game quite often in their tourist-enriched environment. Evelyn's favorite pseudonym was Fran. Edna liked to use Barb. When a brave lad would ask, Evelyn would normally reply with a playful smirk and a hand on her hip, smacking on chewing gum, "Fran.

And what's your name, sailor?" But this time she had been serious and truthful.

Guido answered her question with a sparkle in his eye. "My name is Salvatore Carmine Antonio Lorenzo Capone, but they call me Guido. Call me anything you want, beautiful, just as long as you smile." This handsome new fellow appeared to have a brain and some manners, an unusual three-part combination for Evelyn's typical clientele.

Bo J had downed two more hot ones and gulped half of his Coke, showing no particular interest in the flirtatious conversation. Two truck drivers slumped on their stools at the end of the counter. They were staring at Evelyn, waiting for their next coffee refill, casually smoking. Since they were apparently considering homesteading at this end of the restaurant, Evelyn was not bothered by their obvious growing impatience. Both controlled their urge to interrupt, sensing any pleasure they might gain from more coffee could be offset by the wrath of these two huge men. So they waited, took another drag off their filtered Marlboros, and fingered the sugary crumbs on their doughnut plates; neither had a particularly original thought to share. Wisely, silence was maintained in their corner.

"Haven't I seen you here before? I mean, you have come in a time or two, haven't you?" Evelyn was now slightly flustered and growing uncomfortable with customers watching her and Guido as they sought to introduce themselves and discover some common ground. Such personal intimate and vulnerable moments were difficult in private, but impossible on the public stage of the doughnut counter.

Normally, she could simultaneously carry on a multithreaded coquettish dialogue with three or four rowdy customers at the counter and two at the register and never miss a lick in the doughnut-house banter, but this flow was awkward. She felt a strange tingle inside, awakening a dormant feeling remembered from teenage years, a giddy young love. She bit her lower lip.

"Yes, I've been here a few times, but I've not seen you. I would've remembered that...I mean, I would have remembered you." Even Guido was stumbling from his normal smooth delivery. Evelyn's eyes had captured him. Guido met enticing women all the time, but in his own work environment, where they were typically drunk or out for a wild fling. It was not the environment where serious relationships bloom and grow to full flower. Guido had a good feeling about this lady.

Bo J had finished all six pastries and was chugging down the last of his Coke. He put the bottle down hard on the counter and burped, signaling the completion of his feast. He slouched on his seat, hands hanging straight down, his belly protruding, pulling gaps in his shirt between the buttons. As this sweet treat was the only food Bo J had consumed since the Sinclair Gas Station hot dog the evening before, his blood sugar level was heading off the charts.

His new wardrobe was barely two hours out of the store, and Bo J sat with a sprinkling of sugar crumbs on the front of his suit and dribbles of Coke on his fifty-dollar yellow patterned tie. His coat hung open, and with a slack-jawed mouth and a stupefied stare, he gazed at Guido. Despite their desire to filter out the rest of the world, Guido and Evelyn could not ignore this unwanted attention.

"Well, young lady, as much as I hate to break off this engaging conversation, I think I need to get my partner stabilized before we report to work. Sorry for his sloppy appearance, he's had a rough day. I would like to see you again soon and get to know you a little better." Guido looked in Evelyn's eyes and spoke with sincerity.

"I would love that. Some other time soon sounds great." Evelyn stumbled over the words, but finished with a sweet smile. Get to know you! Is that what he said? Who says that? How many guys wanted to get to know you anymore? Was this guy real?

"How will I get in touch with you? Where do you work? Maybe we could meet after work?" Evelyn blurted all these questions and then thought perhaps she was being a little too forward.

Guido slipped a fifty-dollar bill under his coffee cup, and stood to leave, unconcerned about his unprecedented excess tipping. He whispered a sultry reply, "No worries, I'll see you tomorrow. What hours do you work?"

"Two to ten p.m., and I'll be in the Frisky Rabbit around ten forty-five most evenings, don't work on Sunday or Monday unless we have a no-show." Evelyn looked up at Guido, realizing how big he really was. He was about the same size as Eddie, but thicker. He was a hunk indeed.

Guido and Bo J walked out. They appeared somewhat out of place in their tailored suits, but the sugary crumbs that decorated their lapels identified them as true KK fans.

Evelyn looked down to the counter and picked up the fifty-dollar bill laid on the $6.75 bill. When she looked up, Guido was backing out in a black limo. She ran to the front door and held up the bill.

Guido rolled down the electric dark-tinted window and said, "Keep it, angel. Thanks for the service."

Evelyn really liked this guy. He had looks, class, manners, and money. What's not to like? Lost in her own fantasy, she floated back to her high ground behind the counter. Without a request or a conscious intention, she returned to the monotonous task of refilling the numerous empty coffee cups of her gang of counter-leaners.

Chapter 13

Two days after the Western Sizzler fiasco, Edna was summoned by Darrell Jr. to help open the One-Eyed Flounder. As always, when asked, she pitched in to help. Edna was dependable. Darrell Jr. had called as she was returning from her sunrise walk with Evelyn. She was awake, her metabolic fire stoked with a rich cup of French Roast coffee and a warm, sweet Krispy Kreme doughnut. Three summer workers scheduled for the opening shift at the One-Eyed Flounder had called in sick just moments before opening.

This early-morning sick call was a normal occurrence for the better summer workers. The bad ones never called, they just didn't show up, and when they finally did come in, they acted as if there was no problem. Darrell Jr. had similar character flaws and was accustomed to it. He typically overbooked employees like airlines overbooked seats, with a validated expectation that some workers, like passengers, would not show up. Well, today was no different, just more no-shows than usual.

The tardiness and absenteeism could be blamed almost entirely on a Rolling Stones concert that had captured the attention of the town the night before. Drinking, loud parties, hangovers, and no-show workers were natural derivatives of such an evening. This event was the concert of the summer. Tomorrow would bring its own unique excuses, but today, blame it on the Stones.

This chain of predictable events brought Darrell Jr. and Edna to the One-Eyed Flounder early. Darrell Jr. was barely coherent, for he too had been at the concert. He was driven not by today's profits, even though he was getting a share, but by the fear of his father's wrath, and the ever-present threat to cut him out of the will. His dad was also working early. He had picked up Darrell Jr. to make sure he was on time to help open the store. Dad unlocked and swung open the doors, allowing the employees to stream through, spreading out to work like bees from a hive.

Edna passed by the T-shirt section and noticed steam coming from the press. An employee in a hurry to leave last night must have left it on, she thought. The steam press was used to customize T-shirts by adhering an innovative cliché or a marginally humorous saying that tourists would wear with pride while at the beach. The shirts were quick sellers at 3-for-$10. The press-on lettering quickly took the price of each shirt to ten dollars apiece and a nice profit. Witty tourists selected what appeared at the time to be hilarious phrases like, "I don't suffer from insanity, I enjoy every minute of it," or "Danger, Next mood swing, five minutes." They would chuckle and make an impulse purchase.

Edna turned off the press and moved on past the shark-tooth display, noticing more misplaced merchandise. The store appeared out of order, but given the low quality of the workers this summer, she was not terribly surprised. Edna turned the corner and stopped dumbfounded for a long awkward pause.

It was Tara, the latest wild child to work the tourist trinket circuit. Tara liked to work the evening shift, allowing her the morning to catch some rays and the late night to party. She had settled into the Hutches for the summer and had worked a couple of weeks at the One-Eyed Flounder. As a proud and gorgeous daughter of Tennessee, she often wore orange and sang "Rocky Top" at the top of her lungs every time she got high from any source of stimulant, and that was often. Tara was lashed to an eight-foot-high display rack that held painted coconut heads, a tourist favorite at the One-Eyed Flounder.

Edna and Tara stared wild-eyed at each other until Edna regained speech and screamed. Tara forced a muffled cry into her gag, and her eyes flared with anxiety and fear. Store security arrived and escorted Edna to a nearby chair. She was shaking, suddenly haunted by her uncanny bout with bad luck. What were the odds she would be the first to discover these poor people? She was too close to these attacks to think she might not somehow be connected. Was she being watched or set up? She didn't understand.

Tara was another matter. Security called 911. Disconnecting her from the rack of coconut heads might destroy evidence that the police would need to solve this weird assault, so they watched and waited.

"Myrtle Beach" was painted with red letters across Tara's forehead, and her face had been painted in a similar pattern as the coconuts, with the same red and black paint. Her head and neck were tied in a way that positioned her face like one of the souvenir coconuts on the shelf. Her arms and legs were tied to look as if she had been crucified. Her wrists were lashed with six-foot rubber snakes, the kind sold in the rubber reptile section of the One-Eyed Flounder. Three Slinkys were wrapped tight round and round her ankles. The wire was so tight that it was cutting through her skin. Tara had a bag of pot stuffed in her mouth and secured with reliable, gray, duct tape. Besides a thong made from the store's finest camouflage material, the only garment Tara wore was an extra-large Tennessee-orange, 3-for-$10 T-shirt with big, white, press-on letters that now predictably said, "Go Home."

Tara had black paint around her eyes. Both ears had been recently pierced, each sporting a new shark's tooth earring. Two big shark jaws, filled with the original owner's final set of teeth, had been taken from the front display, tied to the display shelf, and clamped on each bare ass cheek. The scene looked like two sharks had simultaneously attacked her from the rear.

The jaws had been pressed tight until the tips of the teeth had just penetrated her skin. When the police tried to release her from the display shelf, they had not seen the jaws. They cut the rubber snakes, Slinkys, and duct tape, and she fainted, falling forward; but she was held to the display rack by the shark jaws, causing more bleeding. After more work the rescue team was able to pry the jaws apart. Darrell Sr. was supervising on the scene and had instructed the EMTs not to break the valuable shark jaws.

The lead EMT moved quickly, not so much that he felt this was an emergency, but he wanted to check out this shark wound and the potential for infection. As other beach-area EMTs, he had been trained to recognize and treat shark bites, but these bites were slightly different. He cautioned Tara to lie still while he cleaned and dressed her wounds. He took his time now to ensure proper treatment of her plump, well-shaped behind.

Later, Tara answered Detective McKenzie's questions and then was gone that day, back home as fast as she could go despite her extremely sore derrière. She gave only a brief description of the man who did this to her. He was tall, thick, and mean. He wore a ski mask and had promised real trouble if she didn't leave. She had heard about the others who had been attacked and needed no further encouragement.

Booney and Murph collected another rental security deposit. The Hutches had another room opening. Vernon lost another dealer and another lid, and he wasn't happy about it either. Edna was disturbed and scared.

Chapter 14

It was still early in the day when the gift shop closed and the employees were released so the police investigation could continue. With her mind reeling as she sorted through the collage of weird details she had just seen, Edna walked the short distance from the One-Eyed Flounder to her garage apartment.

As she shuffled up the gravel drive, Eddie stepped out of the garage with two black plastic bags for the garbage. Either Edna was feeling vulnerable or she was becoming more suspiciously aware of everyday details, but she had never really noticed how big Eddie was. Or maybe he just seemed much larger at this moment as she stood outside, directly in front of him, face to chest. Eddie was tall, thick, and strong for a man of his age. He must have been quite a beast in his youth, she thought.

"What's all the fuss down at the One-Eyed Flounder, Edna?" Eddie asked with a smile and a nod toward the tourist trap.

"Tara...Tara was found tied up...tied up wearing a shirt that said, 'Go Home'...but I'm not supposed to talk about it." Edna spoke with thoughtful phrases and nervous eyes looking here and there and finally up at Eddie. "Eddie, I'm scared. It's happening all around me; three so far, and I've found them all. I mean, I've been the first one to see all three. I could be next!" Her voice betrayed her rising anxiety.

"You don't have anything to worry about, honey." Eddie spoke with a little too much confidence for Edna not to notice.

"How do you know, Eddie? How can you be so sure?"

"Because you're not a loud, troublemaking, summer worker that sells pot. That's the profile, isn't it?" snarled Eddie.

"Well, I don't know, I, I guess. I've never really heard anyone say that. Until this morning, only two had been scared away. How would you know?"

"I've got my sources, but it's obvious, even with the first two. It's clear that someone didn't like these kids. And they've all had pot in their mouths...bunch of pot-smoking hippies! Good riddance." Eddie continued down the drive just in time to toss the plastic bags in the trash truck as it stopped in front of their house.

When Eddie turned to walk past, Edna noticed a smear of red paint on the back of his arm. She stared at his arm while he walked. For a moment Eddie talked to his friend, the trash-truck driver. They chuckled, and then Eddie walked back up the driveway to the house. The trash collectors moved on to the Hutches to gather the trash, with its overflow of beer cans.

With growing concern Edna turned and walked to the stairs of her garage apartment. She had been confounded by the events of the day, and now she was really scared. She and Evelyn had always looked to Eddie as a surrogate dad, their protector. He had said not to worry, but she was worried. How did he know they all had pot in their mouths? She hadn't said anything about Tara and pot. Was he just talking about the first two? Had he been talking with his police buddies?

She walked past the side porch and saw a freshly painted red-and-black birdhouse, the same colors used to paint Tara like a coconut. A bag of birdseed lay ready to fill the house after the paint dried. Edna felt a sudden relief, but was embarrassed about her momentary suspicions of Eddie. She was still concerned about what might happen next in her little world. She went up to her room, took two aspirin, and lay on the couch with a cool rag on her head. Eddie walked back to the house, sat in his wicker rocking chair, sipped his still-warm coffee, and picked up the sports section from the morning paper.

The garbage-truck crew finished their work at the Hutches, and the truck pulled away. Eddie waved good-bye and noticed a man dressed in a modest, light-gray suit standing across the street beside an unmarked city-owned car. Eddie had seen him around, but didn't know him. He knew most locals, especially the police and firemen in town. This fellow must be the new detective he had heard about, Detective McKenzie. The suit crossed the street and walked up the drive to Eddie's front steps. He rested his foot on the second concrete porch step, pulled his handkerchief from his back pocket, and wiped the sweat from his forehead. The full sun had exchanged the relative coolness of the morning for the heat of the day.

"What can I do for you, young man?" asked Eddie, rocking in his chair.

"Good morning, sir, I'm Detective McKenzie, Myrtle Beach Police Department. Mind if I ask a few questions?" McKenzie requested in a formal, but friendly, way.

"No, don't mind a bit. I'm Eddie Rondell. Have a seat. You're new around here. Want some coffee?"

"No thanks," McKenzie responded as he stepped up on the wide covered porch, glad to be out of the direct rays of the sun. He settled into one of the matching white-wicker porch rockers. He took off his military-style, mirrored sunglasses and sized Eddie up, at least as best he could with Eddie seated.

Attention to detail of everyone and everything, that was his way, and there seemed to be an overabundance of strange details these days. Whatever happened to the standard robbery, car theft, missing "runaway" teenager, or the more complex crimes of passion? This crap was wasting a load of his time, and the captain was getting impatient with him.

"Eddie, you've lived here a long time?" he knowingly asked.

"Yeah, what's up?"

"Well, I'm seeing your nice home and property here, and it looks a bit out of place. I mean, look around. The amusement park two blocks away with a clear view of that old Swamp Fox roller coaster, right there behind Leonard's Beach Service, an eyesore if I ever seen one. I look to the left, where I can only assume in the past was a clear view of the beach, but now there stands a five-story department store and two twenty-story-tall hotels. A look to the right, and you see bars, restaurants, doughnut shops, neon, and asphalt. It must have been something living here thirty years ago without all this development, just you in your nice little beach-town paradise. It seems a mite strange that you'd still be here with all this grown up around you. This property must be worth a fortune."

Eddie stood up, leaned against a porch column, and scanned the 180-degree horizon just described by the detective. "I thought you wanted to ask some questions. Didn't know you were looking for real estate," Eddie replied with a hint of irritation in his voice.

"Have you noticed anything strange in the area recently? Prowlers, late-night noise, strange sounds, screams, or anything unusual," the detective shot back, maybe a little too quickly, with an accusing stare as he rechecked the stature of Eddie.

"Well hell, son, what you describe as *unusual* has grown to become the usual around here. We live on the fault line between a surf and sand paradise and chaotic insanity. There's some unseen force that brings pushy, brain-dead tourists and teenage summer workers, and all of 'em looking for a drunken, pot-smokin' orgy every night, all night. I've had an entire family have a picnic and lay out sunning on my front yard with umbrellas and chairs. They left all their trash when they split. I've come out in the morning to find kids passed out on my lawn. I get beer cans, broken liquor bottles, used rubbers, half-smoked joints, and underwear, men's and wom-en's, all over my yard. I've heard screams, wild groans, loud music, fire-crackers, gunshots, tires squealing, cars crashing into trees, garbage cans, and other cars, sirens, car alarms, ambulances, late-night amusement-park rides, horns honking at all hours of the day and night. I've even caught kids screwing one night in that chair you're sitting in. I'm not sure what you mean by *un*usual! Hell, if this place was quiet one night, then I could tell you I heard something unusual. That unusual thing would be silence."

Eddie wasn't on a rant. He had lived this frustration for so long, the intensity of his response came naturally, calm, more of a boring drone as if he were reading off a grocery list or making a poor attempt to recite a poem, but the tension was there, rumbling deep in his soul.

"Well, hello, I didn't know we had company." A cheery voice eased through the front screen door, dissolving the mounting tension between the men. Vera moved out onto the porch with quick little steps and a welcoming smile. She wore a frilly, white-cotton apron over her pastel-flowered print dress, her blue-white hair set perfectly in place.

"Eddie, why didn't you tell me we had a visitor?" She turned to meet their guest. "Hi, I'm Vera. Can I get you something to drink? Coffee? I've got a fresh pot, or maybe a Coca-Cola?" She waited intently for his selection.

"No ma'am, I'm just fine, thank you. I'm Detective McKenzie, Myrtle Beach Police Department."

Good manners had brought McKenzie to his feet as Vera came outside, and he was now bowing his head slightly in respect for her kind offer. He thought, you're always a friend in the South until you give reason not to be, and even then, most folks would give you a second chance. It was like the Bible said, "Turn the other cheek." He figured Vera had never met a stranger. He marveled at her small stature versus the striking size of her husband, Eddie. She could not have been an inch over five feet tall, and if she weighed ninety pounds, the weighing would have taken place after a Thanksgiving feast. But her heart had to be as big as anyone twice her size.

"I was just here to check if anyone in the neighborhood had seen or heard anything strange last night."

"Why, no, whatever do you mean? Did something happen? We heard all the commotion, but crazy things always go on around here, don't they, Eddie?" Vera looked up to Eddie with innocent eyes and a loving smile. "Are you sure you don't want something to drink, honey, or maybe something to eat? Stay awhile, I've just started to fix some early lunch. Sit down, sit down, relax." She patted his hand and verbally persisted with all her natural Southern charm.

"No thanks, ma'am, I've got to go, lots of work to do. Here's my card in case you see anything, shall I say, different than you see on any other summer night. We have some strange folks around here with a curious sense of vigilante justice, and we need to stop this vengeful activity before someone is seriously hurt or even killed."

"OK, Detective, if we see anything 'different,' we'll let you know," said Eddie with a smile.

"Thanks, Eddie, and good day, ma'am." McKenzie turned and walked down the steps and toward his car.

"You come back now when you can spend some time, have some coffee or lunch with us," Vera called out with sincere intention.

McKenzie smiled. "Yes ma'am, I will." As he turned to walk away, he pondered why the rest of the world couldn't be like that woman. Vera could be the new model for the United Nations as the ambassador of "Nice and Friendly."

Despite the joy shown by his wife, Eddie, however cordial, was mad. He had reason to be mad. He had built his paradise, and other people came year after year, encouraged by developers and "quick-buck" artists. Year after year the crowds had grown to surround his once-remote Shangri-La, his turf near the surf.

Progress powered by greed would kill the cycle. Progress guided by greed was blind to the health of the environment that otherwise nourished its growth.

Chapter 15

⁓

Darrell Jr. was in a tizzy with the potential disaster brewing at the One-Eyed Flounder. He would not be allowed to reopen for business until six o'clock, and he was in a quandary. He had lost a good employee, had a mess to clean up, and would lose revenue for every minute the store was closed.

The slowly budding entrepreneurial spirit in Darrell Jr. recognized an upside to this incident, especially if he could encourage a little radio or TV news coverage. If he could pull off a free promotional event, his dad would surely be proud and might stop hounding his ass for a while.

Someone called in an anonymous tip to local media, and the tragedy vultures soon circled the wounded One-Eyed Flounder searching for tempting morsels of someone else's pain. Their viewers would salivate to hear more details of a story like this one. *"News First at Seven*, get the story exclusively on Channel Two" or "Girl found half-naked and tied up, get the full story at six thirty, exclusive report," or "Shark bites reported at the One-Eyed Flounder, exclusive report, film at six."

The local news stations tantalized their audience with these sound bites like bloody chum tossed in an ocean of hungry fish. Each reporter claimed exclusive reports or film coverage so the audience would not stray from their station's broadcast, and the more dramatic the sound bite, the better. The stations also believed the greater the frequency of these sound bites, the larger the audience.

"Why can't they just tell us what happened now? Why wait till six or seven? Jesus, between injury lawyer ads and these news flashes,

Jerry Springer and *The People's Court* just seem to lose their creative flow," chided a retired lady from Michigan who now lived at the Sea Palm trailer park, two miles inland from the beach.

All of this strategy to generate public interest only worked for the battle to capture the TV audience. The radio stations all reported the news at their next newsbreak. "Get all the news at the hour and the half hour, here on WTGR, Tiger Radio." As the news was reported on every tourist's portable radio on the beach, the customer-traffic strategy Darrell Jr. had put in motion received a big boost.

By five forty-five a crowd had formed and all were patiently waiting in line to see, in person, where the latest summer worker had been assaulted. These tourists knew nothing of the previous attacks except what little they had just heard on the news. They would only be at the beach for a week, maybe two, and they needed some interesting tales to take home to friends.

"Yeah, I saw where they tied her up. I saw those shark jaws too, and they still had blood on them," they would all tell folks back home. "What a vacation, what a thrill, we were there!"

Darrell Jr. had anticipated this reaction. He would keep the store open until 1:00 a.m. to make sure those who missed the "exclusive story" at six or seven, but caught the film at eleven, would have time to drive by the store for a morbidly inquisitive look.

Detective McKenzie had taken the actual shark's teeth, rubber snakes, Slinkys, and a couple of coconut heads from the scene of the crime for evidence, but this lack of authentic crime-scene paraphernalia did not deter Darrell Jr. from his plan.

The budding entrepreneur had taken two more uninvolved shark jaws filled with teeth from the storeroom and put some fake blood prominently on the jawbone and on some of the larger teeth. He had plenty of fake blood in the store's makeup and gag department, and he used it liberally, perhaps too liberally. He opened a new case of Slinkys and a box of rubber snakes and built a display next to the coconut head and authentic rubber Indian spear department. He dribbled blood on the display items and the boxes in a clumsy attempt to make it look like blood splatter. Hell, the tourists wouldn't know; they would just be enticed to make another impulse buy. At least, that was his theory.

Darrell Jr. had brought in extra employees to manage crowd control and to staff the registers. He roped off the area, positioned a couple of rent-a-guards, and had a photographer ready to flash the family photo with the rent-a-guards and coconut heads in the background. At the next stop along the roped path, he set up a glass display case with two "bloodied" shark's jaws, which would present another family photo opportunity. Shark's teeth, shark earrings, and other various artistic attempts to use shark's teeth were placed at other points along the guided path.

All of the coconut heads in the storeroom had been brought out. Darrell Jr. had even purchased every coconut head labeled with Myrtle Beach that he could find at other nearby tourist shops. His competition was glad to move the inventory. Darrell Jr. raised the price and got the displays ready. He was going to make Daddy proud and pick up a little cash from the till while he was at it. At five fifty, just prior to opening, Darrell Jr. had been ordered by the police not to disclose the details of the attack.

At six the crowd poured in as anticipated, and a few photos were taken, but the purchases were not what Darrell Jr. had expected. Earlier, McKenzie had heard the news flash snippets, and had quickly obtained an injunction placing a gag order on disclosure of specific crime-scene information until investigators had time to assess the evidence and maybe prevent copycat crimes. He felt that one person tied with rubber snakes and wounded with shark's teeth would be enough for a while.

The dozens of people who were attracted by the news were mostly curious tourists, but they came with tight pocketbooks. A few purchases were made like any other night, and a few photos taken, but people were not quite sure why the rent-a-guards were standing stone-faced in front of the coconut heads, unless this could have been the spot where the girl had been tied up.

Some sketchy information had been announced on the radio, but when you get your news quick, you get mistakes. Nothing had been confirmed and so it was announced as "unconfirmed reports," especially on the news at six and seven. With the gag order in effect, the stations could air only limited information:

"Girl found tied up and harassed at the One-Eyed Flounder. Police refused to give any details based on the ongoing investigation, but unconfirmed reports described the scene as bizarre, and the victim, whose identity has also been withheld, has reportedly left the state."

"After all the buildup, that's it, that's all they have to say? I hope the film at eleven is more informative, because it would be hard-pressed to be any less," shouted one patron while drinking in a local mom-and-pop bar off the main drag.

The other bar patrons sat relatively undeterred and mumbled in agreement, sipped their brew, and smoked their Marlboro Reds or Salem menthol cigarettes.

Darrell Jr. was pissed. Not only would he take a hit for being closed all day, but also now with the extra help and the extra merchandise, he had the potential for a financial slaughter. Dad would hold his bonus and maybe his paycheck for this disaster.

He jumped into the fray and tried to encourage sales with comments like, "Here's where it happened, folks, get a souvenir of products used on the girl who was tied up and terrorized."

These comments sold a few more family photos. A kid convinced his mom to buy a Slinky, but they returned it before paying. The child was grossed out by a glob of reddish-brown liquid-ishy goo sticking to the box and now his fingers.

The normal number of rubber snakes were picked up by boys and used to scare their little sisters or brothers. They carried the snakes around for a while to use in further sporadic assaults, causing more screaming and pleading to Mom and Dad for help. Finally, the snakes were discarded in various places throughout the store as the harassment game grew boring or their attention was diverted to some other trinkets like fake doggy poop or a fart machine.

With the help of some aggressive, but professional, sales work by all employees, a catastrophe was averted, and a slightly lower-than-normal sales night was achieved at the Flounder. Many of the tourists, who might have come in for a nice seashell candle or a bargain on three T-shirts, stayed away due to the crowd of curiosity seekers. The real shoppers made their purchases in nearby smaller, but less crowded, tourist trinket shops. The same real shoppers noted the shortage of carved coconut heads in all the uncrowded stores. Tonight, they would settle for Asian throwing knives or a Confederate flag, both big sellers. One family got tattoos together. Family fun could be had by one and all on the Grand Strand boardwalk and arcade.

Darrell Jr. finally gave up on cashing in on this crowd and sat depressed on his stool by the main store entrance until he saw a hot, cute, young girl waiting in line. Buoyed by a sudden uplifted spirit, he moved quickly to her and cast his charming smile.

"Would you like to see what really happened here, behind the scenes, I mean?" Darrell Jr. asked with a wink. "You don't need to wait in this line. I'm the owner."

The young girl beamed with excitement. "Sure!" she said while thinking, he's rich, kinda cute, maybe a little chubby, but I can step out of this long tourist line.

Darrell Jr. led her to the scene of the crime and the shark-jaw case. "I can't tell you what happened here in front of these people. I'm sworn to silence by the police department. I wanted you to see the place first, and later, I'll tell you in private what happened."

Darrell Jr. led the scantily clad teen to the back of the store. The girl had bright-red, burned skin, freshly sun-fried in baby oil on this day, her first beach day of the year. He opened a door marked "Private," and they entered his small office.

"I must speak quietly. The place could be under observation by the cops. We have strict orders not to release information to the public." He showed a concerned and serious face as he played to her youthful mind. "The attacker tied the girl to the coconut display with rubber snakes and Slinkys, and then painted her face like a coconut," he whispered.

"What about the shark bites, like, what was that about, man?" she asked with increased interest, vigorously smacking her chewing gum.

Darrell Jr. couldn't help himself—the urge was too great—and he reverted to his favorite sport, but he deployed a more subtle approach than just asking her to fuck. He tried to go more slowly with this young one.

"Before I tell you any more, maybe we should get to know each other a little better," he said with a smirking smile while reaching to lift her loose-fitting halter top.

The moment his hands touched her extremely sore and sunburned breast, just where the red, burned skin met the pure, white skin, she screamed with pain and surprise. She pulled his hand away and bit his finger, inflicting enough pain to momentarily incapacitate him as she moved for the door. The girl raced through the aisles and was lost in the maze of merchandise before he could catch her.

What the hell, it didn't matter. Darrell Jr. put a bandage around his finger to stop the bleeding and went back to his stool by the main door, more depressed than before, and wishing that the bleeding of this whole day would stop. He was ready to leave and go get drunk, when a mature lady in her early forties stepped under the crowd-control rope and looked deep into his eyes. She had probably been a real looker in her day, but too many hours in the sun, coupled with her liberal application of makeup and perfume, chased away any visions of a bathing beauty. He was ambivalent and looked back without interest or desire.

She grabbed both of his hands and asked, "Do you run this place, young man?"

"Yes, how could I help you?" He forced an insipid response.

"You could take me in the back and make wild passionate love to me."

Darrell Jr. thought about the unanticipated offer with a languid spirit and figured why not; the day couldn't get any worse. A few moments later in his office, after disrobing, some cumbersome foreplay, and a few tequila shots, the lady had convinced Darrell Jr. to let her tie him up with a couple of rubber snakes and a Slinky that he had sitting on his desk next to a case of athletic socks. She said tying him would really turn her on, given the events of the day, and now actually being here at the scene of the crime. After being secured with the tourist wares, Darrell Jr. was ready in many ways. She pulled a fluorescent, glow-in-the-dark, prophylactic from her purse, placed it on him with practiced expertise, and climbed on top. Darrell Jr. was enchanted with her enthusiasm.

In her theatrical passion, she clawed eight lines into his flesh with her long, curved, professionally painted nails. She left bleeding gashes over each side of his chest, causing Darrell Jr. to scream in pain. The cardboard case of athletic socks was right in front of her face. She reached in without missing a stroke, pulled out a roll of tube socks, and stuck it in his mouth. After a few more gyrations, she heaved, and breathed a deep orgasm, pulling his hair and slamming his head on the floor with each pulse. As she caught her breath, she unceremoniously climbed off.

There he was on the floor of his office, dazed from the head pounding, his hands tied above his head and secured to a leg of his desk, his legs spread-eagle and each tied to a leg of a heavy wooden cabinet against the opposite wall of the small room. With a roll of socks stuffed in his mouth, eight bleeding scars on his chest, bare patches on the sides of his head where small tufts of hair had been yanked out, bright-red lipstick smeared on his mouth, and a wilting, fluorescent, rubber-covered penis, Darrell Jr. was a sight to behold. She turned on the bright overhead light and got dressed.

She looked down at the confusion and anger in his eyes and his useless struggle to get free and said, "What's the matter, you didn't get off, honey? It was good for me, but I gotta go so we're not going to cuddle." She reached for the tequila bottle and poured it onto the roll of socks in Darrell Jr.'s mouth. She poured until the socks were soaked.

As Darrell Jr. struggled for breath, he bit into the sock and snorted tequila fumes through his nose. Yes, he would at least get drunk tonight. He felt the warmth of the alcohol sink through his body.

She searched through his desk and his file cabinet, finding nothing but a few sex toys and scraps of useless paper. She found a list of names and numbers and thought she had discovered a customer list, but after careful inspection, the list was ripped up and discarded. All names were girls, with their ages, telephone numbers, and notches. The list included the name of her younger sister, which pissed her off, but she found nothing her boss would find interesting. This fellow kept score, and she didn't care to know. The guy was a bigger loser than she had pegged him for.

"Good-bye, Darrell, I hope you had fun. I know I did." She walked out, leaving the office door wide open and the bright light shining on Darrell Jr.'s deplorable predicament.

The door opened to a main aisle and was exposed to the store's shopping traffic. Darrell Jr. struggled to remember if he had known this woman. Was she one of his conquests from the past? His head began to spin.

Several tourists saw him in the next few moments and stopped to look. They thought this was just one more stop on the tour, another example of the assault, though it looked so real. A couple stopped and had the photographer take a picture with Darrell Jr. in the shot, capturing one more unforgettable moment of their vacation. More pictures were taken in a tourist photo-shooting frenzy, more memories to show the folks back home. Who knew the motivation of the lady—lust or revenge? At the moment Darrell Jr. cared not.

Chapter 16

On a calm, blue-sky summer morning, after the Sunday-morning church service, Eddie and Vera mingled for a while in front of the sanctuary, visiting with old friends discovered in the congregational crowd.

"Vera, it seems like we've got twice as many people here as we had last summer. It's good for the church. It's a good thing. Howdy, Hank... Linda, good to see you both. Reverend, great sermon, you touched a lot of people today." Eddie shook hands, and Vera smiled and hugged.

"Eddie, honey, you know, I think you're right. The summer tourists really filled up the pews today. It's such a blessing. Oh hi, Helen. Bless you, dear."

"Excuse me, ladies," Eddie said. "Vera, I'll get the church bus and meet you out front. With this crowd we might not get to the home on time. You know they'll be waiting."

"OK, hon, I'll meet you in a minute," Vera said and turned back to Helen. "How's Fred doing?"

"Better. We're just praying, Vera."

"I'll drop by the hospital this week to see him. Give our love now. Bye-bye." Vera took Helen's hand with one hand and patted it affectionately with her other.

The Rondells left the church and drove directly to the Grand Strand Assisted Living and Retirement Home, where Vera's mother had lived for five happy years. Eddie and Vera enjoyed the visits and activities with the elderly folks at the home, and they continued to share time with them, even after Vera's mother had died. Vera felt joy in her soul when she could help the residents have a good day. To Vera it was not a duty; it was a pleasure and part of her Sunday routine.

Every week Eddie drove the church bus to help transport residents to the Sunday Buffet and Bingo Party at The Blue House Restaurant and Lounge. The bingo trip was the highlight of the week for the residents. Today the traffic had been particularly heavy, and they were behind schedule. Eddie and Vera hurried to help all that could reasonably travel climb aboard the church bus or onto the retirement-home van. Eddie got behind the wheel of the bus, while a nursing assistant drove the van. Both vehicles were full.

Tony, the Blue House manager, had recognized the potential profit in this sector of the bingo market. To establish the Sunday Buffet and Bingo Party, he had worked for six months securing the licenses and permits to allow the event to proceed. Tony paid the right people and with the help of his organizational attorneys from Atlanta, he helped craft the legal mechanism.

On Sunday afternoon, from noon until five, the property of the Blue House was considered an American Indian free trade zone, an extension of the Santee Lake Indian Reservation. Tony hired Indian Chief Harry Running Bear to manage the bingo game. Chief Harry Running Bear was his official tribal name. As the chief had grown older, his friends affectionately changed his name to Chief Hairy Jogging Bear, a playful reference to his growing waistline, declining animal-like agility, and a significant increase in body hair. Tony shared some of the revenue with the tribe.

As the vans pulled up to the Blue House, Tony and his crew stood ready. The wheelchair ramp had been safety checked and decorated with streamers to present a party-like welcome to loyal members. The buffet cost ten dollars, but came with two free bingo cards for the first game. Many local residents religiously attended the popular Sunday-afternoon bingo gathering, and attendance grew every summer.

After eating, Eddie helped Gladis Harfield to her chair. Vera followed them.

"Here's your banana pudding and sweet tea, Gladis. Now, if you need anything, anything at all, you just look to me or Eddie." Vera moved on to check on Mrs. Agnes Faulkner.

As Mrs. Faulkner sat down to bingo, she said, "That lunch was just lovely, wasn't it, Vera?" Vera had to agree, and she smiled.

Chief Hairy Jogging Bear called the bingo game to order with a little music from the movie *Rocky* to help charge the atmosphere and raise competitive spirits in the room. He turned on the bingo machine blower, bringing the numbered balls to life, and they popped about in the glass cube.

Gladis pumped her hands high and shouted, "Bring it on, Chief." Her nurse rearranged the oxygen tank.

Other bingo players quickly finished their desserts of banana pudding, grabbed their sweet iced tea, and shuffled to their tables with visions of Rocky running up the steps in Philly. The bingo attendants began to sell cards for the first game. Most members purchased six cards for each game, but the more-experienced players bought twelve and sometimes more, if they wanted to show off. Eddie watched over his friends Harvey and Basil to help keep their money straight with the card sellers and to see that they played the correct cards for each game.

Disciplined focus was required to ensure all cards were checked for each number called in quick rhythmic succession. Each game offered a prize of fifty dollars, and there was always a winner. On most Sundays a jackpot game served as the finale with a three-hundred-dollar prize, but every three months, a super jackpot game was offered, and the highly contested event was worth a percentage of all cards purchased since the last big game. The pot had grown quickly over the last few weeks with the regular crowd's full awareness each week.

Excitement filled the room as the big quarterly game approached. A periodic tally of the jackpot, growing with each game, was displayed in red lights on a board hung on the wall above Chief Jogging Bear. As expected, today the bingo crowd was much larger than normal.

The mood in the room rose to a mild state of frenzy, or maybe they were just agitated. It was hard to tell; they had been playing for two hours. The jackpot tally showed $2,800 after Gladis won the last regular game prize that had been raised, just this once, to two hundred dollars.

Gladis was so worked up with surprised delight, she fainted. One of the nurses who generally accompanied the group begrudgingly had to stop playing and take care of her. The nurse collected the prize money, revived Gladis with a damp cloth on her face, and coaxed her quickly to a wheeled bed that was always kept at the ready. She gave her patient more oxygen and rapidly checked the elderly lady's blood pressure to validate her recovery. The nurse gathered her bingo cards and moved to a table closer to the patient.

"Gladis, honey, I'm so glad you won, but you should listen to your nurse. Maybe you should skip the next couple of games," Vera suggested kindly.

"Not on your life, Vera. I'm not letting that Elvira win again. I'll... never...hear the end of it." Gladis had to pause and breathe between words. She lay back on the bed, but kept her eye on Chief Jogging Bear.

Vera stroked her hair and checked the oxygen tubes once more.

The air was charged with bingo competitive tension. The crowd bought more cards at a rapid pace and upped the ante on the larger-than-normal super jackpot prize. With the buying frenzy, the jackpot rose to an even $3,000, a new Blue House Bingo jackpot record. Only a full card, with every number covered, would win the jackpot.

Vera returned and sat by Eddie, smiled, and patted his knee. She sat quietly and watched for any elderly resident who might need help. Vera and Eddie really couldn't afford to play multiple cards like many of the folks that they helped, but they enjoyed bingo, so they each played an occasional card, and Vera played one card for the jackpot game.

She got off to a heart-pounding start with a half-filled card, matching almost every number called. She giggled and clapped her hands together. Eddie, looking over her shoulder, gave her a reassuring hug. Lady luck suddenly changed, and the numbers matching her card became rare. She sighed and thought, *oh well, maybe Mrs. Faulkner will win*. She could use a little extra money.

"Bingo!" shouted ninety-five-year-old Elvira Simpson. Groans of disappointment were heard across the room.

"Dammit, I knew it," Gladis barked.

The official card checker took her lucky card for verification as other players held their breath and lamented about their remaining open numbers. Vera needed only two numbers to win, but she just smiled, hoping that this time, Elvira had actually marked her numbers correctly. The checker called out the numbers to Chief Jogging Bear, finding no less than five numbers marked incorrectly.

"Check 'em again," Elvira shouted.

"Sorry, ma'am, but the card is not complete, and that's official."

"You dumb ass." A slur was hurled from an unidentified source in the back of the room.

"All right, we won't have that kind of language. This is a family event, so just settle down." The chief worked to calm the crowd. He could not let the game room get out of control, and that could happen quickly with competitive senior bingo.

Constrained anticipation was restored, and words of encouragement came to Elvira from friends.

Finally the game continued, and two more numbers were called. Each matched a number on Vera's card. She filled it. She didn't announce her obvious victory for a moment, either from surprise or her hope that one of the elderly had also won.

Just before the chief called the next number, Vera timidly raised her hand and whispered, "Bingo."

With Vera's declaration, Elvira shouted, "Bingo." She held the same card as before. One official checker went to Vera and one to Elvira. When the checking was done, Vera had won, and Elvira was still four numbers short.

Mrs. Faulkner, who sat beside Vera, gave her a congratulatory hug and sighed. "I only had one more to go, but I'm glad you won, Vera. I was so close, but...anyway."

"Only one to go? Well, you should get something for that, like second place. I'll ask."

This victory was a first for Vera. Eddie stood behind her as the chief carefully dealt the $3,000 jackpot in unmarked tens and twenties, placing each bill into Vera's extended hands as she counted quietly under her breath. She was beaming and Eddie was shuffling, cycling his hands, first in his pockets and then folding his arms, full of nervous, excited energy, waiting to pick Vera off her feet in a congratulatory hug. Finally, he did. Vera just blushed and shyly smiled, embarrassed by the attention but enjoying her moment. Vera discreetly counted out $500 from the bounty. As the residents rolled and shuffled back to the vans, she stopped Mrs. Faulkner.

"Here, honey, they said this money was meant for the second-place winner. Since you only had one left, you were the second-place winner." Vera handed her the cash.

Mrs. Faulkner looked at Vera in shock, not believing her. "Second place? I've never heard of second place at bingo."

"Oh, it's new, something special for this big jackpot, dear. Enjoy!"

"Thank you, Vera. I'm so happy; it's my first time to win anything."

Eddie cupped the lady's elbow to help her out of the door and to the van. Mrs. Faulkner put the money in her purse, happy with her second-place win. It had been a good Sunday afternoon. The residents of the home all had a great day filled with excitement, whether they had won, lost, or just came in second place.

Frank and Marvin, two nonlocal residents from the home, came walking out with Tony. They shook hands at the top of the wheelchair ramp and stepped to the bus as Eddie was storing the last wheelchair.

"You gentlemen have fun today?" Eddie asked.

"Sure, buddy, big-time fun, thanks for asking." Frank responded for both of them, patted Eddie on the back, and stepped on the bus to the smiles of his retirement-home friends. Tony waved as they drove away.

Chapter 17

A happy bus returned to the home, and the crowd slowly disembarked. Vera helped the last of the elderly ladies and gentlemen off the church bus. Frank and Marvin brought up the rear, and she gave them both a warm smile.

"Hope you two had a good time today. Did you win a game?"

"Ms. Vera, we always win, and thanks for asking," Frank replied.

"Win, what did we win? What are you talking about?" Marvin mumbled as he followed Frank up the walk to the entrance.

"Don't be grumpy, brother." Frank turned before entering and looked at Vera. "I think he needs a nap, ma'am." Frank guided Marvin through the front door.

The two elderly men both had thick northern New Jersey accents, but the locals had welcomed them from their first days at the home. People were not sure why the two men had moved from their northern homes to this particular nursing home in Myrtle Beach. Their arrival was shortly after Tony had opened the Blue House, but none was aware of the coincidence.

While at the bingo buffet, Tony was always particularly cordial to Frank and Marvin. On occasion the two had disappeared from the bingo room, only to return with Tony, laughing and talking like old friends. There was talk of a connection from their past, but the talk was just unsubstantiated rumor. And at the home, there were many unsubstantiated rumors.

Frank, although in his nineties, presented a large, well-built physical presence, too large to confront with demands for explanation. Most people at the home just enjoyed the company of Frank and Marvin and assumed if there were stories to tell, the men would tell them when they were ready. They were good dancers, good card players, good sports, funny, and perfect gentlemen, especially to the ladies, and had over a short time become part of the close-knit retirement-home family.

Eddie made a final sweep of the bus for purses, canes, shawls, or any other items the residents may have forgotten. Under the last-row seat, he discovered a small gym bag. Vera had just returned to the bus.

"Eddie, whose bag is that? Let's just look inside. Maybe...?" Both saw the four bags of marijuana. Without a word they raised their heads and stared into each other's wide eyes, closed the bag, and walked back into the home. Frank was standing by the front desk.

"Thanks, Eddie. Have a good evening, Ms. Vera." He quickly grabbed the bag, turned, and walked down the corridor to his room.

As the disheartened couple drove the borrowed bus back to the church, both were silent. Vera looked out the side window, staring at the passing strip malls, palm trees, and used car lots; all seemed merged in a confused blur. With one hand holding her purse in her lap, and one hand covering her mouth and chin, she struggled to make sense of it all.

"Why would Frank be carrying drugs? Why? It makes no sense. I'm not sure the home is safe. I'm so worried about all of our friends. What should we do, Eddie? What should we do? I am just at my wit's end." The air of suspicion would haunt her, along with worry that something bad might happen to her poor elderly friends when no one was there to protect them.

Eddie was driving the bus with eyes forward in a blank stare, retracing the events of the day. Had Frank taken the bag into the bingo parlor? Why? What else was in the bag? Did Frank buy pot from the Blue House? So confusing. Eddie didn't know who to be pissed at. If Frank was buying or selling grass, would he and Vera be deemed liable or considered accomplices to the crime, since they hauled the group back and forth?

"I need to think about this, Vera. Before we do anything, I just need to think about it."

"Where on earth did he get all that marijuana? Do you think he bought it from Tony? I mean, they were together and not always in the bingo room. Oh, honey, I just don't know. I'm flabbergasted right now. I'm not sure what flabbergasted is, but I sure feel that way right now. I just don't know what to think." Vera sighed.

Frustrated with the incessant stop and go, Eddie navigated the crowded highway, constantly shifting gears to keep up with the pulsing flow of traffic. Periodically, traffic lights had been added to each new busy intersection on the bypass highway. The rampant increase in the number of controlled access streets connected to the highway had been propelled by the cancerous growth of golf courses, subdivisions, and strip malls. This growth had turned the bypass into an oxymoron. A new bypass was needed now, but much farther away from this gridlock.

The traffic lights caused the cars and trucks to move in waves, racing forward, switching lanes, consistent, enduring, one wave of vehicles after another. The haggard, frustrated drivers blew horns, cursed, and aggressively cut each other off as they sought some advantage within the herd of metal beasts, only to be stopped by a red light at the next intersection. As each light turned green, the chaotic rush resumed until the next light, gas station, or some other traffic disruptive nuisance formed an eddy in the flow.

Eddie switched on his left turn signal and eased into the center turn lane, waiting for the next wave of cars to clear the two lanes of oncoming traffic. The constant to and fro reminded Eddie of the beach—the waves sometimes calm and clear, other times angry with foam, frothing, pounding the beach sand. The waves were always forming, the water was always moving.

Eddie snapped out of his contemplative daze as two open lanes finally presented themselves, giving him time to swing the bus into the church parking lot.

Eddie noticed a police car with its doors open parked near the church sign by the road. He knew someone must have talked at the home; the law was onto them. He couldn't recognize the two policemen with their backs turned, so he nervously proceeded to park the bus behind the church.

As Eddie and Vera walked to their car, they were somewhat relieved to see the policemen were busy checking out a hitchhiker with a backpack and sleeping bag. The young man and other young men just like him were a common sight on the bypass and other main roads leading in and out of Myrtle Beach.

Young people coming to live a dream or leaving to escape a nightmare. They were always looking for a better life away from the hellhole they had just left. Every town eventually became a drag to them, but they could never decipher the common denominators that caused their trouble. With their migration inhibited by the constraints of geography, Florida, Key West, and the Caribbean Islands had become overstocked with these wandering souls. Local police tactics were to quickly show them the way out of Myrtle Beach and the road to Florida.

A half-eaten box of Krispy Kreme doughnuts rested on the hood of the cruiser. The two cops had the young man spread his hands and feet across the base of the huge twelve-foot by twelve-foot church message board. The church message of the day, posted in large, black letters on the sign, hit Eddie with its timely thought, resurrecting the events of the day.

"Come On In, Take a Holiday From Sin. Don't
Bypass the Highway to Heaven."

Eddie drove his car from the lot to the highway. He waved at the two young policemen and then looked compassionately at Vera and said, "We'll talk when we get home." Vera just looked back with sad eyes, nodded her head, and again stared out the side window in deep soulful contemplation. Eddie pulled out onto the bypass between the waves.

Chapter 18

The girls sipped their third happy-hour draft beer and were pretty much finished with a rehash of Evelyn's doughnut-shop meeting with Guido when Detective McKenzie appeared at the front door. Edna saw him immediately, but this time in a different light. Previous encounters had been unusually stressful. Edna's first reaction was a deep breath of new anxiety, expecting news of yet another summer-worker victim, but McKenzie didn't seem so businesslike.

The front door of the Frisky Rabbit was adjacent to one corner of the bar. No foyer existed for a casual, unnoticed entry into this establishment. You were in or out, no in-between, much like the crowd who frequented this bar. The Frisky Rabbit was not really a joint for the undecided or for those with questionable self-esteem. You came in because you meant to. You were confident. After work and dinner, patrons enjoyed the rest of the night on the beer-doused shag carpet, with loud music, booze, friends, pool, and foosball. In the summertime, there were no slow nights at this bar.

McKenzie stepped through the door, immediately casting a 180-degree scan of the joint, more from habit than need. He recognized Edna and Evelyn talking at the other end of the L-shaped bar. Their heads were close together as they spoke to each other over the loud music, but they were also looking in his direction.

Even as cool and relaxed as McKenzie appeared on the outside, normal human anxieties of things unfamiliar were at work on the inside. He wasn't on the job, where his position and purpose provided his confidence; right now he was just McKenzie, the civilian. A familiar face in a new place was like gold in the bank, like a beacon attracting you as light attracts a moth. Edna was his light tonight. He slowly edged his way through the crowd and toward the girls.

Edna whispered, "Look what we have here."

As McKenzie reached the open stool just vacated next to Evelyn, Edna flashed a smile, a quick, subtle wave, and a silent hi. Saying hi in this noisy bar was of little value, so mouthing it was a good substitute.

Booney stepped up behind the bar and shouted, "What ya havin', Detective?"

"Beer, please," McKenzie yelled back. The Frisky Rabbit had two types of beer, beer and light beer; if you didn't say light, you got beer. If you want something special, some fancy imported beer, a martini, a manhattan, go somewhere else.

"You're working late tonight," Booney shouted as he pulled back the beer tap and filled a plastic cup.

McKenzie leaned forward to get his beer, shortening the distance to Booney's ear, and said, "Not working. How much I owe ya?"

"You drinking with these girls?" Booney asked, and both McKenzie and Booney looked to the girls for confirmation.

Edna had been watching McKenzie and quickly confirmed with a smile. "Sure, Detective McKenzie is a friend of ours."

Booney said, "OK, twenty-five-cent happy hour for the detective."

McKenzie gave Booney a buck, said thanks, and turned to face Edna. "Thanks. It's good to see you young ladies while not involved with a crime scene."

"What are you talking about? This place is a crime scene!" teased Evelyn. "If you're not on parole, under indictment, or at least have a couple priors, you can't be here. How'd you get in?"

"I'm the acting parole officer for about ten of the young hoodlums I've seen since I walked through the door," joked McKenzie as he took a long first drink of his beer. He wasn't sure what brand he was drinking, but it was draft and worth at least the twenty-five cents he had been charged.

Edna sat at the bar listening to him talk, and McKenzie was looking at her, not scanning the room like most guys that she'd met. She liked his eyes. McKenzie noticed their drinks were low.

"Can I get you girls another drink?"

"Sure, sailor, you're the only gentleman in the joint," Evelyn responded in her Mae West voice, and they all chuckled. McKenzie hailed Booney, the beer-tender poured two lights, and McKenzie laid down two bucks.

Booney took only one and said, "Thanks, Detective, you're gonna spoil me."

Edna, Evelyn, and McKenzie drank their drafts and traded observations about the night's crowd at the Frisky Rabbit. Their conversation competed with a music mix of Pink Floyd, the Doobie Brothers, Elton John, the Stones, Allman Brothers, Steely Dan, and a variety of beach-music favorites. The music permeated the room and the souls of the people in it, with the sound system volume cranked up to over one hundred forty decibels, a noise level harmful to the ears and illegal in many states.

As they got a bit more familiar, Edna asked, "What should we call you when you're off duty? Detective, McKenzie, Detective McKenzie, or what?"

"McKenzie is good. People have been calling me that most of my life."

"What's your first name?" Edna wanted to know.

"Buford."

"What's your middle name?"

"Jerome."

"I like McKenzie." She couldn't see herself calling him Buford or Jerome, and BJ was out of the question. She thought McKenzie fit his eyes. "OK, McKenzie, what do you think of this town, now that you've been here for what, eight months?"

"Well, it's not new to me. I grew up not far from here, in a farming community called Sandy Hill, near Kingstree. I got my criminology degree from Coastal Carolina in Conway. I've always been close to this area. The place has changed a lot since I can remember coming here as a kid. I've seen it grow. I've seen it go in a direction I don't like, so I thought perhaps I could do something about that, so here I am. And to answer your question, I'd like it to be more like it used to be, a smaller, more innocent beach town."

McKenzie dumped twenty years of life motivation in less than a minute. You ask a question like that of most people in the Frisky Rabbit, and the classic answers were "It rocks, man," or "It sucks," or "Yeah, it's OK, but..." Edna was impressed.

"That's incredible, McKenzie," Edna said. "We love this place. We have loved it for as long as we can remember, and we're not happy with the 'direction,' as you call it. So we're glad to have someone else care."

"Thanks."

The humorous and serious conversational chat continued, but was now primarily between Edna and McKenzie, almost as if the rest of the bar had been silenced and isolated behind a glass wall. Even Evelyn, who was sitting next to them, felt detached from the conversation. She was not only OK with that, but happy, happy for Edna.

As it came time for another brew, Evelyn asked to be excused and said, "Actually, I think I'm going to turn in. If we are going to see the sunrise in the morning, I need to hit the sack. I'll let you two keep Booney working. Murph, come outside and watch me walk home."

"OK, darlin', but be quick about it. I've got beer to pour and fights to break up."

She gave Edna a kiss on the cheek and whispered, "Get him, honey," and left. As she stepped through the door, her hand showed the *V* of a peace sign above her head and waved adieu to all who might be looking. After one more beer and some enjoyable conversation, both Edna and McKenzie declined yet another twenty-five-cent draft.

"Let me walk you home?"

"Sure. With all the things going on, I really don't feel safe walking alone, even the half block to my place."

"I don't think you have anything to worry about," McKenzie said with confidence.

"You are the second person to say that to me. How do others feel so sure that I'll be OK with all this crap going on?" Edna asked quickly, almost too fast, too intense, putting a dull edge on the cheap beer love-buzz they both were enjoying.

"Who else said that to you?" McKenzie inquired in a sudden, sobering tone, with his work face on.

"Eddie, my landlord. He said it in the same confident way you just did. By the way, were you hiding in the trees between our place and the Hutches tonight? Eddie thought you were." Now both grew slightly more serious. The smiles were gone, and the distance between them grew with a small buffer zone.

"Yes, I was, as a matter of fact. Suppose my stealth mode wasn't very stealthy. I was hoping to pick up a few clues since that area seems to be the center of focus for our villain. Someone has an issue with these kids living in the Hutches. I want to understand some of what is in his mind, so I can understand his crime."

He eased closer again, speaking in Edna's ear, not so much because he didn't want to keep shouting, but to reduce the chance that ears nearby might be tuned in to their conversation. While he was talking, he became enthralled with the smell and texture of Edna's hair. He caught a hint of her perfume. He liked it.

When they both pulled back from the secret conversational close encounter, their eyes met. McKenzie caught himself, pressed his reset button, and said, "How'd we get this deep into this subject? Let's go back to our good-time beer buzz."

"Yeah, I was thinking the same thing. By the way, McKenzie, if you plan to hang out with us or fit in around here, you can't be wearing your police formal *Colombo, Hawaii Five-0* getup. You've got to lighten up. And don't be going to Walgreens for a new tourist T-shirt and flip-flops. You've got to wear something that looks like you've been around awhile. You'll need a faded T-shirt, shorts, and cheap, worn-out flip-flops. Your shorts or jeans can't be pressed. If the material is worn thin and maybe has a small tear, all the better. You have to look like you really don't give a shit. Then people won't be staring at you like you're a nerd or a narc or something."

"But I am one—a narc, I mean," McKenzie said with a chuckle.

"You might be a bit better at the stealth thing if you dressed more like the natives," she said and noticed McKenzie lose his smile. "OK, sorry, enough on the lectures. Weird, me giving lectures." Edna chugged a drink of her beer, raised her free hand, and screamed her best "Party on!" shout at Booney as the first licks of Lynyrd Skynyrd's "Free Bird" blasted the joint, generating head bobbing and air guitars all around the bar. Four party hounds at a table near the bar let out their rebel yells after each successfully chugged a full cup of draft beer.

The night was middle-aged, and the crowd was growing a raunchy edge after hours of drinking cheap beer. As normal for this time of night, the Frisky Rabbit had grown an obstreperous atmosphere. The noise levels were rising, groups were talking and laughing, couples were dancing. One girl was standing on top of a table gyrating suggestively to her stunned friends. Just blame it on the beach.

Testosterone was pulsing, especially at the hotly contested foosball tables. The pool tables were crowded, and challenge coins were lined up waiting for action. Betting was rampant. Sharks were circling, seeking to engage youthful, primordial hustlers not yet fully schooled in the art. The sharks were quickly and quietly gulping the boastful wager's big-money bet with a sudden, unexpected run of the table. The money gone, the shark moved on, sensing the propinquity of fresh blood at an adjacent table.

Booney and Murph didn't care. They made more money when the crowd got loud and rowdy. All the chairs and tables were industrial strength. The weak ones had been destroyed long ago like weak-rooted trees on the Irish coast. As long as no one got hurt, the rules were, there are no rules, have fun.

This atmosphere was not especially conducive to the intimate conversations of a couple who had just met, each attempting to discover more about the other. Such was the growing dilemma with Edna and McKenzie. Edna had taken her seat again and appeared to have changed her mind about leaving. Sensing that maybe the night had taken a wrong turn, McKenzie leaned over to Edna's ear again and said, "You're right, perhaps I should leave and let you have some fun. The narc look is probably scaring all your boyfriends off."

Edna immediately shook her head. "No, no, don't worry about that. I never meet anybody here that gets my attention. They get younger every year, maybe too young for me anymore. How 'bout you walk me home now, and why don't you tell me about yourself, big boy," she added with her best Mae West accent.

As they walked out the front door, Murph gave Edna a wink and said, "You two be good now." Murph knew Edna was in safe hands.

They shut the door, leaving the mayhem and noise behind. A breeze of fresh salty air was a relief from the smoke-filled bar. Their ears were ringing, but the noise level was now coming from the ambient Myrtle Beach highway and amusement park. A few kids mingled outside doing what they do outside a party bar. McKenzie was oblivious to anything but Edna at the moment. He had been living lonely, focused on his work twenty-four/seven. The young cop knew he needed a change.

McKenzie had moved up in the ranks with his job as a detective at the MBPD, but he was also thinking more about how to separate his work and the rest of his life. He was a good detective because he was good at details and pattern recognition. However, when it came to his personal life, he had blinders on. He could only see those things that were right in front of him, and he didn't interpret them very well. His poor, almost nonexistent peripheral vision of the subtle moments of an intimate relationship left him grasping for answers with the anxiety of a desperate man in a room with no light.

Edna and McKenzie were talking and walking and passed right by her apartment. Both recognized their silly error as they stopped to cross Ocean Boulevard. They looked both ways and crossed over to the entrance of the small boardwalk that ran in front of the One-Eyed Founder. They were drawn to the rhythmic crashing sounds of the moonlit surf. As they reached the beach access steps, McKenzie asked, "Would you like to take a walk on the beach?"

"No, I don't walk on the beach at night with any man," Edna replied as she stopped next to the railing. "I don't know you that well, and rejection has a way of endangering a new friendship."

McKenzie chuckled, stepped closer, and said, "OK." He kissed her anyway. After a moment he backed away and said, "Why don't I get you home? I bet you have to work tomorrow."

Edna got her breath back and said, "Yeah...you're right...and, and...I have to get up early with Evelyn for our sunrise coffee on the beach."

They walked back, not talking, but holding hands as they crossed the Boulevard. They maneuvered through the slow-moving, ever-present, beach-cruiser traffic and didn't let go until they reached Edna's door.

"Thanks for the good time, Edna. I hope I didn't make you feel uncomfortable. Can I call you?"

Edna's sense of humor kicked in to help diffuse the serious tone. She had always felt great anxieties with serious relationship moments. She detected a claustrophobic grip, and distracting humor was her defense.

"Yes, you can call me. My best friends call me Goodtimes," she said again with her Mae West accent. "No, really, I'd like to see you again. Evelyn and I are at the Frisky Rabbit almost every night this time of year, in our reserved seats at the end of the bar." Edna got her keys, unlocked the door, turned around, and placed a sensuously serious kiss square on McKenzie's lips. She turned and went in before he could respond. He stood there for a moment, his nose almost touching the closed door. Women confused him.

He shook his head, turned, and walked down the steps to go home. He watched a brown van race by blowing its horn, with four bare asses pressed against the side window. The van slowed in front of the Frisky Rabbit, with the horn blowing. Unseen people were yelling, curses were traded, tires squealed, and the van was gone. Life was normal at the Frisky Rabbit.

Another day was done in paradise, and the band played the beach tune "Under the Boardwalk." Another love, another unique mind-melded experience between two hearts catalyzed by the seductive serenity of the surf's endless tune and the moonlit foam of each breaking wave, all acting as nature's cupid call.

Edna slipped through the dark living room quietly, trying not to wake Evelyn. As she placed her keys on the kitchen table, Evelyn spoke from the dark.

"Well, how'd it go? Tell me all about it. We don't need a light in here, 'cause you are glowing, my friend."

Chapter 19

〜

With all the crazy events of the summer, new boyfriends, summer work-ers attacked, and other esoteric abnormalities of the beach life, Edna and Evelyn had skipped their early-morning walk for the last three days, but this morning was different. Last night, with the music and crowd rocking, they had vowed to continue their morning routine, and had left their happy hour at the Frisky Rabbit early. They had walked out as the whole crowd in the bar finished a choral rendition of "What Kind of Fool," a classic beach tune by the Tams. It was a rhetorical cho-rus for this crew, but few recognized the close association.

An early-morning rain shower had temporarily washed the dust and humidity away. The air was fresh with a mild northerly breeze. On this clear morning, satisfied with more sleep than normal, the girls felt much better, a new day, a clean start.

Each had initiated a relationship with an interesting man in the last couple of weeks. These were real men, unlike the odd collection of males they had become accustomed to meeting in Myrtle Beach. Typically they met young summer workers, burnt-out beach bums, traveling salesmen, married tourists, and an array of other undesirable candidates who were unsuited for real long-lasting relationships.

The simultaneous discovery of quality men by both women was an extraordinary coincidence. At least they appeared to demonstrate the characteristics of good men—the more sophisticated type, the type that pleased the girls at this point in their life. Each man still had a hint of adventure, but both were anchored to a matured reality.

"Edna, what if you married McKenzie and he gets a better job somewhere else?"

"What do you mean? That's a lot of what-ifs this early in the morning. Geez, we just met each other. I don't think he's going anywhere."

"Yeah, well, how do you know? How can you be sure? What if he moves to another town before you get married? Would you go too?"

"Evelyn, we just started dating. Aren't you jumping ahead with this?"

"No. No, I'm not. I see how you are with him. You may not see it or want to admit it, but I know you, and this man is the one. You'll marry him. I just know it. And then you'll move away and leave me with the Krispy Kreme and the kids at the Frisky Rabbit. I don't know what I would do if you left."

"Oh, Evelyn, you are something else. My goodness, girl. I've been worried about you and Guido too. He's not from here. He could take you back to New York or New Jersey or Italy or who knows where. And I've seen you with him too. I've been worried you would jump up and marry him almost any day now. I mean, I could see you do it with no plans or warning, just marry him and leave and not even wait till the end of the summer. I've always been afraid of you finding someone and leaving. Every summer I think, this is it, I just know it; she'll leave with the next good-looking guy who sits down at her doughnut counter."

"Edna, honey, I didn't know you worried too. I promise I'm not going anywhere unless we talk about it first, OK?"

"OK. I guess we sort of took the happy buzz out of the morning. Sorry, give me a hug."

"No worries, I started it. In the future I promise to talk with you about any marriage or move decision before I do it. I mean, just in case some guy happens to stop by the Krispy Kreme one afternoon to ask for my hand, and we want to jump in his car and drive away into the sunset. Happens all the time." They laughed.

The roots of their lives had been growing together, gradually becoming more entwined somewhat unexpectedly, conveniently, year after year. Alternatives were less appealing. For the moment they were happy, doing what they liked best, sitting on the beach. With an early-morning breeze, they watched the sunrise, sipped coffee, ate hot doughnuts, and talked about the men who had come into their lives. If a good day starts with a happy spirit and a smile with friends, then this was the start of a good day for Evelyn and Edna.

The sun was up, their coffee and doughnuts were gone, and it was time to go home. As they walked up the beach, the wind blew a loosely held Krispy Kreme napkin from Edna's hand. It tumbled along the beach as if playing catch, always landing out of reach and jumping with the next swirling breeze, taunting and evading Edna until it landed behind a large, white, plywood box used by lifeguards to store umbrellas and floats.

Edna chased the napkin. She hated the trash inexplicably left on the beach by so many visitors for nature or someone else to sort out. She reached down to snag the paper before the next gust of wind could move it farther down the beach and stopped cold. Right in front of her was another nightmare, another victim.

A lifeguard was staring at Edna with wide, scared eyes. He was laid out, spread-eagle on his back. His wrist and ankles were tied to umbrella poles driven deep in the sand. He lay between the lifeguard storage box and a four-foot-high cement wall. The placement concealed him from view of anyone on the beach or from anyone at the nearby hotel.

He was naked except for a bag of pot taped across his mouth and an open package of potato chips taped over his crotch. With the growing morning light, sea gulls had begun to hover above him as they searched for breakfast. The lifeguard knew the potential for disaster when these sky rats would start diving on the chips. He had expected the inevitable at any moment.

Edna stood frozen, stunned by the discovery. Evelyn shuffled through the soft sand to see what was keeping her. The gulls were testing their safe distance, forming their ranks as a hovering flock, not yet confident enough to dive for the snack. An elderly tourist standing on the concrete wall looked down at the girls and then the lifeguard. She quickly shuffled to the hotel office to call for help.

McKenzie arrived quickly, no more than ten minutes after the initial call to find Edna leaning against the sea wall, staring blankly out to sea. Evelyn was searching at a nearby hotel for someone, anyone who would help.

"Are you OK?"

"No...no, I'm not! Why me?" Edna covered her mouth with her hand, and tears flowed.

"Why don't you and Evelyn go home and relax. I'll take it from here. Thanks for helping."

"McKenzie, we just found him lying here. We were walking home. I can't believe this."

"It is strange, Edna, but that's all it is." He put his arm around Edna and walked with her up the steps to meet Evelyn.

McKenzie knew the MO; he saw the red paint across the lifeguard's chest that said, "Go Home," the pot, the lack of clothing, the humiliation, the restraints tying him up, and the potential for a catastrophe. But this victim had a profile somewhat different from previous victims. He did not live in the Hutches next to the Frisky Rabbit, but had rented a room across the street at the lifeguard house. The rundown, concrete-block, poorly decorated bunkhouse was home to thirty immature, loud, and obnoxious lifeguards. Guards lived at the guardhouse mostly because it was cheap and easy.

This guard was a recent recruit to Vernon's distribution network. The recruitment had worked the other way around for this young man. The guard had persuaded Vernon to let him be his man. He could sell to the younger set that he attracted and to those who frequented the swash stand on the beach. This guard had learned about the clientele just as Darrell Jr. had learned a few years earlier at the swash lifeguard stand. The umbrella and float rental volume was low, but the chance to sell drugs was relatively high.

Most beachgoers to this location were financially challenged locals with a tight fist on their money, but this market segment's financial grip was oddly flaccid when it came to the unnecessary pleasures of life. This guard became a pot sales leader almost overnight as he serviced a group of customers previously overlooked by Vernon's distribution network. The rookie guard had found his niche.

Through the summer the guard wore his lifeguard T-shirt everywhere to blatantly advertise his job on the beach, and he was likewise not discreet with his financial success. His newfound revenue source had become apparent to most who visited the Frisky Rabbit or the Skee-Ball arcade. The guard took his younger ladies to the amusement park to parade the midway Pavilion and to play arcade games. The age of these girls was so obvious that even Murph and Booney would not allow them in the Frisky Rabbit without their parents.

This guard, trying hard to live his preconceived version of the beach lifeguard, had managed to alienate most around him. His limited posse was composed of two younger lifeguard friends who were less confident, lacking social skills and fighting acne. They followed him everywhere in a symmetric V pattern. They were aptly nicknamed "his wingmen," wore the same outfits in the same way, and funneled young, teenage pot business his way. He would occasionally share a joint with them for their trouble. He was "the man" in his early teenage crowd.

———

Later that afternoon McKenzie completed his crime scene investigative report. The similarities to recent assaults on other young victims were obvious. The attacker was a white male fitting the common perp's profile—large, thick, and strong. He wore a mask and had scared the desire to be a lifeguard out of this boy. As soon as the police released the young guard, he went to the lifeguard house, packed his bag, and drove straight to Highway 501 west to Conway, and back to his home near Paducah, Kentucky.

The young man had been warned just as the others had been. The intensity of the warning was a topic they had refused to discuss. The details of their ordeals were never revealed. Evidence of physical wounds was difficult to detect, but their emotional scars were obvious. They had been humiliated and cared not what happened after they left, knowing only that they had to go and would not come back. No argument.

Another obnoxious, loud, summer worker gone, and he quickly would be forgotten except in the memory of a few too-young, impressionable hearts. Like another wave falling on the shore, a brief splash, a few grains of sand moved, and the next wave falls. The impact of one wave can hardly be noticed, but over time the constant action of a thousand, a million, a billion waves etches the profile of the shore. The turf had been changed, but few noticed.

McKenzie went back to his office to file the report and grab his bag of lunch.

"Hey, McKenzie, did you find your villain yet?" Sergeant Hank Parker asked with a smirk. "Who's the victim here? I mean, really, these are just obnoxious, summertime troublemakers."

"Boy, ain't that the truth," two other officers chimed in with mocking smiles.

McKenzie ignored the lower-ranking officers. "What's your problem, Hank? This is serious. These are felony assaults."

"Whatever you say, Detective." Another sarcastic taunt was tossed for the room to enjoy.

"You gentlemen are out of line. Does anybody work around here?" McKenzie scanned the crowd in the break room and got no response.

"Really, are we out of line, McKenzie? Has a crime been committed here, or are these acts of community service? I'm thinking this guy should get an award or something." Hank chuckled along with five other officers who were watching a baseball game.

"Get a life, man." An unidentified taunt came from the couch.

McKenzie bought a soda and left with his lunch to go anywhere but here. He was beginning to wonder if he had taken the right job. He wanted to help change his beloved beach resort for the better, to keep it safe for people to enjoy as he had. But now he was contemplating the professionalism of his co-workers and was suspicious of their commitment.

He refocused on the criminal attack, the attacker's profile, and common factors that might help lead to the villain or hero; the characterization was based on whom you asked. The guard lived and played at night in the same area as the other victims, therefore the attacker must have some presence in the area, some method for observation of his victims, some profile of his own to catalyze his need to attack. The attacker was comfortable with his surroundings. He was fond of gray duct tape and rope, all common items and hard to trace. He learned the occupation of his victim and attacked them with their job as a backdrop. He knew or speculated these kids had something to do with pot sales. And finally, the most important, consistent fact was he wanted them to go home. Why was he so focused on their departure?

A drug dealer's war was McKenzie's first thought—could be one distributor trying to run off another by scaring the hell out of his sales force. There was no need to really hurt or kill these kids and risk a murder charge. This intimidation had been relatively mild, compared to other torture and murder victims McKenzie had seen.

No, whoever was perpetrating these acts of humiliating terror was just trying to intimidate these young summer workers. If not drugs, what else could it be? Why would someone terrorize them? Is some psycho just pissed at these kids? While this scenario was understandable, based on summer-worker behavior that McKenzie had heard about and was seeing for himself, someone would really be overreacting. But why just here, in this part of town, when summer workers were all up and down the fifty miles of the Grand Strand?

McKenzie decided he would start with another evening at the Frisky Rabbit, where he hoped to see Edna again. He would need to be careful. He liked Edna and did not want her to think he was hanging out with her as a cover for his investigation. But his first priority was a bit of casual surveillance, not at the Frisky Rabbit, but on the other side of town, where more professional criminals might be lurking.

Chapter 20

The Grand Strand Assisted Living and Retirement Home bus was scheduled for departure to the shopping mall precisely at 8:45 a.m. Mrs. Ava Cunningham and two of her friends, Ms. Gladis Harfield and Elvira Simpson, had been up since five and were ready to leave at six forty-five sharp.

"Now, Mrs. Ava, you all know those stores don't open up till nine. We just gonna wait awhile before we leave." Nurse Thelma informed the triad of their schedule for the fourth time today.

"Well, I never," Ms. Ava griped. "I think that is just the most inconsiderate behavior. A successful business needs to open when the customers want to shop, and that is not at nine o'clock; half of the day is gone by then. Why, I remember when the Belk department store in Conway was open every morning at seven a.m. on the dot, except Sunday, of course. They were closed on Sunday as they should be. You could set your watch by when they opened that door. It was exactly seven a.m."

"You could set your watch, yes ma'am," Elvira chimed in.

"Mrs. Ava, Mrs. Elvira, I am sorry, but we cannot leave yet. Why don't you three have a nice cup of tea with Mrs. Gladis?" Nurse Thelma tried to divert their attention.

"Well, I guess we just have to wait, got no choice. We certainly can't walk seven miles to the store, not anymore," Gladis remarked. "We'll just wait." She grabbed her purse and stomped off to join Ava and Elvira in the lounge area.

Finally, they were off, and as they approached the mall, their discussions centered on lunch and where each would like to eat. Gwendolyn Parker was dead set on trying that new Italian place she had heard so much about.

"What time will lunch be served, driver?"

"Same as last week, Mr. Marvin, eleven o'clock."

"Eleven? What the hell? I don't know about these kids today. This tardy service just won't stand. Who can we have a little talk with to fix this thing, Frank?"

"I'll check it out, Marvin. Not to worry, my friend. I'll check it out." Frank smiled broadly.

The availability of food in the mall would prove to be out of sync with the group. The food court operated on a different schedule than the home. The grumbling was widespread but remained under some reasonable control. Many in the group were aghast as if they had just become aware of this injustice, this neglect to the needs of their elderly digestive tracks.

They had responded in a similar manner to the same issues last week and the week before. The loss of short-term memory could be an annoying frustration for those who haven't lost it. The bus driver had learned to cope with this situation early on with his job at the home.

Frank had provided the morning treat, and the high point of the day so far, and all glaucoma sufferers at the home were feeling just fine. Earlier, while waiting for the bus to depart, a group had gathered in the garden outside the home's reception area in a corner hidden from the view of nurses' station, and passed around two huge doobies that Frank had fired up. These folks were not going to wait for lunch; they climbed off the bus, went straight to the candy and snack vending machines, and stood there glued in place, looking at treats, pointing, laughing, and licking their dry lips as they continuously searched their empty pockets for change. The effects of the inhaled Tetrahydrocannabinol, better known as THC, muted their already limited short-term memory, but the munchies drove the urge to search anyway.

The muttering mass was not a pretty sight, but the pain in their eyes was gone, and they were happy, too happy. Harvey Feingold pointed at a

Hersey's candy bar, turned, and laughed at Sue Ellen, who moved closer to the machine.

Frank and Marvin kept their seats on the bus after the other residents and nursing assistants had gone into the mall. Frank handed the driver a five spot, as he called it, and the young man drove them to Santorre's Men's Store at the outer corner of the mall parking lot.

Frank and Marvin were flashy, but not really savvy dressers for men their age. Frank wore mock turtleneck sweaters, polyester slacks, and a sport coat on most days. Over the last ten years, as his eyes had deteriorated, he moved from basic black and blue sport coats to pink, white, sky-blue, and neon-green attire, attempting to model the Miami casual look he so often saw on TV. At one point he went for white patent-leather loafers to match his white patent-leather belt.

His fashion choices had changed dramatically for the worst over the last few years. Frank's clothing decisions went directly opposite of Alonzo's recommendations, but Frank was a stubborn man and raised so much hell about being able to get what he wanted that Alonzo finally relented to the demands. A Santorre's store in Fort Lauderdale usually had the clothes in stock, and when ordered, they were transported north with the next regular drug and cash shipment.

Marvin was typically more subtle and less forceful about the acquisition of his attire. Marvin was more a fan of plaid, different types of prints, and ascots. He always wore an ascot. Once, one of the girls at the home had complimented him on his debonair appearance with a striking peach, silk ascot he wore to a party. The lady who complimented him had passed away, but Marvin had ascots in many colors and still wore them with pride.

He had one for each holiday, one for each season, but he rarely bothered to match them to his clothes. More recently the seasons didn't get the appropriate scrutiny. Last summer he wore his Christmas ascot to the Fourth of July party, but he was happy, clueless, and life was good.

Alonzo met the two men at the door. He knew the schedule for the outing from the home. Alonzo offered these men the respect they deserved as members of the family. Frank was not a high-ranking member or a top boss's close relative, but he had been the "special project" hit man for the family in his time. Frank was no doubt special. When the job had to be done, and done right, they called Frank.

Few in the leadership ranks had ever met Frank, but they knew he existed. For the retired hit man, that world was a long time ago and mostly forgotten, except for a few painful reminders from old battle injuries. He had never failed. Failure in Frank's occupation usually meant death. He was one of the lucky few in his industry to live long enough to retire.

Frank had the respect of the entire mob world, friend or foe. He was no longer a threat, nor was he a target for revenge. He had reached a legendary status in his world. If he had worn a jersey, they would have retired it, quoting his statistics and his lifetime achievements.

Even with all of his secrets, they let him live and sent him into retirement at a home near one of the mob's minor network locations so someone could keep an eye on him. Here he was, still alive at ninety-two. Even his chain-smoking, nonfilter Camel cigarette habit had not been able to kill him, but his clothing selections would be the death of Alonzo.

Alonzo had orders. "Get him whatever he wants. I don't care what he asks for, get it. Frank is a man who helped put us where we are today."

Frank had killed off all the competition in his prime. He executed his tasks with such flare and efficiency that no one dared challenge the boss. Frank helped build this business, and he was to be honored.

Marvin was the boss's wife's uncle. The boss never liked Marvin much, but the price and hassle of not taking heed to his wife's demands were just too much of a distraction. Those demands included taking care of her uncle, despite his shortcomings. The boss couldn't wait to get rid of him so he sent Marvin to keep Frank company. At least, that's what he told his wife.

Marvin was a good sidekick. He played cards, smoked, drank, and talked crap with the best of them. They were the odd couple, but they easily bonded, based on their unique knowledge of the real world behind the facade of every community, small town, and big city.

Frank and Marvin knew the ways of the underbelly of business and politics with all of its money, power, and violence. The real world controlled the structures of the lives of people, and most lived happy and unaware. This dynamic duo was surrounded by the naive unawareness of the other residents at the home.

As a hit man, Frank had a relatively esoteric view of that part of mob life. Marvin was a third-level accountant keeping track of protection payments from merchants in northern Jersey. Marvin stood five foot six and weighed one hundred twenty pounds. Frank was six foot three and weighed two hundred forty pounds. At his prime fighting weight, he had been a lean, muscular two hundred twenty. Marvin had been a pudgy one hundred sixty-five, but now he was shrinking with age. Both were too old now to harm or implicate anyone, and even the mob had some compassion for their elders.

"Frank, Marvin, welcome. Glad you two could come by to see us today. Can I get you some coffee, scotch, or something else to drink? Here, have a seat." Alonzo offered his respectful hospitality.

"No, no, Alonzo my friend, it'll just give me an urge to piss, and that takes too long these days. I am hungry, though. You got any snacks or ice cream around here, maybe a Nutty Buddy?" Frank had a strange wide grin and a manic passion to search the room for something to munch on.

"How's that glaucoma coming along, Frank? Buggin' you much these days?" Alonzo asked.

"What glaucoma?" Frank just kept smiling.

"I want a double scotch," Marvin suddenly shouted.

"You're drinking early, Marv." Alonzo chuckled again and stepped to the bar. "Here you go, pal, double scotch, the best. Frank, I've got some beer nuts and some cheese balls here. Which would you like?"

"I'll take both."

"Frank, you are something. Wish we still had you around working with us. We could use a little of your muscle to get rid of these kids selling pot all over town. They're like fuckin' fire ants; you get rid of one bed, and another one pops up on the next corner."

"Fire ants, eh? I'd like to try some chocolate-covered fire ants just once." Marvin piped in and then was distracted by something floating through the air. Frank popped a cheese ball in his mouth and smiled at Alonzo.

"There's one gang that's been built with summer workers. They are with the tourists in restaurants, bars, on the beach, in gift shops. They've built a real network in a couple of months, and our boys are feeling the heat," Alonzo complained.

Marvin casually re-engaged. "It ain't that hot yet, not this summer." He turned and began to paw through an orderly display of expensive ties without an obvious objective.

Alonzo chuckled but continued. "Seems like there's a whole new generation out there that just don't understand the rules. They just show up, spread out on someone else's turf, and don't realize there will be consequences. We've put some hints on the street, but this group is so fuckin' stupid and naïve, they don't even know there are other people that own this place. This is our turf!"

"Our turf!" Marvin shouted and moved away, searching for something elusive.

"It's like the white man settling North America. All these high and mighty Europeans just waltzed in here, thinking, wow, here's a great wilderness we discovered, we can live here, land free for the taking. Well, what they didn't know was the Indians had been here already. They had already staked out their territory, and here comes the dumbass white man from Europe thinking the land was free for the taking.

"A lot of scalps and massacres down the road, and superior firepower once again won the day. We got to let these ignorant assholes know they could end up like ole Custer if they don't cut it out." Alonzo's intensity rose with each word until his face was red and seemed about to pop. His anger was clear, even if his analogies were a bit confusing.

"Damn, Alonzo, far out...I'm stoned, so I got an excuse, but what da hell you been takin'? Maybe a couple espresso shots too many?" Frank chuckled and started coughing one of those deep coughing fits, bringing up mucus phlegm from some collection point deep down, bringing it up and spitting it out before he could recover. It was not a pretty scene.

"Hey, sorry for the rant. I just get fired up when I think about those punks stealing our business," Alonzo replied and handed Frank a bottle of water.

Marvin was trying on an orange knit hat that did not go with his black-and-white plaid pants or his red-and-green striped shirt. He was standing in front of a full-length, triple mirror, admiring his potential wardrobe addition. An unfiltered Camel with a long, curved ash dangled from his lips. His fly was open, and one shoe was untied, but he was focused on the hat and a new pink silk ascot he had strapped around his neck.

Alonzo was not sure if Marvin's cataracts had not only blinded him to color, but also style, or if his brain had grown progressively feeble, or maybe he just didn't care. He was baffled, but Marvin was the customer, and the boss's wife's uncle was always right. Alonzo made a mental note to clear the store of inventory Marvin could use to create such atrocious outfits. The orange hat had been a special order and was meant for a Clemson football fan, not for finer menswear.

Frank looked at Marvin and then at Alonzo, cranked up his own Camel, chuckled, and shook his head in amused amazement. "Alonzo, what do you know about these wise guys, these punks? Who's checkin' them out?" Frank asked a surprisingly coherent question. He was back in his element.

"They've only recently started to have any real impact on sales. I'm just pissed that they got no respect—they don't know the family, they don't know what family enforcers like you can do to them if they don't follow the natural order and the rules we have fought hard to establish all these years. I mean, this is fuckin' America, it just ain't right! They need a lesson. They're costing us money, and worse, they are making us look like we can't control our turf or our business. The big bosses don't like that, and our ass is on the line. Tony has got to get control of this situation, or he won't be around much longer, if you know what I mean, and I think you do."

"Calm down, calm down, Alonzo," Frank said in a slow, cool, confident way reminiscent of Frank fifty years ago. "We can make these boys heel. Someone just needs to have a talk with 'em, explain a few things." He threw his head back and downed a handful of cheese balls.

"I'll take these." Marvin broke in and put the ascot and hat on the counter.

"How much scotch did you drink, Marvin?" Alonzo asked in a light-hearted manner.

"What da hell you care, I can hold my booze," he slurred. "Shit, I can hold my booze, what the hell..." He repeated himself in a mumble that trailed off, and he looked around, distracted by other things.

"Need anything, Frank? Look around; we have some new Arnold Palmer, silk-lined, green jackets. Looks just like the ones they hand out at the Masters Golf Tournament," Alonzo offered.

"Yeah, I need one that color. You're a good man, Alonzo."

Alonzo got the jacket and helped Frank try it on for size.

Frank ate another handful of cheese balls, spilling unnoticed crumbs across the lapels of the new green jacket. He was, or had been, "the Master."

Marvin put on his new hat and ascot, and they headed out to the bus. The driver was waiting, parked at the front door. The odd couple in turn each reached for the door's safety bar and slowly pulled themselves up the steps and shuffled to their seats.

"Nice hat, Mr. Marvin," the driver said without much enthusiasm. He always told the elderly folks what he thought would make them happy; it was part of his job.

"Yeah, well, screw you, didn't you see my new ascot, you dumb fucker? Don't know nothin' about a well-dressed man." Marvin's words mumbled away, and he looked out his window.

The driver just laughed and drove away, knowing anything he said would go unnoticed or would be forgotten. The driver directed the bus to the front of the mall and parked in the fire lane, ready to pick up the others.

"You boys sit tight, I'll be right back." He left the engine running to keep the air-conditioned interior comfortable for Frank and Marvin. The driver entered the mall to find the glaucoma sufferers in the food court in front of the ice-cream booth; he would need to search for the others.

Frank was looking out of the side window at a brown van parked haphazardly across two spaces among the growing assortment of cars in the front lot. The van caught his attention because it didn't belong here. It didn't fit.

Frank had a sixth sense that had helped him stay alive and able to perform his work like a surgeon. He had been blessed with a special talent to easily detect and accurately assess activity outside of normal patterns—to see things, to pick up hints and clues that other people might not see. It was like the people who wanted to harm him or the people he was after would expose themselves in shades of blue and green, and the rest of the world was color-blind. Frank could pick out the pattern and be ready.

He watched the tall, lanky fellow with coke-bottle glasses and a rag-mop hairdo get out of the van, casually look around, and then open the trunk of a nondescript, white, Taurus rental car. The man casually pulled out two large duffel bags, carried them to his ugly brown van, and calmly returned to the Taurus for two more. He closed the trunk of the Taurus and put the second set of bags in the van.

With the side door open, Frank intently watched as the fellow opened each bag to check the contents. Frank could see bags of pot.

The suspect took a closer look at one plastic bag and then opened it to test the aroma. Satisfied with the quality of his cache, he closed the bags, climbed in the driver's seat, and nonchalantly backed out of his parking spaces as if he were just another mall shopper.

"It's him. It's the pot punk that don't know the rules!" Frank said harshly without taking his eyes off the van. He read and attempted to memorize the license plates for future reference. The North Carolina plates read—"ASS-VILLE." Frank pulled himself out of his seat and climbed behind the wheel of the retirement-home bus. He put it in gear and drove off to follow the pot punk, wondering what idiot would pick a vanity plate that said "ASS-VILLE"; did he mean "ASH-VILLE"?

"What the fuck?" Marvin slurred as he woke up.

"Sit tight, little buddy. I found the punk Alonzo has been so pissed at. I think I'm gonna get his attention, straighten this fellow out. Send the skinny shit back to ASS-VILLE."

Frank was remembering younger days. In his mind this pursuit was just normal business, another mark, another day. This action had been his life, and in his mind, he was still capable. He remembered more about those times when he went after punks like the lanky, pot pusher in the brown van than he remembered about what happened ten minutes ago. The pot he smoked this morning had not helped the short-term memory situation, but at least he could see.

Frank followed the van at a safe distance. He did not want to arouse suspicion.

Vernon casually drove to a small, cheap, one-story hotel called the Ocean Reefer located a few yards off Highway 501, the main highway from Myrtle Beach to Conway and the rest of the world.

This hotel, with its beach resort-like name, didn't fool vacationing tourists who understood the location, but those first-time tourists who booked a week at the Ocean Reefer typically fought for a refund after arrival. Rooms were usually available.

The narrow, short street built by the hotel developer to serve this hotel was named Beech Frontage Road, so the confusion could be expected. The Ocean Reefer hotel management, not unlike other merchants in this tourist Mecca, made a real business based on some minor deceptions.

The outsourced reservation service was paid to say, "Yes, we are very close to the beach. You can even smell the surf." Yeah, you could smell it, if there was a hurricane and you had the nose of a Labrador retriever, or if you drove to the beach from the hotel. But the reservationists lived in Indiana, and said only what they were told. They had never seen the place.

Vernon pulled into the small parking lot, and Frank followed in his pot-induced paranoid stealth mode, a condition more obvious to others than to himself. Vernon was not an intellectual force in the underground drug industry, but he did finally notice the retirement-home bus that was following him. Normally, with any other vehicle, Vernon would have redirected it to another location or would have tried to lose the guy, but the retirement bus did not spook him. It just made him curious.

Just for insurance, Vernon had made a call on the way to the hotel and arranged for a couple of his muscle boys, Harley and David, to get positioned in the parking lot to meet him. Vernon parked and went to his room. His two partners sat and watched from their car. Vernon left the pot in his van for the moment. He would deal with that later.

The bus driver and the rest of the retirement-home outing group stood confused in front of the mall, wondering where the hell the bus might be. The driver was the most worried. He knew what must have happened. He tried to keep the group calm and herded them back to the food court before he called the retirement-home manager, mall security, and the police.

Chapter 21

The thrill of the chase rendered Marvin more coherent, but anxious. As a mob bookkeeper, he had met the tough guys, he had seen pictures of a few bloody confrontations, but he had never been in the action. His heart was pounding. He had stopped looking at his ascot in the rear-view mirror and was now engaged with the pursuit.

"Are we gonna kick some ass, Frank?" Marvin asked with scotch-fortified bravery.

"Maybe. You just stay on the bus and let me check it out." Frank left the engine running, opened the door, and eased down the steps, but he never took his eyes off the hotel door that Vernon had entered.

While Frank was employing his best "casual guy in the parking lot going to his hotel room" routine, Vernon's two thugs were cautiously easing their way from behind the retirement home bus. Marvin was too interested, too naïve, and too intoxicated to just sit and wait. As Frank moved beyond the brown van, Marvin stepped to the parking lot and slowly, quietly, tiptoed behind Frank, not sure if he was more afraid of the guy they were following or of Frank being pissed at him, so he stayed back a safe distance.

Frank forgot that he wasn't packin' heat. His mindset had reverted to his heyday. He was mentally connected to that time when he always had a gun, but seldom needed it. He could typically handle his business quietly with a knife or with his bare hands and brute strength. His senses, keenly aware earlier, were now dulled as he focused only on his single quarry. He did not notice the recent arrival of the two thugs. He did not sense a trap. His sixth sense, like other functions, did not always work properly at his age. He was lost in yesterday and unaware of his diminished capabilities eroded by time.

He knocked on the hotel room door and stepped to one side in case the fellow on the other side of the peephole decided to answer with a shotgun blast rather than an open door and a smile. Vernon, being of the less-aggressive responders, opened the door with a sly grin and saw Frank leaning on the doorjamb, his hand in the side pocket of his new "Masters green" sport coat.

Vernon wasn't sure what was in the hand in the pocket, and even though Frank was obviously very old, he was still quite a large man. Vernon took no chance and immediately brought his cheap, but dangerous nine-millimeter pistol around from behind his back and pointed it at Frank's head.

"Why don't you come on in, sir?" Vernon asked firmly as his two associates quickly grabbed Marvin by each elbow and whisked him into the room. Harley showed Marvin a gun and gave him a cautious warning to remain silent.

Frank was cool. He remembered similar situations, and he had always survived. Punks like this always gave him an opening, a moment when their attention was drawn away, when they became either complacent or too anxious to hurt him, and that's when he would strike. He remained calm and waited for the moment.

Marvin was overwhelmed with anxiety and yelled out, "We ain't telling you punks nothin', come in our territory, come on our turf, sell your pot, you assholes got no respect for the rules, we're gonna teach you a lesson. Don't say nothin', Frank, don't tell 'em nothin'." He mumbled a few last slurred epithets.

"OK, Marvin, I'll make sure I don't say nothin'. Just relax," Frank said sarcastically. He suddenly felt a bit handicapped in his ability to take advantage of any weak or distracted moment that might arise among his captors.

Vernon chuckled. He just shook his head in disbelief, looked at his buddies, Harley and David, and said, "What da fuck? These old bastards are here to teach us a lesson."

They all laughed. This lack of focus was the moment Frank was looking for. He grabbed Vernon's gun with one hand and punched him in the face with his other large, bony fist. Fifty years ago that punch would have collapsed a better man, and Frank would have turned the gun and fired on the other two before they knew what happened. Frank was slower now, and his punch delivered a bit less force. Vernon was quick and moved his head to only receive a partial blow. The safety was still on and protected under Vernon's tight grip on the pistol.

Marvin jumped up and started yelling, "Oh shit! Oh shit! Kick their—" Marvin was out. A pistol whacked the back of his head, and he began to dream of a mountain stream lined with trees all growing brightly colored ascots, there for easy picking; he had gone to his happy place.

Vernon's other muscle popped Frank in the back of his head with a heavy blackjack that he kept in his pocket just for such occasions. Vernon wasn't laughing now.

"Tie these fuckers up, one on each bed, and then you two take that friggin' retirement-home bus to the mall and ditch it. Remember to wear your gloves. Do it quickly; someone is probably looking for these clowns."

Vernon made sure the two elderly surprises were tied spread-eagle, one across each bed. He also put a rope around their necks. The ropes were pulled under the mattress and tied tight, with the knot underneath. Two strips of duct tape were pulled under the mattress and over their foreheads. Washcloths from the bathrooms were stuffed in their mouths, secured with the two-inch-wide gray tape. Vernon kept a supply of rope and duct tape in his van. One never knew when the need to secure something or somebody might arise.

Harley and David searched the bus and found nothing but a couple of cigarette butts, a partially smoked joint, and a white-and-pink knitted shawl. Vernon went inside to watch the two feisty old geezers while his boys took the bus back to the mall.

As the Grand Strand Assisted Living and Retirement Home bus and David's car turned into the mall parking lot, both drivers noticed a crowd and two police cars near the main entrance. Harley figured he would just park the bus in front of the Dillard's Department Store entrance at one end of the mall. No need to raise unwanted attention from the cops.

He turned quickly to the right toward the Dillard's wing, but not before being seen by one of the retirement-home ladies. She was giving her statement to the police while simultaneously being frisked for suspected drug use. She started screaming and pointing at the bus.

By the time the bus sighting was confirmed by the shouts of other retirees in the crowd and verified by a Myrtle Beach police officer, it had disappeared behind a corner of the mall.

Harley quickly parked in a spot near the door and took the keys. He went directly into the store entrance and dropped the keys in the first trash can he passed. Harley was now just another shopper in the busy mall.

David drove casually past the bus to another entrance on the opposite side of the mall. They met in the food court and walked to the main entrance, showing their best tourist-oriented interest in being attracted to all the commotion. Harley asked someone in the crowd what was going on.

"A couple old men from the retirement home drove off in their bus and left all these folks. They were too old to drive a car, much less that big bus. But someone just saw them coming back and driving around the corner over there. It's really not funny, but it's funny."

"No shit," said Harley, staring at the end of the mall where the bus had disappeared, as if it would come back around the corner any second. "So, a couple old boys went for a joyride, eh," David added for good measure to help the crowd rumor mill grow with confident confirmation.

"Yeah, I guess so," someone else said. Harley and David casually but separately worked their way back into the mall, through the food court, and through the opposite side exit. They got in their car and drove back to the Ocean Reefer Hotel with their information on the runaway retirement bus.

Chapter 22

~

Back at the Ocean Reefer, Vernon waited patiently while watching a re-run of *Let's Make a Deal*. He laughed out loud at the contestant that just gave up five thousand dollars, a trip for two to Europe, a new car, and a Maytag washer and dryer for what was behind the curtain. The curtain was opened to reveal a bucket and a one-year supply of hand soap, so she could wash her tears away.

"Greedy bitch, that's what you get, always wanting more, never satisfied." Vernon was exhaling the smoke from his Marlboro Red and mocking the loser on TV as Harley and David walked through the door of the non-smoking hotel room.

"How'd it go, guys?" Vernon jumped up and asked. The three stepped outside for a short conference to update Vernon on their little adventure. "Great job, boys, better than I'd hoped for!" They all went back inside. "Well, you old farts won't be missed. What I want to know is why the hell are you boys following us?"

Marvin had fallen asleep and snored while Frank just stared at Vernon with his piercing, assassin eyes. Fifty years ago those eyes brought most men to their knees with fear. Vernon did not understand the cold intent and promise of the stare because Vernon had no prior dealings with the tough side of the mob, or the fearless tenacity of a man like Frank. He was living in ignorant, disinterested bliss, and without a clue, Vernon was paving a path to his intersection with hell.

"Well, tough guy, I'm gonna run a little test here...on your buddy. You look like a bit more of a challenge." Vernon toked up a reefer and touched the red-hot ash to Marvin's temple just long enough to wake him up, screaming in agony through his gag. As he calmed, his eyes scanned rapidly side to side, struggling to bring his consciousness clearly to the moment. Vernon ripped the gag and tape away in one long yank, plucking away part of Marvin's mustache, prompting another scream that Vernon quickly muffled.

Vernon leaned down close to Marvin's face, looked into his wide eyes, and asked, "Why were you old farts following me?" Vernon drew hard on the joint, bringing the fire end to a bright red. He held the smoke deep in his puffed-up chest, smiled his smirky smile, and looked at Marvin, bringing the hot joint slowly closer to his face. He released the pressure on Marvin's gagged mouth.

"I ain't telling you nothin', asshole!" Marvin shouted.

Vernon pressed the hot joint right between Marvin's eyes at the top of his nose and pushed down hard with his gag, muffling the scream. As Marvin sucked air in through his nose, Vernon released the pot smoke from his lungs directly into Marvin's face, causing him to inhale the secondhand smoke still laden with the mind-soothing drug THC.

Marvin choked and struggled. Frank was pissed, but he couldn't move. As much as he wanted to rip Vernon's head off, his efforts were fruitless. He could not muscle his way out of his bondage. All he could do was watch out of the corner of his eye and wait for his moment to make another move on these punks.

Vernon released the gag and said, "I'm gonna ask you one more time, and then I'm really gonna hurt you. If you answer, then maybe I'll let you go tomorrow after we check out of this dump. Now, just tell me, nice and easy, what the hell were you two old farts trying to do?"

"Kiss my ass!" Marvin barked with contempt.

Although the information that Vernon desired was not a family secret, Marvin knew from years of experience, no one talks; no one gives up on the family. He knew if he gave up info on the family, the torture or pain of death that might come later would be worse than what he felt now. Marvin did not know how to decipher what was secret and what was not.

Vernon administered three more burns to sensitive locations on Marvin's face and cracked one knuckle with the crushing force of the room's heavy glass ashtray. These enticements brought more words of scorn from Marvin. Finally, Vernon opened his small but sharp Swiss Army knife and began to slice off Marvin's nose, one thin skin layer at a time, like peeling a grape. With the second layer removed, Marvin started to sing.

"AAAHHHHH...OK, OK, stop...ahhhh....Jeasusss, OK. We were trying...ahhhh...trying to find out who you punks are. We know you've been selling pot...in our territory. If you don't back off, the boss is gonna kill you bastards, and he's gonna kill you real slow. Ahhhh, man, it hurts, ohhh...I tell you what, the best thing for you is to get the hell out of this town and don't come back. You don't know who you're messin' with! We have organizations in major cities all over this country and the family is not going to let a punk like you move into our territory. Goddamn, my face hurts!" The stress and the pain took away any spunk Marvin had left. His eyes glazed, he became quiet, and began to drift toward an unconscious state and shock.

Vernon taped the gag back on Marvin a bit too tight. He then turned to Frank.

"Well, buddy-roe, I guess we know who you are now. The retired mob, the geriatric connection, the godfather's grandfather," he said, and started laughing. He laughed himself into a chain-smoker's hacking cough. He had to stop himself to catch his breath.

Harley and David, who had been testing a sample of their new delivery of pot from the North Carolina mountains, "Number One Blue Ridge," could only laugh, look at each other, high-five, and eat more potato chips. After another toke, Vernon forgot what he wanted to ask Frank, so he just sat down on the corner of the bed and passed the joint to Harley. Suddenly he remembered.

"So, Frank, are you the only ones? Am I invading your space, or is there someone else to worry about? If you are the boss's hit men, I'm really not gonna get too damned concerned here. So tell me, who sent you?" Vernon ripped Frank's gag off.

"You bastard, you really don't understand who you are fuckin' with here. I'm gonna tell you what poor Marvin told you. The best thing you can do for yourself and all those poor kids you got peddlin' your shit is to get out of town. Disappear and don't come back. Regardless of what you do to us, you are gonna get your ass kicked and kicked hard. Think of me as your best friend when I tell you to leave town now! *Go home!*" Frank issued his warning without a hint of emotion or the slightest waiver in his voice, only a dead-serious, focused instruction.

Vernon looked at Frank with a serious face, listening to every word, attempting to comprehend the message he heard. Vernon kept staring and thinking, battling for cohesive thoughts, but in the end, the pot had taken his brain, and he just burst out laughing, spawning laughter from Harley and David. Vernon was unable to continue to focus on this inquiry and taped the gag back over Frank's mouth.

Vernon was hungry. He could do this crap tomorrow. They had rented the room for the three days' minimum required for summer rentals at the Ocean Reefer. With potato chip crumbs scattered across their bellies, Vernon, Harley, and David all fell asleep while watching *Jeopardy*.

Chapter 23

McKenzie had been watching, listening, and cataloging activity and individuals that he thought suspicious in the central part of Myrtle Beach. He had seen a couple guys in suits, big guys, guys who fit the description of the attacker. Last week he had dropped by the Krispy Kreme for an afternoon pick-me-up, a sugar shocker to get him through the rest of the day. He saw two guys leaving who looked comfortable, relaxed. Either would be the right size for the villain he sought, and neither fit in with the lunch-counter set. They were obvious anomalies in this situation, wearing their thousand-dollar custom suits, in the Krispy Kreme, at three o'clock in the afternoon, with the ninety-five-degree summer heat and thick, humid ocean air. What kind of job did these big guys have that required this attire, this time of year, in this town?

He had seen them at the counter talking to Evelyn. McKenzie was aware that Evelyn had a new almost-boyfriend. Edna had told him. Before he went across town, McKenzie figured he would have a doughnut, talk with Evelyn, and learn a little more about this guy. He got out of his car and met her as she stepped out back to take her smoke break.

"Oh, his name is Guido. He says he works over at the Blue House. He's such a sweetie!" Evelyn answered with a smile on her face and an obvious song in her heart. She even blushed a bit. When McKenzie didn't smile, her lighthearted mood gained weight with concern.

"Why? Why do you want to know? Did he do something wrong? Why do you care?"

"Calm down, Evelyn, I just wondered. He just didn't look like he fit in."

"*Fit in? Fit in!* McKenzie, how the hell would you describe someone who 'fits in' the Krispy Kreme at any time of day? I see it all. We don't have a standard customer profile. Jesus!" Evelyn sighed, took a long drag on her cigarette, and shook her head in confused frustration.

"How about his friend, what's his name?" McKenzie asked with a more relaxed tone to help calm Evelyn.

"Oh, his name is Bo J. He helps Guido. He's really young, sorta learning the ropes."

"What ropes, Evelyn?"

"Oh, down at the Blue House. They help in the restaurant and bar, floor managers or maître d', I guess."

With more concern Evelyn looked around at anything but McKenzie's steady gaze. Her anxiety was building once again. She was growing tired of the questions as a nervous turmoil was churning and twisting her gut. She liked McKenzie, and she knew Edna loved the man, so she didn't want to be rude, but she didn't feel comfortable answering questions about Guido to the police, even if the law was McKenzie.

"Look, I got to get back to work. Maybe we'll see you later tonight at the Frisky Rabbit." She smashed her cigarette butt on the concrete step, leaned on the heavy stainless-steel rear door, and walked back inside to effortlessly resume delivery of sugary delights and coffee to her distinctly loyal and waiting customers.

Chapter 24

When Frank and Marvin failed to show up after the bus returned, Alonzo called Tony, and Tony called Guido. They were not overly concerned at this point, but Tony hadn't got the job running a business for the family by taking things for granted. He would take precautions in case this event was not just a senior moment. Guido was instructed to begin a low-key search for the two wandering gentlemen.

"No telling where that odd couple might be. Probably tried to make a getaway to a strip bar, got lost, forgot what they were looking for, and went back to the mall. Who would know with those two?"

Tony opened a box of Cuban cigars and made a selection with care. He pulled out a guillotine-style cigar trimmer and snipped off one end of the hand-rolled, forbidden, tobacco treat. The razor-sharp trimmer had separated a pinkie or two from their owners; it proved a versatile tool in Tony's trade.

"Maybe they caught a cab and went to a bar or the Boardwalk Arcade. We are checking with the cab companies now, but got nothing yet. Just keep an eye out, take a cruise around town, and see what you can find out." He struck a match and put the flame to his smoke.

"OK, boss, you got it. We'll check around." Guido smiled to himself thinking about those two guys stealing the bus for a joyride. He liked Frank. Guido took a ride to check all the titty bars near the mall; this assignment was very time-consuming. No one had seen the two gentlemen, but most showed their concern.

When Guido stopped by one of Tony's joints, the Happy Snapper Oyster Bar and Strip Club, he talked to Ophelia Butts, a lady he knew well. It was her real name and conveniently a perfect stage name. Her parents had not been so cruel as to anoint her with this title; she had married into it.

Her first marriage had been to a fellow named Roy Good. The daily taunts became monotonous. "What's your name? Ophelia Good? I bet you will." The raised eyebrow, the need to verify her identity with at least two credentials, and all the other humiliating validations were frustrating. She reverted to her childhood nickname, "O." This change did not give relief from the second looks and laughs, but it had reduced the sophomoric harassment a tad.

Her second marriage finally changed her Good last name, but not for the better. When she married Red Butts, it was true love. She was smitten. She knew the hassle that might follow, but love, being a powerful force, rendered her better judgment mute.

The two had a lot in common, as both had endured a lifelong hassle of teasing about their name. Oddly enough, this pain became the bonding catalyst that brought them together. Red wasn't his given name. His real name was Harry. He caught a hassle either way. With very red hair and a red complexion, he was stuck with the nickname from birth, and it would not go away.

Red and Ophelia Butts felt each other's pain and joined their lives by marriage, promising to share their love forever, but forever lasted less than three years for the uncongenial couple. Real life grew increasingly unattractive as the veil of lust wore thin.

When Ophelia kicked him out, she was not prepared to earn a living on her own. In her life she had mostly been married. For all of her late-teenage and adult life, she had used her body, beauty, and good-old-girl personality to get what she needed.

She had recently purchased a new, hot, overpriced Trans Am on credit. She was living in a house on the river that she did not want to give up, and her credit cards were maxed out, at least the ones Red had not canceled.

With a growing sense of desperation, Ophelia responded to a job advertisement in the *Myrtle Beach Sun Times*. The ad was innocent enough, describing a job where a girl could make lots of money and have fun, especially if you enjoyed dancing. The job even offered *benefits*. The benefits included free soft drinks while dancing and a small commission when a customer bought her a high-priced mixed drink.

Ophelia made five hundred dollars on her first night, mostly beginner's luck, with two big Bible conventions in town and generous tippers in the crowd. She decided to keep the job. Her duties required many of the same things she had to do to keep former husbands happy, but at least here, she got paid. The young male tourists she entertained were younger and better looking than Red, so why not. She decided to keep her name, Ophelia Butts; it worked well in her new business.

Ophelia had become one of Tony's favorites. She was country-girl cute, smart, and more reliable than most of the other dancing girls. She proved to be a good source when he needed help entertaining important family bosses or to set up a local merchant or politician with a few compromising photos for leverage. Ophelia had been instrumental in acquiring the cooperation of many esteemed public servants and high-ranking law-enforcement officials.

She had not seen Frank or Marvin, at least not that day. She called around to a couple of the other local joints the boys might visit. Most of the owners and their dancers worked for Tony and knew the elderly men. It would not be difficult to notice their appearance in a club.

No one had seen them, and Guido experienced a growing concern. Maybe they had caught a cab to downtown Myrtle Beach for some people watching on the boardwalk or to get a tattoo or body piercing on the main drag. These guys were old but fiercely independent, especially Frank, who occasionally forgot he was not still in his prime. Frank was not unique.

Guido sometimes pondered on this issue. When would he, or should he, hang up his tough-guy job? He was like many people who have a hard time reconciling the passage of time and the degradation of physical abilities. When does one stop being what one is and defer to the next generation? Eventually, he was likely to meet that strong, young, tough guy who would be able to put him down and thereby endanger those who depended on his protection. As he saw guys like Bo J come along, he knew time was not on his side.

Guido relied on his years of experience and powers of intimidation to avoid physical brawls. He wondered when Frank had figured this out. Perhaps just thinking about it might indicate it was time to choose another job. But Tony and the mob had been his family, so he would just keep doing what he was doing until something else came along, until some other force redirected his path.

Guido climbed in his black Crown Vic to drive to the Pavilion Amusement Park and see if Frank and Marvin were cruising Ocean Boulevard. But first it was time for his daily Krispy Kreme and another visit with his new girl.

Evelyn was at work, waiting eagerly for Guido to drop in. Since they had first met, he had become a daily customer, and she felt a growing attachment to this man, not just for his hunky good looks, but also for his gentle manners. He always said the right things, he always left a generous tip, and he showed up when he promised he would.

Evelyn ignored the other customers while Guido was in. She kept hoping he would ask her out for a late dinner or maybe breakfast. Today Evelyn decided to take the initiative, the step that might possibly move them to the next stage. She was in love and wanted something more than doughnut-counter talk.

"Guido, why not join us for a beer tonight? We meet at the Frisky Rabbit around ten thirty. My friend Edna and I meet there almost every night after work, so if tonight's good for you, that would be great, but if not, you're welcome on most any night, and we'll be at the end of the bar around ten thirty." Evelyn blurted it all out quickly.

She had made an offer guarded to some extent from the public humiliation of rejection. She had a fallback position in case he rejected her advance. She had practiced how she might say it, had rearranged it, replayed it, but at the moment of truth when the words were needed, they just came out in one breath like air escaping from a balloon.

"Well, honey, I work most nights pretty late. I'll see what I can do one Tuesday or Wednesday night. I'm honored by you asking." Guido always said the right things to Evelyn. "Can't stay too long today, love.

I'm looking for a couple of my friends that strayed away while on a group trip from the retirement home." He quickly ate the doughnut and drank his coffee.

"It's time to go, darling." While maintaining eye contact with Evelyn, Guido took her small hand in his massive fingers and kissed it just below her wrist. "Don't work these little hands too hard. Keep 'em soft, just as they are."

Evelyn blushed, drew her shoulders up, and smiled, saying, "Oh, Guido, you're so sweet, must be all those Krispy Kremes you've been eating. Come back and see us again now, y'all hear." Evelyn used her best Scarlet O'Hara accent.

She often used accents and famous words or phrases from notable women when she was feeling good or romantically nervous. And right now she was both. She watched Guido get in his car and drive away. As the taillights of his Crown Victoria disappeared, she yanked off her smock, grabbed her smokes, and went out back for her break. For Evelyn this cigarette was the closest thing to an after-sex smoke that she could remember, and she savored every puff.

Guido cruised along Ocean Boulevard, passing the busy One-Eyed Flounder, the Gallery Arcade, the Pavilion, and the Swamp Fox roller coaster, but no Frank or Marvin. Where did those old farts go?

Back at the Ocean Reefer, the Channel Five *News at Six* blared on the cheap TV. The uneven volume heralded a story, with on-scene reporters and exclusive interviews, about the retirement-home bus missing from the mall. The driver was itching for his momentary celebrity status, but when his chance came, he had little to say beyond, "You know what I'm saying" and "Like-a." The constant drone and mindless chatter of the anchorman was so irritating that it excavated Vernon from the peaceful sleep of his pot-induced coma. He sat up, tortured with a ravenous hunger.

Vernon checked the ropes and gags on Frank and Marvin and rallied his boys to go for food. He was paranoid and driven to focus on his fears and had difficulty maintaining a coherent chain of logical thoughts. They parked his van with the load of pot behind the hotel. Vernon had Harley put the "Do Not Disturb" sign on the room door, locked it securely with bolts and chains from the inside, and all three slipped out the back through a small bathroom window.

Vernon calculated that anyone watching the room would think they were still inside. He didn't want any interruptions. Vernon's last words to Frank were, "Sleep tight, we'll see you old farts tomorrow. Maybe you'll be a tad gabbier then."

Vernon had not offered to let the guys use the bathroom. He had not given them any water. He had not been concerned about their medications. Vernon really didn't give a shit. The trio left the Ocean Reefer and went straight to a nearby Western Sizzler Steakhouse. Vernon ordered "a big ole T-bone," his favorite.

As the night's action developed, Vernon and the boys smoked several more joints, delivered their pot to their distributors, and collected down payments and guarantees. The down payments covered their action with the original growers and left a tidy profit. All the forward money would be more profit for Vernon. This shipment was the largest load by far that the mountain syndicate had entrusted to Vernon.

He was feeling big-time and cocky with this success. He, Harley, David, and several of his suppliers met at the Frisky Rabbit for a little celebration. He put enough coins in the jukebox to select five Elton John songs. "Take Me to Your Pilot" rocked the rafters, and the night was on. They ordered beer and cheap tequila shots, and he led them through a chamber to foosball tables for more rowdy fun.

On the Grand Strand, the breeze was beginning to pick up, with storm clouds on the horizon. "Candle in the Wind" would round off the jukebox set at the Frisky Rabbit.

Chapter 25

At eight thirty that evening, a frustrated Guido drove back to the Blue House to see if Tony had any news on the lost old-timers. Guido's gut feeling was the two had just wandered away for a little adventure; maybe they had been at a bar watching a Braves baseball game on TV. Hopefully, they had caught a cab back to the home.

As Guido walked into the bar, he met Ophelia at the entrance. She had finished her financially productive happy-hour shift at the Happy Snapper Oyster Bar and Strip Club, and was now ready to take her shift behind the blackjack table at the Blue House.

Her dealer's blouse was provocatively unbuttoned to allow players a tempting view of her ample, enhanced feminine assets. Gamblers always filled the seats at her table, and most were distracted while she dealt the cards.

Ophelia had learned how to talk to the players to make them feel relaxed, to make them feel as though she was pulling for them to win. She even apologized when she hit her sixteen with a five or hit fourteen with a seven for twenty-one, while the gambler's cards were showing nineteen or twenty.

She taunted them when they placed meager bets, and the challenge usually drew a couple more chips. When they lost a big hand, Ophelia would order them a shot of schnapps, but their next bet would easily compensate the house.

She played the crowd at her table. She allowed them to win every now and then, and sometimes she gave them a big win to let them think they had the luck on their side that evening. But at the final accounting, the gamblers at her table lost most of their chips and tipped her with those few that were left. Most customers left happy. She was happy. The house was satisfied. Tony really liked Ophelia.

"Guido, I need you and Ophelia to each take a car and go find Frank and Marvin. I'm starting to get worried. Check some hotels and bars down near the arcade. If you don't find them by ten thirty, I want you to spend some time at that damn Frisky Rabbit. I'm betting our new competitor is hanging around down there, and I'm getting a little tired of losing sales to that punk."

"Gotcha, boss." Guido grabbed keys from the desk.

"Ophelia, I want you to spend some time around the gift shops, the arcade, and down by the Gallery Showroom. Who knows, maybe they are just wandering around. And while you're there, give another look in on that lazy dipshit running the One-Eyed Flounder. I bet he's in on selling pot to these kids. That pushy bastard never knows when to quit. He's greedy just like his old man, but different. He's the type to try to work on someone else's turf. By the way, what did you find in that punk's office the other day?"

"Why, nothing, Tony," she sang with her typical Southern charm, "but I could go look again if you want me to."

"No, I don't want you wastin' time playing with him. I just want some information. I want to find out who's screwing up the equilibrium of my town." Tony's voice increased in volume, and his face was edging toward a flushed red. Both Guido and Ophelia took the hint.

"Right, boss, we're on it," they both said simultaneously.

"Remember, Ophelia, I don't care if that asshole, Darrell Jr., broke your little sister's heart. I just want info. See if you can get it without wasting time humiliating the shithead." Tony's voice boomed with anger. "Just get me the facts."

"OK, boss. I'll just sneak in and sneak out, be back by ten or eleven so I can deal blackjack later tonight." Running on the toes of her Bette Davis-style working shoes, Ophelia took short, quick steps and followed Guido out of the door.

As a short-term carpetbagger, Tony had arrogantly claimed this turf, this town as his own. He acted like many unsuspecting new arrivals to the coast. They build houses on the beachfront close to the surf and live boldly, unaware of the inevitable storm that will consume them and wipe the beach clean. Money, greed, and pride made him blind to the lessons of time, the lesson of a land that does not easily relinquish ownership. The turf will always be returned to nature, the rightful owner.

———

Ophelia waited for a family to pile into their van and back out of a forty-five-degree parking spot conveniently located on Ocean Boulevard. Behind her, drivers shouted and honked their horns, urging her to move. The taunting parade of vacationers in rented Jeeps, Vettes, and scooters were eager to continue their destinationless promenade. Or perhaps the harassment was meant to deter her from getting the parking place just like the one they wanted.

Ophelia raised her hand high, honoring their impatience with a backhanded middle-finger salute. She didn't even bother turning around; she knew the face of those behind her. Seen one drunk "my first night on vacation" tourist, and you've seen them all.

She pulled in, parked, and started to cruise the busy central boardwalk and arcade. Ophelia stopped at a couple of open-air food counters to see if Frank and Marvin had stopped in for coffee or a hot dog. She asked one elderly lady sitting at an open-air, worn-out Formica lunch counter, smoking and drinking her endless cup of thirty-five-cent coffee.

The old lady was not new to this seat; her tenure was betrayed by an ashtray piled high with lipstick-covered Salem menthols, all smoked to the edge of the filter. She had a grinding voice, rough as a buzz saw.

"No darlin', ain't seen 'em. Lookin' for somethin' a tad younger myself." She smiled and stared back at the beach and a vivid, distant memory on the night-darkened surf.

Ophelia walked on searching for the two men, but she could not shake the vision of the old woman. The lady was sitting, dreaming, remembering a better time, waiting for her perfect mate, all the while grasping for pleasures from what she had, extracting solace from things that were not so discriminating about who consumed their satisfaction: caffeine, nicotine, and an ocean breeze.

Much like the cigarette and the coffee, Ophelia had given out simple delights to others without discrimination, as long as they had the price to pay. She didn't want to end up a discarded ash in a tray, a stain in the bottom of a dirty cup, or worn out and lonely on a barstool, staring at a memory in the night.

She turned off the boardwalk and walked into the large entrance of the One-Eyed Flounder, scanning for suspicious activity. With her background and experience, she could see a drug trade a mile away. She could spot the look of a nervous buyer, the terrain-scanning stares of an experienced seller, or the practiced choreography of the subtle pass; she had a sense for it.

Her radar was up, suspecting eyes wide open as she moved through the multiple levels and the wandering, confusing aisles of the store. She saw nothing suspicious in a full hour spent picking up items, inspecting, and touching merchandise.

Her intensive manic shopping with a seductively opened blouse eventually caught the attention of the security guard stationed in the back office. The guard was tasked with monitoring a bank of video screens that projected images captured from strategically placed security cameras. While the amateur attempts to camouflage cameras in inconspicuous locations worked for the tourist masses, the spying lens were predictable to Ophelia. She could not help herself, so she gave the security guard a show as she surveyed the store.

———

Darrell Jr. was bored. He watched people shopping and tasting free honey-toasted nuts, peanut brittle, and caramel-covered popcorn, grabbing handfuls, filling their pockets as if these items were entrees in the cafeteria of their last meal. These food-snatching tourists typically purchased precious little as they grazed through his store like a wandering herd.

After he received the third beeping page from the security officer, Darrell Jr. walked slowly to the security-monitoring booth. He really didn't want to get involved. They would be closing in a couple of hours, and these things—these complicated shoplifting thefts—were never easy. What could anyone be stealing that was of value, a shark's tooth, a T-shirt, a rubber snake? None of these things could be worth the hassle.

Unlike his father, Darrell Sr., who would arrest and prosecute someone over a stolen seashell, Darrell Jr. just didn't give a damn. He had been buzzed three times, and records of these alerts were kept. If the security page was due to an injury or a medical alert, and an issue of liability arose, the logs would be checked, and Darrell Jr. would be questioned. He didn't need that hassle either, so he reluctantly responded.

Darrell Jr. couldn't believe his eyes. That bitch in the security video, putting her cleavage on the camera lens, was the same woman who had screwed him and left him tied, drunk, and humiliated a couple of weeks before. What the hell was she up to? His mind wandered, and for a moment, he thought he might try to do her again, but this time he wouldn't allow her to tie him up. Hell, what was he thinking? He snapped back to reality.

This woman was after something. Darrell Jr. decided to stay in the security control room and watch her movements before he followed her. If she tried to steal something, he would have her arrested and strip searched as payback for the humiliation he had suffered.

In Darrell Jr.'s mind, the cruel, devilish behavior of this woman was the reason he was still being teased about how he got "a little tied up at work" one day. He had a score to settle. He wanted to play this cautious and smart, but Darrell Jr. was in over his head.

Pictures of the episode's aftermath were still showing up in weird places throughout the store. Recently some of the factory-installed, smiling-family photos in the picture frame department had been replaced with pictures of Darrell Jr. naked and compromised.

No one had really taken much notice until a couple of nights earlier when a ten-year-old girl standing in the checkout line with her mom, bored and fidgeting through the items on the checkout belt, asked, "Mommy, why is the man naked in our picture frame?" She gazed up at her mom, who looked with shock at the picture, then at the clerk and finally at Darrell Jr., who was bagging gifts for a cute, young, female customer at the next register.

The lady screamed, "It's you, you pervert." She grabbed her bag of merchandise, whacked Darrell Jr. with her purse, and stormed out of the store without paying. Her glare of disgust defied opposition.

Darrell Jr. and his dad were exhausted by the continued harassment. An employee meeting was held, warnings were issued, and the persistent pranks had gradually subsided.

He had thought the worst was over, but now this! Darrell Jr. quickly developed a plan to follow the lady. He got his keys and his car ready to go. The security guard was ordered to signal him when the lady left the store. He was going to follow her and get the story on this vixen.

Within fifteen minutes Darrell Jr.'s beeper burped the warning signal. Ophelia stepped out of the store's front door, scanned the street left and right, and then quickly walked the half block to her car, climbed in, backed out, and pulled away. The cars in the Ocean Boulevard parade honked, and riders yelled as a car stopped and waited for her to exit.

The cars were the same Jeeps and Vettes taking another turn up Ocean Boulevard, only now with more drunken tourists honking their car horns and yelling just for fun. The scooters were now roving in packs, swerving dangerously between the gaps in the traffic. Once again she left them with her backhanded, one-finger salute, still not looking back at her verbal assailants. Darrell Jr. was strategically positioned in a special-permit-only parking area for which he had no permit. He pulled out and fell in with the erratically cruising traffic, two cars back from his mystery woman.

Ophelia was ready to head back to the Blue House. It was almost ten thirty, and she was tired of fake shopping and looking for the wandering old men. They would show up sooner or later. It was time for her to deal, and blackjack customers with money would be waiting.

Darrell Jr. followed her north on Ocean Boulevard to First Avenue South. She turned west, and after a couple of maneuvers to avoid the typical traffic jams, hit Highway 501 on a direct shot to the Blue House Restaurant and Bar.

With all the traffic, even with the shortcuts, which Darrell Jr. also knew, Ophelia didn't notice the car following her. As she pulled into the center lane waiting to turn left into the Blue House parking lot, Darrell Jr. eased his car into the Sinclair gas station lot across the highway.

He could see Ophelia park in a reserved spot and go into the Blue House side door marked "Employees only." So, she worked at the Blue House! Darrell Jr. contemplated the connections. He knew what went on in that joint, more or less, but he was not a member.

His mind started to spin. Should he be worried? Why would the mob send a woman of this caliber to screw and then humiliate him? What was she doing at his store this evening? Had she acted alone, or had she been sent to give him some payback for some transgression he was not aware he had committed? Did she think he was cute, or was it just about kinky sex?

Darrell Jr. was confused, but he was accustomed to that predicament, which rendered him more confident than he should have been at this moment. His pride overcame his circumspection about following this harpy into her lair. Darrell Jr. drove across the highway and parked his car inconspicuously in the middle of the Blue House lot. He walked to the front door.

Chapter 26

Guido dressed in jeans, a T-shirt, and his favorite New York Yankees baseball cap. The hat would be an effective conversational icebreaker in this Southern latitude. He knew he would fare better chasing down Frank and Marvin if he dressed more casually. He planned to make the best of his time by combining the search for Frank and Marvin with his methodical pursuit of the young punks selling pot on the family's turf.

Guido drove to the Swamp Fox roller coaster and Amusement Park, thinking the old men or even the punks may have been enticed by the lights and activity at this popular tourist attraction. He strolled through the crowd, bought popcorn, watched people enjoying rides, and threw three baseballs at circus-rigged bottles on a shelf—two outta three wins. He was just searching, watching for the subtle action that would be percolating under the surface in a way the casual tourist would not notice.

He watched a kid carrying an enormous, well-worn, stuffed bear on his shoulders. Guido followed as the lad wandered through the park, telling anyone who asked where they might try to win a large stuffed animal; it was easy. In his wake kids tugged at their parents and begged for their chance to win the certain prize, if only they could have another dollar, or maybe two.

The fourteen-year-old walked a circular path around the Ferris wheel and the Tilt-a-Whirl and then strolled back to the penny-toss. At the back of the booth, he handed the big stuffed bear to the operator, the operator gave him two dollars, and he drifted back out front and became part of the crowd. After a few minutes, the boy put one dollar down for three pennies. The game required one to toss a penny into a glass plate. If the penny came to a rest on the plate, you won a prize. Make three pennies stop on the same plate, and you win a bear.

The operator moved to one corner of his booth and swapped the plate coated with PAM nonstick cooking spray with a plate sprayed with a sticky aerosol called Stickum, a product favored by football wide receivers for its adhesive qualities. The kid tossed the pennies on the plate, and they stuck. The operator held the plate up, rang a bell, a siren wailed, and he announced, "We have a winner, we have another winner!" In the excitement of the moment, he handed the bear to the kid while simultaneously replacing the Stickum plate with the plate coated with PAM.

The kid, who should have been overwhelmed with joy at his accomplishment, which no one else had been able to do that night or any other night, just took the bear and trudged off without expression to a position out of the spotlight. He lit a cigarette, settled it on the edge of his mouth, and moved on to continue his monotonous routine of the walk and penny-toss.

A couple of stray, barely teenage girls followed him around without interfering, each occasionally grabbing a puff of his cigarette. These followers apparently had less to do than the kid working the ruse.

Guido thought the booth operation would be a great place to start looking more aggressively for information. The big man stepped up and put down his dollar, and the operator handed him three pennies while shouting, "A winner every time, big winners all the time, step right up!"

"Tell ya what, buddy; I'd like a new plate. I'd like the one the kid's been tossing to." Guido spoke quietly but firmly out of the side of his mouth.

"Toss the pennies, sir, the plates are all the same. The last big winner tossed over here at this plate. Give it a shot, pal!"

Guido turned his head slowly and gave his best "I'm serious as death" look at the operator. He then moved a step closer, placing their faces only a few inches apart. Guido calmly spoke again. "Don't fuck with me, or I'll stick that stuffed bear up your ass."

The operator became more attentive. "What can I do for you, sir?"

"You can make me a winner, dipshit. I wanna know what you know." Guido didn't get a lot of information from the operator. He had confessed, at his age, he was out of the loop, but the kid, the kid knew what was going down.

Guido waited for the next cycle of the stuffed bear ruse. As the kid handed the bear back to the operator, Guido grabbed his arm and gave his female remoras a threatening look. Streetwise, even at their young age, the girls melted into the background without a word.

"Hey, man, I don't know nothin'," the kid answered Guido with an irritated snarl. "I'm just trying to make some money for beer and cigs and get laid, man."

Guido popped out the long, sharp blade of his knife and stuck the point to the front of the kid's crotch. "Look, you little prick, I ain't your teacher or your dad, and I ain't gotta put up with your moody mouth. You give me another answer like that, and I'll cut your little smartass dick off and give it to your little girlfriends over there. Now, you wanna get straight with me, or you wanna be a dickless, pimple-faced eunuch for the rest of your nonfuckin' life?"

Guido knew how to get to the point. He was unaccustomed to wasting his time with punks. The kid had no stake in the game, so he immediately shifted gears to a more cooperative tone.

"Sir, I know some guys who sell pot around here, if that's what you want."

"Yeah, I wanna know everybody you know who sells pot around here."

The kid spilled his guts verbally so Guido would not do so physically. "I'm just a lifeguard monkey during the day, man, and I do this gig a couple nights a week. I see a lot."

"What da hell is a friggin' lifeguard monkey?"

"Uh, I, like, help the guards set up their umbrellas, collect floats, break down the equipment at the end of the day, watch my guard's cashbox, help pick up trash, shit like that. I get paid squat, but I get to meet lots of girls, get a free lunch, and put my name in the hat to be a guard when I'm old enough."

The kid shuffled his feet in the dirt and thought for a minute. "OK, so, like, I know a couple guards that sell pot on the beach. I know a couple guys that sell it around here too. They get it from some new guy from Asheville. He brings that mountain weed down every week. It's some good shit—not the best, but good enough."

One of the girls tugged on his shirt; she was bored. He gave her a frustrated look.

"Man." She pouted and stomped back to her friend.

"I heard he's always over at the Frisky Rabbit. I don't get to go in there yet, but I seen his van parked there most nights when I get off here. I walk past there going home."

"Good, son. Thanks. See, that wasn't so bad. Now show me where I can buy some pot. By the way, you don't know me, you never saw me, I was just your nightmare. Unless you want me to be a recurring nightmare, I don't exist. You got me, kid?"

"Yes sir, I get it!"

"Here's a twenty, kid, stay out of trouble." Guido smiled to confirm their pact and went to talk with a pot dealer pointed out by the kid. He had to encourage each of the dealers to share with him, and they all provided a similar story. The sales agents each had a unique method for selling and passing product without being noticed.

One seller was afraid he would be the next to be tied up, humiliated somehow, maybe tied to the Tilt-a-Whirl on an all-night ride. He said he was leaving in the morning, going home and never coming back. He gave Guido his remaining two lids of pot and split that night.

The word was quickly out, and the distributors in the amusement park stopped selling, stopped working their tourist scams, left their booths unattended, and melted into the crowd.

That night most amusement-park pot dealers left the beach for the summer. With this new threat and all the summer's strange activities, they were all edgy. Circumstances made it more apparent that they were on the wrong side of this argument.

Vernon never had any muscle like this guy, even with Harley and David. Those two could be intimidating in a youthful, tough, redneck way, but they were nothing like this guy. It was time to leave.

Guido was content with his visit to the amusement park. This place was an information treasure chest. He walked to the next pot-seller's location. The path was paved and led to a bridge that crossed a canal.

The canal connected a small inland lake to the swash, and the swash ran to the sea and breached the beach at high tide. The tide was running out, being pulled strong by a full moon, drawing the lake level down. The lake was filled with discarded Styrofoam cups, lost balloons, and a miscellaneous assortment of floating plastic debris cast off by an uncaring herd of tourists who were consuming all that this ocean paradise would give. Screw everybody else; they were on vacation.

The lake flushed like clockwork, with the tide twice a day washing discarded tourist crap out for the sea to deal with. It is a big ocean. Who cared?

Guido stopped by two more booths of interest to find the dealers had suddenly disappeared. The tide was changing, and the swash was flushing the backwater trash. Guido knew he had accomplished one part of his mission. His presence had created an undertow, a treacherous submerged force hidden beneath the surf of humanity. Those who know the signs avoid the dangers, and those who don't swim in perilous waters.

Chapter 27

Before he drove to the Blue House Restaurant and Lounge, McKenzie had conducted some critical research in the police files. At ten thirty that evening, he pulled into the relatively empty parking lot and counted twenty-five cars. Once inside he saw only two people eating in the restaurant, with five more patrons at the bar. Something didn't add up.

After an uncomfortable delay, a waitress finally came from behind the bar with a menu, and he reviewed the Blue House cuisine. Faced with a limited, bland, and uninteresting selection, he settled on a chicken Caesar salad and sweet tea. It was obvious to McKenzie that food was not the place's primary business, and he was sure there was no way they would use a big guy like Guido as their maître d' as Evelyn had suggested.

While waiting for his food, McKenzie made a visit to the men's room, and as he moved through the bar, he scanned for details. Guido's young sidekick, Bo J, was handing out towels and mints to bathroom patrons. McKenzie considered that an oversized hand-towel attendant in a thousand-dollar suit was odd, but it was the location of Bo J's towel booth that caught his attention. It was not placed in the bathroom, but in the hall beside a door marked "Private."

Back in the restaurant, McKenzie noticed an attractive, middle-aged woman move quickly from behind the bar and dash across the room. With a red faux-alligator purse draped over her shoulder, she stepped deliberately toward the restroom entrance.

McKenzie's keen eye focused on the lady's frazzled hair. It was tossed about as if she had been out in the wind. But there was no wind to speak of that night, at least not around the restaurant. She could have driven recently in a convertible, or maybe she had the window down. As she had just entered the Blue House, perhaps her beeline path for the ladies room was to straighten her disheveled appearance.

He noticed two bald men enter the restaurant and go straight to the restroom. They did not appear to be in need of a mirror or a hairbrush. The men did not return. It was no crime to spend a long time in the toilet, but it did seem strange.

McKenzie reckoned the Blue House to be one interesting joint as he watched Darrell Jr. ease cautiously through the front door. Darrell Jr.'s eyes were scanning the entire restaurant and the bar. He was looking for someone, and his search appeared urgent. Darrell Jr.'s interest zeroed in on the lady with the untended hair as she quickly moved from the restroom to the bar for a can of Diet Coke and returned to the restroom.

For a moment Darrell Jr. remained in the shadows of the front foyer waiting area, and then moved toward the restroom hall while keeping his eyes on the woman. Was he stalking her?

McKenzie got up and eased his way into a position behind Darrell Jr. Seeking to become less obvious, he merged and blended in with a newly arrived crowd that walked from the front door and collected at the restroom entrance.

Ophelia bypassed the waiting crowd and Bo J to open the "Private" door. Sounds of slot machines and cheering escaped from behind the door and into the reception area as a man emerged from a second interior door just three feet beyond the private entrance. Darrell Jr. went straight for the door, and Bo J stepped in his path.

"Sorry, sir, I don't believe you're a member." Bo J spoke with respect.

"Why do I need to be a member? I know that lady. I need to talk to her."

Darrell Jr. moved toward the door again, only to have Bo J grab his shoulder and say, "Sir, I'm gonna ask you to leave."

Darrell Jr. was not intimidated, although he should have been. He hired guys like Bo J to guard his store, and most of them were just big pussycats. Bo J was not. Darrell Jr. persisted, pushing his way to the door.

McKenzie was waiting at the corner of the hallway and now stepped forward as if to go into the men's room. The "Private" door opened again, a man and a woman came out. Bo J had Darrell Jr. by the arm and was pushing him into the men's room. McKenzie made his move. He stepped to the first door behind the man exiting, grabbed the second door before it closed, and stepped into the private inner sanctum of a full gambling casino.

His unwelcome presence was detected as quickly as he had slipped through the door. As the muscle stepped up around him, he pulled out his badge and told them they were all under arrest. The muscle cooperated too easily, backed away, and raised their hands.

Suddenly the lights went out. Frightened screams and rumbling confusion filled the pure, total darkness of the room. The casino had no emergency lighting, no red, glowing, exit lights, no windows or other means of escape, and would therefore not pass a fire inspection. These thoughts were oddly going through McKenzie's well-trained public servant's head when that same head felt a sharp pain, and his conscious state went darker than the room.

The gamblers were gradually calmed by the voices of Blue House employees. Small flashlights were focused on their eyes, blinding them further to the shuffling activities near the exit. A door opened, and light formed a dim path for customers to exit.

A calm voice in the dark announced, "Right this way, folks, please step this way. Seems we have a power problem. We will need to close for a while. Please step into the bar area, have a drink on the house, and we'll give each of you a one-hundred-dollar voucher good for chips at any table next time you come see us. Our apology, please step this way."

The free drink might have been a sufficient enticement to clear the room, but the one-hundred-dollar vouchers created Blue House goodwill and enhanced the loyalty of their patrons. They all went to the bar, happy and secure.

Tony had responded to the intrusion by this new, not-yet-on-the-payroll cop with polished efficiency. His men knew how to handle unwanted visitors and how to prevent discovery by those who had no need to know. He took care of his golden-goose customers and kept them relatively unaware, safe, and happy.

The Blue House boss took control.

"Ophelia, get a drink for Darrell Jr. and escort him to one of our special 'conversation' rooms. Hector, have the men put this room in order before we have more unwanted visitors." They removed the gambling tables, sliding the gear into custom-made hiding chambers in the floor. The slot machines were quickly moved on their track wheels into a false wall that was camouflaged and decorated with Indian blankets from the local tribe. The bingo tables and chairs and the bingo machine normally used on Sunday were brought out and readied just for good measure.

After the casino was expertly hidden from public view, Tony grabbed Bo J by his silk necktie and tugged him into his office. He slammed the door and backhanded the confused bathroom bouncer with a powerful swing, knocking him onto a large mahogany desk. While he was down, Tony whacked him hard on the back of his head. Bo J held up his arms in defense and surged toward the couch, trying to gain his footing. Tony was quick; he grabbed Bo J with both hands and pushed him down on the couch, standing over him and glaring with violent intent.

Bo J was suffering a reminder of his father. He had been through this drill his entire life, at least as far back in his childhood as he could remember. If he had screwed up in any way, if he had lied, if he had not done his chores exactly the way his dad thought he should, if he had just happened to be in the same room at the wrong time, his dad had given him plenty of this same treatment.

He had hoped Tony would be different, at least after their first meeting. He had assumed Tony had taken him to train, but now the bully seemed to be more like his dad had always been. Bo J was hurt and confused.

"I oughta kill you, you worthless little shithead. You just cost me a load of money, and now I'm gonna hafta pay people to make this shit go away! You got one fuckin' job—watch that fuckin' door!" Tony yelled, reached down, and pulled Bo J's tie tighter around his neck. Bo J was turning red from the combination of anger and constriction.

"How you gonna pay me back for your fuckin' incompetence? You already owe me more than you're worth, you stupid asshole!" Tony's anger was bleeding off, and murder was fading from his thoughts. There were better solutions, but he was still pissed and waiting for an answer.

"Well, punk, that wasn't a fuckin' rhetorical question! How you gonna pay me for all this fuckin' trouble 'cause you can't do one simple job?" Tony spit his verbal venom in Bo J's face with foul garlic-laced breath more repulsive than the bitter words.

Bo J had developed an impervious epidermal facade callused by years of similar mean and physical treatments. He had developed a lifesaving, or at least a pain-saving ability to come up with an answer or a plausible explanation while under stress. Over the last few weeks, Bo J had been thinking about ways to improve his status and demonstrate loyalty to Tony in hopes of being promoted above the bathroom door attendant. He had a partial plan, but he needed to play his card now or be tasked with a debt he could only repay with blood, possibly his own.

"I know where to get a huge load of pot, boss! It's close by, there's lots of it. I know the suppliers, and it's cheap." Bo J blurted out the words even though his throat was closing from the tie's strangling pressure. He had always hated wearing ties, and this was one more good reason not to bother with the useless fashion accessory.

"I've known these dudes most all my life. The weed is really killer stuff, and these boys know how to deliver." Bo J continued in his effort to offer something that might save him from more abuse.

"Oh, you know 'em, do ya? These the same bastards been sellin' pot all over my town, messin' up my business, taking food outta my mouth?" Tony barked. He was not an easy man to please.

"No sir, these boys don't mess around here anymore, mostly Charleston, Columbia, sometimes as far as Greenville. They're more into wholesale. People travelin' I-95 and I-20 pick up big loads and take it to parts unknown.

"But first you have to get into the swamp to get the stuff, and if you ain't from around there, you'll wind up like General Cornwallis's Redcoats. The Swamp Fox will have your ass, I mean; you might not come out of the swamp again, sir."

Business came first with Tony. He started to release the pressure as he agreed to the logic, and his anger cooled to a simmer.

"You see, boss, these boys have their own network and ways of working. There's lots of dangerous things in that swamp that'll naturally make you disappear if you ain't from there. I'm from there," Bo J replied with more confidence.

"OK, dipshit, I'll give you one more chance. You make your play, you take the risk. If it don't work out, I might just make your ass disappear." Tony was smiling, but even his smile could be intimidating. "Tell me about this 'killer weed,' boy, and tell me how you know it ain't what's been goin' round this town." Tony was now all business.

"Well, boss, I tried some of the stuff they're selling, you know, trying to figure out where it came from. The summer workers tell me it's Number One Blue Ridge. That means it comes from the up-country near round Asheville or Boone, somewhere up in the Blue Ridge Mountains. Pretty good stuff, but it's got a mean finish. People always coughing after a toke, but it, like, gives the buzz that makes the kids happy, so... you got that."

Bo J sat on the edge of the sofa and began to relax. With his elbows resting on his knees, he used his hands to help express the intensity of his words.

"But I tell ya what, boss, it ain't close to Swamp Weed, and that's a fact. Swamp Weed is the lowcountry's answer to Number One Blue Ridge, and we blow 'em away." Bo J finished with a proud and satisfied smile.

"What do ya mean, *we* blow 'em away?" Tony grew suspicious.

"Oh, nothin', boss, just one of those upcountry, lowcountry competitive things. We compete in everything—football, basketball, pot, you name it."

"OK, OK, I ain't got time for none of that bullshit. I'm talking about real fuckin' business, boy, this ain't no damn game. Here's the deal. You get me the pot, we'll try it out, and if it's as good as you say, I'll overlook half of what you're gonna owe me for tonight."

Tony moved behind his desk to his large leather chair and sat down, but his eyes never moved from Bo J. "Now get the fuck outta here. Go get some of that Swamp Weed, and if it ain't the best, then you got real trouble for wastin' my time, boy! I don't want you around when that cop wakes up. You better have some samples, pricing, and access in the next couple days, or you're in bigger trouble than you are now!"

Tony picked up his phone, dialed a number, and then looked back at Bo J. "Unless you like swimming with sharks, you better not screw this up."

Bo J left the building to prepare for his new mission. He had picked up the keys for one of the Blue House's new black Crown Victoria limos to make the trip, but thought better of this plan and drove to the Ryder Truck Rental Store and rented a small van. Driving the Crown Vic into the swamp would surely get him shot.

Bo J would drive back to his world in Williamsburg County and to a fish camp on the Black River, not far from the former swampy lair of the famous American Revolutionary War hero, the Swamp Fox.

Meanwhile, the Mickey that Ophelia slipped into Darrell Jr.'s complimentary drink was starting to take effect. She had taunted him to chug his drink while she mesmerized him with a sensuous dance. She opened another button on her shirt and brushed past Darrell Jr. a time or two to help get his blood pumping, expediting the effect of the drug. Darrell Jr. passed out smiling.

Ophelia called for a couple of the guys who had just finished laying out the bingo cards. They tied Darrell Jr.'s hands and feet and put him in a car trunk. Ophelia drove to the Happy Snapper and had the bouncer put Darrell Jr. in a special room in the back of the club. She was not quite finished with him. Tomorrow was ladies night at the Happy Snapper. Darrell Jr.'s prey had gotten the better of him for a second time. Darwin's theory of survival of the fittest recorded another data point of confirmation.

Chapter 28

McKenzie could hear distant, muted sounds, people talking, calling his name, somewhere far off in a gloomy tunnel. He strained to respond but felt numb, paralyzed as in past dreams when he had tried to scream out to warn someone, but could not force himself to utter a sound. He was confounded by the swarm of people that seemed to float about the room and look down at him, carefully gazing, as if studying his face. Some laughed softly, but none demonstrated the urgency he felt to communicate.

And then McKenzie heard his name again and felt someone placing a wet towel on his face. His dizzy head felt like it would burst with a pounding, overwhelming, pain. Clarity finally came with McKenzie's boss, Chief Detective Ricky Driggers. The chief was down on his knees looking into McKenzie's eyes, hovering just above his face.

"Hey, sport. Wake up, wake up. We've been worried about you. How do you feel?"

"Like I got whacked in the back of my head with a Louisville Slugger. Ahhhh! It hurts just saying it. Help me up." McKenzie tried to rise up on his elbows and went right back down. Detective Driggers caught his head before he hit the floor. A paramedic moved in to help. McKenzie turned and puked as the nausea consumed his desire to regain control.

"Here, take these aspirin, they'll help with the pain," the paramedic offered.

McKenzie raised himself up on his elbows and pushed back to support himself against a wall. Finally he was sitting, and his pants felt wet from the floor. He could see water mixed with something red. Was that his blood? He felt the cloth compress already applied to the back of his head.

"What the hell you doing, McKenzie, trying to kill yourself?" Driggers asked while he looked into McKenzie's eyes for a clue to his mental alertness. "You've been having a pretty big night here alone," Driggers chided with an air of disgust.

"What are you talking about, Driggers? I was here investigating. I've seen some pretty suspicious activity. I went through a door marked 'Private,' witnessed illegal gambling, an entire casino, and *bam*, somebody whacked me!" McKenzie said as he became more aware of how much water was on the bathroom floor and how much blood he had apparently contributed to the thick wetness that soaked into his pants.

"Whoa, whoa! What are you talking about, man? You must have bumped your noggin harder than we thought. I'd say whatever you were drinkin' or smokin' might have something to do with it." Driggers chuckled while busily chewing his ever-present wad of Juicy Fruit gum. "I want some of that stuff. Damn, man, it's got you hallucinating!"

"Well, I haven't been drinking, and I did see an illegal casino! Help me up. I put a whole room full of people under arrest. They were all in the next room," McKenzie said with frustration as he tried once again to get to his feet. The aspirin had not yet provided relief, and he was still dizzy.

"Maybe you better just go with the paramedics in the ambulance to the hospital tonight. You're gonna need stitches in that hard head of yours, and I'm afraid you may have a concussion."

"No, look, let me show you!" McKenzie pushed his way to the "Private" door. He noticed a number of uniformed police officers in the bathroom and in the hallway, all relaxed and talking among themselves. Apparently no raids had occurred, and no one had been arrested. What was wrong?

The big guard was gone, his table of restroom amenities was gone, the "Private" door was wide open, and so was the second door. The interior room was well lit, and McKenzie walked in to prove the issue to Driggers. He looked around to see nothing but a bingo parlor. No blackjack table, no roulette, no slot machines, no loud crowds playing craps, nothing but a dormant bingo game set.

With short, unsure steps, McKenzie moved slowly and cautiously around the large room, looking for clues of the gambling he had witnessed. He spied a single five-dollar chip on the floor, wedged in a corner, but said nothing for now.

"Is this the illegal gambling you busted, McKenzie?" Driggers asked sarcastically. Several of the uniformed officers chuckled.

"No, they had this place packed full with people and gambling equipment! It's been changed!" McKenzie said with growing anger.

"McKenzie, I was here in the restaurant for lunch today, and this is how I saw it. I even came back into this room to talk with Tony, the owner. He was in here himself getting this room ready for the retirement-home folks coming in tomorrow afternoon. I swear, McKenzie, like I said, whatever you were drinkin' or smokin', I want some. Look at you, man, you're dripping blood and water all over the floor. You're making a mess. We need to get you outta here and to the hospital."

McKenzie glared at Chief Detective Driggers and growled through clenched teeth, "I wasn't drinking, I was working!" McKenzie decided to say nothing more. Either he was confused by the injury, or this situation exposed potential corruption.

Driggers's lighthearted smile turned quickly to a menacing snarl. "Oh, is that right. Be careful, McKenzie, I've got three witnesses that say you ordered three drinks with your meal, said you appeared drunk when you came in the joint. I got a meal receipt here the waitress gave me that corroborates the witnesses' statement." Driggers held a strip of paper in the air, but didn't let McKenzie see it.

"I got two people that tell me you stumbled into the bathroom, tried to take a piss, and slipped on the water and busted the back of your head. They say you looked dead, and you were bleeding, so they called nine-one-one. They checked your wallet and then called us when they saw your badge." Driggers handed McKenzie his badge, but kept his gun.

"Now you wake up smelling of booze and give me some crap story to cover your ass. You better just drop it, McKenzie. Take the ride to the hospital like I'm strongly suggesting you do and report to the office, sober, when they release you. If you don't, I may just put you on suspended duty. Now, I think you've caused enough trouble for one evening. You are embarrassing the Myrtle Beach Police Department."

Driggers was focused on McKenzie's eyes with an intensity he had never seen from this man. McKenzie was still dizzy, confused by the activities of the night and knew he would do better with this situation on another day. He needed to be sharp. He needed time to think when his mind was not in a painful fog.

"OK," McKenzie said, and walked out with the paramedic. As the ambulance pulled out of the parking lot and hit the siren to move through traffic, McKenzie looked back though the rear-door window and noticed Detective Driggers talking with Tony on the front steps of the club. Tony discreetly passed a small, fat envelope to Driggers, shook his hand, patted his back, and they went back inside.

"Driggers, I pay you too much to put up with this shit. Can you get this fellow to lay off? Assign him to North Myrtle parking meters or Pawley's Island litter detail or something. Damn!"

"Tony, you know better. I think tonight was well handled. We'll just question his credibility. If he doesn't fall in line, we'll set him up, and he'll be gone one way or another. Not to worry, my friend."

"Well, I fuckin' do worry when I lose money, and I lost a lot tonight. I want this shit to stop now! Do you understand that, *friend*?"

The cops left, and Tony went to his office to count his losses and think of some way to make it up. Frank and Marvin disappear, McKenzie walks into the casino, and Ophelia has a stalker. What else could go wrong? Tony had learned not to ask this question out loud lest it come true. Maybe Guido would get some info about these damn kids selling weed around town.

———————

The ambulance pulled under the parking cover in front of the emergency-room entrance at the Myrtle Beach Memorial Hospital. McKenzie walked in unassisted, and the reports were filed to start his long wait for admission.

Despite his apparent concussion, bloodied clothes, bandaged and bloody head, and arrival by ambulance, he would not be taken directly to a room for observation. He was not considered an emergency, as he had no hideous injury gushing blood, no heart attack, no life-threatening gunshot wound, and he was breathing. He answered all the questions on insurance, attempted to resolve the confusion about how his injury occurred, and finally left it at "hit head on hard object."

McKenzie tried to explain his version of the night's events while the admitting nurse read the paramedic's report and smelled his alcohol-soaked clothes. She took his temperature and his blood pressure and smiled as she got up to leave. She made no judgments, at least not to his face.

"Just sit in the waiting room, sir, and we'll call you when the doctor is available."

McKenzie sat in a cheap, uncomfortable chair surrounded by a small mass of humanity, which amazed him. Every time he had been in an emergency room, he had seen this potpourri of the living, the accidents, and the sudden afflictions.

For a night in Myrtle Beach, things were relatively calm. A boy who had nearly drowned was being released. His elated mother repeated the story to the nurse as she led them out of the emergency room to the billing administrator.

He had been revived moments after he had given up, sank under the surf, and sucked water into his lungs. A lifeguard had reached him in time and started his breathing on a raft. He was pulled to shore and carried to the hospital by ambulance. The boy was OK. Finally a summer employee provided a positive impact on the community, but only a few would know, and fewer would care.

The emergency-room scene was decorated with coughing, minor bleeding, a young girl sniffling with a broken arm, a middle-aged tennis player with a busted knee, and some poor, unknown food critic with food poisoning. A drunk whose head had been cracked open by a beer bottle tainted the otherwise innocuous crowd. He was still so drunk, that he wanted to fight even while strapped to the hospital gurney. This night was going to be a long one.

For thirty long, agonizing minutes, McKenzie had to sit among all the sick and injured, and was forced to either watch *All-Star Wrestling* on the small but loud, scratchy TV or stare down at the well-trodden commercial-grade carpet. The TV was controlled by three large, rowdy, tattooed teenagers, who constantly picked at each other while waiting for someone to be treated. McKenzie wasn't feeling like stepping in to relieve the pain felt by most in the room, so he just waited in his fog. Apparently, the triage nurse felt McKenzie's potential concussion and his job as a police detective merited a higher priority than the drunk and a couple of other bleeding patients, so his wait was cut shorter than the norm.

After the doctor checked McKenzie's injury and closed the wound in his head with thirty sutures, they decided to keep him for a couple days of observation. The call from Detective Driggers may also have had something to do with this extended internment.

The nurse pushed him to his room in a wheelchair. They went into the One-Eyed Flounder Memorial Wing. The wing entrance was marked with a plaque identifying its most generous donor. Right next to the entrance was a small gift shop that sold souvenir trinkets allowing every patient or visitor the opportunity to purchase a memento to commemorate his stay at the Myrtle Beach Memorial Hospital.

The One-Eyed Flounder Memorial Wing wasn't so much a wing as an extension, with only one floor offering eight rooms to accommodate the afflicted when the hospital had an overflow of patients.

McKenzie was pushed into the last available, empty, semiprivate room. The nurse said, "You're lucky, this is the last open room in the hospital. If one more patient is admitted tonight, then you'll have a roommate. If you weren't a cop, they would have put you on a gurney in the emergency-room holding area till tomorrow."

"Lucky me!" McKenzie was serious. He lay down, his head still aching and dizzy. With the help of a more potent painkiller, he drifted off into a deep, healing sleep.

Chapter 29

Before he left Myrtle Beach, Bo J called his hometown pot contact, Raymond Raynell, better known as RayRay. It was already midnight, but no problem as RayRay was a night owl; his work demanded it.

RayRay's younger cousin Randy was Bo Jr.'s age. Randy and Bo Jr. had played football and baseball together since they were five. They went through their years of school in the same class, in the same grade. Both were members of the same First Baptist Church, where they regularly attended Sunday school, church services, and Wednesday-night prayer meetings. Their mothers had made sure of it.

In their small town, almost everyone went to church except for the unsociable few like Bo Jr.'s father. On Sunday the community came together at church, where the people sought interaction with their neighbors as well as their God. It was the gathering and social redemption each soul required at least once a week and often twice on Sunday.

Each Sunday after the sermon and the traditional Baptist "call to the altar" hymn, the congregation socialized between the pews and slowly departed. But after the hour of fidgety sitting, Bo Jr., Randy, and RayRay were bursting with energy. They wanted to get out, to run and play on the large manicured lawn in front of the church.

As the oldest, RayRay would navigate a path to the exit, winding between the faithful who waited in line to shake the preacher's hand. As the adults whispered greetings and chatted about football games or social picnics or Wednesday-night prayer meetings, they would move aside for the energetic boys. The town fathers laughed and gave the boys friendly passage. The town mothers smiled and gave hugs or a pat on their heads as they scampered past. They were as one family and one community.

This close-knit community had nurtured the boys in the years of their childhood friendships with a bond similar to kinship. They knew Bo Jr. by his childhood name. He had cared for at least this one family. They were the family of his community, people he could call on anytime for the rest of his life, and they would respond with support, without many questions, because he was family. In the middle of the night, Bo J called RayRay at his farmhouse.

"Bo Jr., good to hear from you, bro. What's up? Y'all need a little somethin'?" RayRay asked with a hazy voice.

"RayRay, I need to come by tonight. I need to talk with you, man. I'll be driving a yellow Ryder van. Be there in about an hour and a half. It's really important, man. Will that be OK?"

"Sure thing, bro. Get your ass on over here!"

Bo J had a strong suspicion that RayRay had been sampling his own inventory, and he hoped he would be coherent enough to deal. He would have to go to RayRay because they could not discuss the details over an open telephone line.

Just before one forty-five that night, Bo J pulled off the bleached-out, asphalt highway onto a county dirt road marked only by a thin weather-beaten metal sign for the Macedonia Baptist Church. He drove with familiar confidence on the sand-clay, washboard road and then turned right on a single-lane road running through the middle of a young longleaf pine-tree farm that belonged to RayRay. A porch light winked through the trees about a hundred yards off the road. Dogs, barking the alarm, came running out to meet Bo J with a menacing ferocity.

The dogs were not the only cautious, watchful sentries of the night. RayRay had a network. Just because he was a local boy didn't mean activities like RayRay's went unnoticed. Like the Revolutionary War hero, the Swamp Fox, RayRay had places in the Santee and Black River Swamps to operate, to hide, to grow, and to store his crop. Law enforcement, who sporadically cared, had attempted to follow him into his domain, but he could lose them and be gone with no clear connection to the illegal plants.

RayRay grew his crop in small plots throughout the swamps; many spots were only accessible by the river in small flat-bottom boats or canoes. Catching RayRay was unlikely, and proving his connection to anything illegal would even be more difficult. Finding a jury that would convict him would be damn near impossible.

The swamp man was still in business because he never became overconfident. His daddy and his granddaddy had run moonshine out of this wet wilderness, and years of evading the law had taught them the lessons well.

Two men stood back in the dark of the tree line, hoods covering their heads and automatic shotguns resting on their shoulders. They were waiting to see who might emerge from the van. Bo J rolled down the window and spoke to the two pit bulls jumping up and scratching the driver-side door, baring their teeth and ready for action. He called them by name, trying to calm their aggressive anxiety and natural urge to kill.

"Snot! Booger! Calm down, boys, calm down." Bo J lacked confidence in their canine awareness and was not ready to put his hand out of the window to allow them to test his scent. With these two he knew he might just pull back a bloody nub.

"Hey, boys, it's me, Bo J. Calm down. Hey, RayRay, call off your damn dogs!" Two shorthaired pointers, three black labs, and a bloodhound joined in the pack's barking chorus. The bloodhound flapped his big ears, put his nose to the sky, and commenced to cast his long baritone howl at the moon. His deep vocal pitch was in a distinct contrast to the sharp, quick, threatening barks from the other dogs in the pack.

A light switched on in the house, and RayRay stepped out of the front door and onto the wooden porch deck. Dressed only in his boxer shorts, he demonstrated natural, but practiced, dexterity by simultaneously scratching his tangled, mussed hair with one hand and his butt with the other. In his sleepy, stoned haze, RayRay had forgotten Bo J had called earlier. He squinted into the darkness, trying to identify his visitor before calling off the dogs.

"Can I help you? Are you lost?" RayRay asked and then chuckled, seeming to forget why he had asked.

"RayRay, it's me, man, Bo J...ah, Bo Jr. Call the dogs, man, and whoever's out there in the trees, it's me!"

"Oh hi, bro, what da fuck you doin' here, man? Come on in, man," RayRay said with surprise and then stubbed his toe on a warped board on the edge of his deck. "Jesus H...and his mother too! Jeez, friggin' deck."

Bo Jr. was not too shocked that RayRay had forgotten his call. Swamp Weed typically played games with one's memory.

"Call the dogs, man, they're actin' crazy tonight," Bo Jr. shouted back.

"Booger! Snot! Come here!" RayRay commanded. The dogs barked once more for effect and then obediently turned and pranced back to shelter under the front porch, turning to look back once or twice to ensure no other danger lurked in the night. The rest of the pack followed.

Sonny and Dale stepped out of the dark shadows of the tree line and herded the other hounds off to the side of the house. Sonny and Dale were well trained and suspicious. Unlike RayRay, they currently had control of all their senses.

These men were not book-trained by some higher institute of learning, but they knew the woods, knives, guns, and dogs. They knew how to handle themselves in a fight, how to survive in nature, and like many of God's creations that lived a life of survival, they were cautious.

They knew Bo Jr., but they had not known he was coming tonight. Could this be a trap, or was he for real? Were others following Bo Jr. and now hiding in the woods, ready to pounce when the time was right? If they relaxed, they became vulnerable. They left with the two pointers and the bloodhound to check the perimeter in case others had followed.

Bo Jr. knew the drill. He knew that they knew he had been gone for a while. Was Bo Jr. working for the cops or some other competitor? Until they were sure, Sonny and Dale would stay where they felt safe, on the edge of the swamp with the guns and dogs.

Bo Jr. called out, hoping to calm their fears, "It's OK, guys. I'm alone. Just come to pick up some weed." Bo Jr. climbed out of the truck with his eyes on Booger and Snot still growling under the porch. The dogs had his scent. It was familiar, and they had begun to lighten up, but they had not truly relaxed. Attack was still a possibility.

The dogs seemed to calm as they continued to categorize the smell of Bo Jr. The last time they had smelled him, the scent was much stronger. This time his scent was mingled with other smells, more like flowers or something the dogs had sniffed when female humans had come around. Booger and Snot now trotted out with their tails wagging, sniffing at Bo Jr.'s new shoes and suit. They sniffed his hand when he offered and accepted their anticipated pat on the head. Bo Jr. was finally allowed to pass to the porch. He stepped up and gave RayRay a simultaneous handshake and hug.

"How ya been, man?" RayRay asked with a semipermanent smile, looking Bo Jr. up and down while continuing to scratch his ass for no particular reason. "Goddamn, you just up and run off, nobody knows where in creation you went. And shit, you show up here, all dressed up like some New York big shot going to church. What da hell you been doin', bro?"

"I've been working with some fellows over near Myrtle Beach. They're treating me real good. Bought me this suit and stuff, gave me a place to live, pay me good, teaching me things." Bo Jr. spoke with pride.

While putting the situation in the most positive light, there was no need to discuss the details. Bo Jr. felt confident back in his element, but at the same time, his short experience in the big city and the big time caused him to question where he really belonged. These people still called him Bo Jr. and always would, no matter what others called him. Even if he wanted them to change, they would not.

"What kind of work makes you wear a suit in Myrtle Beach?" RayRay asked as he stuffed a pinch of Skoal between his cheek and gum. He did not wait for an answer; he brushed the residual snuff off his fingers and said, "Well, it looks like you done good. We can't be havin' a man in a suit standing out here in this damp air. Come on in."

"RayRay, it's great to see ya, buddy, and I'd like to hang around awhile with you and the boys, but I'm in a hurry. I'm bringing you a great deal, cash money, but I need to make it happen tonight.

"My boss is in a real bad mood, and we need to have some of your stuff to help get our customers back. Got some punks from upstate trying to peddle that Blue Ridge crap all over the beach. You know that shit don't hold a candle to your stuff.

"The boss says we ain't gonna put up with that shit, but we need something that competes price-wise. The boss is tired of selling stuff that's been taxed three times before he gets it." Bo Jr. rattled it all out with hardly a breath, almost like what he had been told to say.

"Whoa, whoa, cowboy, calm down. Hell, we ain't even sat down yet. Damn, man. Sit and take a load off. You scare me, boy. I'm a little paranoid right at the moment, as you might imagine." And then he just smiled, and with glazed eyes stared at Bo Jr. like he had lost his place in time. Suddenly he was back again. "Take your coat off, man, have a seat. Shit, I can't take all that info at one time. You gotta ease up, boy."

"But I need some pot to deliver tonight, or it's my ass!" Bo Jr. responded with determination.

RayRay seemed to sober up, looked at Bo Jr., and said, "Shit, if it's that all-fired important, it can wait till tomorrow. Your boss'll understand. Sit down." The last offer was more of an order than just plain hospitality. Then his demeanor lightened up again, and he chuckled at nothing in particular. Bo Jr. placed his hands on the back of a chair, dropped his head, and sighed, resigned to his dilemma.

"Hell, I don't need to be doin' any real business tonight. If you need somethin' for yourself tonight, well, that's one thing, but the rest can wait till tomorrow." RayRay sat down in his old, stained, threadbare, but comfortable red velveteen La-Z-Boy recliner. He fiddled with the tricky side footrest lever, cursed it, and finally it released, and he fell back a little too quickly. He threw his feet up on the rest, picked up a short leftover joint out of an ashtray, and fired it up. He leaned forward and offered it up to Bo Jr.

Bo Jr. knew this process was like smoking a peace pipe with an Indian chief, having chai with the Turks, or schnapps with a Scandinavian. If you don't do it, you will not establish the trust to accomplish any real or important business. Bo Jr. took the joint, drew in deep, and held.

He looked for a clean place to sit, a place the dogs had not been using for chewing or naps. Before the suit Bo Jr. would have just flopped down anywhere, but he viewed himself as more sophisticated now. Finally giving in to the environment, he sat on the couch across from RayRay. All the furniture was equally worn, stained, and covered with dog hair.

RayRay did not exhibit the same obvious suspicion of Bo Jr. as his dogs had shown. Although he too had detected a slightly different scent, he was not in a rush to assess the change. Good dealers sometimes sampled their own products, but they rarely conducted business while under the influence. Those who did didn't last long.

RayRay had been in the business for a long time. He was ignorant of more esoteric and sophisticated concepts of high finance and international trade, but he knew this business. Bo Jr. coughed out the smoke as he felt the buzz start to numb his head. After a couple more tokes, he was smiling. Tomorrow would be soon enough, whether Tony liked it or not.

Chapter 30

Guido slid into the plush leather seat of his Crown Vic and drove two blocks to a parking lot across the street from the Frisky Rabbit. The time had come to identify the ignorant punk who didn't understand the turf laws of the drug business. Tonight, Guido was just here to observe, not to react. The price for the transgression would be paid later.

As soon as Guido stepped through the front door of the Frisky Rabbit, he felt out of place, like a New York Italian in a Boston Irish pub. He drew a glance or two. The place had no foyer for casual entry, no wall to be a flower on; you were front and center for scrutiny by all those in the bar who had staked this turf as their own.

Nightlife predators hovered around the front door, hungry for any fresh meat that might enter their domain. Guido saw an open stool at the end of the bar and headed directly for it. He had planned to order a beer and settle in a dark corner. Being the focus of attention was not recon. He sat down.

Booney stepped over, smiled, and asked the newcomer, "What will ya have?"

"A beer."

"Sir, I gotta warn you, these seats are reserved for a couple of ladies who should be here in fifteen minutes or so, but feel free to enjoy until then." Booney's years of running the bar made him a fairly good judge of human nature, including assessment of the size and power of potential bad human nature. Normally he would tell young tourists to find another place to sit, but he was more polite to this man.

Guido looked up with a mocking smile and a good-natured response. "So what, they got their names on these seats, do they?"

"As a matter of fact, they do. They've been coming here for years, they're our longtime friends, and we like to take care of those dear to us, as you can surely understand. They're like...ah...family." Booney smiled.

Guido got up and looked at the seat to validate Booney's claim. He read "Evelyn" on his seat and "Edna" on the seat next to him, both written crudely on the black paint of the stool with thick, yellow, sparkle ink. A half smile emerged as he thought to himself, Evelyn and Edna, eh. Evelyn said they came here most evenings.

"No shit." He chuckled. "They do have their names on these chairs."

"Yeah...it's a long story, happened a couple of years back after a minor misunderstanding during a discussion much like the one we're having. Thought we would just solve the problem and scribe their names on the chairs. We would appreciate your cooperation. First beer's on the house. Enjoy."

Guido could only smile. "OK, thanks, pal."

With a beer in hand, he got up to cruise the bar and check out the action in the back rooms. He was not surprised. At the foosball table, a magneto of intense competition charged the atmosphere. In another room with pool tables, quarters were lined up on the rails, each coin reserving a young challenger's future chance to play the table winner. Guido looked around. There were some real players here. He could sense the hustlers prowling. Someone sank the eight ball after a three-ball run, faked surprise—what luck—and five twenties were passed from the loser's hand with a glare.

These hustlers were kids by appearance, but they had a world of pool-shark experience under their belt. When the bets were placed, this aura of youthful innocence dissolved any pretense of suspicion by their prey.

Bells rang in pinball machines, and reward points were chalked up on a glowing red digital display. Darts were flying, the music was deafening. This place rocked. Guido had noticed the squishy feeling under his shoes as he walked on the beer-soaked lime-green and yellow shag carpet. No cost had been spared on the ambiance, he thought sarcastically to himself.

As he scanned the rear of the bar, he noticed a line of flirtatious young girls working the room while waiting to get in the small restroom with a single toilet. Young men circled the area, darting in and out, hunting like a school of hungry sharks. The prey seemed ready and willing, flaunting their edible delicacies.

The men's room door stayed open, with a stream of uninhibited young males recycling their draft beer into the toilet and the wall urinal; later in the evening, the sink would become fair play for those with a more desperate need for relief.

What a crazy fuckin' joint, Guido thought. He moved his attention to the walls that were adorned with six-foot-high paintings of rabbits performing a variety of soft-porn sex acts, as if this place needed any more suggestive tactics to stoke the sexually charged atmosphere. This place was a testosterone-pressurized, college-age, pickup party joint, and it seemed fun.

Smoke filled the top half of the room with a cloudy haze that would spread ceiling to floor before the night was over. Secondhand smoke was not a concern to this young crowd, although it filled their lungs and permeated every pore of their bodies. At this age they knew they were invincible.

Guido saw a lot of uninhibited behavior, but he saw no one who matched the profile of the flamboyant dealer he sought. He decided to just wait and observe awhile longer. He moved back into the main bar as Evelyn and Edna walked through the front door. Guido stopped in the shadows of the darkened poolroom to watch the girls. He wanted to observe them in their own comfort zone.

They laughed and joked while the bartenders smiled and welcomed them. A beer for each was placed on the bar at their seats before they sat down. Guido watched Evelyn light up a Marlboro Light, take a deep draw, and exhale upward through the side of her mouth with practiced perfection. She crossed her knees, held the cigarette out to the side of her leg, sampled the beer, and leaned over to talk with Edna.

He watched as they laughed, talked, and high-fived the bartender. The girls were temporarily distracted as they checked the rear ends of a couple of young guys leaning over the bar. Edna gave Evelyn a satisfied nod of approval and then immediately went back to their animated discussion. They were in their happy place, on their turf, enjoying life.

Guido did not really want to disturb their happy-hour high, but thought, what the hell. He had promised to drop by, and he was in the mood for Evelyn's engaging humor. He stepped out of the shadows and eased over behind Evelyn, unnoticed. He leaned close to the back of her head and said, "Mind if I buy you a beer, darlin'?"

Evelyn knew his voice. She didn't turn around immediately, but took a moment to compose herself, giving Edna a look of openmouthed surprise. She turned and casually replied in her best Mae West accent, "Well, sailor, why don't you pull up a chair and sit awhile." She finished the taunting invitation with a suggestive smile and a wink.

"Guido! How are you, sweetie? I'm so glad to see you finally made it to our secret little getaway bar." She didn't want to appear too aggressive, so she gave him a barroom-party friend hug and cheek touch. "Meet my best friend, Edna. Edna, this is Guido. You remember I mentioned him coming by the Krispy Kreme occasionally to keep me company."

Edna looked at Evelyn with a "get real" glare and sarcastically said, "Yea, I vaguely remember you mentioning him, just every day for the last month or so. Hi, Guido, it's a pleasure to meet you finally. I feel like I already know you."

"Oh stop it." Evelyn blushed and gave Edna a friendly shove. "I swear you exaggerate, girl."

Booney could not help but notice Evelyn acting like a teenager. He had not seen that type of behavior from either of these two in quite some time, except when Edna was in the bar with McKenzie last week. He thought about how these women had grown older but still showed that "starry-eyed young girl" response to love.

The party turned more festive for Guido. He forgot the reconnaissance mission and joined the exchange of jokes and humorous dialogue Edna and Evelyn had going. All three were really unwinding, each having had a stressful day in their own way, in their own place.

"It's been a crazy day. Two elderly gentlemen from the retirement home hijacked a van, went on a joyride, and just vanished. I've been looking for them all afternoon." Guido sighed and shook his head.

"Oh no!" said Evelyn. "Who? Eddie and Vera will go nuts when they hear. They love those people."

"Yeah, they go to the retirement home all the time," Edna chimed in. "They take them to bingo at the Blue House."

"Vera's mother lived there for years." Edna and Evelyn traded lines.

Guido listened as if he knew nothing of the bingo scam at the Blue House. He knew of Eddie and Vera. He knew them as caring supporters of the elderly, but he had never had a reason to connect them with Evelyn.

"You know, I've seen Vera and her husband before on Sunday at bingo," Guido admitted. "Heard people in the crowd mention their names."

Guido was learning a whole new side of Evelyn in an environment away from her identity as a Krispy Kreme waitress. Tonight he was seeing more of the young Evelyn, more of the Evelyn that must have existed when she first came to the beach. He liked this Evelyn.

"That's so sweet of you to look for them," Evelyn said. "But why you? Do you know them?"

"Some friends of mine know the family. They asked me to help. So I did. No biggie."

They returned to their more lighthearted discussion. Evelyn told a joke about three old men at a lunch counter. Guido was caught up in the conversation and laughter when the front door exploded open, and three loud, stoned men stepped in, scanning the room like vandalistic crows at a picnic.

"I want a fuckin' beer!" shouted the guy in front. He was wearing thick, black-rimmed glasses complemented by a bowl-cut mop of hair hanging over his eyes.

"Me too," each of his two wingmen simultaneously declared to anyone who might be listening.

Guido leaned over close to Evelyn and said, "This reminds me of an old western movie: Prospector strikes it rich, makes a grand saloon entrance, gets drunk, gets obnoxious, and gets shot."

"It's a good thing no weapons are allowed in here, or that guy would have been blown away long ago." Evelyn looked briefly and turned back to her beer.

The three loudmouths stepped up and leaned over the bar, waiting for their beers. Vernon turned around to face the room, threw both elbows behind him, and slouched, resting his back on the bar. He was scanning the crowd for young female prey, assessing the potential of the night. He took an exaggerated toke on his Marlboro and blew the smoke high to the ceiling.

"Vernon, here's your damn beer, you fart head," Harley shouted. "Let's play some foosball." The three marauders migrated to the foosball room with a cloud of commotion and noise in their wake. They were like a desert dust devil with no direction or purpose, just kicking up sand.

Guido's recon radar perked up. He had his man. All the descriptions fit. Now he just needed some time to watch and learn. If this was his competition, this situation was now even more depressing. He knew that the life and reputation of a warrior could be measured by the quality of the enemies he had defeated. Bringing down this competitor would surely subtract from his average score of more noble victories.

The night played on, and it was nearing closing time as Vernon and his wild tribe moved toward the door to leave. A few more loyal worshipers of this summer's self-proclaimed drug czar had joined his boisterous gang. He was basking in his royal status among these drunken vassals, but was oblivious to the limits of his kingdom. For him this place was the whole world, as he could comprehend little beyond this limited realm. Ignorance equaled bliss for Vernon.

Guido was having fun and didn't want to appear too conspicuous in his pursuit of this band of underworld wannabes. The trespassers were either too stupid, too naïve, or both to understand the dangerous ground on which they strutted with the arrogance of peacocks.

A few nonobvious moments later, Guido said, "Ladies, I must go. Tomorrow I'll be up early to search for Frank and Marvin and then back to the restaurant tomorrow evening. This has been fun. We should do it again."

"Oh, we hope they show up soon," Evelyn responded and touched Guido's hand.

"You let us know if we can help," Edna chimed in and patted his shoulder.

Evelyn was a bit dismayed. She had thought this might be the night. This might be her first time with a man since she could remember...but he had to go. He had always been such a gentleman to her; maybe this was his way of proceeding at a proper gentleman's pace. Most guys she met in the bar tried to get in her pants at the first possible moment, but Guido was different.

"We'll walk you to your car," Evelyn said. "We need to go as well. This place is about to close."

"You two go ahead. I'll finish my beer, be along in a minute," said Edna. She knew the romantic value of this moment, and knew they didn't need a third wheel around.

Guido opened the car door for Evelyn and then walked to the driver's side. He settled in, looked at Evelyn as he cranked the engine, and then drove his Crown Vic the seventy-five yards from the parking lot to her apartment. He cut the ignition.

"Listen, gorgeous, I really hated to break up the party, but I'll need to be on my toes tomorrow if those two don't show tonight. The pressure from their family will really be intense."

"Their family? You said you know their family. They seem to be really different. Are they related?"

"Well, sorta. I guess you could say so. But no matter. I would rather talk about you and me right now. I'd like to get to know you better. Believe it or not, I'm looking for something serious, a relationship, and I'm thinking about you and that relationship."

Evelyn was bursting with joy, but held her breath while he spoke.

"How about you? Are you interested in a try with a guy like me?"

"A try? Sure, a try would be good. What's a try?"

"Why don't we talk about it on our next date? I really must go, love."

As Evelyn began to hyperventilate, Guido got out, walked around the car, and opened her door. Evelyn gathered herself and stepped out, her eyes gazing up the full length of his imposing body, all the way up to his eyes. She stood. He was only inches away, not moving back to allow space for her to shy away from the moment.

Guido was in a hurry, and Evelyn was not going to wait any longer for him to make a move. She looked up, and they immediately kissed, but Guido pulled away too soon and said, "Darlin', as good as that was, I really must go. I hope we can do this again soon. I always keep my promise."

"Really, I hope so. And I appreciate that in a man." Evelyn thought she might be babbling and released her double-arm grip around his waist. She walked sideways to the base of the stairs leading to her apartment, never taking her eyes off him. She turned and scampered up the steps.

Guido waved good-bye, climbed into his Crown Vic, put it in reverse, and started to back the car out along the darkened driveway. He had his windows rolled up and a Frank Sinatra classic playing at a high volume on his stereo system. His luxurious vehicle was a comfortable ride. It moved smoothly down rough roads, brought on significant power with only a small bit of pressure from the driver's foot, and filtered the irritating noises of the outside world when he desired the solitude. Like Guido himself, it was smooth, powerful, and quiet.

He didn't hear the horn honking and the yelling. He didn't see the brown van speeding in its getaway from the front of the Frisky Rabbit, but Evelyn did.

She stood on her apartment steps stunned, knowing, hoping Guido would see them coming and stop. She watched, frozen in time, helpless to avert the inevitable, as he backed out of the driveway fast.

Vernon smashed his heavy van into the driver's side door of Guido's Crown Victoria. He hit it hard enough to propel the large sedan sideways and send it rolling over and over. The van careened to one side and rolled over twice, finally skidding across the rough asphalt road to a stop on its roof. Bare asses were hanging out, wedged in the broken side windows. Although trapped and momentarily stunned in the mangled metal, no one was seriously injured in the van. The Crown Victoria was another story.

One week earlier Vernon had gathered four of his dealers and two new recruits. He was fueled by an intense desire to create himself as a local beach legend and was driven by a need to solidify his place as the coolest dude on the Grand Strand. He had planned for a surprise moon-attack as the Frisky Rabbit closed on Saturday evening. Vernon had parked his van down the block in the dark end of a vacant parking lot.

His van was not a sexy, custom-painted love machine. He had purchased this two-tone brown vehicle from a church in North Carolina. The van had been used to shuttle God-fearing members of the Hendersonville Third Baptist Holy Revival Church until it had chalked up over 180,000 miles and began to burn excessive amounts of oil.

The van was an extended version with uncomfortable bench-seating accommodations for twelve. The vehicle had panoramic viewing windows that wrapped around both sides and the rear doors. Vernon had used a third tone of brown to paint over the church's name, but the letters could still be seen upon close inspection.

He had considered removing his hasty paint to further camouflage his illegal activities under the guise of a church van, but he didn't. As usual, this little plan was just something Vernon thought about one night in a smoky haze, but only for a moment. The thought was forgotten as quickly as it was proclaimed.

The stage was set on this night. Vernon was aware of the prime time to perform his stunt. On Saturday night state law required bars to close at midnight. At this hour the rowdy crowd had been required to exit the Frisky Rabbit, but typically people hung around outside in loud, drunken groups all looking for a chance to score in some measure. The crowd had formed in front of the bar, working on what private party place to hit next.

Vernon had gathered his gang in the van and had given careful instructions for the execution of their stunt. With Elton John blaring from his amplified head-banger stereo, he had jammed the accelerator to the floor, and the van sputtered and swerved wildly toward the front of the Frisky Rabbit. Throwing caution and a cloud of blue smoke to the wind, Vernon had raced past the edge of the crowd, honking his horn, with six bare asses pressed against the van's viewing windows to the port side. All outside the Frisky Rabbit had been stunned, shocked, or delighted by this awkward display of stupid young manhood. It was not a pretty sight.

After the moon-attack, Vernon had parked the van and returned with his gang to the scene of his crime. Vernon had assumed he would become "the man," but even though the drunks were still laughing and talking about those assholes in the loud van, most did not realize it was Vernon. The obnoxious act had been so quick and surprising that most people focused on the bare asses and the blaring, kick-ass cut from Elton John's live, early release of "Rocket Man." Vernon and his van had moved by in a haze, a frame out of focus to the crowd.

But people talked about how great that prank was—"only at the beach," they said. Vernon would need to fix this lack of recognition and appreciation for his artistry. He had an idea, but it would have to wait until this same time next week, when the crowd was gathered once again at midnight outside the Frisky Rabbit.

———

At eleven forty-five Saturday night, Vernon readied his crew for a second, more visible run. He had added two additional bare-ass followers to his crew. The plan required this additional duo to stick their asses against the two rear windows as a parting view. He had hand painted the van on one side and added another one hundred watts and two speakers to his stereo. He had rolled down the driver's side window so he could wave to the crowd as he passed.

Earlier he and his crew had mingled with the crowd inside the Frisky Rabbit to raise awareness of the potential for another multiple full-moon night.

"Hey, did you see those wild and crazy dudes last week, shooting a moon to the crowd?" Vernon's dealers asked over and over. Vernon had given detailed instructions on how to build the expectations and "create buzz."

With a belch, one bar patron said, "Yeah, I saw those stupid assholes."

Vernon quickly had one of his guys challenge the antagonist. "They weren't assholes. Those guys are cool."

The patron would not be swayed in the recollection of what he had seen, even in his drunken state. "No, man, I mean...I actually saw their assholes. They shouldn't lean over so far when they shoot a moon. If I see them again, I'm going to stick this pool cue right up one, teach them a little lesson."

This patron was a muscular six foot four and seemed to mean what he said. Some on Vernon's crew who heard the discussion began to rethink their upcoming prank, but they knew Vernon was counting on them and would demand their participation. There was no backing out now. They would just be more careful of their level of exposure.

At 12:05 a.m. Sunday morning, with the doors to the Frisky Rabbit recently closed and the maximum crowd gathered out front, Vernon once again threw caution to the wind. For a moment his van roughly idled in a cloud of blue smoke, as he prepared to make a run for glory.

Vernon cranked up Elton John, and "Take me to Your Pilot" filled the air. He rolled his window down and jammed the accelerator; his brown machine swerved, spitting street pebbles and squealing its tires, as he rolled past the Frisky Rabbit.

Vernon had one hand on the horn, his head and shoulders fully out of the window, and waving one hand. The crowd saw a line of asses passing, starting with Vernon's smiling face and then six bare ones pressed against the side windows. Only this time the asses were not poised so high, presenting a more modest exposure, with just cracks visible in the windows. Why ask for trouble?

The visual atrocity finished with two asses pressed against the rear-door window. Vernon moved his upper torso back into the van just in time to see the wide eyes of the driver in the Crown Vic.

Chapter 31

Frankie, a lifeguard monkey during the day, had just finished his night job involving the mind-numbing, cyclic routine of winning a big stuffed bear at the penny-toss booth and walking around with it on his shoulders before returning the bear to the booth and later winning it all over again.

After work, as the park was going to sleep, he lingered with the two stray young girls who had idolized him all night. They were happy to just follow him mindlessly, amazed at how cool he was. They shared a joint, and each girl took a chance to make out with him behind the Tilt-a-Whirl. The grinding orthodontic braces sliced his lips and made the experience less enjoyable than his jealous friends assumed it was.

None of the three really had the experience to get into too much trouble. But one day soon, a careless fling would put them in the same difficult situation where their older cousins and friends had unwittingly wandered.

For now Frankie just kissed the girls and felt each one's shirt for a while, but he discovered nothing definitive. He grew bored and decided to walk home. He was required to be on the beach at seven thirty to help his lifeguard set up the umbrella rental stand. A good monkey was always at the guard's stand before the guard arrived. The boy needed some sleep. His meeting with the big New York Yankees fan had been intense, stressful, and tiring.

Frankie walked out of the side entrance of the amusement park and across the yard in front of the lifeguard bunkhouse. He was walking in the middle of the yard when he heard the shouting, the horn honking, and then the crash. He ran in the direction of the wreck and was standing next to the Crown Victoria as it came to a rest. He looked in, and even though the man looked horrible or maybe dead, he recognized him from earlier—the Yankees fan who was looking for drug dealers.

A small satchel lay at his feet next to the overturned car. It was open and contained four plastic bags fat with pot. He had seen the dealers with these large bags before. The kid knew where this stuff had come from that night. He picked up the bag, quickly looked around, and saw two women running his way. Now others were running from the bar to the wreck. They were yelling, but not at him.

He moved toward the van and away from the rapidly approaching crowd. As he passed the wreck, he saw another, larger duffel bag. On a hunch he grabbed it, raced behind the guardhouse, and hid between the concrete building and a chain link fence, eight-foot high, and densely covered with honeysuckle vines. He looked into the duffel bag and saw it was filled with bags of pot.

He pondered the situation for a moment. Drug dealers would hurt you over the theft of a couple joints. They would kill your mother and rip your eyes out for stealing this much pot. But he really wasn't stealing it. He was holding it. He was doing these guys a big favor. If he left the pot, the cops would get it when they came to the wreck, and then these poor bastards would have more to worry about than their injured bodies and wrecked cars. He was a minor, no big risk. There was money in this deal, no matter how he played it.

The kid thought more about where to put the stash. His lifeguard's stand was nearby in front of the Lemon Tree Inn, only one block to the darkness of the beach and two blocks south. He had a key to open the umbrella box, and he would be back in the morning before his guard arrived.

He was the one who normally removed all the umbrellas and humped the heavy canvas through the sand to their assigned places in a long straight line. He would also have all the floats stacked for rent in the rack behind the guard stand before his guard ever came dragging out on the beach, ruffled and hung over, fighting the effects of booze and a party the night before. The guard always had a night before.

Frankie was a loyal monkey who knew the morning drill. As an unselfish apprentice, he had saved the guard from being fired at least three times this summer. Each morning precisely at eight, the managing guard drove to the beach to inspect the stands. And each morning Frankie's guard sweated through the nausea of his hangover and waved, faked a big smile, and plugged "chutes" in the sand. Each time the manager had waved and shouted, "Let's get an earlier start tomorrow," and then he was gone.

The monkey followed the chain link fence back toward the side entrance of the amusement park. He knew this place like the back of his hand, all the secret paths and hidden trails. He raced through the shadows of the park and followed the swash channel to the beach. It was low tide, and he was able to run under the four-lane street bridge of Ocean Boulevard, through the swash drain and onto the beach. A short run south, and the bags were locked away in the umbrella box. Tomorrow night he would dig a hole and bury the bags under the box for safekeeping.

The monkey left and headed home, skirting around the wreck investigation with all the flashing lights and sirens. Tomorrow would be another day on the beach, and everyday on the beach in the summer was an adventure.

Chapter 32

On their way back to the station from the Blue House, Chief Detective Driggers and some of his boys decided to stop by the Krispy Kreme for a hot doughnut celebration, their wallets a bit thicker due to tonight's unexpected bonus from Tony.

The celebrating police team had just stepped out of their cars when they heard the squealing rear tires of the van speeding out of the parking lot and racing in front of the Frisky Rabbit, horns blaring. The noise momentarily caught their attention, and they all looked straight up First Avenue North as the van accelerated. They heard and saw the crash. The celebration was forgotten as they hopped back in their cars and called for an ambulance. The police cars fishtailed across Kings Highway, racing to the scene, sirens blaring.

Edna had just walked out of the Frisky Rabbit to see the bare-bottomed full-moon shots of Vernon's crew as the van raced past. She and the other Frisky Rabbit patrons who had lingered in the front lot had all chuckled, thinking, "What a bunch of losers." But what the hell, it was all summer fun. Tonight's fun quickly turned tragic.

Edna couldn't see the crash as her sight was blocked by a row of trees and shrubs, but she could hear it. No screeching brakes, just a solid metal-crushing impact, metal scraping on the asphalt as cars rolled away from the collision. She ran to the accident as flashing lights accompanied the urgent wails of sirens racing up the street.

Evelyn sensed the event. For some reason, as she watched Guido back out of the drive, she shivered with a premonition of danger and had walked back down the steps from her apartment. She saw and heard the approaching vehicle but was paralyzed by the anxiety of the moment, unable to yell a warning. Her mind was processing the action, anticipating the inevitable collision, but her brain could not transmit a signal to her vocal cords. As the cars crashed, her brain released the vocal lock, and a scream erupted. She ran down the steps, scared of what she would find.

———————

Before the wreck Eddie had not been sleeping well and had heard the Crown Victoria pull into the driveway. The car in his driveway was just one more invasion of his space. Driven by a compulsive anxiety, he rolled out of bed quietly, not disturbing Vera, and peered through the shades.

His frustration quickly subsided into curiosity as he saw Evelyn with a man. Normally Eddie would have been pleased, but one of those "fatherly protection urges" compelled him to monitor the situation. Evelyn's visitors were typically beach boys, an older lifeguard, or the occasional mature tourist, but none had ever exhibited signs of success or radiated a presence like this one. Something about this guy was different.

He was up and fully awake now. The surrounding sounds of the summer celebration were more vivid and thus more irritating to Eddie. He wanted to make sure Evelyn was OK. He was still watching through the tilted window blinds as the Crown Victoria backed out of the drive and into the street.

Eddie never backed into the street. Long ago he had learned it was impossible to see cars coming as they gunned their engines and raced up this side street at twice the legal limit. The treeline and hedges that he had let grow around his yard to block the intrusion of noise and neon light also blocked the view of traffic. He felt the inconvenience a fair trade.

The Crown backed out blindly. Bending metal, dust, sparks, and rolling vehicles filled the street. Eddie dialed 911, woke Vera, and ran out of the house.

All responding parties were equally anxious and horrified at what they had just witnessed. Few saw the young boy running to the scene and escaping into the night. If they had, it would be a confusing and seemingly unrelated detail they might recall later as odd, but his presence would not register as relevant to the situation. The focus for the moment was directed to the occupants of the vehicles, especially the badly damaged Crown Victoria.

The driver's side of the black limo was crushed inward with such force that the body was now more in a U-shape. The car had also rolled over as a result of the blindsiding force, knocking out windows, crushing the roof, and knocking out lights. The engine was running but smoking as leaking fluids evaporated off the hot metal. The car was upside down with the tires slowly spinning a warped path, emitting a monotonous, repetitive, clinking sound with each full rotation.

Chief Detective Diggers, Edna, and Evelyn all reached the scene at approximately the same time, with Eddie only a few steps behind. Evelyn was attempting to crawl in the driver's window, reaching for Guido when the cops emerged from their car. The police officers recognized the need to isolate civilians from the scene and quickly pulled her from the wreck, but not before Evelyn saw Guido's broken, bleeding, unconscious body.

"Lady, lady, please come over here and settle down. We'll take it from here," said one of the officers.

"Help him! Help him! Please, help him!" Evelyn cried and pleaded, distraught and helpless in her struggle to return to Guido. Eddie grabbed Evelyn.

One of the officers crawled halfway in through a broken window. He checked for breathing and a pulse and crawled out backward. Pushing aside the entirety of his sensitivity training, the officer shouted, "We got a live one." The approaching ambulance siren blared over his second honest but insensitive comment, "But maybe not for long."

Edna relieved Eddie and held Evelyn off to the side as the fire department and the Grand Strand Rescue Squad utilized their new Jaws of Life tool to carefully extract Guido from the car. The removal of his massive body was difficult and time-consuming.

While the emergency crew worked to stabilize and save Guido, Chief Detective Driggers moved to a much less serious, but equally repulsive, scene with Vernon and his crew upside-down, asses shining against the light of a full moon. Despite the serious nature and tragedy of the moment, Driggers could only chuckle at this scene.

Eddie was pissed but could do little at the moment. He could only watch as the rescue workers took care of their business and the police kept the curious crowd in check. Eddie took note of the young men as they were extracted from the van with their pants still around their ankles. Some were so stoned on weed, they just laid down on the gurney and laughed as they were loaded into the ambulances for a trip to the hospital. The frozen smiles on each face scraped a raw nerve, but Eddie held his rage one more time.

A somber, hushed mood merged through the crowd of firemen, police, and other rescue workers. Some had known Eddie all their lives, and others were the children of his friends. He was like family to most and was allowed to freely wander around the accident scene. The image of this misguided group under the full moon was the perfect example of the never-ending series of mindless events fueling Eddie's festering anger.

Concrete and hotels had replaced sand dunes and natural protective shrubs. Car horns, loud bands, tires, yelling, and amusement-park noise had replaced the calming music of the ocean. When would this annihilation of nature stop? Only when people like these kids, with their own selfish "live for today" attitudes could be eliminated. For now he would keep these thoughts to himself.

Eddie went back to Edna, Evelyn, and Vera, who were all watching as Guido was carefully loaded into an ambulance. Eddie became more steadfast in his resolve to respond. He felt these punks would never be aware of the emotional pain they inflicted on others, nor would they care. Eddie's mind was digging deeper into his disgust and hatred for the morass that had taken over his paradise. He needed to refocus on caring for his girls. He had the mental strength to do so, to filter his hate and frustration and return to the needs of his distraught family.

Chapter 33

Eddie and his family got into his square-bodied, white Chrysler sedan and exited the rear of the property onto the next avenue north of the accident. Eddie and Vera owned three acres stretching a block north from First Avenue, allowing them access to the less-crowded Second Avenue.

This land was not only an escape route, but also served as their buffer zone to the encroachment of tourism, an unrelenting force that grew around them like centipede grass on steroids. Three acres were not nearly enough. Tonight this driveway allowed them to avoid all the emergency crew trucks and to more rapidly reach the hospital to be with Guido.

Eddie pulled in behind the ambulance as it raced north on Kings Highway, maneuvering through a maze of late-night cruising tourists, making its way to the Grand Strand Memorial Hospital. By the time Eddie parked and they made their way through the crowded emergency-room parking lot, Guido had already been wheeled back to a treatment room for immediate care.

The nurse at the counter, accustomed to the arrival of frantic friends and relatives, directed Eddie, Vera, Edna, and Evelyn to the admitting receptionist to handle the paperwork for Guido. The receptionist looked up briefly over her bifocals as she pushed the clipboard with multiple forms through a small passage, under the bulletproof glass and onto the counter.

The receptionist's job description did not require her to show compassion for the family members of the patient. However, it did require her to identify a responsible adult with insurance or cash and to complete administrative forms. She seldom strayed from the basic requirements. Her monotonic speech provided instructions to the frantic group, ending with a sigh of disgust to express her disdain of their presence, which just meant more work for her.

In Evelyn's anguish she could not comprehend the instructions, but the woman dutifully recited the details and repeated the instructions in the same flat tone each time Evelyn did not respond or meekly uttered, "What?"

"Are you related or responsible for the patient?"

"No, I'm not related, but he's my friend, and we just want to know how he's doing. Is he OK? Will he be all right?"

"We can only provide that information to family members who have been approved by the patient for distribution of the patient's medical status."

"But how can the patient who is unconscious and maybe dying approve something like that? We just want to know if he will be OK!" Evelyn was growing more frantic by the minute.

"I'm sorry, ma'am. We are not allowed to give out medical information or status to anyone without the patient's approval, especially to nonfamily members. You shouldn't be filling out the forms I just gave you, unless, of course, you have his insurance information." The receptionist knew her assigned priorities.

Eddie and Vera stepped up behind Evelyn to help. The receptionist recognized Eddie and nodded, but when she saw Vera, a smile cracked her indifferent face. Vera often helped the folks from the retirement home when they made visits to the hospital. In the past Vera had volunteered one day a week at the hospital, helping visitors find the rooms of their loved ones or to just hold hands and pray. The receptionist knew how kind Vera had been toward frantic family members. Vera had diverted a lot of hassle that the receptionist would have otherwise endured. Her demeanor softened.

"Oh hi, Vera. Are you here to volunteer tonight, or are you with this lady?"

"Not volunteering tonight, Stella. We came with Evelyn. This young lady rents our garage apartment. She is like a daughter to me. Her boyfriend was just in a bad accident. We saw it happen. We just need to know how he's doing," Vera explained in her compassionate, motherly way.

"OK, Vera, I'll see what I can find out."

Detective Driggers walked through the sliding-glass emergency-room doors, followed by seven rolling ambulance cots loaded with seven stoned, slightly injured victims. Eddie turned and went straight to Driggers.

"Detective, could you help find out about the fellow they hit? We can't seem to get approved for release of medical status or some such crap. The girls here are about to go crazy."

"Sure, Eddie, what's his name?"

"I think Evelyn said Guido."

"Guido? The Guido who works for Tony down at the Blue House?" Driggers leaned in close and half-whispered the question to Eddie. Driggers was interested in knowing how well these folks knew Guido and why. He was at the accident; he knew full well who Guido was, but he had a part to play.

"I don't know," Eddie responded. "Now that you mention it, I think I've seen him a couple times at the Blue House when we go for bingo with the folks from the retirement home. I know Tony, but don't think I've met Guido."

"What's his last name?"

"I don't know. Let me ask Evelyn." Eddie turned to Evelyn. "What's Guido's last name?"

"I...ah, well, he just goes by Guido. I never really asked. I should have asked, I just never really thought it was important, yet. Oh wait, he told me once. Let me think...he has a really long name, I mean lots of names. Oh, I can't remember them all, but I think he told me his last name was something like Capo or Capone. Maybe that's it." Evelyn's face started to scrunch up. Her eyes grew wide, and Eddie could sense an imminent outburst of tears.

Eddie couldn't believe she didn't know his name, but now was not the time to push it. He turned back to Driggers and shrugged. They both understood what they did not understand about women and let it be.

"I'll see what I can do. Got to take care of these bums first. While I'm back there, I'll find out about your friend."

"Want me to help watch these fellows for you? I'll make sure they hang around."

"No thanks, Eddie. I got officers coming in."

The EMTs were transferring Vernon and his crew to hospital beds in a waiting area offset by curtains. When the transfers were complete, the EMTs returned to their ambulances and the rest of the night. Driggers was on his cell phone calling Tony while he walked into the patient care area.

As the standard emergency-room confusion continued, Eddie eased over to the holding area and snagged the charts with identification from the beds of Vernon's crew just before the two officers walked through the automatic emergency-room doors looking for their detained patients. Driggers eventually emerged from the treatment area, spoke to the reception nurse, checked with the officers, and then came over to Eddie and the ladies.

"Well, I've spoken briefly to one of the doctors who stabilized Guido. They have him in surgery, say he's pretty banged up, but appears like he'll survive. No guarantees. For now his whole left side is broken—arm, leg, pelvis fractured, cheekbone, shoulder, one collapsed lung, and two broken ribs. His foot is going to need some work. I think those were the major issues. Of course he's unconscious, and they're not sure of any brain trauma, could be a concussion, but from preliminary tests and X-rays, he seems stable. He's going to be in the hospital for quite a while and then therapy. Guido's going to need some tender loving care."

"Thanks, Driggers, appreciate the update. Do you think we should wait or come back later?"

"It's late, Eddie. What is it, two a.m. already? He'll be in surgery and recovery another couple hours, they said. Why don't you come back tomorrow morning if you want? We'll have someone aware of what's going on here, and we'll call if anything changes tonight. Go get some sleep. He's in good hands."

"Yeah, OK, thanks, maybe we'll see you tomorrow," Eddie said quietly as he walked back to his girls. He shared the news that they were breathlessly waiting to hear.

"I'm not leaving. I'm staying right here! I mean, he's stable, right? What does that mean? They didn't say he's OK, or nothing to worry about. They said stable. That's not encouraging; anything could happen. I'm staying," Evelyn announced as if she were a stubborn six-year-old.

"But, honey, you can't do anything but sit in this room and wait. You need your rest so you can help him later when he's finished with surgery. That's when he'll need you." Vera's voice was compassionate and empathetic. Her wisdom on this matter was hard to argue, but emotions are rarely ruled by logic, and Evelyn declined to leave. She wrapped her arms around herself and stared aimlessly at the floor.

"Honey, come on, we'll have you back here as soon as he is allowed visitors. When we get home, I'll make you some nice tea, and we can talk. Why, I hardly know anything about Guido. You've been keeping him a secret." Vera was the best mother any renter could have.

"Thanks, Vera, but I can't leave. Y'all go home and rest. I just have to be here when he gets out of surgery. I don't mind. I couldn't sleep anyway."

"Well, hon, if you're staying, then I'm staying. Can't leave you here alone."

"Me too. I'm staying too," Edna chimed in.

Eddie was outnumbered. "OK, girls. I'll leave the car and catch a ride with Driggers." Eddie left as the sky opened up with a hard late-night thundershower.

The night had started with so much promise. The sky had been clear, providing a perfect stage for the brilliant full moon to shine in all its glory. Hopefully tomorrow's sea breeze would blow away the dark clouds, and the sun would shine on a new beach-perfect day.

Chapter 34

The Myrtle Beach Memorial Hospital was full. As the night went on, patients continued to arrive seeking medical attention due to traffic accidents, bar fights, drug and alcohol overdoses, night-surfing accidents, babies being born, emergency appendix removal, sunstroke, a head injury caused by a horrible golf shot at the "Hit till Midnight" driving range, and a young couple who had been scraped and cut by barnacles and nearly drowned while skinny-dipping under a pier.

Sometimes the intensity of activities at a beach resort such as Myrtle Beach could overwhelm its public infrastructure. People tended to live on the edge when they came for their one week a year at the beach: too much sun, too much alcohol, too much testosterone, too much of an opportunity to do things no one from back home would likely ever know about. And often someone got hurt.

This high-intensity resort environment now gave Guido a less-than-ideal-care scenario. After two hours of surgery and another hour in the recovery room, Guido was moved, not to the intensive care unit, but to the only bed left in the hospital, in the One-Eyed Flounder Memorial Wing—the same room as McKenzie.

The room was dark and quiet. McKenzie's bed had the privacy curtain drawn, with only a low-voltage night-light on the wall and the red-and-green diode lights of medical monitoring equipment to provide soft shades of illumination.

Overhead florescent lights in the hallway lit the entrance as the door opened and Guido was quietly wheeled in. Guido was engulfed in plaster casts and bandages. Tubes and monitor wires were plugged and patched to his chest, in his nose, and in his arms.

His nurses floated around the room, arranging Guido's bed and the necessary equipment. They connected bedside monitors and linked the vital-sign devices to the monitoring station. One more check of the IV drip and a cursory look at the patient's cast and breathing, and the nurses left the room, gliding out like the compassionate angels of the night they were.

The doctor stepped into the waiting room to provide Guido's status to those anxiously waiting. He found Evelyn and Edna sleeping uncomfortably on sofas under a TV displaying another exciting episode of paid programming.

Two scantily clad workout instructors hosting the show were verbally climaxing over the virtues of some incredible new workout equipment. What marketing study convinced manufacturers that a sufficient number of potential customers would be watching this program at four in the morning? It played to the emergency-room waiting area.

Vera sat with her eyes closed, napping in an equally uncomfortable chair, silently miserable from joint pains and the lack of a good night's sleep. She was the first to speak with the doctor, her eyes popping open, alerted by his approaching steps.

"How's he doing, Doctor?" Vera asked softly. With the doctor's first words, Evelyn and Edna both sat up and rubbed the sleep from their eyes.

"Ladies, we've been able to stabilize him. There's no internal bleeding but some broken bones. We'll know more tomorrow after more time for observation. His body received a significant amount of trauma, but he's a strong man. He's done well so far, all things considered. Are any of you related to him?"

"No, there's no family that we know of, but I'm his...well, we're all just good friends," Evelyn stammered.

"I see. Well, he will need individual care for a quick recovery, if his relatives can be found. Or perhaps one of you could help, at least initially," the doctor offered.

Vera stepped in knowing from experience that emotions like those racking Evelyn might adversely influence her most logical responses.

"Doctor, none of us is legally responsible for Guido, but we know of his employer, and we'll commit to be here for him when allowed."

"Thanks, ma'am. If you'll give the nurse here your names, we'll make sure you have family visiting privileges. Do you have any more questions for now?"

"When can we see him?" Vera remembered to ask.

"Later tomorrow morning, but only for a short visit. I guess it is tomorrow already, isn't it?"

"Thank you so much, Doctor, you've been a real help and comfort. We appreciate your time," Vera said sincerely with her soft Southern charm.

"You're welcome, ma'am." The doctor turned and left. Vera and the girls had a group hug and went to their car.

The girls were tired but awake now, so they stopped by the Krispy Kreme and picked up their usual morning treat, with a matching portion for Vera. They parked near the beach for their early-morning ritual of watching the sunrise. Conversation was in short supply this morning as all three sat, savored their coffee and doughnuts, and stared out at the profound beauty of the early-morning ocean as the first gray light ushered in the day.

The glassy waves crashed on the hard-packed sand of a cleansed beach. Yesterday's sand castles and footprints had been removed by the night's high tide, putting the beach back to its natural order. Sandpiper flocks were scampering up and down the edge of the surf, driven to move left and right by some silent, secret, sandpiper command. Pelicans glided in a perfect beak-to-wingtip flight formation, skimming over the peaks of the waves. Sea gulls squawked their familiar racket as they searched for morning breakfast scraps. Early-bird tourists, hunting shells and shark's teeth on the declining tide line, announced the beginning of another day—another day for this ever-changing paradise to endure the growing human onslaught.

"Ever notice how each morning after a high tide, the beach wipes away all reminders and scars of the day before, like no one had been here?" Vera mused while staring at the continuous roll and crash of the surf. "Like an Etch A Sketch, God just sends in a good high tide to put the beach back like he intended it to be. And if man gets too aggressive with buildings and houses, then God sends a hurricane and puts nature back where it belongs."

"I wish a high tide could wash away what happened last night," Evelyn said as a couple tears appeared on her cheek. "I really like that guy. He's the first man I've ever cared for. I mean really cared for as a person, since I can remember. I think I love him."

Evelyn let the tears flow. Vera and Edna each put an arm around her and let her release her grief, secure in the presence of her best friends. After a few minutes, Evelyn raised her head, wiped her eyes with the back of her forearm, took a bite from her Krispy Kreme, and regained her composure.

"Well, ladies, I've got to take care of some business so I can focus on taking care of Guido," Evelyn said, throwing her chin up in a sharp newfound determination. No more lying around moaning and groaning; she had things to do.

They headed back home for showers, fresh, clean clothes, and a new day. A sea breeze was blowing, cleaning the polluted air from the night's boulevard cruisers. A few dark, ominous clouds were still hanging in the sky on the horizon. The beach resort was waking to another summer day, another day full of action.

Chapter 35

McKenzie was awake by seven and ready to go, despite the generous supply of pain-killers administered the night before. During the night he awoke only briefly as a patient was brought into his semiprivate room. The nurses had been quiet, but McKenzie was on edge even in his drug-enhanced sleep. He was determined to resolve the mischief at the Blue House. He held a new suspicion for his boss and almost every other cop at the Myrtle Beach Police Department. McKenzie knew he would need to proceed with caution and a clear head. He punched the nurse's call button, but with the turmoil of a shift change, it was almost seven thirty before a nurse was available to respond.

"Whatcha need, hon?" she asked with a smile.

"I'd like to check out. I want to be released as soon as possible."

"Well, hon, we're gonna need to get the doctor to OK that. You got yourself quite a knot on the back of your head, and stitches too." She sounded like his mother. "Have you tried to walk to the bathroom yet?"

"No ma'am."

"Well, why don't we give that a try? It'll be a good first test to see how you're doing. Don't want to rush these types of injuries; they can surprise you. Here, let me help you."

McKenzie pulled the sheets back, threw both legs over the side of the bed, and tried to stand up. He felt dizzy, a bit wobbly in the legs, and immediately sat back down on the bed as the nurse grabbed his arm.

"See, hon, you need to be careful now. This time stand up slow."

McKenzie reconsidered her suggestion. He might need more time for recovery, but he wasn't happy about it. He used the toilet and made his way back to the bed and waited. An hour later the doctor completed his evaluation of McKenzie.

"Detective McKenzie, do you have anyone at home to watch over you today? Maybe your wife, a friend, or a family member could stay with you."

"No, not really. I mean there may be someone...I'm not sure." McKenzie struggled to come up with someone he could call on, at least long enough for the doctor to be convinced to release him. No one trustworthy came to mind except Edna, and he didn't feel confident making that call.

"Detective, I'm going to keep you here one more day. I also want an MRI to make sure we didn't miss anything last night in the emergency room. I'll see you tomorrow morning." The doctor marked his chart and left. McKenzie lay back in his bed and closed his eyes.

When McKenzie awoke from the morning nap, he became more aware of his roommate. From the other side of the curtain, he heard only periodic muted beeps and chirps from the array of monitoring equipment. He noticed the traffic in the hallway was gradually increasing.

Familiar voices chattered outside his room, and he smiled at the unmistakable banter of Edna and Evelyn, his new favorite duo. Both ladies were talking to the nurse as if they were one voice. One would begin to articulate a thought, and with a pause, the other would finish. Their minds were in synchronous harmony.

How did they know he was here? Had they called the station looking for him? Maybe the relationship had grown more serious than he had realized. Why would they be discussing his injury outside the room? Was this blow to the head more serious than he thought? McKenzie was confused.

Edna and Evelyn moved their conversation with the nurse into the room, but with a whispered tone. McKenzie remained in bed sitting up, smiling and waiting for the obviously worried duo to walk around the cloth curtain barrier separating him from his unknown roommate.

But they stopped on the other side of the barrier, looking at the other patient.

"Edna." McKenzie spoke in a matter-of-fact tone.

Edna turned and glanced over, suspicious of the patient who knew her name. She did a double take and turned toward McKenzie in utter surprise.

"What in the world? McKenzie, honey, what are you doing here? What happened to you? Why didn't you call me?" Edna took a breath, waiting for answers.

"I got knocked in the head over at the Blue House. Thought I'd be out of here this morning, but here I am. What are you doing here?"

"Evelyn and I came here to see Guido. He's in the next bed." She eased back the curtain for him to view. Seeing Guido's condition was worth a thousand words of description.

"Wow! What happened?" McKenzie asked as he stared at all the casts, tubes, bandages, monitors, and other medical devices that were attached to this one patient.

"He was in a car wreck last night, backing out from our house, after dropping Evelyn off," Edna whispered. "It was horrible."

"Tell me more about Guido. I didn't know Evelyn was so...I mean...I didn't know she had..."

"Yes, McKenzie, as we discussed before, this is my new boyfriend, Guido. What else do you need to know?" Evelyn looked around the curtain. The curtain was a poor conversation barrier. "Guido and I have been seeing each other, sorta secretly for months...OK, maybe for a month. I didn't let anybody know because frankly I didn't think it was anybody's business. He's been coming into the Krispy Kreme almost every afternoon. It's the only time we could get together with our schedules. His work is so demanding. I think it's important to get to know someone mentally before you get to know him otherwise, if you know what I mean. We were just getting serious, and then this..." Evelyn's red puffy eyes started to seep tears again, and Edna gave her a hug.

"Sorry, Evelyn. I'm sorry to hear that. I really am. I didn't mean to pry."

"How did you get hit in the head at the Blue House?" Edna changed the subject back to McKenzie. Edna sat on the end of McKenzie's bed.

Evelyn went back to her chair beside Guido.

"I discovered illegal gambling in one of the back rooms. Just as I tried to put the people in that room under arrest, the lights went out, and that's all I remember till I woke up on the men's room floor."

"Oh my God, that's horrible. Someone hit you?"

"Yeah. Driggers, my boss, and other police officers were there telling me everything was OK. When I got up, the gambling tables were gone. No one seemed upset about the whole deal, but Driggers got real pissy with me when I told him what I had seen. Something doesn't seem right about the whole thing, but with my head, a lot of things are mixed up right now."

"Oh my. That's terrible." Edna was concerned for numerous reasons.

"Don't tell anybody what I just told you. I want to clear up a few issues before I start sharing the details." McKenzie wished he had just said he got in a fight with a couple of drunks in the parking lot. That situation would have been more believable and easier. Edna looked at him with puzzled, nonjudgmental compassion. He sensed his story was less than convincing.

"But you just told me, McKenzie. Am I supposed to keep my lips zipped too?" Evelyn added sarcastically from behind the curtain. Edna waved her hand at Evelyn with a "forget it" smirk.

"Guido works at the Blue House," Edna told McKenzie. "But he wasn't there last night. He was with us at the Frisky Rabbit and then, of course, the accident."

"What does he do at the Blue House?" McKenzie asked.

"I don't know. Evelyn, do you know?" Edna talked to both sides of the curtain.

"No, I don't," Evelyn replied. "He doesn't talk about it, but he wears really nice clothes and tips really well. I'm sure he's like a manager or something."

"Well, I'd like to talk to your friend when he's conscious and feeling better," McKenzie said with a more serious business tone.

"OK, but that might be a few days. I'm sure he'd be happy to talk with you when he's better. You two would get along just grand, I'm sure," Edna interjected quickly before Evelyn could respond. She finished with a friendly, cordial smile and a soft, caring hand on McKenzie's leg, trying to diffuse the growing tension.

"Edna, I need to get out of here. I think I can leave first thing tomorrow morning. The doctor says all I need is someone to keep an eye on me. You could do that if, of course, that's all right with you." McKenzie paused to evaluate Edna's reaction. "But I need to get out of here and finish what I started, before all the evidence is gone," he almost pleaded. "This situation is really serious."

Edna wasn't confident of her ability to detect the subtle signs that might warn of a brain swelling, or any other medical problems, for that matter, that could develop with a patient who had received blunt head trauma. She was nervous with the thought of being responsible for oversight of any person with a prognosis that was labeled with caution. She had no medical training, but she did have tomorrow as a day off, and she didn't mind watching this man. So with conflicting thoughts, she agreed to serve as McKenzie's medical guardian.

"OK, I'll do it. If you promise you're OK."

Chapter 36

Bo Jr. was dreaming of bacon and eggs. The dream was so real, he could smell the bacon cooking, and he could hear it too, hissing and popping in the pan. The aroma was thick and inviting, but quickly gave way to a new horrible taste in his mouth. His face felt damp, and a foul, humid breath seemed to pulse on his cheek. Something was tugging on his leg. Now it was bouncing. He didn't like this dream anymore and struggled for a way out.

Bo Jr. gradually rose into a white haze somewhere between sleep and awareness. The warm, foul breath and the attack on his leg gnawed at his previous bliss. Bo Jr. rubbed his nose with the back of his hand and opened his eyes with confusion, not quite knowing where he was.

A low menacing growl inches from his nose bit into his haze, and he was awake, but didn't move. Booger threatened attack with steely eyes and a rumbling growl. Snot humped Bo Jr.'s leg. Where the hell had these dogs come from?

RayRay yelled from the kitchen, "How ya like your eggs, boy?"

Bo Jr. hesitated to answer. As he returned Booger's stare, the dog's lip curled, exposing stained, pointed teeth. RayRay stepped into the living room and started to laugh until a cough overwhelmed him. He hocked a loogie sending his morning phlegm out the front door and then returned to the scene with a smile.

"Goddamn, Bo Jr., they like you, but I believe old Booger's jealous. You better put that other leg out and give him some too."

Without moving his lips, Bo Jr. hissed, "Get these dogs off me, man!"

"What, and ruin their morning wood? Let 'em finish, they'll be your friends for life."

"Get them the fuck off me!"

"OK, OK. Booger, Snot, get over here."

The dogs just kept at it. RayRay grabbed two pieces of raw bacon and called the dogs again, this time waving the bacon over their noses to divert their attention. Booger followed the scent, but Snot stayed with it. RayRay whacked Snot in the head and grabbed his collar to pull him off Bo Jr.'s leg. He pulled and Bo Jr. kicked while Booger, with bacon grease dripping from his chops, was barking and trying to climb on the other leg. RayRay finally stopped laughing, grabbed both dogs firmly, and yanked them back together. The two dogs barked ferociously, standing on their hind legs, straining against their collars and RayRay's firm hold.

"What the hell's wrong with those crazy dogs, man? Damn," Bo Jr. griped and pushed up from the couch. He moved farther from the dogs and brushed his clothes, but it didn't help. RayRay put the dogs outside and went back to the stove, cracking and pouring five eggs into the iron skillet, greasy with the remnants of crispy, brown bacon.

"Fried or scrambled?"

"It don't matter." Bo Jr. slumped down into a kitchen chair and rubbed both eyes with the palms of his hands. He was hungry and tired, and was not happy about waking up as the victim of two vicious, horny, nondiscriminating guard dogs. Humiliation had dominated his morning.

"How 'bout some coffee? It'll perk you up."

"Sure."

RayRay placed a steaming cup of coffee under Bo Jr.'s nose; the better part of his morning dream was coming true.

"Bo Jr., those dogs keep me safe and sane. I don't worry about lying down to a good night's sleep with those two on guard. Whatever they do, they do together. If they kill a rabbit, they kill it together, and each one gets his share. If they chase off an intruder, they do it together. If they catch some bitch in heat, they each take their turn. That's why they were after you, pal, they both wanted a turn. Must be that new sweet smell you have with those expensive suits." RayRay laughed again.

"Well, if they come after me again, I may just kill both of them together. I'm pissed off right now. Killing those two may be a good way to start the day, settle my nerves a bit," Bo Jr. said in a calm but menacing tone he had learned from Tony.

"Whoa, whoa, buddy. We got to eat breakfast before we do anything, much less killing." RayRay laid down two plates, each with scrambled eggs, bacon, hot biscuits, and a large mound of buttered grits. "Eat, young man." Bo Jr. didn't argue. He devoured the meal before it could start to cool. He burped.

After an appropriate time and a second cup of coffee, RayRay leaned his chair back, balancing on its hind legs, and focused on Bo Jr., almost the same way Booger had been staring at him.

After a moment RayRay said, "So you want to do a big deal, eh? How big? Is this a onetime deal, or are we talking about a full-time supplier? How do I know you won't just take my stuff and lose it or turn it over to the man?" His voice got louder, and each question came more quickly.

"Hang on, RayRay, hang on a minute." Bo Jr. jumped in. "Look, man, I stuck my neck out to my boss, told him I knew some local fellows who could supply us so we could compete with a new dealer from upstate. So he gave me a chance, and here I am."

Bo Jr. took a sip of his coffee and fingered a toothpick from a salt-shaker converted for the task. "He gave me some cash, and I'm probably dead if I don't bring back a load as good as I said it was. RayRay, this is real money, not just some local folks with a few bucks to spare. We could be talking, like, a national distribution or something."

"Tell ya what. I hear ya on the big distribution deal, buddy, and I'm grateful you thought about your old pal RayRay, but I'd like to start slow at first, and then we can look at bigger deals—you know, later on down the line after we establish a relationship, an understanding." RayRay laid it out and stood up as if business was finished; for him, it was.

"Wait a minute!" Bo Jr. pleaded. "I need some now. I need to get a sample to show the man."

"I know, I know, we're gonna take care of you, brother. Now don't get all fussy like a little girl. Today, we gonna need two grand. You got that much?"

"Yes sir, I do." Bo Jr. started to pull the money out.

"No, no, not here, asshole. I don't do business here, and we're just talking. It don't mean nothin'. Just talkin', talkin' and that's all." RayRay held both hands up in the air and away from the money. "One of my men will ride with you when you leave, and you boys can do whatever business you need for two grand. Maybe he can be your fishing guide for the day. Have fun now."

"RayRay, these guys are the real deal, man. They don't play around."

"I know, I know, Bo Jr., and believe me, if it wasn't you, old buddy, we wouldn't be talking, 'cause you know I'm serious too. I don't mess around either, so don't be bringing any help, or your ass might disappear in the swamp along with your new friends. Come alone and we'll be fine, just like we've always been. Now go have fun today and then get on back and sell the deal to our new good buddy." RayRay walked Bo Jr. to the door.

Bo Jr. backed the Ryder van out of the driveway. One of RayRay's men was standing on the road and climbed in as Bo Jr. stopped to shift into drive. They took a ride down a white sand road guarded on both sides by thick stands of pine trees and underbrush. The road went farther into the swamp for another mile and ended abruptly on a high bank overlooking the Black River. They were in a clearing surrounded by large cypress trees rising from the edge of the river and stately live oak trees spreading a thick cover on the higher ground. From the high bank, he could see the tannic-brown river below flowing to the sea, draped on both sides by thick trees covered with Spanish moss.

"Come down here," Dale ordered. "Get in the boat."

"Where are we going? I need to get this deal done today, man."

"We're going fishing. Get in the boat." Dale took his shotgun off his shoulder and held it in Bo Jr.'s direction.

"All right, all right, no need to get riled up."

Dale climbed in the flat-bottomed boat after him, cranked the small outboard engine, and pushed off. They moved upstream for thirty minutes and then turned into a small creek hidden from the river by overhanging tree limbs. Carefully he snaked the boat through narrow unmarked cuts between the knees of giant cypress trees until they emerged into a small lake in the swamp. Dale ran the boat onto a white sand beach. Under the treeline sat a raised hut, with a ladder for stairs.

"What's this, one of your fishing camps or what?"

"This is where you stay until I get back. This is the fishing trip you paid for. There's food, water, and fishing gear in the hut. Here, take this cooler. It's got some beer in it."

"What the hell, man. I got on my suit and all. You just gonna leave me here?"

"I didn't tell you how to dress, that's your problem. Let me see your money."

"Bullshit, man. This is bullshit. I don't see no pot, and you want to leave me here and just go off with my money."

"Give me the money, or I ain't gonna come back." The shotgun came up again.

"This ain't no way to do business, man." Bo Jr. counted out two thousand dollars in new, crisp, one-hundred-dollar bills and put the cash in a bag sitting behind the bow seat of the boat.

"It's how we do business. Just stay here and don't try nothing. I'll be back."

Dale pushed back into the water and guided the boat farther into the swamp. Bo Jr. could hear the engine for a few minutes and then nothing but the sounds of nature. He took off his jacket and climbed up into the hut. It had a bed and was well stocked with some magazines and plenty of food. On the small porch, he found fishing gear and a chair; it looked like they meant for him to be here for a while. Bo Jr. went fishing.

The next morning Bo Jr. rose to the sounds of the small outboard. It was Dale. Bo Jr. was pissed, but controlled his urge to attack. He brushed his wrinkled pants to no avail and grabbed his neatly folded suit coat and tie.

"Did you have a good fishing trip?" Dale greeted him with a snide smile. "You'd be surprised what some people would pay for a fishing trip like this."

"Cut the crap, Dale. You left me here all night. That wasn't the deal, man."

"Yeah, what was the deal? Get in the boat before I leave you again."

They pushed off and returned through the swamp and downriver. Dale pulled up to the bank where they had started the adventure the day before and said, "Get out. Your truck is right where you left it."

Bo Jr. climbed out onto the sandy bank, and Dale left, quickly guiding his boat back upriver. Bo Jr. climbed the trail up to his truck while thinking that Tony was going to kill him when he got back. Tony did not like explanations or excuses.

He walked to his truck and opened the door. On his seat were two brown Piggly Wiggly shopping bags. Bo Jr. looked into one bag. The aroma confirmed the contents. He picked up the bags and estimated the weight of each bundle at about two pounds. The price was good for the quantity, but then, the first purchase was always fair in this business.

He was tired, dirty, and mosquito bitten, but he might live after all.

Bo Jr. put the bags in the back of the rental van and headed out of the swamp. He was a little more than an hour's drive from the fast-paced, crowded madness of Myrtle Beach, but this place was so different, it could be on the opposite side of the earth. He drove the dirt road to the farm-to-market road to the main highway, confidently following the roads he'd known in his youth, roads he didn't need to think about to navigate, gliding through the transition from one domain to the next. He emerged from the world of his youth to a new world that was uncordial and foreign, one that would require a map and guidance. If he wanted to live, he would need to get better at reading the caution signs in this new world. He drove back to Bo J.

Chapter 37

Vernon and his gang were low on the emergency-room priority list, but had finally been evaluated by members of the Grand Strand medical staff. Abrasions were cleaned and bandaged. When the van rolled, the windows had exploded into thousands of little sharp pieces, and the roof had collapsed, trapping their crowd-mooning bare derrieres with sharp, glass-studded metal. The patients had been released to the Myrtle Beach Police Department, who provided them with a free ride, a free room, and free meals at the Myrtle Beach Detention Center while they waited for their turn to go before a judge.

Vernon's gang pleaded guilty to indecent exposure and public intoxication. The county prosecutor had tried to stick drug charges on each of them, but the small amounts of pot found scattered on the ground near the wreckage were deemed inconclusive evidence. The city took what they could prove. Each paid a two-hundred-dollar fine and was sentenced to time served and forty hours of public service. They were assigned to a highway trash detail, a fate reminiscent of the days of county chain gangs, only without the chains and shotgun-toting prison guards.

Vernon was charged with drunken driving, reckless operation of a vehicle, assault with a vehicle, speeding, reckless endangerment, drunk and disorderly, public drunkenness, destruction of property, disturbing the peace, violation of the city noise ordinance, driving without a valid inspection sticker, and two counts of driving a vehicle unsafe for highway operations. The police had noticed the tires were worn, and both side-view mirrors were broken. The mirrors might have been explained by the crash, but the tires would make at least one count stick. Vernon had also been warned that if the other driver died from injuries sustained in the accident, the assault charge would be changed to vehicular homicide.

Vernon was in trouble, so he had called home to his suppliers, seeking assistance. They sent Daniel Gaffney, their best defense attorney from upstate. Mr. Gaffney, Esq., knew the local good-old-boy network. He had attended law school at the University of South Carolina with a couple of Myrtle Beach attorneys and one prominent local judge. He also knew the police had leveled every charge possible except littering, but he wasn't going to bring that up.

"How do you plead?"

"Not guilty, Your Honor!" Vernon replied with unwarranted confidence.

"Not guilty, eh? Humph! Due to the potential addition of a vehicular homicide charge, and this court's concern with your obvious despicable behavior, we want to be assured that you will be here for your trial. Your bail is set at two hundred thousand dollars, and you are not to leave this county without approval of this court and proper notification to law enforcement. Is that understood, Mr. Henderson, Mr. Gaffney?"

"Your Honor, the two-hundred-thousand-dollar bail seems extreme and will be impossible for my young client to post. His desire or ability to flee this jurisdiction is highly unlikely. The young man is a summer worker here in Myrtle Beach, and his parents have limited resources." Mr. Gaffney stepped out from behind the defendant's table and walked the floor in front of the judge's bench with his hands raised in the air for emphasis.

"Incarceration for months with hardened criminals while awaiting trial would be detrimental to this young man's development. In anticipation of posting bail for the charges brought here today, his parents have leveraged their mobile home, their small family farm, and their retirement funds in whole and have only been able to raise one hundred thousand dollars. It's all they have. The defendant is acutely aware of their sacrifice and support. I have complete confidence that a lesser bail amount would be sufficient to ensure my client's total compliance with the court's orders in this matter." He looked down at poor, misunderstood Vernon with sad eyes and then back to the judge with a hope for mercy.

"The defendant's parents are nearly destitute, yet you are here," the judge said. "A destitute couple has hired a thousand-dollar-per-hour defense attorney. OK, I cannot and will not spend the court's time to validate your claim, Mr. Gaffney. You are well known to this state and this court and with your difficult-to-believe but passionate plea, I will offer you this option: one hundred thousand of the bail to be fulfilled by your personal guarantee and one hundred thousand by the defendant or his family. If you are so confident of your client's commitment to this court, you can have a stake in the game. How say you, Counselor? Is it agreed?"

"Yes, Your Honor," Gaffney mumbled, slumping his shoulders like a kid who had begrudgingly agreed to clean up his room.

"Let it be so, this court is adjourned." The gavel cracked against the desk. The sound echoed like a rifle shot in the empty canyons of Vernon's head.

Vernon and Gaffney signed all the appropriate papers and posted the bond with cash and collateral guarantees, and Vernon was released. As they drove away from the courthouse, Vernon started to laugh.

"Wow, what a story. My parents, that's great! I heard you were good, but I didn't know how good. Where do you come up with this crap?" Vernon had tears in his eyes from laughter. Gaffney was not nearly as amused.

"You are one stupid asshole, Henderson. Where do I come up with this crap? Do you think I just started getting punks like you out of trouble? Your ass is mine, son, mine! That judge has a marker on me for a hundred large, and I will skin you alive with my own hands if you try to jump bail on this one. I will personally hunt you down! If you go to jail, I've got plenty of incarcerated friends who owe me and would be pleased to extract payment from you. Your friends put up one hundred grand and guaranteed my ten-grand fee. I'm sure they'll be right beside me coming after your worthless ass. I'm not sure of whom you should be most afraid. Am I clear on this issue, you son of a bitch?"

"Yes. Crystal. I thought you were here to help me, man. What gives?"

"All right, listen up, because here's how it works. Your 'friends' sent me to solve this little problem you created because it's too hard to build another sales network this late in the summer season. They want to salvage what's left. Fortunately for you, your sales have been good, or your ass would still be in that jailhouse. My bill comes out of your cut until it's paid in full. So now I got an interest in getting you out and working again." Gaffney pulled to a stop in the airport parking lot next to a car rental office.

"I don't like to wait for payment, punk, so you better get aggressive. You'll pay back the bail commitments over time with interest. Nothing is free in this world, kid, and you're in debt to some bad people. Work hard, be loyal, and you might live to laugh about this someday. But for now keep that shit-eating grin off your face and get serious. I brought another load for you, and I want it sold by the end of the week. Now quit screwing around and get to work!"

Vernon rented the cheapest car available from the Airport Low-Budget Rental franchise. The rental car company had classified the car as a midsize but had it discounted as part of an advertisement campaign called "The Family Beach Vacation Special." The car was barely big enough for Vernon. His knees forged a snug fit under the steering wheel, and only one duffel bag could fit in the trunk. It was not good for a distribution vehicle, but it would have to do. Vernon cranked up the engine and pulled away to push some pot.

He met with each of his sales agents and searched for more willing summer workers. Just after he had delivered two pounds to a lifeguard in front of the Landmark Hotel, a thought struck him like a mosquito on a windshield. What about the old farts he left in the Ocean Reefer Hotel? The huge, flashing, red-neon sign in front of a real beachfront hotel, more accurately called the Ocean Reef, was the reminder. He had left the men for three days, but the room had only been rented for two. He had used a false ID and a stolen credit card, but he had been seen. He needed to find out if the men were still tied up or what. Throwing caution to the stormy northeasterly wind blowing off the coast, he gunned the sputtering engine and headed for Highway 501 and the Ocean Reefer Motel.

The waves were getting bigger, the sea looked angry, and the under-tow was fierce.

Chapter 38

At seven fifteen the next morning, McKenzie was wheeled down the hospital corridor to the exit and Edna's waiting vehicle. McKenzie stood up confidently from the wheelchair, walked with a focused effort through the automatic sliding-glass doors, and sank into the passenger side of Edna's car just as he began to lose his balance. No one had noticed the minor stumble at the end, and with his apparent success, he was released.

"Please take me to the Blue House; I need to get my car," McKenzie said with focused intent on a predetermined plan.

"You shouldn't be driving, at least not by yourself," Edna objected quickly.

"OK, OK, let's just go," McKenzie agreed. He desperately wanted to get back to his car, the Blue House, and the right of a wrong.

Edna pulled away, feeling hurt by McKenzie's intense obsession with his job and his disregard of her. But she was also glad he trusted her.

Edna's life had been boring for too long. This bit of excitement, this change from the monotony of work, her brief mornings on the beach, and her happy hour at the Frisky Rabbit, fueled a heart-throbbing sensation as they raced together to confront the unknown. Edna needed something new in her life, and she was off to find it. Edna turned into the parking lot of the Blue House. McKenzie's car was still parked where he left it, but with a police notice taped to the windshield warning that the car would be towed in twenty-four hours. She parked, turned off the engine, and said, "Now what?"

McKenzie had been quiet during the ride, attempting to solidify a plan to deal with a crime that was morphing and growing with the prolific tenacity of a kudzu vine. Kids assaulted, abused, tied up, and terrified; drugs, gambling, and now the possibilities that police corruption was supporting the illegal activity he had been trying to stop. He needed help.

"Edna, I need to make a call. Please stay right here. I'll use the pay phone right over there in front of the Blue House." He did not want Edna to be concerned about the dizzy and confused feeling he still fought.

McKenzie turned and walked with a quick pace toward a pay phone. He wanted this call to be untraceable. He dialed the number of one of his best, lifelong friends at the South Carolina Law Enforcement Division headquarters in Columbia, South Carolina. Based on the events of the previous forty-eight hours, he didn't trust anyone in local law enforcement—not local police, not the local US Marshal, not the sheriff's department or anyone else within the local system. He had not been in town long enough to know how far this corruptive cancer might have spread its malignant tentacles. His friends at SLED might be his only hope.

Chapter 39

Officer Harry Floyd, McKenzie's childhood friend, had answered his call and made hasty but comprehensive arrangements to come to Myrtle Beach. SLED, the state's top law-enforcement investigative agency, handled statewide crimes, including those involving the corruption of public officials. He took the call seriously because he trusted McKenzie.

With confidence that help was only a few hours away, McKenzie knew he needed more hard facts to convince others who might be assigned to the investigation, and eventually those hard facts would provide the evidence to seek convictions. Bo J was an obvious choice to check out, and oddly enough, at that moment he saw Bo J driving a yellow van past the Blue House. The van slowed, stopped, and backed up to the garage of a cottage house next door.

McKenzie turned with his back to Bo J and the house. He motioned for Edna to stay in the car and slipped around the opposite side of the building to a thick hedge of cedar trees. McKenzie moved closer to the garage, maintaining a secure position within the trees.

He watched as Bo J removed two brown grocery bags from the van and put them in the garage. McKenzie figured that with this van, Bo J had hauled a full load of something illegal, something like marijuana. He waited, but Bo J didn't come back for more.

McKenzie slipped down the hedge, aware that in the daylight, he was not well hidden. Quickly he stepped up to the truck and looked over the front seat into the empty cargo department. He was surprised and miffed; what happened here? Had Bo J dropped off the primary load before coming home, or was he preparing to make a run to pick up another load? Or was he just acting on an overzealous speculation? Was his mind playing tricks? Was he too aggressive?

McKenzie had nothing, but he knew this still water had dangerous undercurrents. Studying a crime scene that wasn't obvious was like looking at deep, calm, running water and thinking it was safe. All these bits of data might help, but to truly know, a sensor was needed to accurately gauge the turbulence below the calm surface.

McKenzie needed to get some help and somehow get a sensor deep in the backwater of these currents. He needed to get Edna someplace safe and uninvolved, out of this menacing undertow. He turned and went back to her car.

"We need to leave. This place is dangerous."

"What do you mean? There's no one here but us. What were you looking at back there?" Edna didn't get it, but she respected the fact that McKenzie was a trained law-enforcement officer, so she didn't press the issue any further.

"McKenzie, are you sure you're OK?"

"Yes. Why?" He didn't want to share his suspicions with anyone. He was not sure whom he could trust, but he wanted to trust Edna.

"You seem agitated, and I thought maybe...oh, nothing. Why don't we go back to my place, and later I'll fix you some lunch?"

"I'd love to, but I've got to go by my place first. Maybe later."

"But I thought I was supposed to watch you."

"Right, but I've got to take care of some business first, and it's just too dangerous for you to be involved."

"But—"

McKenzie quickly climbed in the car. "Edna, I know this seems strange, like I used you just to get out of the hospital, but it's not. I mean I needed someone to get me out, and you're the only person I trust in this city at the moment. But it's more than that—with you."

"More than what—with me?"

"This is the wrong time to have this conversation. There's not enough time, but I want you to understand."

"Understand what, McKenzie? Are you OK? You're talking in circles."

"It's because I don't know how to say what I'm feeling, especially now, with all of this going on. It's like I'm pulled in two directions." McKenzie looked down at the floor of the car and squeezed his hands together nervously.

"Just tell me. If you trust me, you would share. I want to know so I can help." Edna studied McKenzie with empathetic eyes.

"I really like you, Edna. From the first time I saw you, I've been hooked." He looked up briefly, but was too shy to hold her gaze. "I've never felt like this with anyone. You're the first and I'm not sure how to handle the feelings. But I'm caught in this thing and someone could die, or be seriously injured if I don't fix it."

"Let me help."

"No way, it's too dangerous. As soon as this mess is over, I want to talk about us. I don't want to lose what I think we have going, and I need another kiss like the one we had on the boardwalk."

"Me too."

"I'll see you soon." He kissed her. "Thanks."

Chapter 40

A drug-induced haze clouded Darrell Jr.'s mind as he regained a scant consciousness. He was sleepy, uncomfortable, and perplexed about his situation. His wrists were shackled with thick metal bracelets, and a tight-fitting rubber mask covered his head. The mask had two holes for his eyes, one for his nose, but no opening for his mouth. The shackles on his wrists were chained to poles, stretching his arms outward in opposite directions with precious little slack. He was bent over a plastic-covered upholstered stool with his knees on the floor. Upon further self-assessment, he found his ankles were also shackled and chained on a short leash to heavy metal hooks that were anchored to the floor. Not a good sign, he thought.

The room was dark and quiet. Through the rubber mask, he forced out muffled mumbles for help. He couldn't move his lips. No one answered. Hoping this was just a very vivid dream, he finally gave up to his plight, and his narcotic fueled sleep returned.

A woman's voice whispered, "Wake up, honey. Wake up." He was no longer feeling particularly amorous. He was confused. The room was bathed in a soft, red-hued light. Directly in front of him, an odd scene was reflected in a large glass mirror. Red velvet was on the floor, on the wall behind him, and on the stool to which he was bound. Again he heard her voice whispering seductively against his ear.

"OK, honey, it's show time. Show 'em how you like it!"

"Uh, mmmm!" he mumbled through the tape covering his mouth under the rubber mask. What the hell was going on here? He could feel her hands on his bare ass. What the hell was he doing naked? He strained to look forward into the mirror and saw his own wide eyes and that woman standing behind him. She was naked except for red leather garters, red fishnet stockings, red stiletto heels, and a red leatherette mask of her own. In her hand she had a round, red, leather strap or a whip of some sort. He thought the whip looked a bit more substantial than the ones he sold to tourists for their kids. No, this piece of bound leather was much more substantial, and he thought it a strange topic to dwell on, given his predicament.

Darrell Jr. heard a noise that sounded like coins dropping into the slot on an unused soda machine. He lost count of the echoes of metal clinking into an empty metal container. Next he heard a whoosh sound like an airlock or a door sliding. With this sound a bright light came on in the room, and he saw that woman moving seductively behind him, looking at the mirror glass like a lover. She brought the leather whip down on his ass with a depraved sexual vengeance. He tried to scream, but could only deliver a muffled groan. With wide eyes he watched in the mirror, suspicious of her next crazed action. With the high-quality bondage gear expertly applied, he was helpless to react.

She knelt down and gently caressed the ass cheek she had just whacked. "Fire and ice," she whispered. He did not trust this woman and did not interpret this action to be any sort of apology. With a viper-quick action, she struck again. His ass was red and burning now. She stood up straight, balled fists at her hips, glaring down at her prize with a predatory dominance. The swooshing sound came again, and the bright light dimmed. She stepped over, put her hand on his back, and whispered in his ear again.

"Come on, baby, you need to participate. Our guests are gonna love you out there. They love that wild look in your eyes. Either you play along, or I'm gonna get mean with this strap."

Darrell Jr. was still thinking, "What the hell?" when he heard the coins clinking through the device and landing in a metal container in the wall. The whoosh sound and the bright light re-energized the woman and her whip. She added a few more S&M dominating tricks this time, and finally he felt relief when he heard the whoosh sound, and the lights dimmed. Darrell Jr. prayed whoever was dropping coins would get bored with this show and leave. But the whooshing sound and the bright lights continued with unpredictable repetition throughout the night.

After the first couple of hours of this treatment, she had lightened up on the ferocity of her swings, but only after Darrell Jr. had agreed to play along with the act, showing loving, painful reactions and dedication to his dominator. She finally pulled off his mask, ripped the tape from his mouth, and gave him a glass of cold water as his reward. Darrell Jr. could not speak. His throat was so dry, he could only drink the water.

He looked at her in the mirror and demanded, "What the hell do you think you're doing, you bitch? Take these chains off of me." As he spoke, she became blurry. The last sense he could distinguish was the faint smell of oysters roasting.

"Oh no, not again," were the last words he muttered before succumbing to her sleeping potion.

Chapter 41

The listless hotel manager was unfazed by the "Do Not Disturb" sign that had hung on the door of room 112 as a constant sentinel for two days. He didn't care; the room had been paid for, in advance, and the occupants would be allowed the privacy they desired, but their time was up.

"Jolene, I need you to go get room one-twelve cleaned up," the manager barked to a maid over his two-way radio.

He wished more hotel guests would use "Do Not Disturb" signs, which would mean fewer towels and sheets to wash and less work time for the maids, whom he paid with cash. Cash payments helped reduce the cost and administration required to deal with sticky issues such as payroll taxes, health-care benefits, and minimum wage. A "Do Not Disturb" sign meant more profits.

The maid would need an hour to clean the room for the next unaware tourists who expected proximity to the beach. When the new guests arrived, they typically complained vigorously about the deceit of the advertised location. The manager would use every tactic before he gave up revenue for a room due to late checkouts.

Discreet arrivals and departures occurred often along this highway strip of unattractive, inexpensive, but overpriced hotels. So the maid knocked twice.

"Maid service. Hello. Maid service."

She waited a considerate two minutes with no response from the room and inserted the passkey. The dead bolt was engaged, so she used a second master key.

"Uh, oh, something ain't right," she mumbled to herself.

Guests could only utilize the security of the dead bolt by turning the lock from inside the room. The locked bolt meant someone was still in the room. Jolene pulled her walkie-talkie out of its belt holder.

"Hank, we got a problem here. Dead bolt was on, and nobody answered. Should I go in? Over."

"Yeah, get 'em outta there and quit bothering me." He went back to his *World Wide Wrestlers Special Edition* magazine.

She turned the doorknob and attempted to open the door a small crack to once again announce her arrival. The door yielded only an inch when the internal safety-chain lock presented the next line of defense.

"Hello, maid service, can I come in? Checkout time!" The only response was a smell that almost knocked her down. The pungent odor poured from the room like water over Niagara Falls.

Jolene was not happy. With a smell like this one, she knew her job would not be pleasant. She was continuously amazed by the weird and disgusting things guests would do to a hotel room. Did these people always live this way, or was this deviant behavior stored up to be unleashed on the unsuspecting small hotel owners and their hardworking maids?

She called to the office. "I think you should bring the bolt cutters. The chain lock is hooked, no one answers from inside, and this room smells like death." She closed the door and stepped around the back to check the small rear window. The window had been shut, but not completely.

As she came back around the hotel, she met the manager at the door. "The rear window is open, so maybe they slipped out."

"That's crazy. Why would someone sneak out of a room that they paid for?" Hank knocked once more, cracked the door open slightly, and said, "Manager. Open up." The odor hit him immediately. He pushed the door hard against the security chain. He quickly cut it with the large bolt cutters, often used at their hotel for this task. Two men lay motionless, tied to the beds.

Without entering Hank surveyed the rest of the room and called out to the closed door of the bathroom.

"Anybody in there? I'm calling the police." No one answered. He was holding his bolt cutters as a weapon should some deranged maniac jump out from hiding.

"Call nine-one-one from the next room," he said quietly while backing out of the room. He did not want the blame for contamination of a crime scene.

"Are they dead?"

"Smells like it, looks like it, but I don't care." An assessment of the health of hotel guests was not in his job description. This problem would be left for the professionals. If the police and rescue squads could not help these men, then the coroner would take them away. He only hoped he could get it resolved, the men removed, the questions answered, and the room cleaned up and aired out before the new guests arrived before six o'clock. He would need to encourage the emergency vehicles to leave quickly to allow parking for his future guests. Police cars, ambulances, and fire trucks in the parking lot rarely helped business.

Chapter 42

Within five minutes of the 911 call from the Ocean Reefer, Myrtle Beach Police squad cars, two ambulances, and a fire truck arrived on the scene. Five minutes later Detective Driggers's cruiser came skidding around the Ocean Reefer entrance sign and screeched to a stop in front of room 112. When Driggers heard the original officer report over the radio, "Two elderly gentlemen, one dead, one alive," he knew who it had to be.

He pulled on his latex gloves and stepped directly to the room as the other officers cleared a path. The man who had been first on the scene provided a quick update. While listening to the report, Driggers looked over to see the EMTs administering lifesaving medical attention to Frank. The battered elder had an IV injected into his arm and a clear-plastic oxygen mask strapped over his nose and mouth. The medics were checking his basic vitals once more before placing him on their gurney.

Driggers looked to the other bed to see Marvin, who was hopelessly dead—confirmed by sight and by smell. He had obviously been dead for a couple days. Driggers moved over to inspect the marks of torture and the restraints used to hold these men down. Driggers had a difficult time controlling his hate-filled anger at the grisly scene. These old men had been tortured, and the work was sloppy. Amateur punks had treated these fine old men with unconscionable brutality.

Tony had called Driggers the night Frank and Marvin disappeared. They had been afraid of this outcome. They would find out who had perpetrated this heinous act, and then justice would be administered slowly and painfully. The retribution would send a message to any other stupid punk who might stick his nose in Tony's business.

Driggers called in two of his best detectives, who were also receiving financial aid to ensure Tony's unencumbered business operations. All the right people had been paid, and cooperation with the established turf was widespread. But all it took was one or two who wanted to go another way, who wanted their own action, who wanted to follow the rules. All it took to upset the equilibrium was one straight, dedicated, do-gooder cop or some stupid punk criminal. Driggers went to his car, retrieved a private cell phone, and called Tony.

"Marvin is dead and not due to natural causes. Frank is still alive, but unconscious. He is being stabilized before they transport him to the hospital. We should have him in the emergency room within the half hour. They think he'll survive. Marvin was messed up a bit. He's been dead a couple days. Not a pretty sight."

A scary silence held the line, and Driggers could sense Tony's anger boiling!

"Tony, you still there?"

"Yes!" Tony growled. "You find out the son of a bitch who did this, Driggers, and you find him fast! I'm gonna take care of another little troublemaker in the meantime. I've got to answer to the boss on this one. Marvin was family, and the boss ain't gonna be happy. He may come down himself to watch the justice served to the prick who thinks he can do this shit and get away with it...Dammit!"

"Tony, I've got two good men working the evidence. I'll go to the hospital with Frank. When he comes around, I'll get the info."

"You better! I want the assholes who did this, and I want them tonight!" Tony hissed. Driggers could hear teeth grinding.

Driggers gave instructions to his detectives, emphasizing the demand for immediate results. He climbed in his car to follow the ambulance hauling Frank to the hospital. As Driggers sped out of the parking lot, he almost collided with a small rental car driven by a curious, rubbernecking, dark-haired tourist who stared back through thick black-rimmed glasses. Driggers was pissed, grew impatient, gunned his engine, and passed the ambulance. He raced to the hospital to ensure immediate attention would be available for Frank.

Driggers knew Frank, the big, tough ox. He was old, but he was still as strong as most men half of his age. He would pull through, he would come around, and he would give the information needed to identify these punks.

One hour after arrival at the hospital, all that could be done for the old gangster had been done. Driggers went to intensive care, stood over Frank, and inspected his condition. He looked peaceful, like an old man sleeping soundly, dreaming a good dream, resting weary bones.

"You tough old dog, you," Driggers said softly.

Frank's eyes fluttered and then opened. He looked up and around like a man cast through time to a distant, unfamiliar planet. He tried to speak, but his lips were dry. Driggers quickly administered a few ice chips and a wet cloth left by the attentive nurse.

Frank recognized Driggers and became aware of the hospital surroundings as signs that he had survived the ordeal. Just before he had passed out, he had remembered thinking this stupid, ill-advised chase would be his last. He had let the punks get the drop on him, and now his buddy Marvin had suffered as a result of his failure. His survival had been fueled by a desire for revenge, his desire to even the score. Frank would only be satisfied by a death of honor, one dealt by an equal or by nature, not by some stupid punk. Frank's survival was fair by all the laws of the jungle.

"Frank, do you remember anything about the people who did this to you?"

"Vernon, Harley, and David. They've been selling pot to tourists and summer kids. Vernon is the leader of the three stooges. He's a skinny bastard about six foot two, dark-brown hair, thick glasses, a real redneck, has a hillbilly-punk accent to his voice. He's driving an old brown van with some lettering on the side covered over by a bad paint job." Frank laid it out like he knew Driggers could use it. Driggers's eyes lit up on the mention of the brown van.

"Was it a long van with glass all around?" Driggers pressed for confirmation of a detail he knew would be true.

"Yea, you know him?" Frank asked with a puzzled look.

"He drove that van into Guido night before last," Driggers said. "Almost killed him. Guido's here in the hospital. You get some rest. I've got work to do."

"Get him, Driggers! Don't make me get out of this bed to avenge my friend, Marvin. Get him, and let Tony have him!" Frank said with new strength in his voice.

Driggers smiled, gave the thumbs-up sign, and left to call Tony.

"I've got people looking for this jerk tonight," Tony told Driggers.

"They just let him out of jail. The bum has got multiple felony counts, but the judge let him go. He got a high-price lawyer from upstate. Someone from that part of the state or in the Asheville area is backing the boy. They posted his bail." Driggers worked to explain what he knew about Vernon. "They got a man making money for 'em, and they want to finish the summer out with his little network. They'll give him up and let the courts have him as soon as the summer is done and they get their bail money back."

"I want that punk and his two friends now! The courts can just keep his bail money, 'cause what I got planned ain't gonna leave no body for them to cash in." Tony was persistent and edgy. "The big boss himself is coming here tomorrow. He wants to look in this man's eyes while he's dying, and that's a direct quote." Tony slammed the phone down to emphasize his point.

Driggers put out an all-points bulletin for Vernon, Harley, and David. From this point forward, this misguided trio could only hope that the good cops would get them first.

Chapter 43

Edna parked her car next to the garage below her apartment, knowing McKenzie's warnings of danger must be true. She knew he was trying to protect her. And she was anxious to finish their talk.

After checking on her apartment, she walked down to the One-Eyed Flounder. Darrell Sr. was frantic, and the store's atmosphere seemed to mimic his mood.

"Edna, thank God! Can you work now? Can you help me? That little prick, Darrell Jr., just up and left the night before last. He didn't collect the cash, he didn't close out the registers, and he didn't lock up or anything. If it hadn't been for Ms. Carlisle taking charge, the store would have been left open for all the bums and crooks on this beach to rob us blind. He didn't come back yesterday either. I know it's your day off, but I need help." Darrell Sr. exhaled with frustration as he scanned his prize, his life's blood, his store.

"Sir, I can help for a couple hours, but we've all got a lot of problems today." Edna promised herself two hours max.

"Have you seen Darrell Jr.? No one seems to know where he is," Darrell Sr. said as he pulled another cash drawer from a register, placed it on his cart, and headed back to his office. Edna shrugged and straightened taxidermied alligator heads on a shelf.

He stopped and turned back to Edna. "By the way, three of our summer workers haven't been to work all week. Billy, Steff, and Barb, all absent for a week. It's early for them to start going home; the summer's not over. I don't know about these kids; the desertions seem to start earlier each year. For Christ's sake, it's only the first week of August. It just doesn't make any sense for these kids to leave a good job just as they are finally becoming productive."

He bent over and picked up a fluorescent rubber dragon from the aisle. "Oh well, you know, I'm not sure those three were ever going to amount to much anyway." Darrell Sr. just shook his head in dismay and frustration.

Edna could not believe how clueless this man seemed to be. He had built this store from nothing, had made a lot of money, had lived in this seasonal paradise employing summer help for years, and yet still didn't understand the tendencies and motivations of the teenagers he hired.

Darrell Sr.'s reality was in another time period when kids were required to work, to earn their own spending money, to save for college or to help with the family business. In that more naïve and different time, people had respect for authority, their elders, and generally they followed the rules. Much like the out-of-date merchandise he sold, Darrell Sr. had not followed the trends.

These kids had been at the beach for two months, working and playing, burning the candle at both ends. As the hot, breezeless, dog days of August wore on, the kids lost their enthusiasm for the beach. They had to cut back somewhere, and walking away from a party was just not feasible in their minds, so the work suffered. Some got homesick, some got bored, and some fell in love. For many reasons the summer workers started to disappear, and by Labor Day, all but a few diehard beach lovers would be gone.

"I'll ask around, sir, maybe Dianne has seen them. I think she hangs out with that crowd." Edna continued to work at an efficient, methodic pace to straighten up her department. Darrell Sr. walked to his office to count his cash. Edna worked her way to the front of her section, where custom-made T-shirts were sold right on the boardwalk. This spot gave her the occasional view of the beach and ocean.

The T-shirt department was located in this part of the store to maximize visibility for tourists strolling along the boardwalk. As they waltzed their evening waltz, full of oysters, shrimp, and other seafood favorites, licking their ice-cream cones or biting caramel-covered apples, they would stop to read the humorous sayings one could have steamed on a cheap cotton shirt. These selections were tourist-impulse buys and nothing more. People not on vacation had the common sense to bypass such retail temptations. What other explanation could be found for a couple to purchase matching shirts, one shirt stenciled with the phrase "I'm with Stupid" and the other shirt with only one word, "Stupid"? Where else, in what other universe, would a happy couple decide to spend their money for these items, and wear them?

Darrell Sr. had earned a good living based on this odd phenomenon of mindless, irrational fun. Edna looked up from her work and saw Frankie walk past the store.

Frankie was the most senior lifeguard monkey on this end of the beach. The boardwalk at night was Frankie's place, his Frisky Rabbit. Frankie was too young to hang out with the guards in joints that served alcohol, but the beach had plenty of entertainment for underage kids. He was an expert at all the arcade games, including his mastery of Skee-Ball. He had helped many young girls with their first game away from parental supervision.

Frankie could dance. At an early age, his mother had taught him the synchronized shuffles, twists, and turns of a dance for couples called the Shag. The Shag was the only dance acceptable for truly cool people while at the beach, listening to Carolina beach music like the Drifters, the Tams, or the Swinging Medallions. Frankie had the day off and was on his way to Big Daddy's, the no-alcohol teen and preteen haven, an afternoon and early-night, beach-music, dance joint where many young beachgoers created memories of their first dance, or their first kiss with their first summer love.

Frankie had been the focus of many a young girl's dreams and memories. He was a young teenage legend. Frankie wasn't shy, and he was quick to ask the best-looking girls to dance and to thrill them with the complex turns that only the better Shag dancers had mastered. He rarely just danced with one; he liked to play the field.

He usually traveled with a loyal collection of admiring young girls and younger guys who all wished they could be cool like him. Frankie was passing the One-Eyed Flounder with his posse when Edna had spotted "his coolness" through the sales window.

"Frankie! Frankie!"

"Yeah, hi, Edna!" She had always been nice to him. She knew his mother and had been Frankie's baby-sitter on occasion. Frankie would not reveal that bit of trivia to his friends, and they would assume this lady calling for Frankie was just another mark of his coolness.

"Frankie, have you seen Billy, Steff, or Barb lately?"

"No, but I heard they split town. They were kinda lame, if you ask me. My guard says almost everyone staying at the Hutches has left town. After the water torture, those three split with everyone else. They didn't want to be next."

"Torture? Are you serious? What torture?"

"Hey, it was just some rumors. Maybe you need to ask Booney. He should know."

"Frankie, you look tired, buddy. Your eyes are all bloodshot. You been getting enough sleep?"

"Yeah, yeah, I'm cool. Look, I'll see ya later, Edna," Frankie responded a bit too fast, a bit too paranoid, and with a little too much of a smile on his face.

Edna was worried but let it go as she saw him with his crowd, walking away, smiling and being cool, the master of his own dimension. He rejoined his group with youthful confidence, leading away his harem of early teen girls and his cast of young male protégés. They would soon be the almost-legal teens and young college summer workers. The beach and its nightlife would be their domain. Their time would come.

Edna just smiled and went back to work. She needed to finish and go find Evelyn. As she folded and straightened the mass of shirts people had been picking over, she pondered how a kid Frankie's age gets pot.

Chapter 44

Four hours after McKenzie's first call, SLED Officer Floyd guided his unmarked SLED vehicle off Highway 501 and into the Conway Piggly Wiggly parking lot, the agreed rendezvous point twenty miles west of Myrtle Beach. McKenzie was waiting and quickly briefed Floyd with more detail than he had revealed during their first telephone call. Floyd informed McKenzie of actions he had initiated with a small group of trusted officers at SLED headquarters.

"It appears we have the potential for a number of investigative cases here. This situation is complicated with multiple crimes by multiple parties, including organized crime, illegal gambling, corruption, conspiracy, kidnapping, illegal substances sales, illegal alcohol sales, and possible state and federal tax evasion."

Officer Floyd closed his notebook, took off his mirrored sunglasses, and looked at McKenzie.

"If we can substantiate charges of federal tax evasion and kidnapping, this case may even draw attention from the FBI, but I just can't say yet. We need more details to clearly identify all of the suspects, and we need more evidence before we let the legal dogs out. You seem to have walked into a hornet's nest, my friend."

"Well, I believe we may have a way in, but we'll need a wire and authority to use it. I've got the mole identified, but we'll need to convince him to cooperate. I don't believe it'll be too hard. First, we need confirmation of what I saw, but I can't go back in. They know me now.

I can brief you on the layout and the illegal activity, and hopefully you can get confirmation."

McKenzie felt betrayed by those around him, and as a small-town lawman, the one thing he disliked more than a wife-beater or child molester was a crooked cop. He was intent on justice, but after bringing in SLED, this place and this job would not be safe.

They wasted no time as McKenzie described the situation that Floyd should expect to see that evening inside the Blue House. They dropped by the local Goodwill store to purchase a nondescript, average-guy outfit for an undercover disguise. McKenzie and Floyd spent the remainder of the afternoon in a library conference room on the Coastal Carolina University campus in Conway. They both had concluded that a university library was probably the last place they need worry about being seen by the guys they were after. McKenzie repeatedly drilled Floyd on names, descriptions, and their suspected criminal activity. He had no pictures or written files, but he could describe the details and the people from his precise memory.

McKenzie took Floyd on a reconnaissance tour to check out the Blue House while there was still daylight and no activity at the joint. Floyd viewed the situation, not as a single crime spree, but as two separate activities. He had more experience than McKenzie with city criminals, organized crime, narcotics, and kidnapping.

McKenzie's experience had been in small towns. He knew country folk and the crimes more associated with rural poverty: alcohol, spouse abuse, child abuse, petty theft, and the toxic disaster caused by the plentiful supply of cheap homemade drugs. He also knew agriculture and the new highly profitable crops of the South. In his community he knew the growers, the distributors, and unfortunately the overusers. He knew the addicts that fried their brains early in life and became nothing but trouble as they reached adulthood.

"Man, I have to tell you this deal really irks me. I got in this business because I felt like I was doing something to improve and protect my town and the people I grew up with." McKenzie pushed away his notes and sat back in his chair. Frustration showed on his face. "But I've watched my friends, people I knew in school and the people in my little town, go down the wrong path. They're growing marijuana, and some are even cooking meth and crack."

"I hear you, brother. I see it every day too, but we have to keep fighting the good fight."

"I know, I know, but it's hard when you keep arresting people you know and then you arrest them again. I mean, I've seen their kids crying and their wife begging, and the drugs are right there in their house." His people were going bad, and he did not want to be the man imposing the law on family and friends.

"That's why I joined SLED. I wanted to stop the drugs."

"Yeah, but after you arrest people you know in a small town, their wife and kids ain't got nothing to live on. Their relatives look at you with a stare like hate, and I can't get those looks and those kids begging out of my mind. That's why I'm here. I couldn't take it anymore, and now this crap."

McKenzie's recurring struggle with his home and his belief in the law and in justice was a personal nightmare. Many of his friends became suspicious and uncomfortable when he was around. When would you arrest your hometown friends? How could you sleep at night?

He felt he had to tell Floyd about Edna and Evelyn. Was he suspicious, or was this just full disclosure? How well did he really know them? Why had Edna and Evelyn always been there first to find most of the victims? And now they turn up at the hospital with a mob goon. Coincidence?

"So now I get here, and I meet a woman, thinking this is a new start, a new home, but I've got questions. Edna and Evelyn have been first on the scene several times to find these kids tied up. I think Edna and Evelyn are fine young women, somewhat caught in a teenage-dream time warp, but good, honest, hardworking folk nonetheless." McKenzie mused that perhaps these two had held on to a lifestyle for too long, but they were not criminals. Evil was not so clever that it might easily hide within these two women.

"I don't know, McKenzie. These ladies don't seem to fit the profile. I think they've just been in the wrong place at the wrong time."

Guido was a wild card. From Edna, McKenzie knew the story of Evelyn's courtship, but was it a coincidence or what? Was Guido using the girls to get information, to better fit into the summer-worker scene where he normally would be avoided? He worked at the Blue House, but McKenzie had no proof that Guido was connected to the mob or any crime. Was Guido working twenty-four/seven, or was he just another guy who got in the way?

Just then McKenzie's police radio chatter kicked up. He heard about the discovery at the Ocean Reefer Hotel: two old men tied up, beaten, one dead, one barely alive. He heard the unusual response by Driggers and his suspected loyal officers with a quick arrival. Driggers's quick arrival was complemented by a quick departure. This procedure was highly unusual. Was his assessment of the response accurate, or was he being overly suspicious again?

McKenzie suspected that the mood tonight at the Blue House would be tense. He decided to leave Edna out of the profiled list of suspects. He really liked that woman, and he didn't intend to let his suspicious mind get in the way of a future with her. If she was involved, her connection would be obvious when they arrested those he determined were more dangerous. McKenzie turned his attention to the immediate plan.

Chapter 45

Edna finished her tasks at the One-Eyed Flounder within her two-hour, self-imposed limit. She told Darrell Sr. about the rumors of the three summer workers leaving town. He was frustrated and told her thanks while he kept counting the cash and receipts from the previous day. Edna left and walked down First Avenue North, past her apartment and the unnaturally quiet Hutches, and stepped into the Frisky Rabbit.

"What's going on, Booney?"

"Hey, babe. What's with you droppin' by so early?"

"Just wanted to talk to you about things going on at the Hutches. Three of our summer workers just split. It's really quiet next door. What's up?"

"I thought you knew. I mean, you were first to find all the others... that's kinda freaky, by the way...so, ah, I thought you knew about them all." Booney chuckled as he teased Edna. "What ya drinkin'?"

"How 'bout a Pepsi? What are you talking about, knowing about all of them? I found four, and you have more than that living next door. And what's this I hear about some kids being tortured?"

"So you missed the big news? Edna, you've been working too hard or something, 'cause last week someone used water torture on four of our tenants. They were tied to their beds. Each had a plastic milk jug full of water with a small hole, and a plastic tube in the bottom was set up to drip water on their foreheads. Whoever did this painted "Go Home" on the bottom of the jugs. The kids were staring at those words as the water dropped."

Booney cycled between wiping the bar, eating potato chips, and thrusting his hands in the air for added emphasis to his story. "It was Chinese water torture, man, with a message."

"That's crazy, Booney. Are you sure?"

"That's what they told us. Anyway, after a while, they were anticipating, and finally, afraid of each drop. They were damn near crazy when we found them that next morning. One of our other tenants had been out all night. He came in to change clothes for work and found them all. Each one had 'Go Home' painted across his chest with red paint."

Booney finally pulled Edna's Pepsi from the cooler and plunked it on the counter. He stuffed another handful of chips into his mouth and continued.

"The kids were gone as soon as their clothes were packed. They didn't want cops. They just wanted to leave. We didn't argue. We've got their August rent and their security deposit. They would leave after August anyway." Booney just shrugged, wiped the bar again, and smiled with chip crumbs speckled across his beard.

"Booney, come on, man, sure you care. I mean, these people have been terrorized, assaulted, threatened. This is serious stuff, and I can't believe you didn't tell me before! Geez, what's up with you?" Edna questioned, not understanding his blasé mood.

"The new cop dude told us to keep it quiet. Didn't want us to tell anyone, supposed to keep it on the QT or a strictly 'need to know' basis, or something like that."

"He what? This craziness needs to stop. These kids should be protected!"

"Edna, they come and go. Just like the tide, it's high or low, in or out. Every summer they come, they think they are the only ones, they think they are the first ones to do what they do. They have no respect for others. They just want to party to the extreme. Every year they get worse. They drink, they destroy, and they walk away."

He jammed another handful of chips in his mouth. "Our paradise takes the hit, takes their intrusion, and then attempts to heal during the winter, but it cannot, it *cannot*. The sooner we get them out of here, the better, dude."

"Whoa there, Booney...buddy...dude, sounds a bit heavy. Were you the one who tied them up?"

"Hell no, but I ain't complaining. You know I make a lot of money on these punks, but I worry about the future of our beach town. Seems like we got a good thing here, but the atmosphere is changing. It's changing, I tell you. The special place that both you and I came and stayed here to enjoy is not the same. People find a paradise and use it to death! They don't care about preservation or the long run, it's only, 'Where's my piece?' and 'Watch my fun today.' I don't like it, Edna. I tell you, I don't like it."

He pounded the bar, and his drink fell on the floor. He stared at it and then refocused. "They're screwing up the things you and I love about this place. We need a balance."

"Booney, dude, you've been smoking weed."

"Yeah, well, what ya gonna do? I'm hungry."

"Booney, I'm scared. I think I might hibernate at night for a while at least until this thing is over. So don't be surprised if I miss a happy hour or two. See you later. Be safe."

Booney just smiled and wiped the counter again.

Edna left and crossed Kings Highway to see if Evelyn was back at work at the Krispy Kreme.

"You made it in today. How's Guido this afternoon?" Edna asked with a smile.

"He's still unconscious. I came in around two, and I'm leaving at eight. The tourists don't care about our troubles. They want their Krispy Kremes. Vera is at the hospital in case he comes around. Some big goon from the Blue House is hanging around. I thought he was kinda creepy, so I didn't mind taking a break, but I'll be back tonight." Evelyn's lack of sleep had her giddy but still coping.

"Where's Eddie?" Edna asked, suddenly aware that she had not seen the big omnipresent man since the wreck. "I haven't seen him today."

"Vera said he was sleeping, not normal for him. Maybe he just wants to be ready in case he's needed tonight. Those two are such good people, always watching out for us," Evelyn said with a weak smile and a pause for sincerity. She wiped a small section of the clean counter with a practiced circular motion.

"Maybe he's tired, and he's retired, so he can sleep when he feels like it," Edna joked. "Evelyn, I'm worried about McKenzie." Edna was more somber with this remark. "He's got some really strange things going on. He won't tell me most of it. I'm not sure he's over that bump to his head. I dropped him at his car at the Blue House. He used the pay phone and got really weird, touchy, and then made me leave."

"What's he doing now?" Evelyn refilled coffee cups at the end of the bar without looking away from Edna.

"I don't know, wouldn't say. He just didn't want me to be around, said it wasn't safe. He's such a gentleman, so protective but serious, almost too serious sometimes. But he's a good kisser. We need to get him and Guido to be friends soon. Trouble is...I think McKenzie is suspicious of him and thinks something is going on at the Blue House."

"Like what? Guido's such a sweet guy. I'm sure it can't be anything he's doing." Evelyn was dismayed by the potential of Guido being in trouble. She delivered two hot doughnuts, took money from a customer, and put another pot of coffee on to drip.

"Well, whatever, I'm sure we'll figure it out and bring them all together. We'll be like one big, happy family!" Edna smiled. "I'll see you when you get off. Maybe we'll go to the hospital together."

"OK, see you round eight." She cleaned the spotless counter again.

Chapter 46

Tony returned to the Blue House. He was beyond being pissed off and was now focused on a plan to get even. He could not let seething anger monopolize his thoughts or dictate his actions, because he also had a business to run. The family would be extremely upset to hear about Frank and Marvin, but they could be unforgiving and violent if the business was shut down for the night. Priorities were priorities, and profits came first.

As he pulled into the empty lot, typical of early afternoon at the Blue House, he saw the van parked next to Guido's house, reminding him of Bo J and the money he had given him. Where had he been, and what the hell was a bright-yellow rental van doing in the yard?

Tony parked and walked directly to the house. The front door was unlocked, allowing Tony to waltz right in. He heard snoring, loud and dramatic, emanating from a bedroom. He walked to the noise and found Bo J lying on his back, slack-jawed and making a noise that sounded like a buzz saw. Tony walked into the kitchen and found a large pan, filled it with ice and water, walked back to the bedroom, and dumped one big gush of cold water in Bo J's mouth, soaking his whole head. Bo J sucked in, gasped for air, and came up from the bed swinging, coughing, and fighting for his life.

"Where the hell you been, boy?" Tony yelled while slapping Bo J across the top of his head, knocking him back down onto the icy, wet bed.

Bo J instinctively held his arms above his head, collapsing in a fashion reminiscent of a protective fetal position often used in his youth to survive violent, angry, drunken onslaughts delivered by his father. Bo J's father and now his new father figure seemed to always beat him when they were mad about something else. Bo J was tired of being the whipping boy, but he hadn't discovered a way out yet.

He had assumed his life was like everyone else's. He had assumed someday he would have kids and take over as the new tyrant. For now he was more focused on the present and his own survival. He had been trained by a master in a double-wide dojo. He was still a student, but with a new master.

"What? What's your problem, man? I was gettin' the pot like I told ya I would!" Bo J growled. His mind was quickly clearing from the deep sleep, and his confidence was growing as a man who could defend himself against this bully.

"You dumb, hick punk. I needed you here! While you were gettin' high with your redneck buddies for two days, I got senior family members being murdered, and Guido was almost killed by that fuckin' trespassing maniac who's trying to deal in my territory." Tony moved closer and got in Bo J's face. "I swear you're like the plague. Since you showed up, I got nothing but trouble!"

Tony poked him in the chest hard with a stiff finger. "I should have killed you the first night you tried to rob me. If Guido hadn't taken you under his wing, I woulda snuffed your ass already. Nothing but fuckin' trouble." Tony was still pissed at the world, and Bo J was the only country in sight.

"Well, 'Trouble' is about to save your ass with some bodacious, permanent smile-generating, head-numbing pot. Your ass will kiss mine after you take a toke of this stuff, man," Bo J snarled back at Tony. "This shit is the trial pack. Like it—put up the cash, and we get it by the truckload." Bo J arched his shoulders back, stood erect with more confidence, and poked a finger into Tony's chest.

"You little dipshit." Tony pulled out his pistol and slammed Bo J beside his head with a hard backhand, knocking him down and carving a gash in his forehead. Bo J scrambled up to strike back and met the long, cold barrel of a cocked forty-five aimed between his eyes. The threat of the weapon had the effect of a stone wall. Bo J froze.

"Get your ass dressed and get over to the club. We are shorthanded, or I'd pop you right here, right now! Next time you think you want to talk smart to me, boy, remember this moment, 'cause it will be the last thing you'll ever do. You still owe me, and that means I own your ass. Now get ready. Bring the pot with you; I've got some friends I trust to test it. We'll talk more later." Tony released the hammer, lowered the gun, and stepped away from Bo J. He turned and walked out of the front door.

Bo J collapsed on the bed, frustrated, wounded, and bleeding. How could a beach paradise be more of a hell than what he had endured at home on the farm? At least at home, he had all his friends—friends who had a common bond like family, friends who would accept him for who he was and care for him as part of their community. Friends who still called him by his real name.

Tired of wallowing in his own self-pity and wet bed sheets, he got on his feet, cleaned up, and dressed for work, as he was told. What choice did he have? He felt like a man trapped in purgatory, a man without a country or a family. Bo J picked up the pot, walked through the treelined portal, and went to work at the Blue House.

Chapter 47

Bo J carried the pot directly to Tony's office, knocked on the door, and entered to find him leaning back almost horizontally in his executive leather chair. His feet were resting on the edge of his desk. Two ladies were sitting sensuously on a broad, plush, brown leather couch. Tony was smoking a Cuban cigar and blowing perfect smoke rings that floated in lazy circles to the ceiling, where each gradually lost its shape. A small cloud hovered around an overhead light. This man had an entirely different demeanor than the angry bully Bo J had encountered such a short time ago.

"Come in, young man. Meet two of my favorite ladies, Ophelia and Tina." Tony waved his hand in admiration toward the ladies.

"Tony, Darrell Jr. ain't the mastermind ringleader we thought he was. He may be like a lower-level dealer, but he ain't the leader. He just don't have the right stuff." Ophelia continued her report as if Bo J were not standing in the doorway.

"We'll keep him for now until we're sure he's not connected. If it turns out he's just an unfortunate dumb ass, drug him and drop him at the amusement park one night."

"OK, boss. But first I want to play with him a little. A girl's gotta have some fun."

Tony waved off the comment and looked at Tina, who gave her reconnaissance report.

"I'm planning to pick up Vernon tonight. He's the one, or at least he wants everyone to think he is. I watched him at the Frisky Rabbit last night. He's definitely selling pot, and they were laughing about the wreck with Guido."

Tina was the right age to hang out on the beach, buy pot, and question the dealers without raising suspicion. She had a way with the young, cocky drug dealers. Last night's visit to the Frisky Rabbit had been the ticket.

For now, as any good enterprising manager might do, Tony was thinking about another issue, the pot Bo J had purchased. When they got rid of this drug-pushing kid, someone would need to fill the void. Tony meant to have his supply line established when that void developed.

"Bo J, I want these ladies to test your stuff. They're my experts and know the quality I expect, so let's see what you've got."

Bo J opened one bag of the fragrant, sage-green cannabis and emptied a portion on the conference table. "You girls like me to do the honors, or you roll your own?"

"I'll do it. Don't want you licking my joint. We don't know each other that well yet," Tina sassed back in her typical high-pitched, but sensuously brassy, voice. She waltzed to the table and bent over, giving Tony a provocative view of her ass. Tina was street-smart beyond her young years, and she had the body to get whatever she wanted in Tony's world.

She rolled two fat joints with casual expertise. This girl carried her own rolling papers in her bra, and Bo J was impressed. Tony offered her a silver engraved lighter to get things fired up. With her first deep hit, her eyes rolled back in her head. She held on and then blew it out; the smoke joined the cigar exhaust loitering below the overhead light.

"Hot damn, man! That's some smooth shit!" Tina was impressed and took another long hit before passing the joint to Ophelia.

"Damn, that's fine." The girls never made it to the second joint. By the time Tina roached the last bit of the first joint, she was lying back on the couch, laughing. Ophelia was numb and sported a broad, frozen smile. She was standing in one spot and could not decide which way to move, so she just looked back and forth from Tina, laughing on the couch, to Tony, kicked back in his chair.

"Tony, this is some of the best pot I've ever smoked. Oh man!" Ophelia finally decided which way to move and slid over to Tony.

"OK, dipshit. Appears you might be right, but I don't trust you or your suppliers yet. This sample is apparently good, but I need consistent quality. I want you to prove this ain't no onetime, setup deal." Tony's playful mood with the girls had quickly changed 180 degrees again.

"Tomorrow I want you to work on getting me a truckload of this stuff, and if it ain't the same, you and your boys are dead. I'll even give you half the money in cash to cut the deal, the other half plus five percent at delivery, if it's the same quality. Now get your ass back to work." Tony turned to play with his giddy ladies, and Bo J returned to his post next to the men's room.

Chapter 48

That evening Floyd was sitting casually in a nondescript, white Ford F-150 pickup truck in the Blue House parking lot. The truck had seen many hard workdays on a construction site and had a worn, rusty trailer hitch on the back. The rear cab window sported a University of South Carolina Gamecocks sticker. The bed of the truck had an accumulation of scrap building lumber, nails, a rusty hammer, and some empty crushed beer cans. This truck fit in. No one would notice it, even if it were the only vehicle in the lot.

The cheap tinted windows obscured the view of anyone walking past, and if they glanced at him, he would fake a slug from a Pabst Blue Ribbon beer can. Floyd knew how to pose as invisible in a crowd. When two separate groups of men left their cars, he got out and headed for the entrance, timing his pace to arrive with the small crowd.

Floyd wore a pair of worn jeans, a white, short-sleeved shirt, and black cowboy boots. Wearing nothing specific that would be noticed, nothing that later might mark his identity, he easily blended in with the group. Floyd needed to verify what McKenzie had witnessed, and be sure that SLED should be involved versus the local law enforcement. He needed to be sure this call for help was not just a turf war within this local jurisdiction.

He merged with the herd now forming in the bar area. He stepped forward, ordered a Bud, and moved in another path, through the crowd, toward the men's room and Bo J's post. McKenzie had briefed Floyd, and so far everything was exactly as described. He was well trained and skilled in undercover reconnaissance and blessed with an uncanny ability to collect and mentally record the infinite details of a room, a building, people, or any number of situational environments. He was the right man for this job.

Bo J was standing at his post, his back against the wall, wearing his goon suit, his hands crossed in front, with a serious, pissed-off look on his face and a bandage on his forehead. Floyd could sense tension in the ranks. On his first look, he had merely passed by, not staring, just casually looking around and checking the crowd. Floyd dropped a quarter in a pinball machine located in a far corner of the room, played a game, and then headed back toward the bar, moving with the crowd.

He noticed a heavy black curtain behind and to the left side of the bar. He positioned himself directly across the bar from the curtain and under a TV tuned to a Turner Satellite Station broadcasting an Atlanta Braves and Cincinnati Reds baseball game. He had noticed the occasional bartender or waitress pass in and out of the curtain with large quantities of liquor bottles and cases of beer for the bar. Floyd surmised a storage room and maybe an office were concealed behind the shield.

Moments later the curtain opened, and Tony strutted out, smoking a huge Cuban cigar. Following him were two women, one good-looking, middle-aged lady with a frozen smile tripping along entirely too giddy, and the other, a well-endowed, too-young, cheaply attractive girl exposing her trailer-park heritage. The ladies were red-eyed and laughing.

Floyd recognized the symptoms; the evidence was visually apparent, but not enough to initiate an arrest. Even the unlit joint tucked behind the young girl's ear was insufficient for a SLED task-force deployment. He recognized Tony from McKenzie's description. While the curtain was held open for the girls to pass through, Floyd saw a door down the hallway past the kitchen. Tony escorted the ladies off into the crowd.

At the end of the bar was a large collection tray that the wait staff used for stacking dirty plates and glasses. Floyd stepped over and expertly lifted the half-full tray to rest over his shoulder. He headed for the kitchen just like he knew what he was doing, acting as a helpful busboy. With every worker in the bar moving fast and furious, serving the crowd, no one took the time to question his helpful action. He set the tray down with the other dirty dishes on a stainless-steel table in the kitchen and glided through Tony's office door in one smooth, continuous movement.

He could smell the residual, mingled fumes from the pot and the cigar. Two bags of pot were open on the table. He snapped pictures with his miniature camera and moved over behind the desk. He pulled a kit from his back pocket to capture fingerprint samples and then quickly opened the desk drawers. Two handguns, a nine-millimeter, a forty-five caliber, and a blackjack were in the first drawer, an account book in the next drawer. Floyd snapped more pictures. He checked the telephone speed dial for Tony's important numbers. He recorded the top five and then snatched a few New York and Chicago numbers from the Rolodex. It was time to move on. As Floyd grabbed the office door handle to exit, he heard Tony's laugh coming from the hallway. With his exit blocked, he turned, looking for a quick second refuge. The room had two other doors. The first he opened was a small closet with shelves. He went through the second door and closed it as Tony stepped into his office.

Floyd's focus switched from the anxiety of his narrow escape to his present circumstance. He found himself in a full gambling casino: blackjack, roulette, slot machines, craps, the whole nine yards. The joint was full of loud people gambling and drinking. Floyd quickly gained his composure and moved to blend in the crowd. He watched how they played, where the money changed and the pit boss, all while acting as a casual observer, no eye contact, no obvious stares.

Floyd glided through the crowd. He watched a man exit through a door marked "Bar and Restrooms." He calmly walked to the exit and left. As he went out the door, he passed Bo J, walked through the men's room, into the restaurant and out the front door with enough information to call in the rest of the SLED team. Floyd climbed in the truck and cranked it, with a puff of blue smoke belching from the tailpipe. He backed out of the parking space with the engine sputtering, jammed the gearshift into first, stepped heavy on the gas, popped the clutch, squealed a tire, and scattered gravel as he fishtailed out of the lot. Again he was unnoticed, blending in perfectly with his surroundings.

Chapter 49

Red-eyed, toked up, primed, and full of youthful, misguided testosterone, Vernon, Harley, and David sat in the Frisky Rabbit guzzling pitchers of cheap beer and celebrating their release from jail. Their clueless minds were not burdened with the future consequences of their recent activities. Vernon was not one to fret over such mundane issues as the pending, multiple, felony charges, not when an opportunity to party presented itself.

Vernon was in his element, stoned in a raunchy bar, raising hell, surrounded by his team, all of whom appeared to adore him as their charismatic leader. He loved the lead-dog position and the admiration of his new crew. No police force, judge, or jury was going to dampen his buzz.

He was "the man" in this Frisky Rabbit world, with this crowd of dealers all working for him, expanding his domain, developing concentric defenses to his turf like the dukes, lords, and knights to their king. The attendants to this drug king's court grew as the night progressed. Vernon funded the feast of chips and cheese-salsa dip and enhanced the bar banquet with a bounty of large pitchers of beer. Predictably, the free beer attracted a hoard of freeloaders.

Vernon had dressed appropriately for this celebratory occasion. He wore cutoff ragged denim shorts that were too short, with holes in all the wrong places. Fortunately, he had also selected a complementary oversized white T-shirt that said, "I'm with Stupid." A partner would be easy to find in this group.

He strutted effortlessly through this tight crowd, with his lanky, awkward physique exaggerated by permanently hunched shoulders. An invisible force emanating from the free beer tightly bound the swirling school of fair-weather party friends. Vernon worked the crowd and ordered more beer to refuel the force. With a smile Booney brought two more pitchers to the table and wisely demanded cash. Vernon moved directly in front of each party participant, pushed his black, thick-rimmed glasses up on his nose, held his fist high in the air, and shouted, "PARRR-TAYY!" The reply was always the same: the repeated shout back, a raised glass, a raised hand, and a slap on the back. Neither intellectual nor intimate personal conversations had a place here.

Beach music, heavy metal, and Southern rock permeated every corner of the bar. A thick layer of secondhand smoke merged with the fibers of the bar patron's clothes, while the music settled into the fiber of their souls. Queen, the Doobie Brothers, Black Sabbath, the Allman Brothers, Steely Dan, the Tams, the Drifters, and Lynyrd Skynyrd all played at the Frisky Rabbit that night. Air guitars and mass singing to popular lines were common, as the tunes and words were well-known. The bar rocked; it vibrated with music, and the crowd loved it.

Vernon stepped over to fill his beer cup and waited his turn behind an almost-legal, bleached blonde oozing with the aroma of suntan lotion and clean hair. He was stunned, love struck. She was just his type...tonight. Her tight, threadbare, Daisy Duke denim shorts were just short enough to expose the tight lower curve of her buttocks. Her skimpy halter top contained some portion, but certainly not all, of her thirty-six D-cup breast. She stepped confidently in what appeared to be uncomfortable white stiletto heels with crosshatched straps laced up her ankle and calf. Even at her illegal age, she carried the confidence of an experienced woman, and wearing her "fuck me" pumps was the exclamation point to her packaged appearance. She was clearly hot for some action and was throwing her tempting chum to the nightspot sharks. Vernon read the blunt message correctly. If necessary, he would learn her name and the color of her eyes later, but for now he was applying for the obvious open position.

He stepped forward with his standard "PARRR-TAYY!" greeting and received the complementary response from the not-too-recently christened blonde. Vernon's eyes never met hers as he stared directly at her abundant cleavage and shouted his best pickup line over the final notes of "Free Bird." It was a rare occasion when he interrupted his air-guitar accompaniment of this tune, but this young lady gushed with the persona of his favorite type of woman.

"What's up?" Vernon said with a smile.

The young lady did, however, notice the color of Vernon's eyes—red. She had been observing the dynamics of this group since entering the bar with her fake ID. The doorman was slightly suspicious of the validity of her credentials with what appeared to be altered print under "DOB," because he was reasonably certain that the DMV did not use a pen to scratch in a date on a license. But the maturity of her smirk, the size of her breasts, and her hand on the inside of his upper thigh helped resolve any questions, and she entered the Frisky Rabbit. The free beer was just a bonus.

"You got any pot?" she asked.

The fake blonde was not one for mixing words, playing mind games, practicing verbal jousting, or using suggestive innuendoes, unless it got her what she wanted. To fit in the popular social cliques while growing up in her small hometown, she had often feigned an inability to have a coherent conversation, only occasionally blending a word or thoughtful phrase between "like, ah," "ya know," and "ya hear what I'm sayin'." She was, however, considered the most intellectual of her gang. She wanted and needed more, so she had moved to the beach.

For the last few weeks, she had been earning her spending money dancing at the Happy Snapper, and now Tony had her assigned to this extracurricular activity. She had moved up, quickly propelled by her hypnotic sexual swagger. What she lacked in highbrow social graces and a classical educational résumé, she made up with a natural genius to manipulate men, especially young, unsophisticated braggarts like Vernon. He was her type. They were perfect for each other.

"Sure, baby, I've always got pot. You ever want some, just come see old Vernon or one of my boys." Vernon draped his arms around the necks of two of his comrades and squeezed while smiling at his new love. His knights grimaced but stood rigid at his side. Wanting to be part of the conversation with the hot blonde, one of Vernon's young pot-selling dukes stepped up to Vernon, laughing and asking if they had heard about the two old men found tied up in the Ocean Reefer.

The young duke laughed. "They're looking for three suspects, and here's the weird part, the descriptions sounded just like you three. But one of the old geezers died, so I knew it couldn't be you, but it was weird, man." The accumulated effect of the pot and beer was not good for this young man.

Vernon laughed. "Are you shittin' me, man? It *was* us, asshole!"

She had her man. "Like, ah, what's your name, handsome?"

"Vernon."

"Ohhh! I like that! So you are, like, the pusher-man around here."

"Yea, that's me, baby! So what's *upppp*..." Vernon's verbal skills were often limited, especially in these circumstances. His mind was not occupied with the complexities of romance.

"Well, I, like, ah, you know, I want some now, man. Ya see what I'm sayin'?" She stepped up, grabbed Vernon's belt, and pulled him closer, positioning her cleavage just below his nose. The man was helpless.

"Well, OK, darlin', let's go."

Vernon put his arm around her neck and chugged the rest of his beer as they headed for the door. The beer dripped from the edges of his cup and down each side of his chin. He stopped, slammed down his cup, turned, put one hand with a split-finger peace sign high in the air, and shouted a parting salutation.

"PARRR-TAYY, motherfuckers!" He grabbed the blonde and left.

"That son of a bitch is gonna leave us here with no ride. Asshole!" Harley recognized that the party, the free beer, and his ride all walked out the door with Vernon. As the beer gradually disappeared, so did the adoring crowd. No one offered to buy the next round. A trip to the toilet, and the beer, the bonding, and the newfound party friendships were all flushed away.

Chapter 50

Evelyn left her shift early and went to the hospital to continue her nightly vigil over Guido. As promised Vera had been standing guard over Guido's large, broken, comatose body.

"Vera, honey, why don't you go on home? You look exhausted. Go home, get some rest, and see that man of yours."

"Oh, OK, dear. I suppose Eddie wonders where I am. You know he worries about me so. And lately I've been worried about him. His mind seems to be somewhere else, and he is so cross with the world. After I take a nap, maybe I'll fix him some nice soup. I don't remember him ever being like this."

"Vera, I think I love Guido."

"Oh honey, you sure act like it. I'm betting he loves you too. How could he not?"

"But I'm afraid. I'm afraid that me being with Guido and Edna with McKenzie will cause Edna and me to...to go different ways, and I don't want that. But we both...I guess sooner or later we both would end up growing apart, or we would just end up old maids in your garage apartment."

"Oh honey, you two will always be great friends, you know that."

"I just wish all of this turmoil would end. Someday soon I would love to have Guido and me and Edna and McKenzie all sit down together for dinner at the same table and maybe go out to a movie together, just like one big happy family."

"Oh sweetheart, you will, you'll see. It will all be just perfect. Eddie and I love you girls like you were our own."

"Well, Vera, things have been pretty weird lately—we'll be OK soon. We love you and Eddie too. You are so good to us. Now get on home and get some rest."

Evelyn picked up the bedside telephone and called Edna. "Edna, hon, you stay home. I can handle this. Don't you worry."

The emotional bond that had solidified through the years was now showing a slight separation. Edna and Evelyn were faced with a conundrum: the diametric forces of new love and long-loved family.

Evelyn crawled into the hospital bed and maneuvered her small frame against Guido's massive body, hoping her warmth and affection would give Guido the extra strength to survive, wake up, and be a smiling face again. Tony's henchman assigned to watch Guido stepped into the room to check on him. Even this heart-hardened goon felt the tenderness of this human bonding and quietly melted away to allow the couple the private serenity of this moment.

Evelyn ran the tip of her finger along Guido's cheekbone and softly sang, "Under the boardwalk, down by the sea-eee-yea, on a hospital bed with my baaaby, that's where I'll be."

Guido smiled a short but distinctive smile.

She saw it and picked her head up, leaning on his shoulder and trying to confirm what she had just seen, but he now lay stone-faced as he had before. This small movement had been the first anyone had seen since the wreck.

She sang the verse again. "Under the boardwalk, down by the sea-eee-yea, on a hospital bed with my baaaby." This time Guido moved his lips to the verse and smiled. Evelyn's eyes went wide. She squealed a soft, high-pitched, "Guido, honey, are you there? Can you open your eyes? Guido?" Evelyn was now sitting up, hovering over Guido's face.

His eyelids fluttered, and he smiled as his consciousness floated back through a foggy tunnel to a light of marginal awareness. He could hear her, but he could not quite gather the clarity sufficient for a response. His view gradually adjusted as Evelyn's face appeared, framed by a fuzzy circle. She was pulling him into the conscious world. Her words were far away in a tunnel, but getting closer. He wanted to see her clearly, talk to her, but like a dream, he struggled with all his soul.

Evelyn whispered his name again and brushed her finger over his lips and cheeks. His eyes opened. He smiled, but could not talk, not yet. Evelyn hugged him with a careful, tender intensity. She wanted to do no harm to his battered body. She looked at his face, and his eyes were open, blinking eyelids and dilated pupils searching for the way back. His mouth and lips were dry. She got up and grabbed a cup with ice chips, tenderly placing a few wet flakes on his lips.

"Evelyn," Guido said hoarsely. "What happened?"

"I'm so glad you came back to me. You're going to be OK, I just know it. I'm right here, honey, right here."

Guido was now awake, but tired. She talked. He mumbled responses. She told him about the wreck. She shared details of the last two days. She asked him why he had a personal goon guard, but she got no answer. Evelyn sang softly again until Guido fell asleep. She continued to snuggle by his side and gradually drifted into a relieved slumber, calm and satisfied.

Chapter 51

Vernon was both chemically and emotionally high. Within the irresponsible realm of his mind, he had no troubles and not a care in the world. He was in his prime physically, but his mental development had unfortunately maxed out. He had developed a loyal following among his group of like-minded boys, and now he had a hot young girlfriend, at least for tonight. That's the way he liked his girls—just for the night.

He watched her strut out of the bar as he shuffled along a cool distance behind. She knew it and let him follow, and follow he did, like a lion on the prowl, stalking his tender, young prey for this night's conquest. The hunter became the hunted. Vernon had no clue that he was being controlled, pulled out like a bull with a ring in his nose. He was pulled by an invisible chain, tethered with links built by the potential for sex.

As they went through the doorway, she turned around and said, "Let's smoke in my car. I like to drive while I'm getting high. It makes me horny." The girl taunted him with irresistible bait.

She was driving a candy-apple-red, convertible Chevy Camaro with a 327-cubic-inch engine and a chrome Hurst four-speed shifter that was adorned with an eight-ball knob on the top. A pair of fuzzy pink-and-white dice hung from the rearview mirror. To complete the package, a three-inch-high plastic, Hawaiian, grass-skirted dancer was glued to the dashboard, dancing her dance as the car rumbled out of the parking lot.

Some of Vernon's gang had come out under the guise of seeing him off, but more likely they wanted to get a toke of what he and the girl would be smoking. As the car threw rocks, smoke, rubber, and caution to the wind, Vernon turned around and got up on his knees in the seat. He held both hands high above his head, his fingers formed peace-sign Vs, and he shouted his best rebel yell to announce his exuberant departure.

"Yeeeehaaaw, mutha fuckersssss!" He was pure class. Vernon turned around beaming and sat in the passenger's seat. The girl gave a casual glance in both directions before peeling out onto Kings Highway. The rear end fishtailed, leaving two parallel strips of hot, melted rubber and the requisite plume of blue exhaust. The night was young, and so was she.

The girl downshifted and braked to a stop at the next red light, handling the vibrating, raw power of the car with an ease beyond her years. The car shimmied in a metallic dance, keeping time with the powerful engine. She reached over and pushed a classic-style, eight-track tape of Elton John into the still-working eight-track player stereo, and the four speakers blared out "Take Me to Your Pilot," the early Elton days, the radio-station, live-studio version.

"Light the joint, honey; I want to get high and horny." She was vigorously smacking her chewing gum with nervous excitement, staring ahead at the light, hands gripping the steering wheel at the ten and two positions, focused like a dragster waiting for the green-light countdown.

Vernon was in absolute heaven. He could see the cold-blooded mischief in her eyes, like a shark easing up for the kill. He watched as she revved the engine and moved her right hand from the wheel to rub her palm on the eight-ball shifter.

She was anxious to jam the gear in place, stomp the aftermarket, chrome, foot-shaped gas pedal to the floor, and test the raw power of this machine one more time. Just before the light turned green, just as her senses said it was time to move, she slowly turned her head with her eyes wide open and cast an intense laser stare into Vernon's mesmerized eyes. She slammed the gear into first, popped the clutch, and gave the machine all the gas it could drink.

The power and positive traction laid them back in their seats. Without a flicker of her eyelids, without a glance to the road ahead, she calmly said, "Light up the goddamned joint or get the fuck out!" She slammed the Hurst shifter into second and squealed the tires again as the engine rose to the occasion, responding obediently to her demand for speed.

Vernon thought out loud, "I'm in love." He was considering keeping her around for a couple of nights or maybe for a whole week.

"Well, exxcuuussse me, baby! Sorry!" Vernon laughed, reached in his pocket, and slipped out his pack of Marlboro Reds. He pulled out what appeared to be a cigarette, pulled off the filter, and stoked up the doobie, choking on the first potent hit. He reached over and passed the joint as she shifted to fourth.

She cruised through another green light while pulling two long, head-numbing hits. Staring straight ahead, timing a clean run through the next light, the girl asked, "Are you man enough to chug a shot of tequila?"

"Why, hell yeah, darlin'!" Vernon answered.

"Reach in the glove box."

Vernon popped the glove box to retrieve a quart bottle half-full of Jose Cuervo Gold, pulled the red hat-topped cork stopper out of the bottle, and took a long chug.

"Honey," she said with the joint hanging out the corner of her mouth, "grab some salt and those lemons outta there too. I come prepared. I love a man that's got that tequila wildness in him. Makes him a superman."

"Jose has always been a friend of mine," Vernon said as he licked the salt, chugged the tequila, and bit into a lemon wedge.

The girl pulled through the last stoplight before merging onto an open unimpeded section of Highway 501 West. She let the engine have its fill of ninety-eight octane and moved on into the cooling wind of the night. Vernon, driven by desire, reached over to grab her thigh. She laid her leg open to his touch.

"Hey, baby, take another shot of that tequila. If you're the man I think you are, you will." Vernon was just about at his limit, but the tether to the ring in his nose was pulled tight. One more hit on Jose, and Vernon saw only the blur of strip-mall lights.

"Here, honey, try this, it'll really make you a wild man." She slipped the white tab in his obedient mouth, and he swallowed with another chug of Jose Cuervo. Vernon never knew what hit him as the dark night grew darker, and he fell into a cavern of deep sleep.

A few moments later, she whipped the Camaro into the parking lot of the Happy Snapper Oyster Bar and Strip Club. She drove past the parked rental cars of the tourist patrons and behind the building through a gate marked "Employees Only." Elton John was singing "Like a Candle in the Wind." The mob now had Vernon. His wet dream would become a stormy nightmare.

Chapter 52

~

Closing time at the Frisky Rabbit found Harley and David alone playing a pinball machine. The energetic swirl and hearty camaraderie of the party crowd was gone and quickly forgotten, but a bloated beer buzz lingered as a loyal confidant. The drinking had not stopped with Vernon's departure, but the remaining holdouts had to pay for their own beer. While playing the last ball, they slammed the sides of the pinball machine until it tilted. Game over!

"OK, fellows, time to go, the party's over. Gotta close this place." With a helpful nudge from Booney, they left to find a way home.

"Hey, man, we need a ride home." Harley really didn't know the guy, but he had been drinking free beer with them for three hours. The only response was the squealing of tires leaving the parking lot.

"Hey, there's Rick. Hey, Rick, we need a ride, man. Help us out, dude?"

"Sorry, guys. Got a late date. See ya." Rick whipped his car across two parking lots, crossed Kings Highway without looking, and disappeared into the night.

David stepped in front of a car with Debra and Dianne, two inebriated young ladies who had been sitting very close to them while the beer had flowed.

"Hey, babes, we need a ride. We are only fifteen blocks south. Can you help us out?"

"Hey, dudes, we're only going twelve blocks south, so that's kinda out of our way. Can you move, or am I gonna have to run over you?" He didn't budge. She backed the car up and drove around, music blaring, windows down, and the girls dancing in their seats.

The lot was almost cleared. They were too drunk to continue pleading for a lift. They gave up and walked away happy, singing loudly, zigzagging generally in an eastward direction toward Ocean Boulevard and the beach. They might hitch a ride from someone cruising the boulevard at two in the morning. People were always cruising the boulevard.

Harley and David would need to walk two blocks along First Avenue North to reach the boulevard. This section of the street between Kings Highway and Ocean Boulevard was shadowy dark, with no streetlights, and had been the site of their accident just two nights before. They didn't care.

As they stumbled along, they repeatedly sang a single verse from their favorite Tams song. "What kind of fool do you think I am? What kind of fool do you think I am?" Although many answers would be correct, no one was around to respond. They were singing loud, off-key, and could not remember any other words of the song. Harley randomly confused the words of a song by the Drifters, "Under the Boardwalk, down at, down...ah, the sea, yeah," and David sang, "What kind of fool." They were bad but were not aware.

As they passed the Hutches apartments, Harley stopped by a high Ligustrum hedge.

"Hey, man. Look over there."

"What?"

"I hear, ah, I hear 'Smoke on the Water,' dude."

"What?"

"Yeah, the Tilt-a-Whirl, man. The Tilt-a-Whirl. That's crazy, man." In the darkness of the amusement park, the lights of the ride were easy to see.

"Wow, weird, man." David stared at the park.

"I gotta piss, man." Harley stumbled off the road and groped his way along the hedge that bordered Eddie and Vera's yard. He unzipped and started to pee. He tilted his head back and looked at the stars. Smack! His lights went out and he hit the ground.

David quickly grew impatient while standing in the dark street, looking up at the stars and humming a tune he was not sure of, trying to keep his balance. He too had the sudden urge to pee, and in his current condition, he was not nearly as shy as Harley about where he relieved himself. He took two steps off the street and unzipped while standing in the Rondells' front yard.

Merely urinating would have been too mundane for this party night; David decided to paint figure-eight patterns in the sand and grass bordering the asphalt street. In his hazy euphoria, singing loudly, poorly, and repetitively, David held both hands up to the moonlit starry night while moving his hips back and forth, splattering lines in the grass. It was not a pretty scene. David finished his uninhibited performance, zipped, and turned to go find what the hell Harley was doing. As he turned, mumbling the chorus to "Smoke on the Water," he saw the silhouetted outline of a man standing deeper in the shadows of the trees and hedge. He thought it was Harley.

"Hey, man, what the—"

The man said, "Hey, punk," just before stepping forward with a huge fist, and planting a powerful punch firmly on David's jaw. Lights out, and down he went.

When David came around, he had a sore jaw and an aching head. He felt the pain of tight, heavyweight, fishing line cutting into his wrist and ankles. He was lying in the back of an old truck. He attempted to move, but his body was covered with a heavy, waxed, sailcloth tarp and concrete blocks. He was lying on his face and gagged with a rolled cloth and duct tape. Breathing was difficult. Something moved beside him, and he struggled to turn his head to see Harley, gagged and wild-eyed with drunken fright.

The old truck turned down a dirt road and bounced hard in and out of large water-filled potholes. Harley and David were tossed about violently. David's head slammed against the rough, splintered, plywood board that covered the truck's rusty bed. On the next bump, he turned his head slightly to avoid hitting his cheek and came down hard, cracking his nose. Blood gushed from one side as he struggled to breathe. He tried to turn, but the tangle of bodies, tarp, ropes, and fishing line yielded no mercy. After being struck by a flying concrete block, Harley flopped about unconscious. David bounced and suffered.

The truck did not slow down as it twisted and jostled wildly down the muddy, bumpy, dirt road, heading farther from the highway and deeper into the swamp. As the truck skidded around a sharp curve and hit a deep, muddy hole in the road, another concrete block bounced up and came down hard on David's side, cracking and bruising rib bones. He felt a new pain taking his mind off his headache and busted nose. Finally, mercifully, the truck stopped.

In the swamp the early-morning hours were inky dark. The trees blocked out the minimally illuminating effects of the subsiding, sleepy moon. David was dazed, but he could hear the truck door slam and the tarp covering the bed of the pickup being removed. The man said little as he went about his work. David was glad the brutal ride on the rough dirt road was over, but he wasn't ready to endure whatever might happen next. Common wisdom would suggest the worst was yet to come, but David was not blessed with common wisdom. He tried to speak, but only mumbled in the gag.

David heard the clank and thud of heavy metal and wood banging against the truck bed, scraping the tailgate on the way out. He listened to a periodic metallic squeak as his captor went about preparation—for what, David could not imagine. He had no idea why this man was doing whatever it was he was doing. David felt a large, rough, abrasive coil of rope being dragged across his shin and out of the back of the truck.

Harley had finally come around to a painful consciousness. He began twisting and tugging frantically against his bonds.

The big man returned, grabbed Harley by his ankles, and pulled. His head banged on the tailgate before his body dropped to the ground.

David could hear the muffled groans as Harley was dragged through the dirt and underbrush. The metal squeaked again; he could hear more muffled screams.

David's heart was pumping hard; every pulse was a hammer hit pushing his headache back into a competition for the most painful part of his body. Fear and pain battled for his attention. David lay still and listened for what seemed an eternity; this eternity was too short.

The captor grabbed David's legs and pulled him from the truck. Again David suffered excruciating pain from his busted ribs and his broken nose. The man pulled him by his bound ankles through the muddy road, underbrush, and aromatic, mucky, pluff mud on the edge of the brackish river. David was lying on his back looking up and around anxiously at a railway trestle, cypress, trees and a tidal river. He could see ropes and pulleys attached to the base of the bridge.

The man worked methodically, not wasting any time with indecision about the details of his task. Either he was a professional, with very specific instructions on techniques to terrorize his victims before killing them, or a crazed, psycho, serial killer with way too much free time to plan his tortures. In either case David assumed he was screwed. He couldn't move, he couldn't scream.

The man placed a set of stainless-steel handcuffs on David's wrists. He then cut away the now-redundant fishing line and attached a galvanized anchor chain to the cuffs. The chain was attached to a rope that had been threaded through a pulley on the train trestle. The man yanked the opposite end of the rope, put a strain on the pulley, and dragged David, with his hands above his head, to the edge of the water.

"Son, you come to my town, you abuse it and act like you own it. You get drunk, get loud, and piss in my yard. I keep trying to warn you punks to go home, but I guess you're just too damn hardheaded to get it. So I'm going to make it clear for you tonight. I'm going to help you understand the error of your ways."

While Eddie talked, he kept working to complete his mission. He pulled out a knife and cut off David's shirt and shorts. The mosquitoes gathered to feast on his naked body. He pulled two putrid, raw, chicken necks from a plastic bag and tied one around David's head, causing the chicken neck to dangle between his eyes. It smelled. The second chicken neck was tied around David's waist, with the smelly meat hanging to his crotch.

"Crabs just love chicken necks. All the crabs downstream will smell this meat and come get it. Trouble is, they can't see very well, and there's only a little meat here on this string. Truth be told, they aren't all that discriminating. I'm sure they will like you just as well."

Eddie started to pull the rope to drag David to the river.

"You smell too. They'll go for the soft tissue first, like your eyes and balls. When this tide goes in and out a few times, all kinds of fish, crabs, alligators, and maybe if we are lucky, a bull shark or two may find their way up this river. The sharks follow the bait pods that come up here from the marshes. After a couple tide changes, you'll be wishing a shark gets you. It's about low tide now, so have fun. I hope you learn to hate this place."

David could see Harley was already in the river, tied and struggling against the outgoing current. The captor put the rope over his shoulder and started walking, pulling David across the pluff mud and oysters, slicing his back and legs before he hit the sting of salt-tainted freshwater. The man kept pulling the rope through the pulley until David's feet and legs were in the river. His arms were pulled above his head, his lower body from waist down was in the water, and he was not comfortable.

Chapter 53

In the morning Vera had gone to the retirement village, where she had empathized and tended to the lugubrious mood of the seniors, many distraught by the loss of their friend Marvin and the injuries to Frank. The elderly duo's friends at the home had been wringing their hands, some sobbing and continuously shaking their heads as they attempted to comprehend the villainous nature of a person who would cause harm to these fine gentlemen. They had lamented in the deterioration of the morals of mankind. What had happened to their happy, fun-loving paradise?

Vera had just hugged them. She had no answers, but as always she gave them unconditional love and affection. She gave them hope and encouragement. She gave them strength. She had listened. Someone outside their retirement-home world cared, and they felt better.

Before Vera had left the retirement home, she led the group in a prayer asking for peace, love, and caring, asking that Frank be quickly healed, and that Thelma's children might finally come to visit. The last request had come as a quiet suggestion whispered by the head nurse. Vera knew they all cared for one another. Their friendships in the home were mostly all they had.

She had already been emotionally tested by the time she arrived to monitor Guido. He was quiet, so she had read and knitted, but the process had still been exhausting.

After turning the care of Guido over to Evelyn, she happened to see a friend from church following a medic as he quickly pushed a patient in from an ambulance.

"Amy...what on earth?"

"Ralph had a heart attack, I think."

"Are you OK, hon?"

"No, I'm not. Thank God you're here. Lord knows I needed someone to talk to."

Vera stayed until finally a nurse came out with good news.

Vera arrived home around one in the morning, weary from her long day of caring and ready to enjoy her own peace and quiet. Just outside, the noise and the cancerous growth of progress in paradise engulfed her hope for restful peace. She looked out her kitchen window and longed for the solitude gained from a walk in a forest isolated from the noise pollution of humanity, isolated from the sound of cars racing on the highway with the unrelenting chorus of their asphalt and rubber song. She longed for the solitude of a long walk on a remote winter beach, where only sea gulls and the fiddler crabs would compete with those seeking the seclusion. Vera turned and surveyed the quaint and subtle comforts of her home. She loved the security and its meager sanctity, but it was no longer a romantic cottage in paradise. It was just home in the noisy city.

Eddie was not home. He had been sleeping late the last few days. She thought perhaps he had been feeling ill. Lately he had seemed so detached, or maybe depressed. Why was he out so late? She was too tired to think about that now, and tomorrow would be another full day. She thought maybe he was night fishing on the pier. He often fished late on the pier, especially when his mood was down. She walked to the bedroom and found a note on her pillow. "Gone fishing—Love, Eddie."

Vera got ready for bed and collapsed under the solace of the familiar quilt that her mother had made. She was asleep shortly after her head hit the pillow.

Vera had neglected to read her Bible verse for the evening, but Vera was an angel. She could skip the Bible tonight, and God would understand.

Before dawn Eddie turned off Second Avenue into his back driveway, killed the truck's engine and headlights, and rolled to a stop. He stripped to his undershorts, stepped into the outdoor beach shower, and washed away the mud and sweat from the night. Eddie quietly eased into the house and into the bed without waking Vera. He had some small bit of self-satisfaction that had curbed his anger and released some of the stored tension that fueled a dangerous anxiety. He was exhausted and quickly joined Vera in a deep sleep.

Chapter 54

Skeeter McGill was running a load of pot for RayRay. He maneuvered two flat-bottom riverboats around the tight curves of a marsh creek. The second camouflaged boat was tied behind the first with a ten-foot anchor line. Skeeter knew the shifting currents, the deepwater channels in each turn, and the hidden dangers below the surface of the river. He had memorized the locations of all the oyster beds and the paths through the maze of channels near the coast.

Skeeter had instructions to meet a shrimp boat two miles upriver from the coast. He anchored and waited in a small muddy creek perpendicular to the main inland coastal waterway. He didn't want to arouse suspicion, so he fished while he waited. The empty second boat, with its duck blind of marsh reeds attached, was tucked away in a narrow, high-tide creek, hidden from the river.

When he spotted the shrimp boat's signature rigging and pulsing diesel exhaust towering over the marsh grass, he quickly pulled in his lines and retrieved his hidden boat. Skeeter accepted the illicit load packed in large black plastic bags, filling both johnboats from the shrimp boat as it chugged steadily up the waterway at five knots. With the transaction quickly completed, he pushed off, gunned the motor, and within minutes was headed home, concealed by the estuarial maze. The shrimp boat, a silhouette on the moonlit marsh, churned forward on its slow, monotonous pace bound for its home dock, three miles farther along the coastal waterway.

Skeeter guided his boats along a hidden creek fenced on both sides by marsh mud and thick, high grass. Two white egrets launched off the bank, flying to safety. The creek eventually joined back with the main river ten miles farther inland.

As he skimmed upriver in the dark, he passed his favorite river house situated on a high bluff, a well-selected haven typically safe from storms, floods, and the swamp's high water collected from the runoff of heavy rains. Skeeter loved the house and was amazed by the contradiction of this luxury in the swamp. The lot offered a view down a stretch of the river that provided a perfectly aligned stage for the setting sun. He passed this spot on the river often, but he could not remember ever seeing anyone on the property. He found it curious that the grounds and the uninhabited river mansion were so well maintained, but rarely enjoyed by its absentee owners.

The stretch of river that carved a path by the house was near enough to the coast to recognize the tidal change. The water that flowed back and forth was brackish. Three miles downriver was saltwater, three miles upriver was freshwater. The house was uniquely located at the juxtaposition of the river's life, the ending of one ecological environment and the beginning of another, a flexing barrier, a place where creatures from two worlds lived. Sometimes crabs, sharks, or even porpoises would venture upriver in pursuit of food, until the diluted salinity of the freshwater caused them to suffer, and they would return to a more hospitable environment. Catfish, bass, sunfish, and alligators would venture downstream until the salinity drove them back home.

The barrier was not well defined, but the creatures sensed it and were affected by the changes. While the natural curiosity, adaptability, and hardiness of each species set the limits of their ventures into an inhospitable environment, this neutral zone was a beautiful paradise conducive to the needs of both worlds. For whatever Skeeter was, he respected and admired the forces of nature, and he knew how to survive on both sides of the line.

After several big bends and another mile up the river, Skeeter approached an easily identified river landmark, the Atlantic Coastline Rail Trestle. In the scant moonlight, he saw two unusual lines hanging from the railway trestle down into the river. Not wanting to get tangled in ropes or nets, he slowed to a crawl, holding a slow, steady pace moving upstream against the current.

Two large forms struggled in the water, splashing in the current. His first thought was that a couple of gators or some large catfish had been caught. People in this area often tied heavy-duty fishing line to trees or other structures spanning a creek branch or even over the main river. They baited large hooks with smelly, rotted meat to entice their prey and would leave the tempting lures for a couple of days. The fishermen's trap normally yielded a large river creature.

Skeeter was always on the lookout for such dangerous devices when he guided his boat along the murky waterway in the dark. He didn't want to take anyone's catch, or tangle with an angry alligator, or whatever these two huge, splashing creatures were, so he kept a safe distance in passing. His curiosity, however, forced him close enough to at least identify the hooked prey.

In the dark Skeeter could make out a human form, the feet and legs lashing furiously at the surface of the water. He closed in-between the two forms, his boat engine idling at a speed equal to the current, holding a steady position between the two hog-tied humans.

He was cautious and took a little time to contemplate the situation. He heard the distinctive sound of a large gator splashing off a nearby sandbar as it raced for the safety of an underwater tree stump. Skeeter guessed the gator had been watching and waiting for these two to settle down and die and their flesh to ripen to his taste. His dinner would be easier to consume and digest after the meat softened a bit. Gators could be patient predators.

Skeeter also considered that whoever had put these two here was powerful enough to do it, and angry enough to want them to die a slow and painful death. This setup was a torture killing, intended to send a vivid message to others who might think about crossing the wrong line. Like the life of the river, these drug creatures normally did not wander far from their natural habitat.

Skeeter could not imagine what these boys had done to the predators on the human side of the brackish line, but he knew what the predators, large and small, on nature's side could do to them, and it wouldn't be pretty. Regardless of their transgression, no matter whose turf they crossed, they didn't deserve this slow death. If he saved them, he could meet a similar fate.

Skeeter's mental ping-pong game finally scored a point for humanity, and he decided to cut them down, but he would not give them a ride. He pulled out his knife and eased his boat over to the rope closest to shore. He grabbed the rope and looked at the naked man tied and gagged. Small crabs had already caused damage to his face. Several of the little pincher carnivores were crawling around his eyes, ears, and neck. Skeeter cut the main rope and tied the fellow's hands to a handle on the front of his boat. He expertly maneuvered to the other man, whose head was covered with small fiddler crabs, and cut his rope, likewise tying him off on the portside bow cleat. He maneuvered his boats to the sandbank where the gator had been waiting.

The two men were wounded, bleeding, and exhausted. Skeeter ran the bow of his boat up on the bank, dragging the two men onto the sand, half out of the water. As they crawled and squirmed out of the water, Skeeter released their ropes, threw an old fish fillet knife, sticking the blade in the sand, and quickly backed his boat off into the river again. He wanted no part of any piss and vinegar these guys might still have.

He pulled away and said, "There's a house about a mile down the river. It's best to just float downstream. The current will take you there on this falling tide. It's the only place around. Good luck. Whatever you boys did to get here, I'd suggest not doing it again."

Skeeter pushed the throttle forward and guided his boats upriver at full speed. In a few hours, forty-five miles up the river from the coast, he would deliver his load of pot.

Chapter 55

Harley and David had survived. They were miserable, but at least they were still alive. The crabs had picked away a portion of Harley's eyelid and some of the membrane around the edge of his eyes. David had similar damage but not quite as severe. His nostrils had been picked raw, and his crotch was bleeding. Both were paranoid about the gator that had been sunning on the sandbank all day and watching them with an unnerving, deathly stare. They had never been sure at what moment the reptile would decide to have dinner. Luckily they were still too alive for the eight-foot predator.

Both men were tired, naked, and hungry. More small fish, crabs, and insects had nibbled on them than they cared to count, and at the moment, large bloodthirsty mosquitoes and small sand gnats were sinking miniature pinchers into their skin and devouring their blood. They didn't want to put their shriveled bodies back in the water, but the bloodthirsty insects were insatiable. Large black horseflies joined the insect feast, intensifying their agony until finally the men decided to move.

David used the knife that Skeeter had left them to help Harley cut and remove the ropes that were tangled about their arms and legs. They pulled off their gags, but were still handcuffed. Even with their fear of the creatures that had attacked them without mercy, their pain and desire for survival forced them back into the tannic-brown water to float with the current as their rescuer had suggested. Anything was better than sitting here, being slowly sucked to death by millions of hungry, relentless insects; at least they believed nothing could be worse.

David and Harley floated side by side, easing into the river's current. The tide was pulling strong to the ocean. Still handcuffed, they couldn't swim so they used their remaining strength to tread water. Based on their experience with the river while being tied to the train trestle, they knew that at some point, the current would gradually slow after the tidal flush had taken what the river would give it, and eventually the moon-driven flow would give it back.

"Man, we need to kick, 'cause this water is slowing down. We ain't gonna make it to that house. What the hell is that?" Near the water's edge, a pair of glowing eyes floated with them on the surface. The eyes submerged, with a ripple cast in their direction.

"Where did it go?"

"Shit! Start kicking, man. Kick!"

Gradually exhaustion drained what little strength they had left. They slowed their frantic churn, and both rolled over to float on their backs, silent except for heavy breathing and groans of misery. With quiet they heard foxes barking, owls hooting, birds screeching, and other sounds of the night woods that were not easily identified.

"This place is spooky, man. If I get outta here, I ain't never comin' back, never!" Two large brown water snakes slithered on the surface, crossing their path undeterred just an arm's length away.

Two hours later as the tidal current was beginning to ebb, they saw a sandbar and a house on a bluff silhouetted by the cloud-filtered moonlight.

"David, I got a bad cramp, man. Help me, dude!"

David grabbed Harley's hair as he sank below the surface. He kicked twice more and felt the shifting, coarse sand with his toes. He dug in, pulling closer to the beach, and pushed Harley to the bank. They crawled and climbed onto a sandbar, wet, sandy, and covered with mosquitoes. After a moment they stood, testing the strength of their wobbling legs. Harley's leg cramped again, and he went to one knee until the twisted muscle released its painful grip. He pulled himself up on the dock.

Cautiously, they walked up the set of wooden stairs to the yard behind the house. There were no dogs, no lights, no cars, and no evidence of anyone home. Both men were in pain and bleeding from their ordeal. They were exhausted and desperate to return to their side of that invisible, flexible barrier of life, desperate to move upstream to their more hospitable home turf and a surprising survival.

David quietly climbed the steps to an unlocked screen porch, a potential haven from the relentless biting bugs. Harley was still picking fiddler crabs from his hair. David broke a windowpane in a French door, unlocked the dead bolt, and slipped in. His senses focused on the potential presence of life or alarms, and he found neither. He went straight to the kitchen, with Harley three steps behind.

Confident no one was home, David relaxed and moved to find a pantry and a light. With a bit more boldness, he discovered a treasure of canned goods. They ate soup and canned meats and vegetables. They drank fresh water and juice. Although he was full, a visceral force kept David rummaging through the well-stocked pantry until he discovered a panacea in a bottle: eighteen-year-old scotch. David took the bottle and announced his treasured discovery to Harley. They were still cuffed, but after more searching, they found shorts to cover their wounded genitals and shirts to drape over their shoulders. They headed for the screen porch. The porch was cooled by a night breeze whispering off the river, making it cooler than the stuffy air in the house. Two cushioned straw lounges served as perfect beds, and after drinking the quart of scotch, they crashed.

Chapter 56

All night Bo J had boiled with the anger of humiliation and rejection after Tony had mocked him in front of two women. The younger lady had caught his eye and his interest with her seductive persona. He hated that he had been treated with such disrespect, especially in front of her. Didn't they know he was the one who had brought the pot they so enjoyed? Why hadn't Tony shown some gratitude? Why had he been cast out as an unworthy servant?

As if to solidify his degrading message, Tony had put him back on bathroom door-attendant duty, the worst job in the joint. All of these new guys, these Yankees who had suddenly come in from God knows where, and immediately they get the good jobs. Bo J was pissed, but on Tony's turf, he had no choice for now.

This deal with Tony was like living at home, harassed, beaten, and humiliated. At home he had no choice.

It was like school when he was younger and smaller, before he could defend himself against older bullies, until he became the bully. At school he had no choice.

He had grown into the position of head school bully as naturally as a palmetto tree grows on a Carolina beach. He knew all the tricks and all the methods utilized to belittle and embarrass those who were weaker in some way. He knew it, because he had endured it all himself. As a bully, he had no choice.

He had received no sympathy at home. If he had complained to his parents, his dad would kick his ass for being a weak punk, a baby who couldn't stick up for himself. There was no escape, so he learned to take it and later, to give it, and he gave it often.

He did not intend to live in this quagmire for very long; something would change one way or another. He would make a new choice. Bo J had seen enough to know that a rebellion would not be easy here, in fact; it could be deadly. Bo J still owed Tony money, and he assumed those markers would continue to move out just beyond his reach, ensuring his indentured servitude. Tony was a curmudgeon who seemed to enjoy Bo J's suffering. So he knew he had to play it cool. He had tasted the wrath of this group when he had tried to skip out on a few dollars. He knew they took few prisoners, and right now they were beating the war drums, gathering their tribal warriors, and he was not considered one of the tribe.

Deep wounds were being reopened for Bo J. He had thought about it all night, but he had to get the big load of pot for Tony. If he didn't, he would not only lose respect with Tony, he would look bad in front of RayRay and his homeboys. His friends at home were the only people who currently had any respect for him, and even that respect was suspect now. Bo J knew he had to do this deal despite his anger and fear. He had no choice.

Just before dawn Bo J clocked out with the last of the restaurant employees, exited through a rear door, and headed home to his lonely cottage. He missed Guido not being around. At least Guido had given him some encouragement, some hope, some respect. Bo J's mood was dark and vengeful. He planned to get some sleep and call RayRay later.

Bo J unlocked the side door to the cottage and moved inside. He shuffled through the kitchen, turned into the hall, and stepped into the barrel of a thirty-eight revolver pointed directly between his eyes. He took a step back, and his droopy eyes popped wide open. He struggled to catch his breath. He felt another cold barrel in his back.

"Easy, big fella. Have we got a deal for you. But you're gonna need to be quiet and listen. Put your hands above your head," Floyd instructed from behind and then patted Bo J for concealed weapons. "Put your hands behind your back." He cuffed him just in case.

Bo J recognized McKenzie behind the barrel of the thirty-eight. "OK, but aren't you the cop who was in the bar the other night? You got my ass in trouble, hoss." Bo J spoke with a growing confidence that he was not going to be wasted on the spot by these intruders, but with a town full of crooked cops, he was not going to get overly bold. "So what do you gentlemen want?"

A very official, formal voice delivered a response. "I'm Detective McKenzie, Myrtle Beach Police, the detective who still believes in the law. Behind you stands the honorable Sergeant Floyd, a well-respected officer of the South Carolina Law Enforcement Division, SLED to you. Sergeant Floyd is here to corroborate my allegations concerning certain activities within the club where you are employed. He has done so. We are here to further develop this evidence with you." McKenzie lowered his weapon and moved between Bo J and the door.

"We believe you to be a central figure associated with a variety of major felonies including assault, kidnapping, illegal gaming, drug sales and trafficking, and perhaps a murder or two. If you're lucky, you're looking at life in prison. If you're not so lucky, maybe the electric chair. It all depends." McKenzie blended the facts with a little fiction and mixed in a touch of conjecture to cook up a hot stew for Bo J to wallow in. The pressure cooker was on high.

Bo J was exhausted, frustrated, humiliated, caught in a corner, and had no defense. Now these bullies were talking about prison, the ultimate bully, and a hell for the rest of his life, one circumstance he would not easily grow out of. In a moment all his visions of a more peaceful future had been destroyed. Now he had to make a choice that would be more permanent.

The fire was too hot, and Bo J broke down. He collapsed to the floor and started crying, like a kid in school after he had been mocked and beaten up. He reverted to those days not so long gone. He was trapped and accused of something he could not control.

Bo J, a six-foot-four, 275-pound ball of muscle, dressed in his expensive, tastefully gray suit, crying like a baby on the floor was not the sight McKenzie or Floyd had expected. They had anticipated a fight or some smartass, attitudinal resistance, but they got none of that. These two highly trained lawmen were much better suited to deal with a more physically violent response than this raw emotional reaction! What should they do with this blubbering kid?

269

They had known he would be the easy one to crack. Most of the thugs working with Tony were sworn blood-family who would go to prison, endure torture, or even die before turning on the family. Bo J was the easy way into the close-knit crime circle headquartered at the Blue House. McKenzie handed his gun to Floyd and knelt down beside Bo J. He took his arm and helped him up and onto the couch in the living room.

"OK, son, it's going to be OK. All right, come on now, let's talk. Maybe we can help you out here. Appears you've got some things going on, some real pressure on you. Why don't you tell us about it, and we'll see what we can do." McKenzie spoke calmly.

Bo J wiped his eyes on a couch pillow and returned to himself, the Bo J of today, not a ten-year-old kid. Gradually he told them his story. He told them why he had come to the beach. He had been seeking an escape. He had wanted the good life at the beach that he had always heard about. For a while it appeared he might find his dream, but things had gone south in the last few days, with all the murder and mayhem and his friend Guido getting hurt. He told them Guido was not like the others; he was a good man caught in something that wouldn't let go of him, just like Bo J.

Bo J even told them about the pot purchase he had been instructed to handle. But here Bo J secretly drew the line. He didn't mind Tony getting nailed, but he would not rat on RayRay. The loyalty to his childhood friends was much like the family loyalty Tony enjoyed from his employees. Bo J had family too.

He regained some of his composure and sought to negotiate the terms of his confession, but he was at some disadvantage. McKenzie and Floyd understood relevance and position within the crime scheme better than Bo J knew himself. They were only interested in Bo J as a baited hook to help snag the others. After hearing all the young man had to say, McKenzie made an offer he felt Bo J could not refuse.

"Wear a wire, and we'll help you get a new start away from Tony and his gang." McKenzie suggested the choice with a face of fatherly wisdom. He gave Bo J a path out of his corner.

Bo J now had an option. His mind quickly turned to revenge. Not only could he get out, but he could also punish the bully. Bo J thought he would finally have the last laugh.

"We have a surveillance device that is difficult for anyone to detect. We'll be following you and listening. We'll always have several heavily armed undercover agents around you, ready to pounce and protect. We have placed a tap on your phone. We are on you, boy, like white on rice. This is your way out," McKenzie said firmly and conclusively.

Bo J was ready to play a new game. "OK, let's do it."

Chapter 57

Edna woke Evelyn early to revisit their morning-doughnut-on-the-beach ritual that had been derailed by the strange events of the past weeks. Evelyn had come home late after she had talked to Guido until he fell asleep. She was afraid he might return to his comatose state, but the nurse assured her he was only sleeping. Finally, exhausted herself, she opted to sleep the night in her own bed, rather than in the uncomfortable chair in Guido's room. Edna and Evelyn talked about McKenzie and Guido as they watched the sun rise through a cloudy horizon. The conversation kept them on the beach much longer than normal.

As they walked back to their house, the girls saw the police converging on the amusement park. Earlier, as they were walking to the beach, they had heard the Tilt-a-Whirl's signature music, the same music that blared from the amusement park ride each time the ride cranked up and zoomed riders round and round. But they were so engaged in conversation, they had disregarded the relevance of the park ride running at such an early hour. Maybe secretly they feared another discovery, and neither cared to admit it, or maybe at the time, they just didn't care. Edna diverted her path closer to the park, with her curiosity falling in the "what now" category. Evelyn followed, relatively unconcerned and immersed in her own thoughts.

Curiosity won the battle for their attention, and the girls walked over to the Tilt-a-Whirl. As it was slowing down, the ride was still announcing its repeated challenging question, "Do you want to go faster?" On any normal night, after this recorded question, the ride would then accelerate, thrilling the riders with its rapid, rolling, spinning rush around a track of music, whistles, and mirrors. This day would find four young rookie lifeguards strapped naked on top of the cars, with "Go Home" painted in red on their asses. After hours of riding, the young men had heaved all their stomach contents into the car seats. Bugs were splattered all over their backsides, like a car windshield in Florida during lovebug season.

"When will this crazy person get caught or get tired?" Evelyn asked with frustrated disgust.

"I guess when the summer workers go home," Edna answered. "From what I hear, that might be a bit early this summer. Several kids working at our store have already left. Booney tells me that almost all of his summer tenants have gone. You know we get some early quitters, but not this many and not this early. I guess they figure, why take the chance."

Detective Driggers pulled in, momentarily scanning the scene, automatically knowing the story.

"Where's your friend, McKenzie?" he asked Edna with a suspicious smirk.

"How would I know? He doesn't work for me, Detective!" Edna shot back with a tone exposing her newfound dislike for this man.

"Whoa there, young filly, y'all seem a little uptight this mornin'," Driggers said, still wearing the smirk and pleased with the possibility that he had hit a nerve that was perhaps festering from a lover's quarrel.

"Please don't refer to me as 'young filly,' and it's none of your damn business what I feel like this morning. Why don't you get to work? Looks like you have a crime to solve." Edna bristled and refused to back off.

"Well, I'm working on it right now with you, aren't I? You always seem to be at the scene of each one of these summer-worker crimes. Pretty suspicious, don't you think?" Driggers took a drink of his coffee and looked around at the Tilt-a-Whirl. "That's a profile indicator, you know. Perpetrators like to show up to watch the reaction of others as they see the results of the crime. McKenzie has been in charge of these investigations, and he hasn't come up with a damn thing. And now he's stickin' his nose in places he don't belong. That careless little diversion got him hurt, and now here's another crime scene, and he ain't here. But you are."

Driggers spoke with arrogance but intended intimidation. Driggers couldn't care less if Edna was involved; he just needed to discredit McKenzie and get him under control. Driggers didn't need some new guy rocking his well-funded boat.

"I believe he might be protecting you. You best be careful, Edna, especially careful with who you keep company."

"Get a life, Driggers," Edna said as she turned to walk away.

Driggers didn't take the time to respond. He moved back to the crime scene, made sure one of his men was working the details, and then left. He knew what the report would say. He was anxious, but it was too early. Something was up. Tony had called a morning meeting with Salvador and a couple of members of the local organization. Driggers went for a hot Krispy Kreme while he waited.

Four more summer workers left town that day; word was spreading fast, and a full-scale summer-worker desertion was on. Merchants up and down the Grand Strand were suffering, struggling to staff their temporary summer jobs. Deposits were down in branch banks, but the effect was most notably felt by businesses within twenty blocks of First Avenue North. The onslaught and loss of workers was most obvious in this area. The mayor's office was pretending to put pressure on local police officials. Most officials put on a show for the small merchants affected, but this community issue had not yet hit the pockets of anyone who could make a real difference. Money talked, and few cared if a number of summer workers left their beach jobs a couple of weeks earlier than normal. Nothing would change.

The real money pot that controlled municipal political powers was fueled by the development dollar and contributions from folks like Tony. Permits would be issued, business licenses would be approved, and liquor sales and strip bars would still exist. The tourists wanted it that way, and this city existed for the pleasure of tourists. The tourists were unconcerned with the city infrastructure and town hall as long as the resort pleasures were available in full scale for their vacation. The growth that supported this political engine was obstreperous, with no regard for those forced to live within it.

Chapter 58

Wired with SLED's most advanced micro transceiver, Bo J stepped to a pay phone to call RayRay. He didn't mind if the police heard this call to order the pot, but he wasn't giving up his homeboys. No traceable numbers would be used, and he knew from experience that RayRay would devise a pickup scheme with no clear connection for police to track. Once RayRay had his cash secured, he would not care what happened to the pot.

"RayRay, your stuff passed the test, man. The boss wants to crank things up a notch or two. I need a thousand pounds, and I'll need it by tomorrow noon. You'll get half the money now, and the other half on delivery." Bo J laid out the deal as directed by Tony.

"Well, dude, you're not too fuckin' demanding, are you? You think I got a thousand pounds sittin' around waiting on the hopes you'd call? Shit, man, that's gonna cost you if you want it by tomorrow." RayRay responded just as Tony had warned. Like most dealers RayRay always answered demands for large orders this way; he wanted to see the money first.

"Hey, can you do it or not, man? That's all I need to know. We're playing big-time and we'll need to act big-time!" Bo J responded with more confidence.

"Well, ain't you stepped up, big dog? Those are awful tough words from the Bo Jr. I know. Tell you what, hoss, when y'all get tired of playing with those Yankees, let me know, I might have a job for you."

"Can you do it or not?"

"Now listen to me, son. I'm gettin' a little irritated. You get half the money and put it in a gym bag with a lock. Put wax over the keyhole on the lock and along the zipper. Take the bag to the Sand Dunes hotel at Thirty-Third Avenue South before three thirty. Stand in line with the maids and workers waiting for the bus to Hemingway. Get on the bus, sit in the back row, leave the bag under the seat, and get off at the next stop. Got it?"

The details of RayRay's plan demonstrated some experience with this part of the process. At least he had thought about it and had prepositioned couriers ready to receive. RayRay was country, but he was no dumb-ass beginner.

"I got it, man. But how will I know where to pick the stuff up?"

"We'll let you know." The telephone on the other end of the line disconnected.

Bo J went to get the money ready. RayRay went to order some more pot to supplement his stash. No one knew how much RayRay had or where he kept it, and that's the way he wanted it.

Chapter 59

~

Tony, Alonzo, Driggers, and three members of the Atlanta-based family met to make preparations for visits by bosses from New York and Chicago. The family leadership was coming to show their respect for Marvin and Frank. They would take Marvin's body back for burial in New York, but they would also drop by to see Frank. They all knew him or knew about him. Frank had a reputation as a loyal but elusive member of the family.

Tony suspected that the real purpose of their visit was to assess his ability to handle his territory and his ability to grow his business—but most important, to test his obedience to the pandects of their operation and to the family. The series of problems Tony was experiencing brought all of these issues into question. The cash from free-spending tourists was too easy to pass up and would not be conceded. The family had plans to expand gambling and gentlemen clubs in the area. Their current investment, the Pink Party Pony, was scheduled to open next summer. They wanted no impediments. Problems meant delays. Delays meant lost revenue. The bosses wanted to make sure Tony had things under control.

Expecting to find Tony alone, Bo J knocked and quickly entered his office. He was anxious to get the cash for the delivery of the down payment to RayRay. Driggers and Alonzo looked nervous when Bo J entered the room. Three well-armed family members, sitting on a couch, casually moved to defensive positions behind Bo J. Tony didn't want Bo J knowing more than he needed to know, and these nervous reactions were the catalyst for unwanted suspicions. But Bo J's dull talents of perception didn't interpret the mood shift caused by his arrival as anything abnormal.

"Relax, gentlemen. Keep your seats. I think you have all met our man, Bo J. He's working to connect us with a new source for product. We're entrusting this kid with a large investment today. We expect to take delivery and begin distribution as early as tomorrow. If it all works out as planned, this product could establish a whole new expanded business model, doubling our profits while reducing our risks. I want you gentlemen to help ensure Bo J performs his job without any difficulty."

The muscle moved back to their seats. Tony stood and put a confident hand on Bo J's shoulder.

"Failure to perform on his part will bring a heavy price for all of us. I will hold each of you responsible for success. Alonzo, after this meeting I need you to take a couple guys out to the river house. Get it ready. Take some summer clothes for our friends coming from the north. We want them comfortable. Make sure the place is stocked, aired out, and ready to entertain our family. Bo J will deliver us a large shipment of pot tomorrow evening. This is quality stuff. We want the exchange to go down with no problems. Got that, Driggers?"

"Gotcha, boss!"

"Yeah, well, that new guy McKenzie better not be messin' things up, or he's gonna get more than a bump on the head," Tony growled.

Floyd and McKenzie were listening. They had not expected to record incriminating evidence so quickly. Their timing for this surveillance couldn't have been better. In this brief exchange, they had conspiracy, drug trafficking, and corruption, all with the potential to snag multiple suspects. It seemed too simple. One well-placed wire and a few hours of waiting had yielded the potential for legendary police work. They had a feeling that this recording would only be the surface of this raging crime river. They knew the undertow was always more dangerous than what could be seen on the surface, and right now they were only watching a calm breeze blow ripples on the surface.

"By the way, gentlemen, my girls brought in one of those scumbags we've been lookin' for. We already had one that we suspected, but I want to be sure before we engage. If we got the wrong guy, we'll just let him go."

"If we release them, they'll be pissed," Alonzo said. "Might try to call the police and press charges."

"Driggers will handle that, but since the girls caught them using their God-given talents of seduction, what charges could they file? The first one we got has some local political connections, so we need to be careful. We need to be sure. I want this trespassing idiot neutralized by tomorrow. A little revenge show for the family should set things straight and gain our operation some respect. I'm going over to check out our two captives later today. I'll let you know if we have found our boy. Let's get to work!"

The huddle broke for both teams. Floyd and McKenzie heard them call the play, but some of the details were not clear. Floyd would need to plan a multiphased defensive formation to ensure SLED could respond to what might occur. Floyd looked at McKenzie.

"Game on, brother!"

Chapter 60

Vernon woke up in a room so completely dark that he couldn't have seen a hand in front of his face—or for that matter, not even his own hands, which were securely handcuffed to some unmovable object on the floor. He didn't need to see the handcuffs to know what bound his wrists; he had sufficient past experience with similar constraints.

This moment was not a first time for Vernon to wake up and not know where he was or how he got there, and perhaps it would not be the last. He had been out with wild women of many different persuasions and often found himself in strange circumstances the next morning. He thought perhaps his current state was a remnant of the forgotten wild night before. He was still dressed, so the evening that he didn't remember must have resulted in mixed reviews from the minx he was beginning to recollect.

He heard someone move in the dark space and thought it might be the mysterious seductress. His mind was still cloudy from the night before. He couldn't remember the name of the young bombshell, and his experience told him this memory lapse might be dangerous, or at least unpleasant. He decided to take a positive approach.

"Honey, is that you?" Vernon asked softly.

"Who the fuck are you?" a male voice responded harshly, squashing Vernon's hopeful mood. Darrell Jr. had lost track of time with the mind-numbing darkness and silence. His senses were confused. He had also heard movement in the dark room. His experience since enslavement warned him to leave well enough alone, but he was Darrell Jr.

"Hey, sorry, man, I thought maybe you were the chick who put these cuffs on me," Vernon replied with a slightly nervous laugh.

"Man, you don't really want to hang out with these ladies. They got a weird mean streak. Takes some getting used to," Darrell Jr. replied, a bit too blasé.

"Oh yeah, well, how long you been in here getting used to it?" Vernon quizzed. "Where the hell are we anyway?"

"You'll find out soon enough."

At that moment brilliant lights flooded the room, pinning Vernon in the glare of a stage spotlight. After his eyes adjusted to the light, he squinted and saw the mirrored glass. He saw his own rumpled reflection, chained to the floor with bright chrome handcuffs and matching chains that were not exactly police issue. In a far corner, dimly lit by diffused light from the beam, was a man strangely dressed in some a poorly fitting, silky-something leftover from a Victoria's Secret full-sized sale. Darrell Jr. was cowering in the corner like a trapped and beaten puppy.

Inaudible and invisible to Vernon and Darrell, Tony was standing with Ophelia and Tina on the other side of the two-way mirror. "It's apparent they don't know each other, otherwise this little discussion wouldn't be taking place," Tony said.

"The new one's name is Vernon," said Tina. "He's the guy causing all the trouble, selling pot, killing Marvin. He didn't know he killed Marvin, but the dumb ass just laughed when he heard another idiot talking about it. At the Frisky Rabbit, he was bragging about his business." Tina recounted some of her not-too-difficult discoveries.

Tony sneered and stared at Vernon with disgust and contempt. Well, no sweat, this irritating distraction would all be handled tomorrow at a family gathering. Tony had only hoped his competition would be a more impressive adversary. This punk would pay dearly, and Tony would make the payback impressive.

"Keep these boys locked up in the dark, but I want them separated. Ophelia, after we take this one away, you can do whatever you want with the one you caught. You can keep him or let him go, I don't care. My boys will come for Vernon. Give 'em all he wants to eat and drink, but pass it under the door, no discussions. Leave him in the dark."

———

Later that night, a cute young lady walked up to Bo J while he stood watch on the men's room at the Blue House. She handed him a sealed envelope.

"That man over at the bar asked me to give this to you," she said in her local Southern drawl. "He gave me five bucks, I figured, what the hell."

Bo J looked and asked, "Where, who, which one?" But the man was gone. "Thanks."

Bo J opened the note. It simply said, "Drive to Hemingway, be at the pay phone at Oakland Avenue and Main Street at 10:00 a.m. You'll be riding on a river, so bring a boat."

Bo J had to hand it to RayRay; he took no chances. He left no trail for anyone. Even the pay phone would not give much help to the folks who had him wired. He knew the conversation would be short and untraceable. Riding on a river could mean anywhere up or down one hundred miles of river or along one of the uncountable tributaries in the surrounding swamps of three rivers, each a short drive from Hemingway. Roads from Hemingway could put you at a boat landing anywhere from Lake Moultrie to the Atlantic Ocean. RayRay would be able to detect any undercover force of any size. The swampland of low-country rivers was RayRay's territory and virtually impossible to compromise with a stealth force. RayRay was the Swamp Fox of his time. The note-delivery girl was lost in the crowd. She left with others and drove to her home on the bank of the Black River in Williamsburg County.

Chapter 61

~

Alonzo gathered his five men and went to the river house immediately after the meeting in Tony's office. They had a lot of work to do. The place would need to be spotless and comfortable for the bosses. They brought fresh food and a resupply of other basic provisions and scheduled the services of one of Charleston's well-respected Italian chefs. He would be brought in from Anson's Restaurant later in the afternoon to prepare their private supper. Everything would be perfect for this meeting.

Alonzo parked in the back of the house to allow the men easy access for transfer of the groceries directly into the kitchen. As they walked up the steps and into the screened porch, they saw Harley and David still cuffed and passed out on the porch chairs. The sleeping pair did not move.

"Well, well, look what we have here, boys!"

Harley and David were dead to the world, with an empty bottle of the house's best scotch lying on the floor between them. Two of Alonzo's crew went inside, following a trail of damages left by the careless pilferage of these intruders.

"These boys had quite a night, but look at them. They've been cut up and handcuffed. This one has a leech on his leg, and looks like something has been eating on 'em. My God, they're a mess."

"Well, it's gonna get worse," Alonzo said with disgust. "They broke into the wrong house. We'll let Tony handle them with the other punk. I better call Tony. He's gonna love this!"

The men went to work preparing the house. Alonzo had the muscle drag Harley and David, with their hangovers and other bodily pain, out to a shed in the pine thicket near the edge of the river. The shed was the same where others had met their maker and Bo J had first met Tony and Guido. The disheveled pair were gagged and chained to hooks on the wall of the shed.

Both men dangled against the wall, exhausted from their ordeal and throbbing with pain. The momentary pleasure gained from far too much scotch was now being repaid double by the sickening misery of a hangover. All of this, and they were still oblivious to the danger of their predicament. They both fell asleep again.

Chapter 62

In the constant darkness, Vernon had lost track of time, but he had been well fed. His most recent meal was his favorite and just what he had ordered: "a big ole T-bone" steak. He had eaten it with the gusto of a starved refugee. He had been drugged, kidnapped, and chained in a dark room, but that did not mean he would ignore a good meal. He was unaware it might be his last.

With little light and no sound, the short-term sensory deprivation started to work on Vernon's psyche. He did not understand why he was in this place or when he would be released, and the uncertainty left him anxious and fretful. A spiked mixed drink was passed through the small door. Vernon was thirsty, and it was one of his favorites, a margarita. He thought, yeah, this will settle me down. Three minutes later Vernon did not fret with conscious thought. He was out, resting in a dream world, and Tina was to blame once again. Later that day Tony and his men dropped by the Happy Snapper Oyster Bar to pick up Vernon for his last ride.

Vernon's next conscious thought was the realization of tight ropes around his ankles, a gag in his mouth, and a bouncing movement. He was still in the dark but now in a more confined space. He could smell the new rubber of a spare tire. Blindfolded and groggy, Vernon deduced he was in a car trunk moving on a road.

The car continued for a short distance over a rough road and came to a stop. Vernon was working hard to clear the cobwebs from his mind. He suspected he would soon need the clarity. This situation had progressed way beyond the desires of a weird, sexually aggressive, local teenager.

Vernon struggled with his confused thoughts. Did he owe someone money? Who had he pissed off? Well, OK, he thought, lots of people, but who would get this worked up about it? Maybe it was the lawyer who had bailed him out of jail? That logic did not seem right, because his ability to make the court date would be the ticket for the guy to get his money back. Was he just locking him up to make sure he went to court? If he was locked away, he couldn't sell product, so that didn't make sense. Vernon really didn't like to think with this intensity, so he gave in to his current plight. He just relaxed and let his mind drift to his happy place.

Vernon's mental dilemma was solved moments later when two huge men of Italian persuasions dragged him out of the trunk and into a building. As they took his blindfold off, he heard David shout, "Vernon, man, thank God you're here, man! You don't know what's been goin' on with me and Harley, man! I swear to God, you don't, man!"

"You know these bozos?" the muscle asked Vernon. Vernon did not respond.

"Why, hell yeah, he does!" David shouted. "He's the man! That's Vernon, man! We sell for him, man! You assholes better let us go now, or there's gonna be hell to pay."

"Yeah man," Harley chimed in. "I swear to God, man. Hell. To. Pay!"

"Shut up, you boneheads," Vernon barked. His head wasn't clear yet, but he was still more cognizant of the danger they were in than his two dimly lit cohorts could decipher.

The muscle punched David in the jaw and backhanded Harley across his face. They hoisted Vernon and tied his cuffed hands to a hook above his head.

"So you punks know each other, do you? You guys have a run-in recently with a couple of old men?" The muscleman laughed as if he thought it was funny.

"Yeah, the dumb old goats were trying to scare us, telling us they were after us for selling pot. They were crazy, man, acting like they were some kind of mob or something. Crazy bastards," David blurted out with pride and a laugh, thinking he was gaining some trust and maybe a little respect from these toughs.

"Shut up, David!" Vernon said again. "Un-fuckin'-believable."

"What? We did it. Nobody messes with us, man! That's what you always say." David was a bit miffed and frustrated with Vernon's lack of bravado. He had never seen Vernon when he didn't show it.

"So you were the guys, eh? Did you get anything out of them; did you get them to talk?"

"No, those old bastards didn't know nothin', I swear to God, man! They were just dreamin', trying to play tough. We showed 'em tough. They'll just go back to the home, won't bother nobody no more," David bragged, still not aware of the hellhole he was digging.

"Well, you sure are right about that, son, 'cause one of them is dead, and the other one, well, we're gonna make sure he has better care. But we're also gonna get rid of his problem, and that would be you and your buddies here." The muscle punctuated his response with a driving jab into David's already injured ribs. The pain was debilitating. David screamed with pain, puked, and passed out. "Looks like somebody else had a problem with you before we came along. We're just gonna finish the job."

The other two Italian brothers joined in with a few punches on Vernon and Harley. They wanted to spread the pain around. These three could not adequately express the anger within the family over the harsh treatment of Frank and the death of Marvin. They would remain under control and do their duty as instructed. Make it painful and make it last. They were just getting started.

Chapter 63

Twenty minutes before the time scheduled for RayRay's call, Bo J drove the rented truck into Hemingway. He wanted to make sure he was at the right pay phone at the appointed time. McKenzie had briefed him that undercover officers would be positioned discreetly, watching from a distance. Bo J was aware that some of these same officers had been in the Blue House the night before, but despite the fact that he knew they were watching, he had not been able to determine who they were. He knew they had not been able to ID the guy who had paid the girl to give him the note, so at the moment, he wasn't exactly confident about their abilities to protect him. No one had suspected the girl.

The location of the pay phone had been well selected. It was surrounded by open property. A city park with ball fields was on one side of the road, and a vacant parking lot and a large grass yard were on the other side. Hiding agents would be difficult within three blocks in any direction.

Bo J was parked on the street next to the telephone, and the appointed time was now only one minute away. He was confident, but anxious as he watched a crow pick at a dead squirrel in the middle of the road. A city police cruiser glided slowly past Bo J. The more Bo J tried to appear casual, the more suspicious he looked. The officer slowed to a stop, contemplating a need to check on this fellow. Hemingway was a small town, and Bo J being parked here with a rental truck pulling a boat was odd. There was no apparent reason for him to be here unless he was bringing trouble or was looking for it.

As the officer opened his car door, he got a call for emergency assistance five miles out of town on Highway 51 North. He responded quickly, leaving Bo J to a ringing phone. The officer would not find trouble on the highway, and Bo J's trouble would be gone when the officer returned. An alert undercover SLED team had made the bogus emergency call that kept the game in play for the moment.

Bo J answered the phone on the third ring. "Hello?"

"Take Highway Fifty-One South to Highway Forty-One. Go to the Santee River Bridge, cross it, immediately turn right, drive to the boat ramp, and follow the dirt road down the river for two miles. Put your boat in and head downriver. Take the rest of the money with you. Don't waste any time; go directly to the river. We're watching, and we won't wait long for you to get there. You done good on the first drop. Don't mess up, and you'll get what you need. Now get movin'."

"But what are—" Bo J started to ask questions but heard the click of a disconnect on the other end. He knew time was critical to meet whoever was waiting for him on the river. He attached a piece of red tape to the telephone stand, climbed into the cab of the rental truck, and headed south. Red was for the Santee River and Black was for the Black River. One of Tony's men would drive by later to get the signal and provide a pickup team.

Bo J was familiar with the directions, and he knew he would be picking the pot up in the swamp, in RayRay's territory. The SLED support team could not help him. Tony's thugs could not help him. He was on his own.

A young lady walked her dog at the far end of the park and watched as Bo J drove away. She took note of other movement and cars heading cautiously south in pursuit.

Tony had instructed Bo J on delivery points, including the potential of a Santee River pickup as the most likely. With the correct hunch, after the pickup, Bo J was to continue downriver for a mile past the railway trestle to a house on the north side of the river. Tony said he would have people waiting. He warned Bo J that there would be consequences if he screwed this up. Bo J knew the river and he knew the railway trestle. He could do this.

Bo J followed Highway 41 and crossed to the south side of the Santee River. He turned off the highway and followed the paved road past the boat ramp and under the bridge. The pavement soon turned to a rutted dirt lane that got rough quickly. He had made the trip from Hemingway to the river in less than thirty minutes. He had time to negotiate this rough road at a reasonable speed. The rental truck bounced and swayed as it struggled over the bumps and mudholes of the neglected road, while the boat trailer danced behind in an uncoordinated pursuit.

The dirt road ended after two miles, and Bo J stopped in an opening between large cypress trees. After dragging his boat down to the riverbank, he found an empty gym bag. It was the bag he had used to deliver the down payment on the bus. A note attached read, "Take it, fill it with the cash, we'll let you know where to drop it."

Bo J quickly launched his boat and started downriver. The SLED agents tailing him could not follow without detection. They could put a boat in the river, but the closest launch was an hour's drive west and a long way upriver. Overhead a Cessna observation plane tracked a beacon hidden on Bo J's boat. The beacon was constrained by distance and battery life, but for now it served the purpose. Tracking Bo J, however, would have limits in this swamp.

A few miles downriver, Skeeter powered his two boats out of a small side creek and pulled alongside Bo J. They moved the boats over to a sandbar and traded rides. Skeeter took the gym bag filled with cash, climbed in Bo J's boat, and quickly disappeared upstream into a cypress swamp tributary laced with a maze of flowing water channels. Bo J was now standing on a sandbar, miles from the nearest road, minus a large amount of cash entrusted to him by the East Coast mob, plus two long riverboats filled to capacity with bundles of high-quality pot. He knew the boat with the tracking device would be tied to a cypress knee and abandoned deep in the swamp.

For Bo J this event was the national championship; there was no time on the clock, the game was tied, and he was in the open field, running to the end zone. All he had to do was get the ball across the goal line without tripping or fumbling. History would record him as the hero or the goat, because at this point, there could be no tie.

He was on his own with miles of river to negotiate—no one to watch, no one to criticize the details of how he would accomplish his task. This was his chance to move up the ladder of respect. There would be no one to blame but himself if he failed. For RayRay, Bo J had already delivered.

Chapter 64

Today Vera was determined to visit the Grand Strand Assisted Living and Retirement Home, with or without Eddie. She had no idea where he had gone, or when he would return. Despite her frustration, she got dressed, fixed her hair in a perfect, untouchable, white-blond, starched do and then put on her makeup. She selected a pair of white faux-leather shoes and a matching purse with shiny, gold, strap hinges. Vera liked to look her best for her friends at the home.

Edna was walking back from the One-Eyed Flounder. She had helped to open the store again this morning. She was helping Darrell Sr., until they could find out where Darrell Jr. had gone this time. Vera opened the kitchen door, stepped to the carport, and opened the car door.

"Vera, you look so nice. Where are you going by yourself, sweetie?" Edna asked with some surprise at Vera's stern face.

"I'm going to the retirement home—without Eddie! I can't find him, and I need to take some of the ladies over to the hospital for a visit. You know they're all sweet on Frank, and they were just devastated when they heard about him and poor Marvin. They've made some cakes and pies for Frank and they've got no one to take them. No one who understands how they feel."

"Well, wait a minute, hon, and I'll go with you." Edna raced to get her purse. "We'll meet Evelyn there. She's already gone to see Guido again."

Vera was feeling better already. Edna was one who could always lift her spirits.

Smiling, Edna drove the car, and Vera sat in the passenger seat with both hands resting on the top of her purse perfectly poised in her lap. She said nothing and stared out the window. Edna knew Vera was troubled, but she wouldn't ask. She would wait until Vera was ready to talk.

After a few frustrating miles of stop-and-go traffic lights on the bypass, Edna turned off Highway 501 and into the parking lot of the retirement home. Vera quickly arranged for the use of the home's transportation bus and collected Sam and Ralph who were Frank and Marvin's card-playing buddies and four women, Ms. Naomi, Ms. Thelma, Ms. Gladis and Ms. Agnes, who were their very close friends. All six were dressed in their Sunday best. The men sported pastel ties, white patent-leather shoes, and sports jackets that absolutely did not match their plaid slacks. The ladies wore their best yellow, white, pink, and blue dresses, heels, and matching purses, and of course, formal, broad-brimmed, summer hats. Edna felt slightly underdressed, but she was committed to this endeavor.

"I brought this pie for Frank. I know how he loves rhubarb pie," declared Ms. Thelma.

"And I've baked this chocolate cake," Ms. Naomi announced. "He just loves chocolate cake. I'm sure it's his favorite."

"He'll be so happy to see all of you," Vera said. "Now let's everybody get on the bus."

"We need to get my cake to him as soon as possible. It's best when it's fresh right out of the oven."

"I've got him a cold beer in this bag. Thought I'd sneak it in past the nurses. He loves a cold beer," Sam said with a cheerful face.

"Now Sam, you know you can't drink beer," Vera chided.

"But Frank can, if we can get it past his nurses."

"We must hurry, my rhubarb pie is getting cold."

They got everyone in the bus and left to visit Frank, who was resting and healing in the One-Eyed Flounder Memorial Wing of the Myrtle Beach Hospital.

Meanwhile at the hospital, Evelyn settled into the chair next to Guido's bed after giving him a kiss and hug as best she could with his cast, bandages, tubes, and monitors. Guido was smiling, now fully awake from his comatose dream-state.

"Evelyn, thanks for coming. I'm really glad you are here. Let me introduce you to my old friend and new roommate, Frank." Frank had vastly improved since entering the hospital. He was sitting up in his bed and preparing to give Guido and Evelyn a few minutes alone.

"Pleasure to meet you, Evelyn. Now if I may excuse myself, I'm going to take a walk and get some exercise. I see we have a new set of nurses on the day shift. Think I'll go introduce myself."

Tony's muscle, who had been watching the door, had been instructed to help stage the surprise family visit. He now had to stop Frank from leaving the room without him noticing the goon's uncharacteristic caring efforts.

"Frank, before you go out, you might want to check the back of your gown. Got a little too much exposure."

Frank retied the open rear flap and checked his efforts in a wall mirror.

"How's that look?"

"Well, I got to tell you, it ain't pretty," the goon said while shaking his head in disgust.

Frank checked again.

The sentry could not contrive a strategy to casually keep Frank in the room while encouraging Evelyn to leave. This ruse was his best spur-of-the-moment delaying tactic. His talents were more involved with fear and intimidation, not with social manipulation, but his delay proved to be sufficient. Tony met Frank at the door, and moments later the bosses arrived as a group.

The mobsters surrounded the bed, edging Evelyn out of her chair and to the door without apology. Neither Frank nor Guido dared question or correct the actions of the bosses, especially with the honor of their surprise arrival and obvious show of respect. The two rear guards watching the door helped complete her journey from the room. Guido looked to her and gave a muted smile of apology. He watched her as she moved to the door and out of his sight.

"Why don't you take a walk, lady?" one guard, with a thick northern-Jersey accent, said quietly out of the side of his mouth. His eyes moved up and down the hallway, looking over Evelyn's head. She was ticked off now. The mean-looking goons that Tony had brought in appeared seriously scary and exhibited absolutely no positive social manners. They were obviously not local. Evelyn left, huffing with indignant anger.

McKenzie and Floyd had pulled into the hospital parking lot behind Tony and his crew. They had discreetly followed the bosses into the hospital and separated on alternate routes, feigning only casual interest in any observation of the group; disinterest was their disguise. Tony knew McKenzie, but he had been too busy leading the group, maintaining the attention of the bosses and demonstrating his leadership, to notice him.

The visit with Guido didn't last long. The big man was given a few moments of respectful gratitude for his past service. His loyalty and contributions to the family were not in the same league as Frank. The condolences were reserved and mechanical.

Frank, by contrast, had dedicated his early life to the needs, whims, and the successful dominance of the family. Frank was not "the man," but he was the man who helped make "the man" who he was, and these men knew it. Tony jumped in to take advantage of the moment.

"Frank, you're unbelievable. You look almost fully recovered, and for a man your age, that's some magic, my friend, some magic." Tony announced his assessment to the room and then moved closer and whispered to Frank, "We've got him. We've got Vernon."

"Get me outta here, Tony. I want another shot at that punk. I've got a score to settle."

Tony held a short and spirited discussion with the nurse. Frank got dressed and walked out of the hospital with the group. For this encounter with Vernon, Frank would own the high ground.

Edna, Vera, and the folks from the home were driving into the hospital lot as Frank and the bosses came out. Edna maneuvered into a parking spot and watched. Everyone on the bus stared with stunned disbelief. As they began to shout out to Frank, Edna noticed McKenzie and Floyd exit the hospital. They were acting weird with some false casual demeanor. Edna saw their subtle glances tracking Frank, Tony, and the group. Watching them walk separate paths to the same car confirmed Edna's suspicion.

"Everyone, please sit quietly," Edna announced to the bus. "It appears Frank is already out of the hospital, and he's leaving. Of course, this quick recovery is great news. Perhaps we should wait to see him when he comes home later this afternoon. I think his family must be visiting."

A noisy buzz percolated within the bus. Frank's elderly friends were curious, but cautious. No one was aware of Frank's family. He never talked about them. He had no pictures. It had all been just intriguing gossip. But now...

Edna was focused on the action in front of her when a sudden sharp tap on the driver's side window almost made her heart explode. She jerked around to confront the noise, and her eyes met a frustrated, angry Evelyn, who was in a fuming snit.

"You see those guys!" Evelyn shouted in frustration. "They kicked me out of Guido's room, told me to 'take a walk' or hike or something like that." She mocked the "take a walk" line with snide sarcasm. She threw her purse strap over her shoulder, put her left hand on her hip, and took a long drag off her cigarette. Her anger was focused through a laser-beam stare at Tony's entourage.

In her distraction she hadn't recognized the occupants of the bus. The calming effects of her cigarette and the proximity of comforting friends helped clear the steaming glaze from her eyes, bringing the elderly group into focus.

"Oh, I'm sorry, I was just so upset, I didn't notice. I mean, I didn't—"

Vera interjected. "That's OK, honey. I suppose we're all a little frazzled right now." Multiple comments from the group blended with a communal welcome.

"Oh, don't."

"It's OK, darling."

"No worries."

"Evelyn, why don't you get in with us?" Edna suggested.

After rubbing out the glowing ember of her cigarette butt with three quick twists from the pointy toe of her high-heeled shoe, Evelyn climbed on the bus. She always wore heels when she visited Guido.

Two white limos filled with the bosses, Tony, Frank, and bodyguards drove out of the lot onto Kings Highway. Without being noticed, McKenzie and Floyd eased their car out in pursuit. The bus followed a few moments later. Edna forgot to turn off the big, orange, blinking turn signal as they sped in pursuit of the entourage.

Edna had a variety of interests in this sudden set of events, including McKenzie's involvement. He was injured. Why was he doing this? He should be home in bed.

Evelyn was focused on what connection Guido might have with this group. She wanted to know more about them.

Vera and her elderly crew were just concerned for Frank. They missed him. He could show photographs and tell them all about his family some other time, when he was ready, of course. But they had baked goods and beer to deliver and it needed to be delivered before it got cold or hot, depending on the pleasure.

The disjointed caravan headed south down Highway 17 through a monotonous string of cross-street stoplights, following an unending, pulsing line of cars and trucks. Tourists populated the landscape, crossing the highway at each light, wearing their flip-flops, sunglasses, and swimsuits, carrying their towels, coolers, and rafts, children in tow, heading for the beach or their hotel room.

Other tourists lined the sidewalks on their way to eat at local fast-food stands and restaurants. Many were wandering about looking for entertainment and finding some semblance of satisfaction while shopping at the endless array of discounted beachwear, trinket, and tourist souvenir shops.

The limos stopped for a red light at First Avenue South, and the men watched the amusement park in full swing. The Swamp Fox wooden roller coaster was packed with screaming thrill seekers. The kiddie train chugged under the roller coaster's supporting struts, providing young children and their parents a pleasant memory for life. The motion of cash being freely spent was evident and mesmerizing.

The odd convoy continued south, passing through the condos and strip malls of Surfside Beach and Garden City. They passed the entrances to golf-course communities at Litchfield, the beach houses of Pawley's Island, and the restaurants of Murrells Inlet. Finally, as they reached the unimpeded four-lane track passing Brook Green Gardens and Hunting State Park, the group of vehicles began to spread out. The traffic moved on, gradually thinning, with the pace picking up as they continued south on a memory-forming trip of their own that would be more thrilling than any of them could have anticipated.

Chapter 65

〜

Before dawn Eddie had gone fishing on the Myrtle Beach Pier. He had needed some time without interruption to ponder his actions over the last few weeks. Years of contemplative fishing had taught him that it would be easier to corral his thoughts while immersed in the hypnotic music of waves rolling through the wooden pilings beneath the end of the pier.

He was frustrated over the deterioration of his lifestyle in the beach community that he had always loved. But his dogged approach to gain some resolution may have been too extreme. He had blamed the growth and sprawl of an entire resort city on the summer workers. Summer workers were merely responding to a demand for seasonal help and summertime adventure. They weren't the force behind the growth, just an irritating by-product.

He put some bait on his line and tossed it into the sea. He secured the rod in a white plastic tube attached to a wooden railing and sat back in his chair. Just as Eddie was about to nod off for a nap, Fred Ladd, the most common face on the pier, came strolling up.

"Eddie, buddy, where you been? Haven't seen you here much this summer. Can I cop a seat here beside you?" Fred, buzzing with his usual high energy, put a chair down too close for Eddie's comfort.

"Fred, are you really homeless and we don't know it? I mean, really, don't you have a home, or is this it?"

"Hey, what's eating you, buddy?"

"Ah, nothing, just trying to get some sleep."

"Bull. Something's bugging you, man. Tell old Freddie all about it. By the way, you got an extra beer in that cooler?"

"So that's what you're here for, or are you just out snooping in everybody's business, like usual?"

"No, no. But I'm a good shoulder to cry on, like a bartender."

"Yeah, like a bartender without beer."

"Maybe. So what's up? Come on now, tell old Fred."

"Well, I guess you won't go away till I tell you."

"You got that right, bubba." Fred popped the top on his newfound beer.

"It's these summer workers; they're taking this place over. They're destroying this beach, running around drunk all the time, raising hell. They're driving me crazy." Eddie gazed over the pier railing at a surfer riding a wave a little too close to the pier and to his fishing line.

"Ah, buddy, you know better than that. Hell, they're just like we were when we were kids. They're just having fun like they can't find no place else. 'Cause there ain't no place like the beach. Ain't that why you and I are here?" Fred smiled and took a slug of his beer.

"Nope, I'm here to enjoy my retirement, and I can't enjoy it with all this damn noise and commotion. They are in my space, *my space*, dammit. I wasn't like these kids today. They've got no respect for authority."

"The hell you say. I know you, Eddie. I've known you a long time, and I remember a time when you ran with the best of 'em. We all just settle down when we get older, think everything is ours and should be our way. The people who are running around change, but this place stays the same, more or less." Fred took another drink of his beer and settled himself in his chair, with a relaxing calm taking over.

"Hell, I don't know about that," Eddie replied. "Seems like it's changed a lot to me."

"First of all, the businesses need these kids; they're cheap labor. And B, if these kids didn't have these jobs, they'd be sittin' home bored, lethargic, watching TV, buggin' their parents to drive the car and get into trouble in their nowhere towns. So number three, they come here, and everybody wins." Fred, satisfied with his argument, pulled the bill of his cap over his eyes.

"Everybody wins, eh? I'm part of everybody, and with you bugging me now, I'm not feeling like a winner."

Fred was silent now. He had fallen asleep. Eddie laid his head back and in a moment, joined the snoring party at the end of the pier.

In a dream Eddie drifted back to memories of his youth, living in a small town and his desperate desire to get a summer job in Myrtle Beach. He had heard that the beach jobs were available and longed for the opportunity to be a summer beach bum. Without the beach he and his friends would sit home all summer searching for some minimal level of excitement in their otherwise quiet, boring hometown. They would sit on their parked vehicles in the remote parking areas of a shopping mall or on cracked concrete lots neglected by a deserted business.

They would waste their glorious teenage years with this summer-night boredom. Maybe they would meet a nice girl, or get in a fight, or maybe they would just sit in the lot, smoke pot, drink, and go home. They all talked of their longings for something, anything to magnify the fleeting moments of the most impressionable times of their lives. It made them crazy and somewhat irrational. They were all seeking extremes to satiate their internal hormonal engines.

He remembered even earlier years when his family went to the beach, and they saw the large numbers of children and teenagers from Ohio, West Virginia, Michigan, Kentucky, Tennessee, Virginia, and the entire Southeast enjoy a vacation at Myrtle Beach. His friends talked about people they knew who brought back tales of wild parties, the surf, the amusement parks, a new summer love, and a good time.

The lies and the truths merged with time and distance to become general knowledge forged into fact by the cool crowd. These legends from the promised land were forces that convinced these kids, including Eddie, to abandon the security of home for a chance to experience the joys of the beach for an entire summer. In his dream he remembered the unrelenting urge that drove him to leave home when he was eighteen. He never went back to that small-town home.

He got a job, met his wife, and made Myrtle Beach his home. He had defined this location as his own, his paradise. But that time was a long time ago, and the place was more innocent then, quaint, less crowded.

At least, that's the way he remember it. His turf had changed with the tides of time to a beach resort he no longer recognized as paradise.

In his sleep his subconscious rolled this conundrum around and around. Fred had spoken some truth; Eddie had been considered a rebel and a rabble-rouser in his time. He had driven muscle cars up and down the main drag, squealed a tire now and then. He had been out all night drinking, making noise. Was he holding these summer workers to a different standard? They were different and more extreme, but this time was different, and today was more extreme. He realized that he, in his youth, was somewhat like them, and maybe he shouldn't be so harsh.

He was confident that by now the young men he had hung in the river were scared and intimidated, at least enough to ensure their rapid departure for home, back to whatever small town that might be. In the dream he saw them vividly, swinging from the bridge, dead, gruesome. They were looking at him. They were talking to him.

"Did we really deserve this? Did we really? Come on, man."

"Maybe not, maybe not," he replied. He just hoped, he prayed they were still alive.

With a jolt he awoke from his afternoon slumber with a conscience resurrected; he needed to fix his latest attempt to scare off the summer workers. He collected his gear and went home. There had been enough "fishing" for today.

Eddie slid his twelve-foot canoe into the back of his pickup truck. The canoe was built with a reinforced square stern to allow for a small motor. He carefully positioned the two-horsepower gas engine beside the canoe and departed immediately for the Santee River train trestle.

Eddie knew the night would be closing in on the narrow river channel by the time he would arrive. The thick woods growing in the low-lying swamp would be dark, but Eddie calculated those shadows of dusk would allow him to release the boys with a minimal chance of recognition. He maneuvered his rusty truck through the afternoon tourists, rumbling from stoplight to stoplight in the afternoon heat. As he powered south down Highway 17, passing Murrells Inlet, the strength of a late-afternoon sun illuminated the low clouds on the horizon. An orange summer sky warned of the dark to come. He hurried.

Chapter 66

Earlier, Tony had called with final instructions on how to deal with Vernon and his recently discovered cohorts. The advanced support team of bodyguards and muscled intimidators proceeded with the second stage of their plan to show the bosses that Tony's turf was secured and well-managed and to demonstrate that Tony knew how to deal with unwelcome intruders. Driggers had arrived at the river house to ensure some finesse was employed in the execution of the plan. Timing and visual impact would be important attributes weighed in the judgment levied by the bosses. Mercy was not on the mind of anyone from Tony's crew.

Vernon, Harley, and David were cut down, and all three collapsed to the floor of the shed often used to deal with traitors, competitors, or kids who tried to skip out on tabs at the Blue House. Vernon's face was bleeding from numerous lacerations around his eyes and mouth. His nose was bleeding and broken. Harley and David were in similar shape, but suffered the added pain of bruised ribs, crab-eaten eyelids, and uncountable mosquito bites.

Vernon pondered the situation. These men had asked them no questions, and no deals appeared to be lurking behind the violent treatment. What did they want? He had tried to ask and had tried to bargain, but all he got was another hard fist to his face for each attempt at negotiation. Surely this gang didn't intend to kill them without a discussion. Why would they? Vernon remained clueless and had grown quiet with despair. Now what?

Driggers directed the men to pick up the three captives and toss them in the bed of a pickup truck. Vernon and his two sidekicks lay motionless and suffered, wishing their ordeal would soon end. Harley and David felt a painful sense of déjà vu coming on. Vernon went on another short mental journey to his happy place, where he drank beer and gulped tequila shots with the buxom blonde from the night before.

The goons drove the truck along a two-lane path through a pine thicket and into a clearing where the trail ended near the river. A flock of black vultures scattered as the truck pulled up to a grassy low bluff that bounded a turn in the river. A long sandbar provided an inviting view. The idyllic setting provided the property with a unique picnic and swimming area perfect for boat launching, fishing, or other summer fun on the river. The only picnic planned this day would be for the vultures.

Driggers had the men drag their captives out of the truck by their feet. Each young man was tied spread-eagle to a crude wooden raft. Planking had been laced to blocks of Styrofoam sufficient to float a body. One man stood over Vernon with a long, razor-sharp fillet knife. He bent over and cut Vernon's shirt and trousers open. Without hesitation he pulled the knife across Vernon's stomach and then again below his waist, slicing the skin only an eighth of an inch deep. Vernon screamed. The flesh wounds bled profusely, but no internal organs were exposed; that job would be left for the vultures to finish. The man moved with practiced precision to David, performing a similar epidermal surgery, yielding a bloodcurdling scream that was heard only by these men, the vultures, and the swamp. The man stepped over Harley. As his clothes were cut away, he passed out from fear fueled by anticipation. The sadistic surgeon walked away.

One of the goons threw a bucket of river water in Harley's face, bringing him back to a terrified conscious state. Driggers leaned down and whispered a cold message in his ear. Harley heard him even above the painful, crying howls and pleadings from his partners.

"Son, you are one dumb son of a bitch, and you caused trouble in the wrong place. You need to go home. I want you to warn others, including your supplier or whoever the hell you think you might discreetly share this message with. If you go to the cops, I'll know, and then your next meeting with me will be more painful than this one. It will be terminal for you and your family. I know who they are." Driggers grabbed Harley by the nose and yanked his face so they were eye to eye. "Do you understand me, son? Are you grasping the impact of your future course?"

Driggers's monotonic message was chilling. Harley thought he understood, and even with his limited capacity for comprehension of these issues, he got the big picture. He was going to live to warn others not to sell drugs at Myrtle Beach, or anywhere even close.

The goons retrieved two odorous deer carcasses they had picked up along the highway. Both deer were bloated from a few days in the summer sun and were ripe for consumption by the abundance of black vultures that inhabited the area.

The carcasses placed in this field to attract the vultures had worked. A vulture's prime dessert, the rear half of a deer with intestines, was placed over Vernon's chest and abdomen. The same vulture banquet was laid on David. The sight and smell was truly repulsive, even to the hardened team helping to write this message in Harley's memory.

"Boys, do you know why we are draping these ignorant felons with this stinking roadkill?" Driggers asked.

"No, boss, tell us," one thug obediently asked on cue.

"Because black vultures act as mother nature's garbage crew. For the benefit of our young bullies, let me tell you a little about these unique birds. When death is imminent in the wilderness, vultures come together in surprisingly large numbers. They arrive from places unknown and wait for an injured or sick animal to die for an easy feast. Sometimes they just wait until their prey is immobilized; depends on how hungry they are. But regardless when they start, vultures are rarely in a hurry to consume their prey." Driggers walked around Vernon and his hapless crew, strutting and waving his arms in the air like a Baptist preacher at an outdoor revival.

"Their beaks are not well suited for chewing, so they favor the soft entrails and organs of their victim. They poke and rip the abdomen open and wait for the remainder of the animal to cure into a soft pulp. Their persistent and methodical consumption of the dead and decomposing rids an area of the smell. They make efficient use of what is no longer useful to others. They are patient, systematic, and tenacious in their task to serve their place in nature's plan. And that, my friends, is what you have to look forward to. Seems almost like nature's way, don't it?"

Two thugs laughed at the enthusiastic preaching.

"We will rid ourselves of the stink of deteriorating, useless flesh like these bums. Can I get a hallelujah?" Driggers cried out.

"Hallelujah." The thugs played along.

"Now boys, you're really gonna love this part. It's dinnertime for our vulture friends. You have their meal resting on your bleeding guts, and I'm sure they will have some difficulty determining the point where the deer stops and your belly starts."

David howled with pain. Another vulture floated down to a nearby treetop to watch.

"They will probably not give a damn, now that I think about it. It should be interesting for you to watch. How long you live will depend on how hungry they are, and how many can get at you at once. Why, I've seen these birds sit over a carcass for three or four days, sometimes a week before they finish. In a day or so, we're gonna float you down the river, where some other swamp critter may decide you're ripe enough to consume before the vultures finish you off."

Driggers wanted to make sure Vernon, Harley and David were clear on their fate to minimize the guessing and maximize the horror of the slow, painful death to come.

"Next time you pick on a couple of old men...wait, I guess there won't be no next time. I guess you boys are just up shit creek." Driggers laughed at his own little pun, but no one else did. The men pulled the rafts with their vulture delights closer to the edge of the sandbar and on top of two enormous fire-ant mounds.

"Oh, we have just a little more pain for you boys. These fire ants look really pissed off. You messed up their nice little dirt mound. These nasty, mean, little devils will finish off what the vultures don't get."

The men all climbed in the truck and drove through the woods and back to the house.

The vultures had found safe haven in surrounding treetops, cautiously watching their meal. They were patient creatures. Slowly, one by one, they began to return closer, landing on the edge of the field and completing the cleanup of roadkill morsels left behind. Two were circling effortlessly overhead. Time was on their side, but they looked hungry.

Chapter 67

Two limos slowed on Highway 17 and turned left onto an unmarked, paved, secondary road. As the single-lane road entered the tree line, the pavement thinned to gravel and then to a washboard-rippled, white-sand road. The cushioned suspension of the limos buffered the road's impact, easing the transition from the city to the swamp.

After a two-mile ride down the winding, tree-draped road, the limos eased into the well-manicured yard surrounding an elegant riverfront house. Dusty ribbons of sunlight cut diagonal paths through the trees of the river's swampy woods.

The bosses were impressed with the sophisticated luxury compatibly nestled within this unspoiled wilderness. These men could recognize quality and appreciated fine accommodations reserved for the upper class. They expected nothing but the best, and this place was the king's palace of river houses. The isolation would allow their private business discussions without interference or prying eyes. They appreciated the peace and quiet of the sequestered riverside paradise. The bosses climbed out of the cars and moved onto the wide porch that wrapped around three sides of the yellow clapboard house with a tin roof. Detective Driggers and the assembled staff greeted them at the large double-front doors.

"We have the trespassing, pot-selling punks who hurt Frank and killed Marvin. If you would like to see them before they go, it won't take but a few moments." The group returned to the cars. Driggers quickly briefed Tony that the scene was set.

The massing of vultures continued, and the flock patiently waited for their time. The muscle, watching the captives from a distance, heard a few random screams and monotonous whimpering. The limos drove through the pine thicket to the end of the road.

The more aggressive black vultures had already moved to the edge of the floats and their aromatic prey. Cold, dark, unwavering eyes focused on dinner, not quite sure if it was time to eat, but the buffet banquet was set and ready. Vernon, Harley, and David had watched as the vultures gradually moved closer. One lead bird had jabbed his beak into the deer carcass on Vernon's stomach. Vernon screamed, and the vultures retreated a few feet, but were undeterred. Another vulture joined the first. The horror was building. Vernon and his doomed gang saw more vultures coming in to join the flock, and the birds were getting restless. The carrion birds were swarming like flies and gradually moving closer—cautious, waiting. Patience was their rewarding virtue; patience brought their prize, and patience provided their meal ticket. The gray light of dusk gradually doused the afternoon's golden glow.

The family and their thugs emerged from the limos. The vultures scattered only slightly, some rising to their treetop waiting areas, yielding to these larger beasts for the moment. Frank walked in front, with Tony and Driggers trailing close behind. He had the right to be first to inspect the family's retaliatory action. Frank stood over Vernon and looked down with disdain and anger derived not so much from his own suffering, but from the callous treatment dealt to Marvin. He gazed with admiration at the setting Tony had prepared. He could not help but smile at the symbolic artistry of this macabre scene.

"Tony, you done good, brother; shows originality. You'll leave a message, and that's what's needed." Frank patted him on the back and stepped forward to peer down into Vernon's eyes. The wretched stench of rotted deer carcass, held captive in the buggy, late-afternoon heat, permeated the entire clearing. The strength of the smell and the density of biting deerflies increased in direct proportion to the proximity of each of the victims. Frank seemed unfazed by the gore or its sensations.

"Well, punk, good to see your sorry ass again. You killed my friend, and you made me just a damn bit uncomfortable." Frank spoke evenly with his hands on both knees, leaning over Vernon's face.

"Let me up, man, these vultures are picking at us!" David pleaded.

Frank stood up, moved over to David, reached down and picked up a scrap of fly-covered carcass, and stuffed it in David's mouth. He pulled out a barber's razor and sliced David across the gut, a bit deeper than the cuts made before.

"Well, that's the point, son! Maybe that'll help 'em get to you a little faster. These birds just love intestines!" The bosses laughed, their men laughed, Frank laughed, and David puked out the rotted deer hide. His misery increased as a remaining deerfly crawled into his nose and bit. Frank moved back to Vernon, slicing his belly and leaving a Z-patterned bleeding wound. Both victims were crying with new pain.

"Even Zorro can't save you now, son," Frank said.

"We'll wait a couple of days before we put them in the river," Tony said. "Give the birds a chance to get the job started. I want them to get stranded in a side creek off the main river. Let nature finish the job. We'll send a boat to make sure that happens. Bo J can help with that after he arrives. Have him pull these boys up a swamp creek where no one will find them," Tony instructed Driggers.

All the men had returned to the house and were admiring the view of the river from the back deck as Bo J glided up to the low wooden dock that stretched from the large patio out into the river. He secured lines from the bow and stern of the boat to cleats on the dock. He held his head high, proud to deliver this one boat fully loaded with pot. Tony and a couple of his men walked down to check the haul.

"Well, that looks good, son, but where's the rest?" Tony asked in an unfriendly tone.

"It's up the river about four or five miles, boss," Bo J answered respectfully. "I was having trouble getting both boats safely over some river rapids. Thought it would be smart to get this load here and then go back for the other."

He was hurt and embarrassed again by Tony, in front of the others. When would he get some respect? When would he be able to do something considered right in the eyes of this man or any other older man in charge? Bo J's lower lip protruded slightly, his eyes began to moisten, but he would not let them see this weak moment. He turned and focused on unloading the bails of marijuana onto the dock. Someday he would be in charge. He would be the bully, just like in school.

"Well, hurry up and get your ass back up that river, and do it now," Tony barked. "I want the rest of it back here tonight. Anything happens to that load, and it's your ass, son!"

Tony turned and walked up the dock and back to the rear of the house. The group was migrating from the porch into the well-appointed living area. As they entered, they were greeted with wine, beer, and cocktails exactly to their tastes. Tony entered, smiled, and welcomed the group to the family's river plantation. Happy hour was underway.

Chapter 68

As the limos turned into the woods, McKenzie and Floyd elected not to follow. They glided down the highway, crossed the bridge over the wide expanse of the north and south branches of the Santee River, and eased off the asphalt into a roadside picnic area on the southwest side of the bridge. Floyd checked his recently printed, high-resolution satellite map.

"Here's the bridge where the river splits, and along the north bank that road ends at a large house on the river. This section of the river and the house are secluded. There are a couple of fish-camp trailers and a small boat landing between the highway and the house, but that's it. One way in, one way out, except for the river, and that wouldn't be the normal mode of transportation for this gang," Floyd said with confidence.

"Should we notify the rest of the team?" McKenzie asked.

"We'll let them know where we are. The teams are spread out, so it'll take some time to bring them together for a bust here."

McKenzie tried his radio. He got static. His cell phone had no signal. This area was one of those rare radio coverage voids. "Of all the times for the radio to crap out, this is not it," he snarled. McKenzie knew how to do many things, but electronics was not his strong suit.

A widespread grid of communications towers to serve a variety of law-enforcement organizations established the public safety radio network. But despite the critical service it provided, there were still coverage holes.

"We've got nothing but static now. All of that mundane chatter we've been listening to, and now we get squat."

"Might be that big thunderstorm coming out of the southwest. With this swamp and river, the next antenna tower would be in the direction of that big cloud."

"Yep, that storm is giving the radio tower a beating."

Another lightning bolt, and the radio crackled with electronic static. The reason didn't matter; they had no service.

"We need to check these guys out some more before we bring in the whole team anyway," Floyd said and looked at the sky again. "We'll go down the road and get more intel, then we'll call backup. No sweat."

"You know, we could do this on our own," McKenzie said. "They only have two cars and about ten people, maybe a few more already at the house."

"Right, but we'll call later," Floyd reminded him. "No need to take a big risk when we have help on the way."

"Sure, we'll need help to transport all of them and someone to deal with the house."

"Let's go in and check on our little gang of trouble," Floyd suggested.

He cranked the car and returned across the river. They checked their weapons and disconnected their seat belts to allow for a quick exit from the car if they got surprised on the way in. Twilight came quickly as the growing dark clouds robbed the southern sky early of its dwindling afternoon light. They turned off Highway 17 following a white sand road. The swamp swallowed them as the car entered a canopy of thick, moss-covered oaks. The white sand reflected what evening light seeped through the trees, allowing Floyd to drive without headlights. Approaching the house with headlights in the woods would result in quick and easy detection. Stealth was required for now.

About a half mile into the woods, Floyd drove past a small dirt drive leading to a fishing trailer and had just rounded a curve when a deer jumped into the road. He jerked the steering wheel quickly and stomped on the brakes, but couldn't avoid hitting the deer in the hindquarters, forcing Floyd to turn more sharply to the left, slamming the car squarely into an unmovable three-foot-wide oak tree. Floyd and McKenzie simultaneously crashed into the windshield at almost twenty miles an hour, rendering them both unconscious and bleeding. The car's momentum rolled it sideways into a deep drainage ditch, smashing the side windows into crumbled bits of glass. After the impact their radio no longer crackled with static. There was no sound, only smoke.

Chapter 69

Edna, Evelyn, Vera, and the elderly folks from the retirement home had not planned on such a long drive. When they reached Georgetown, they had to stop for gas and a trip to the restroom. With the small restroom and its difficult door lock, the short stop turned into fifteen minutes. Edna grew more agitated as time passed and the gap between their bus and McKenzie increased.

When they finally started south on Highway 17, Edna was concerned that to continue might be useless. With the gas stop, the limos could be ten or even fifteen miles ahead, unless they had turned off the road. If they had left the main highway, Edna doubted they would find them, but her determination, and the support of the whole group, gave her the faith to press on.

"Evelyn, I'm afraid we may have lost them. They've got quite a head start. What are we going to do?"

"We have a long, open stretch of road ahead, and there's not much here except the Francis Marion National Forest for about fifty miles. Where on earth are they going? Charleston, maybe?"

"Are we going to eat at Murrells Inlet or Georgetown?" an oblivious Ms. Naomi asked from the rear of the bus.

"Oh, Georgetown can't compare, honey. We just must eat at Murrells Inlet. I am so tired of instant potatoes and canned peas, I could just puke." Thelma offered her two cents with her best aristocratic Southern flair.

"Thelma, you are not the only one, dear. I hear Georgetown has some pretty good restaurants on the river," Gladis chimed in. "Oh, by the way, it's time to take my medicine."

Sam jumped in the fun. "Let's stop at that bait shop yonder and get some beer. The one I brought is already warm. We need some ice-cold beer if we are going to ride all over creation."

"Sam, you hush now, you know you can't drink a beer."

"Well then, I want some fried shrimp and oysters, and I want some pretty soon, or my blood sugar is going to go off the charts, I'll tell you what. It sure is." As they passed the bait shop, Sam's voice trailed off. He watched with envy as a fisherman walked to his pickup truck and boat with a six-pack and a quart can of worms.

"My pie is getting cold," Thelma blurted out.

"Where does Frank's family live," Agnes asked. "Do they live in Charleston? Is that where we're going?"

"My pie will be cold if we go all the way to Charleston."

"OK, folks, we have to drive a little more to see if we can catch up with Frank. We'll get you something to eat directly now. I promise." Vera stood and walked down the aisle, patting shoulders and checking closely for any real signs of trouble. Most were just teasing or griping to be part of the fun. The elderly group really didn't care where they went—they were just glad to be out—but their focus was somewhat out of sync with the intensity of the chase being felt by Edna, Evelyn, and Vera.

This section of road was overpopulated with highway patrol officers anxious to stop the endless supply of speeding drivers on these remote, flat, four lanes of asphalt. Edna drove the bus at a speed slightly over the posted limit. She wanted to catch up to the strange entourage but keep her passengers safe. She traveled faster than she should have, but more slowly than she wanted.

"Edna, honey, I do believe you're speeding. Should you be driving so fast?" Thelma asked and looked around for support.

"There are more state troopers on this road than Carter's got little liver pills," Ms. Naomi said.

"Go faster, Edna. I need the speed." Sam laughed. Irritated Thelma huffed in a breath.

Evelyn and Vera looked down each side road that they passed, inspecting each gas station and small restaurant, but found no sign of the limos or McKenzie. Ten miles south of Georgetown, a growing black thundercloud brought an early twilight and a growing anxiety to the group. Edna and Evelyn were focused on the traffic ahead.

Vera had lost her intensity with the pursuit and was gazing at the wooded land that she knew bordered the Santee River. She loved this area. It was a peaceful respite from the hustle of Myrtle Beach. With the waning strength of their commitment to what now seemed a hopeless endeavor, they passed McKenzie and Floyd, who were slowing in the northbound lanes with a turn signal blinking.

"Girls, isn't that McKenzie? That's his car turning down that road," Vera said somewhat casually. The unmarked police car turned onto a side road. Edna and Evelyn simultaneously snapped their heads to the left, catching a glimpse of the car as it disappeared into the trees.

"Glory be and hallelujah, we found them. Now we can go get some seafood." Sam cheered.

"No one is watching the road," Thelma chided. "We could wreck."

Evelyn glanced back and said, "Thelma, please."

"Where can I turn? Quick, we need to turn," Edna shouted. She looked forward desperately at the median, seeing only the river and the long bridge ahead. At the speed they were traveling, she had no time to pull over. She had to cross the double bridges spanning both the north and south branches of the river and its wetlands before she could turn around. She accelerated and searched for a paved crossover connecting to the northbound lanes.

A mile past the bridge, Edna saw a small reflective sign indicating the turn lane and the connector to the northbound highway. As she turned left and accelerated back across the bridge, the first huge drops of rain, warning of the coming storm, began to strike the windshield. Edna quickly crossed over the river again and turned off the highway, cautiously following the road into the woods. The rain was now a torrent. With shocking urgency the dark clouds flushed their stored, freshwater gift on the earth below.

"Honey, don't you think you should turn on the headlights?" Thelma asked. "It's awful hard to see."

"Thelma, please ma'am, let Edna focus on driving," Vera said with a tense voice.

"Edna, please turn on the lights," Evelyn agreed quietly.

Edna slowed the bus to a crawl and searched the dash for the head-light switch. Without any additional help from the rear seats, she sensed the new danger of this journey. As she guided the bus around a curve, they saw a car on its side, half-wedged in the ditch and half-hanging in the air.

Edna stopped the bus and said, "Vera, stay with the group." She and Evelyn jumped out.

They dashed across the dirt road to the wrecked car. The hard rain strained through the thick layers of the forest canopy, dousing the girls as they went to the rescue. The engine was still running, with an exposed rear wheel slowly turning in the air.

Edna looked over the crumpled hood through an opening where the shattered windshield had been. She saw McKenzie and Floyd in the front seat. McKenzie was unconscious, slumped over and bleeding from his forehead. Floyd was dazed, but moved with weak awkward efforts when the girls shouted to them. The dashboard that had been pushed back on their thighs trapped the men, wedging their legs to the seats.

Edna climbed through the windshield, searching for any sign of life from McKenzie. He was breathing slowly and had a pulse, but would not respond to her voice or touch. She was careful not to move his head in case there might be some more serious injury. Evelyn jumped behind the car when lightning struck a tall pine tree near the edge of the river with an explosive crack, demonstrating the godly power of the storm positioned directly overhead.

"Evelyn, this ditch will be filled with the runoff from this down-pour," Edna shouted over the rain. "We have to get them out of here quickly."

"You must be Edna," Floyd said with a grimace, overcoming the pain.

"Yes, how do you know? Who are you?" Edna responded, somewhat surprised.

Floyd was still dazed from the knock on his head but appeared to be recovering.

"Are you hurt?" Edna asked.

"Yeah, it hurts, but I think I'm going to be OK if I can get out of here," he said, gasping.

"Where does it hurt most?"

"All over." Floyd braved a chuckle. "This dashboard has trapped my legs. McKenzie told me about you. You must be an angel, just like he said."

"He said I was an angel?" Edna asked with rain pouring on he head.

"How else would you be here?" Floyd said. "But hey, we need help. I have an army of SLED agents ready to come arrest the men we're following. They are really nasty characters who can't be allowed to escape. You've got to help get the rest of my team here as soon as possible."

Floyd stopped struggling and just lay back, saving his strength to help Edna help him.

"But no, we can't," Edna blurted out, confused by Floyd's priorities. "I mean, we need to get you two out of here and..."

Evelyn had eased around the vehicle, evaluating the predicament of the two men. She was standing in the ankle-deep, fast-flowing water that was filling the ditch, and the rain fell harder. The deafening rainstorm drumming the car attacked Evelyn's senses and reminded her of Guido's wreck, where there had been more help than they needed. Evelyn had only watched and worried. Now, it was up to Edna, Evelyn, and Vera to rescue these men.

"Edna, I need you to call this number. Tell the dispatcher where we are, and the SLED unit will handle things. Please do it quickly!" Floyd handed her a card and gave the instructions with the greatest urgency he could muster through his clenched teeth. "Our radio is toast, and there's no telephone coverage in this swamp. Please go to a phone, quickly!"

"No way. I'm not leaving McKenzie to drown in this ditch. I'm staying right here; maybe we could pull you out or something!" Edna pleaded, uncertain of what to do next.

"You stay with them," Evelyn blurted out. "I'll drive the bus back and try to find a phone that works. We passed several stores just outside of Georgetown. It's only a few miles. We could be back in thirty minutes or maybe less."

She understood Edna's dilemma, and she understood Floyd's message. She looked for a solution that suited both, and she knew the busload of senior citizens could not sit out here for half the night. She grabbed the card.

"I'll be back as soon as I can, dear," Evelyn said. She hugged Edna and then climbed around the wrecked car, out of the now knee-deep water, dashing through the rain back to the bus. She opened the door and climbed directly into the driver's seat. She was covered with mud, and her hair and clothes were dripping wet. With fire in her eyes, she struggled to back the bus to the small driveway they had passed on the way in.

"Vera, honey, would you help me back up? Could you look through the back window? I'll use the mirrors, but in this rain, I need your help too."

"Sure, hon, I'll do it. But my goodness, what's going on out there? Where's Edna? Are the two boys OK?" Vera asked with an anxious concern.

"I'll tell you on the way, Vera. Just help me get turned around."

With some considerable effort through several attempts, Evelyn finally got the bus backed far enough to turn around and drive out of the woods on the wet road. She quickly pulled onto Highway 17, gunned the engine, and headed back to the first telephone they could find in Georgetown. Ms. Naomi, newly self-appointed spokeswoman for the group, moved up to the seat behind Evelyn and next to Vera.

"We've all decided we'd like to eat at Lee's Kitchen in Murrells Inlet on the way back, hon. It is way past our normal dinnertime, and most of us need to take our medicine soon. It's best to eat first, so let's go on to dinner now. Is that all right with y'all?" Naomi stated the group's desire with an authoritative conviction.

"Now, Ms. Naomi, we're going to help those young men who were hurt back there in that car," Vera answered with compassion. "After we help them, then we can get something to eat. I know it's past dinner-time, but those nice young men need our help."

After Vera got Naomi seated with the others, she came back up front with Evelyn. Evelyn quickly explained the situation and their need to get to a telephone to alert the SLED agents who were supposedly wait-ing somewhere to help Floyd and McKenzie. Vera thought a moment about the best way to make the contact with SLED. They needed a tele-phone and someone who had law-enforcement connections.

Vera knew the area, as Eddie had worked at the paper mill in Georgetown for thirty years. Most of his friends from work still lived in the Georgetown community. She could get one of them to help. Then it hit her. Vera had the perfect solution.

"Drive, Evelyn, drive! I've got an idea! In another mile you'll see a stoplight. Take a left, go a half-mile, and you'll see a Kmart. Pull up to the front door. One of Eddie's best friends, Harold, was a security guard at the mill. He's retired now, working security at Kmart. He'll know what to do. Here, turn here!" Vera spouted the plan with com-plete confidence.

Evelyn did not wait for a green light. She pulled into the turn lane, checked for traffic, and gunned through the light. Thelma and Ms. Naomi took careful notice that Evelyn had run the red light. They coughed softly under their hankies and looked about at the others with stifled indignation, but neither said a word. They just held onto their pastries.

Evelyn stepped hard on the brakes, and the bus skidded to a halt in the fire lane in front of Kmart's main entrance. Both Evelyn and Vera ran into the store and went straight to the service desk.

"Would you please page Harold, your security guard? It's an emer-gency!" Evelyn shouted.

"OK, just wait a minute, ladies. Shoppers, we have another Kmart BlueLight Special on men's socks. Look for the flashing blue light in the men's department. Hurry now, the sale won't last long." And with a voice lacking all the enthusiasm of the BlueLight Special, she announced, "Harold, please report to the service desk, Harold to the service desk."

The service associate turned and shuffled through a plastic bag and looked at her co-worker. "Do you know how much overtime I had to work last week? Lord, I tell you what, I just can't be doing that anymore. They gonna have to get somebody else to work these hours now."

"I hear ya. I can't wait for my shift to get over, I am soooo bored, you know what I mean?"

"Uh-huh, I sure do."

They were obviously unfazed by the sight of a soaking-wet, muddy woman and her little motherly companion who had rushed into the store urgently requesting the security guard. Apparently, this sort of thing was not out of the norm for the Kmart in Georgetown.

Harold emerged from the back, slightly perturbed. He had been watching the end of the Atlanta Braves baseball game. They were ahead in the ninth, with two outs. As he trudged to the front mumbling in frustration with this distraction, two ladies from the bus came in looking for a bathroom. Evelyn couldn't take the time to collect them. After brief introductions and hugs, Vera asked about Harold's wife and family. Talking about family was an odd nicety at the moment, but Vera was Old South, and manners took precedence, even with the urgency of this situation.

Evelyn burst in. "I'm sorry, Vera, but we need to make this call now!"

Vera and Evelyn explained to Harold what they knew. Evelyn cut the explanation short and pleaded for Harold to call. As Vera had told her, he knew what to do.

Harold was not an impressive sight, with a potbelly straining the buttons of his poorly tailored uniform. Coffee stains and doughnut dribbles didn't help either. He carried no weapons or shiny handcuffs or a nightstick, but despite his current appearance, Harold was well trained and experienced in the methods of state law enforcement. He quickly grasped the severity of the situation. He took the ladies to the main office upstairs and made the call.

With an intimate knowledge of the area, Harold was able to precisely identify the location to the dispatcher. He offered to meet the SLED team in the parking lot of the Kmart and lead them to the spot. Harold was on fire with excitement. He was back in the action.

While Vera, Evelyn, and Harold were busy with the call, most of the elderly passengers had wandered from the bus to visit the snack bar and were now shuffling back to their ride. They did not want to miss the rumored trip to Murrells Inlet for a big seafood dinner at Lee's Kitchen. Evelyn and Vera guided them onto the bus and drove off, heading back to help Edna. A large multi-disciplined SLED task force, a SWAT team, and a bus from the Myrtle Beach Retirement Home were all en route to save two "officers down" and to make the bust of the decade.

Chapter 70

Eddie arrived at the river as dusk dulled the afternoon light. As a safety precaution, he used the boat landing located a couple of miles upstream from the trestle. Thunder and encroaching dark clouds signaled that a nasty storm was coming. A boat motor whined in the distance, moving fast upriver. Eddie was undeterred by the threatening weather and was solidly committed to the decision to set the young men free. He prepared his small boat and launched it just as both the dark and the rain fell on the swamp with a vengeance.

He loved this place. He had often fished the Santee and camped many nights on the numerous high sandbars dotting this stretch of the river. If Eddie didn't live at the beach, this watershed would be his choice. This paradise would be a perfect substitute for his home: a place where his need for solitude and the quiet pleasures of nature could be met.

As he eased down the river, his poncho kept him dry even as the rain pelted and soaked everything around him. A bolt of lightning struck a tall pine on the riverbank less than a half mile ahead. He saw the bolt attack the tree, thumping the ground as the electrical current followed the sappy conductor down to its taproot deep beneath the surface. This storm was angry and dangerous.

He approached the train trestle with a woodsman's caution, searching the bank on both sides, quietly paddling, looking for any clue that he might be under surveillance. When he was satisfied he was alone on the river, he edged farther along the bank under the limbs of overhanging trees. The main thundercloud had passed over, and the rain eased to a drizzle. In the low light, he could make out the loose ropes dangling from the bridge. His victims were no longer tied where he had left them. Eddie maneuvered his boat over to inspect the ropes with frayed ends just touching the surface of the river. Someone had cut the boys loose. Someone else knew.

With his cautious approach, Eddie had been on the river for a couple of hours. The rain had almost stopped, but new clouds and thunder promised more. Mosquitoes were making use of this brief torrential reprieve to swarm their prey. The poncho helped, but he was still aware of the relentless bug attack to suck his blood.

Eddie wanted to be sure about the two men, so he continued his search. He knew about the fishing camps and a yellow plantation house not far downriver. Maybe they had escaped to a sandbar. Maybe their handcuffs and remaining ropes were entangled on a submerged tree limb, and they needed help. Eddie needed more factual confirmation to satiate his recently discovered guilt.

As he approached the plantation house, he saw a rare display of lights, inside and out. He had fished this river over a hundred times in the last five years and had never seen a person or even a single light at this house. He had thought it to be a waste of prime real estate. This activity was an odd and curious sight.

He eased to the opposite bank and grabbed a low-hanging tree limb to watch. Had they found the boys? What was going on here? He heard loud voices, men moving quickly, reacting to a truck pulling up. Two men and a woman were yanked out of the truck bed and forced into the house. Eddie saw guns. This situation looked bad and was growing stranger by the moment.

He released the tree and floated downstream and across the river. He knew of a sandbar that would provide easy access to the house for a closer look. These men were dressed in suits, and he doubted they would be able to catch him in this swamp or on the river. The Santee River swamp was clearly not their turf. Eddie tied his boat to a tree on the downstream side of the sandbar, positioned for a quick getaway.

Chapter 71

~

Two members of the family's perimeter guard sat in a truck parked on the dirt road halfway between the house and the highway. When the group had first arrived, these thugs had been posted to ensure they had no surprise visitors. The road was private from their position to the house, and they were stationed to ensure it remained private. The two men had watched the slow creep of darkness over the woods and the ominous approach of the thunderstorm. They had suffered from the increasing swarms of mosquitoes.

Just after dark, as the rain began to fall, the men saw headlights. They discussed the potential source as a young couple parking for some secret romance, someone on the wrong road, or maybe just someone going to a fish camp. They tried to reconcile the erratic behavior of the car. The men watched the lights back up, turn around, and rapidly drive away.

Something about this luminous display bothered these men, who were paid to be suspicious. They drove their truck forward without headlights. In a few moments, they discovered the wrecked car, flipped on their headlights, and cautiously surveyed the scene. They drew their pistols and approached the vehicle from opposite directions. The men found Edna struggling to keep McKenzie's head above the ditch water now flowing through the lower side of the car.

With a distressed face, Edna looked up and said, "Thank, God. Can you help me?"

"Sure, lady. Move away from the car."

"But his head, he'll drown."

"Your choice, lady. You better be moving when we pull it out."

The men threw a chain around the rear axle of the car, hooked it to the trailer hitch of the truck, and extracted the wrecked vehicle from the ditch. Edna held McKenzie's head until the car started to move and then she jumped clear and landed in the rushing ditch water. The men were not so concerned about McKenzie drowning; they just wanted to get these two guys out of the car and this wreck moved and report back to the boss. They wanted to avoid wreckers, ambulances, and police snooping around.

With extreme effort the larger of the two men released the jammed seat adjustments and forced each front seat back, helping to free both men from the car. One at a time, he yanked and pulled and finally squeezed them out. He picked McKenzie up and tossed him in the bed of the pickup.

"Be careful," Edna said with surprise. "What do you think you are doing?"

"Shut up!"

"Take your hand off me!"

"Get in the truck, lady, and shut your mouth," snarled the smaller thug, who with a nervous hand waved a shiny, nickel-plated, forty-five-caliber pistol in her direction.

The guards had little regard for the injuries the men had sustained. A search of their wallets produced police and SLED IDs. The big thug kicked Floyd, picked him up by his shirt collar and belt, and tossed him in the truck bed like a sack of potatoes.

"Stop that. He's hurt. What's wrong with you people?"

"Shut up, lady."

"Don't touch me, you jerk."

"I said shut up, lady."

The guards' anxiety rose to a dangerous pitch. The discovery of law-enforcement identification created a new sense of urgency. One man sat in the back of the truck with his gun on the three intruders, while the other drove them back to the house.

The big thug drove the truck wildly, weaving along the serpentine dirt road, racing to the house with their news. The sentries posted outside the house saw the truck coming fast, heralding trouble, evoking a frantic response. They prepared for action. The rapid movement on the porch transmitted a sudden ripple of tension onto the tranquil surface of the dinner party. The most senior boss turned to his bodyguard, silently soliciting an explanation.

The truck brakes were vigorously applied, causing the truck to skid across the rain-soaked drive and wet grass, throwing mud and gravel on the neat pastel-colored suits of the guards who had raced to meet them. The driver opened the door, ready to jump out even before the truck had fully stopped. He raced to report the presence of a SLED agent and a local policeman.

Until this moment Tony's stock had been rising, with kind words and praise from the bosses. But his newfound respect and confidence now melted like a warm slice of butter on a plate of steaming grits. The family leaders, who only moments before had toasted him for his accomplishments, were now nervous, standing huddled with their lieutenants and obviously rethinking their previous assessment.

When they saw the badges of the men just discovered, they grew suspicious about this meeting. Had Tony set them up, had he sold out, had he brought them together in this remote location on unfamiliar ground to make capture less complicated? The minds of these men worked much the same; they trusted no one, not even one another. They held a quiet caucus.

Who else could have done it? Who else knew enough to put them in this situation? The bottom line was Tony and Driggers had set this meeting up and they were responsible. They had to be setting the bosses up. They felt betrayed and vulnerable, trapped like rats. Frank was divided in loyalty because they had all been good to him. No one doubted Frank, but everyone else was in play.

The boss called the room to order. The two blindfolded lawmen and Edna were on the floor. Edna was kicking and struggling, cursing into her gag.

"Unless they tell you what they're doing here and who tipped them off, shoot them in their joints until they do. Take them and take Tony and his cop buddy down by the river. Do any of you men got a problem with dis?" He looked around briefly, knowing the answer would be a unanimous shoulder shrug, signifying a "No, of course not" response.

"But, boss, I didn't—"

"Shut up, or I'll shoot you myself, right now!" The boss had pulled his own gun and jammed the barrel to Tony's forehead. "Now get him outta here. Tie Tony and the other guy to one of the rafts and push them down the river. Shoot them first, but just wound 'em. Let the vultures have 'em too."

Edna used her chin and tongue to move the gag. "I'll tell you their plan, you bastards. You're surrounded, so you might as well untie us, and give it up."

The group chuckled in unison. "I'm sure we're much more concerned now, sweetie. Take them to the river, and let's get on the road, just in case someone cares where these clowns are." The boss spoke, and people reacted.

Three goons tossed McKenzie, Floyd, and Edna in the back of the truck again. A moment later Tony and Driggers landed on the steel bed of the truck, tied up and gagged. Two goons climbed in and drove the truck down to the river. The rest of the group got the pot loaded and the limos ready.

Chapter 72

After Eddie had secured his boat, he stepped quietly up the sandbank and into the edge of the woods surrounding the clearing where Vernon and his boys were being served as the main course for the scavengers' dinner. In the dim twilight, he could see the mass of large black birds patiently standing, watching their prey. He could hear the eerie cries and gut-wrenching groans of the tortured men. He looked up to see the trees bending with the weight of a horrible horde of birds sitting, watching, and waiting for the time when their prey was too weak to resist. The dinner bell was about to ring. Two of the more aggressive birds were standing on Vernon's legs, digging their claws into his shivering flesh. The acrid air enhanced the horror of the scene that Eddie was beginning to comprehend.

His experience told him not to rush to the rescue. Whoever had done this to these men was more pissed off than he had been. Eddie's patience was rewarded, as he was still hidden when the truck approached. He looked around quickly, finding a fallen tree limb the size of a large baseball bat, but he needed a more lethal weapon.

The birds squawked and flew back to the safety of the trees. With the turmoil of the truck and the birds, Eddie moved through the woods and out of the headlights. He moved to the side of the truck and behind the men.

The two goons pulled the five bodies, one at a time, from the back of the truck. Eddie recognized the captives as they crossed in front of the headlights. When he saw Edna being roughed up, he got mad, but he maintained his composure and his cover, watching, waiting. Rushing these two thugs, who no doubt were well armed, would surely get him shot. The right moment would come.

McKenzie was conscious and quickly becoming aware that he was in trouble. As he lay on the damp ground, blindfolded and hands tied, his mind struggled to recollect what had happened. What was the last thing he remembered—the car, the dirt road? He knew these men must be henchmen for Tony's bosses.

Bam! A scream! One of the thugs shot Tony once in the shoulder after securing him to the raft with Vernon. The more aggressive vultures had not flown to a tree when the humans had arrived, but now they moved away with squawks and flapping wings. The huge perturbed flock shrieked, squawked, and flew about, generating an eerie, angry, mob-like ruckus.

"Hot damn, did you see that? Those birds are pissed."

"We're messing with their dinner."

Both thugs laughed loudly. One moved to Driggers. "How did one of your detectives know to come here tonight?"

"I don't know, I swear. He's trouble. I tried to—"

Bam! Another scream as the thug shot Driggers in the knee. McKenzie became more focused on the present than on how he had gotten here. One of the men stepped over and pulled the blindfolds off McKenzie and Floyd. Both men leaned over, one face to face with Floyd and one face to face with McKenzie. One placed a nine-millimeter pistol on McKenzie's right knee, and the other put a nine-millimeter on Floyd's right knee.

"Now, gentlemen, we're going to shoot you in each of your joints, one at a time, until you tell us what you know about us and why you're here. You get one chance. You go first—"

Thump! *Thump*! The two men went down like limp sacks. Tony was screaming with pain. Driggers chimed in and held his knee. Edna, still blindfolded, was shivering with fright, unsure what had just happened. She heard the first shot and Tony wailing and the second shot with more screams. She heard the threat to McKenzie and Floyd. She expected another shot, but the sounds and the ensuing confusion did not make sense, made her mind frantic with anticipated fear and quickly engulfed her in a wave of disoriented anxiety. She screamed.

Eddie's tree limb had been broken by the second whack, but it had served his immediate need. He grabbed the guns from the two unconscious thugs. He quickly freed Floyd, McKenzie, and Edna. Eddie and Floyd pulled the thugs to nearby trees and handcuffed the men with their arms above their heads and around a tree. They found two more guns in ankle holsters. Eddie picked up two pieces of deer hide and stuffed it in their mouths.

Floyd checked Tony's gunshot wound. The bullet had bored a clean hole through the shoulder. He ripped off a shirt from one of the thugs and dressed the wound. They retied Tony's hands to the raft anyway. McKenzie was sore and dizzy, but capable to help do what was needed. With Driggers's own handcuffs, McKenzie cuffed one bloody hand to Tony's ankle. He pulled Driggers's belt off and created a tourniquet above his wounded knee.

"OK, Tony, if you don't want to bleed to death nor have these vultures eat you for dessert, you better hope we get the rest of your buddies, and quick. Now! How many are in the house, how many guys do they have guarding them, and where are they?" McKenzie quizzed with a tight jaw. Through the pain Tony told what he knew.

Eddie was calming Edna. He gave her one of the guns he had taken from the goons. "You stay here and shoot any one of these clowns if he moves. The chamber is loaded, and the safety is off, so be careful."

"Let us go, man, help us," Vernon pleaded.

"Get these fire ants off me, please, man. Come on, I'm dying here, dude!" David pleaded to unsympathetic ears. The vultures hovered and waited their turn.

"Cut these ropes, and we'll go home right now, man!" Harley said with conviction.

Harley and David had seen Eddie coming up behind the thugs. They had been shivering in fear ever since, and wanted out of this swamp and out of Myrtle Beach.

"Quiet," McKenzie growled in a hushed tone. "We'll get to you later. Just lay there and keep your mouth shut!" He had neither the time nor disposition to deal with crap from these idiots.

Floyd, McKenzie, and Eddie checked their weapons and then huddled close to discuss a plan to take out the guards, one at a time, with the least amount of force. With a fear of the obvious danger, Edna stopped them and explained to McKenzie and Eddie how she happened to be here and her faith that help was on the way.

"The backup teams might not get here in time. We need to do something to slow these guys down." Floyd sounded confident, but he was worried.

"Evelyn and Vera will come through. They took the bus and went back to Georgetown to call your backup, Floyd. They can do it, I know they can."

Floyd and McKenzie simultaneously began to calculate the chances for successful delivery of the alarm message to the right person, who would be able to alert the SLED teams, who no doubt were anxiously searching for them now. Eddie stepped in to add his two cents.

"Don't worry, boys, Vera will come through for us. Now, let's go kick some ass!"

Floyd, McKenzie, and Eddie climbed in the truck and drove without lights, following the road to the house. They stopped prior to the last bend in the road and shut off the truck. All three men had grown up hunting and fishing in river swamps like this one. They were at home in this environment, and their enemy was not. The recent downpour from the passing thunderstorms had soaked the woods, leaving the wet leaves and underbrush muted under their steps. The trees were still dripping rain, and a brisk, cool wind suggested more rain was on the way.

As they approached the house, they could see the activity to prepare the limos and the bosses moving quickly onto the porch. The entire group they wanted was about to get away, and if they succeeded, they could easily be absolved of any connection with Tony and his illegal activities. They already had enough evidence on Tony, but an arrest of the entire gang would be legend. More importantly, they hoped this arrest would kill the local corruption beast and would put a halt to mob activity along the Grand Strand.

Floyd, McKenzie, and Eddie could easily see the clearing around the house as they quietly worked their way through the woods on the border of the large yard. As they moved into place, the bosses turned and proceeded down the steps. The guards collected around the vehicles with their automatic weapons drawn. McKenzie, Floyd, and Eddie did not stand a chance. The men climbed in the limos, and the last guard gave a glance down the road to the river.

Chapter 73

～

Evelyn and Vera were focused on the dark, winding road. They were cautious, knowing the dangers McKenzie had already encountered. They were looking with the hope of finding Edna, McKenzie, and Floyd safe and waiting, but the scene of the accident was not how they had left it. They were confused. Floyd's car had been pulled out of the flooded trench, and no one was waiting on the road.

Evelyn slowed the bus and stopped beside the car to check the possibility that one of the injured might still be inside. The trees were dripping rain, and the air was fresh, but as Evelyn peered into the wrecked and abandoned state-owned vehicle, with blood on the dash and a shattered windshield, she smelled trouble. She climbed back into the driver's seat of the bus and pulled the handle to shut the double folding doors. Evelyn sat thinking and watched a silhouetted fox trot across the road and disappear into thick underbrush growing along the ditch bank.

Out of the dark night, bright headlights rounded the sharp curve in the road and blinded Evelyn. The approaching vehicle swerved in an effort to stop before hitting this unexpected roadblock. The first limo crunched into the front of the bus, and a moment later, the first was rear-ended by the second limo. All occupants were stunned, steam emerged from radiators, and an owl hooted somewhere in the swamp.

Bodyguards gathered themselves after the impact and quickly emerged, checking their perimeter. No evidence of a trap or ambush was obvious, but these men were paid to be vigilant. They were suspicious of what they could see, and they did not trust what they could not; right now they were all on high alert.

With experienced stealth, Eddie, McKenzie, and Floyd had been following the limo taillights. Their eyes had become accustomed to the dark and were helped by the occasional dim, blue glow of moonlight peeking between the thinning, scattered storm clouds. The red taillights had intensified, signaling a sudden, hard, braking action, and then the car stopped. Floyd stopped the truck, and they listened.

McKenzie and Floyd needed to delay this gang until the SLED cavalry arrived. If they could immobilize the limos, this group would be arrested and found guilty through association. If the group got back to the highway, this little river-trip vacation was a nonevent, and arrest with a conviction would be difficult.

Frank emerged with the goons, who quickly surrounded the bus with guns drawn, safeties off, and ready to rumble. The bosses remained in the bulletproof limos and had taken the unusual step of quietly drawing their own guns. Frank's reaction was programmed. Even at his age, he knew the job; it was difficult to forget.

Frank recognized the vehicle immediately. Evelyn turned on the interior light. She and Vera were up, moving about attending to their elderly passengers as the first bodyguard climbed in through the rear emergency door, gun drawn and ready. Ms. Thelma and Ms. Naomi had fallen from their seats, one lying on the legs of the other, neither able to get up. The chocolate cake had fallen on top of the rhubarb pie. The gunman didn't know how to react.

Frank appeared at the front-glassed bifold door and casually slid his gun behind his back, under his jacket, and fit it snugly into the stretch waistband of his pastel slacks. Vera used the driver's door lever to open the way to the passenger stairs for Frank to climb in.

"Oh, Frank, we're so glad you're here," Vera said in her normal, compassionate voice. "We brought all your friends from the home to visit you, and we've just had the worst time. We've all been so concerned."

"Relax, Al, these people are my friends," Frank said softly.

Al shouldered his weapon, helped Ms. Naomi from the floor, and retrieved her purse. She slapped his hand and snatched it away.

Ms. Thelma barked at him, "Don't just stand there; help me up! Where are your manners, young man?" The guard responded as instructed.

Frank was a bit flabbergasted at his friends, who were all dressed like they were going to a Sunday social. As they got resettled in their seats, they simultaneously greeted him and voiced their concerns for his health.

Ms. Thelma and Ms. Naomi pulled their pastries apart.

"Look Frank, I brought your favorite; chocolate cake," Ms. Naomi said proudly.

"I do like chocolate. Thanks Naomi," Frank said as he drifted from his mission for a moment.

"Oh, Frank, looky here, I brought you chocolate-covered rhubarb pie. I know you'll love it. It's something new I made just for you," Ms. Thelma announced with a smile.

He didn't know whether to shout or cry. These kind people, his closest friends, did not understand the danger they were in.

Sam said, "Great, Frank's here. Now we can go eat at Murrells Inlet, get some shrimp and beer."

Frank took control of the situation. His mind was operating in the present, and he knew that the less these people knew, the less danger they would be in. So far they had only seen one guy with a gun, who had already jumped out of the rear door. They had been in a wreck. Frank could say it was his car and a friend from a hunting trip.

He climbed into the driver's seat after asking Al to help him back the bus into the driveway just twenty yards off its rear. The radiator fan had been damaged, and the fan belts loosened. The squealing noise and steam signaled a limited future for the engine if unattended. Frank only needed a few more minutes of power from this wounded vehicular beast. With some effort he backed the bus down the drive to the fish camp and farther from danger.

"Now everyone just sit tight. Let me check on the other car, and I'll be back to help in a moment." Frank would come back. He loved these people. They were his family now.

The limo drivers had checked their vehicles. Both had damaged front ends; the trunk of the first car was crushed forward but appeared drivable.

The leaking gas tank went undetected. The bosses were anxious to move and get the hell out of this swamp. They ordered their men back into the cars.

Eddie and Floyd had flanked the vehicles, hoping to somehow create a further delay. They traveled swiftly and quietly in the rain-soaked woods. They were not sure what had stopped the limos, but their fears were confirmed as they got close enough to see the wreck. As they watched Frank back the van, they both knew they needed to move forward toward the highway and perhaps create another obstacle to the exit. They needed more time. Both men continued through the woods, meeting as planned a couple of hundred yards closer to the highway.

"I crossed a big log just on the other side of the ditch," Floyd reported. "Looks like somebody cut it clean from its stump and moved it out of the road. I think we can move it."

They moved swiftly without further discussion. The fallen tree was twelve inches in diameter, heavy, partially dried out, but not rotted. Whoever had cleared it from the road had removed the upper limbs and left them with a fifteen-foot-long oak pillar. They both grabbed the smaller end and tugged, dragging the log across the road. They raised the log up onto the higher bank, where the road had been cut out of a three-foot rise in the terrain. The log spanned the road as it had when it had first been blown over, lying three feet above the road, wedged against a tree stump on one side and in the ditch on the other. They crept into the woods, thirty yards back on both sides. As prearranged, McKenzie would follow with the truck if he saw the limos move, and they did.

The drivers were focused and cautious, but they had clear orders to "Hurry the hell up." The lead car made the turn traveling at thirty-five miles an hour. The log smashed the driver's side headlight. The log popped up, driven by the unyielding force of the vehicle, and crashed down onto the windshield as the car moved forward, changing its speed from thirty-five to zero in one second. The occupants were not so quick to reduce their momentum. They were vaulted headfirst into various inanimate objects in the vehicle. Moments later they were rammed from the rear. A fire erupted between the limos. A horn was blaring in the night, challenging the frogs for the loudest sound in the woods. Floyd and Eddie watched and waited.

Chapter 74

Harold met the SWAT team helicopter in the Kmart parking lot. He eagerly climbed aboard. The clearing thundercloud would allow them to search the river. Support units were heading north from Charleston and south from Myrtle Beach, and others approached from three smaller towns to the west. When the call had been made, the closest unit was twenty minutes away.

Harold strapped himself in the chopper. Five minutes after becoming airborne, they were hovering high over the house on the river. They saw the cars move fast along the dirt road headed to the highway and then stop too quickly. A decision was required. The only drop zones for the SWAT team were near the house and at the highway; a three-man team was dropped at each.

A disorienting downpour of rain had slowed most of Bo J's trip with the second load of pot, but now he was doing his best to hurry. He was determined to deliver as promised and receive his fully justified reward of respect. He had done more to help with Tony's profits than any of the guys who just stood around looking tough. Bo J would show them how valuable he was. He was a "connection," not just a bouncer, not just a bathroom attendant. He would deliver despite the police surveillance. Now that was the sign of a pro, he thought.

As Bo J eased the boat past the bridge pilings under Highway 17, he knew another two miles of river would put him at the house. He could hear sirens in the distance, but he was unconcerned with these remote alarms. The boundaries of the river and the darkness of the swamp cloaked him from detection by anyone on the highway. The rain had subsided, allowing him to use the river current to his advantage, and he picked up speed to quickly cover the distance remaining.

Bo J's confidence collapsed when he saw the military-style helicopter hovering near the approach road and then over the house. He heard more sirens, but this time the sounds were coming from the north. Bo J quickly interpreted their intent. He guided his boat toward the bank on the opposite side of the river from the house, sliding under the cover of overhanging tree branches.

Sirens were louder now, ubiquitous and echoing to all corners of the swamp. The whining horns and chirps were everywhere. Bo J floated to a spot in the river directly across from the house, just as the SWAT team helicopter dangled thick ropes and dropped a team onto the clearing in the side yard. Bo J silently eased on down the river with his boatload of pot. He did not look back.

Eddie and Floyd moved to the road and met McKenzie at the truck, where he provided the rear guard. SLED agents converged from all directions on the wrecked limos.

Edna sat in the dark with a gun she was unsure how to use, watching a group of seriously injured men in various states of bondage, and she was frightened. She had watched the morbid dance of the vultures, a dance undeterred and unconcerned with activities elsewhere in the swamp. Dinnertime was near. She sat silently, guarding, watching the birds fly in one by one, hopping closer, soliciting shouts from Vernon, Harley, and David. She sat and watched, almost feeling like one of the black vultures that had refused to leave.

She heard all the sounds echoing through the swamp. She heard the crash, the owl hooting, the second crash, the horn, and finally the helicopter and the sirens, providing some easing of the tension that was becoming unbearable. She watched the silent silhouette of a man in a boat drift silently down the river, apparently uninterested in and oblivious to all the noise and disturbance so unusual to this tranquil watershed. She did nothing to interfere with the surreal, morbid scene that played out in front of her. What could she do? One of the wounded screamed from the pain of biting fire ants. Her life was no longer boring repetition.

Ten minutes after the helicopter and the sirens, McKenzie came driving to the clearing to relieve Edna. More SLED agents followed. Frank decided to stay in the bus, protecting his friends, ensuring they would be able to get back to the home. Evelyn helped settle the elderly group, calming their fears, promising they would have dinner in Murrells Inlet as soon as the road was clear. Eddie joined Vera in the bus; each had some explaining to do. Eddie drove the bus slowly back to Georgetown.

Floyd directed the arrest and cleanup operations. The SLED helicopter returned Harold to an admiring crowd in the Kmart parking lot. After thanking the pilot and waving good-bye, he called the Kmart service center mechanic for some after-hours repair on the retirement-home bus. While the group waited for their ride, they all walked across the Kmart parking lot to the Krispy Kreme for coffee and doughnuts. Later they would have fried shrimp, deviled crab, hush puppies, slaw, and green beans for dinner at Lee's Kitchen in Murrells Inlet, on their favorite turf.

Epilogue

~

The mob bosses went to jail. The first round of charges leading to incarcerations was based on drug trafficking, conspiracy, kidnapping, and attempted murder. Other charges would come as investigations continued. This one enormously effective arrest brought down not only the local mob affiliate's illegal gambling and drug trafficking, but it also brought down a significant amount of crime family activity in Chicago, New York, Miami, and their major connections on the East Coast. Floyd was promoted and received national law-enforcement recognition.

Three years later, in Williamsburg County on the banks of the Black River, all was ready for a Thanksgiving feast.

"Skeeter, why don't you put the dogs in their pen? I see a car coming, must be the gang." RayRay pulled a cold six-pack of beer from the fridge and walked down the steps of his new river house nestled deep in the Black River cypress swamp. The high bank presiding over a wide curve in the river was a perfect spot for a home with a view. A large Cadillac SUV, with the horn honking, pulled up to the house. Bo Jr. stepped out from the driver's side, shook Skeeter's hand, and walked around to open the passenger door. Tina jumped to the ground, gave Bo Jr. a kiss, and grabbed two cold ones from RayRay. Ophelia opened the rear door and struggled to maintain her dignity as she stepped out in her Bette Davis heels and short, tight, red-sequined dress. Darrell Jr. removed his signature Happy Snapper rubber mask and velvet handcuffs and obediently followed behind her.

"Welcome, comrades, welcome. Have a beer." RayRay peeled off two more and tossed them to Darrell Jr., who popped the tops and gave one to Ophelia. The group moved to a screened barbeque shed and sat around a wooden picnic table.

"Boss, the barbeque turkey is ready, so I'm going to get the oysters steamed up, and we can eat," Skeeter informed with pride.

"Well, all righty then. Y'all ready to eat?"

"Bo Jr. is always ready to eat," chided Tina and gave his belly a hug.

"RayRay, after dinner we need to talk. Got a proposition for you."

"Oh yeah, that's great. But first let's enjoy this feast while it's hot, and then we can talk some business." RayRay smiled and passed a joint as an appetizer. Skeeter mixed up some of his secret hot sauce for oyster dipping. Darrell Jr. opened a box of One-Eyed Flounder oyster knives and passed them around.

They finished two more six-packs, and the meal was a success. Skeeter brought down a cooler full of beer and ice to lubricate the after-dinner discussion.

"How are those trailer parks doing for you, Bo Jr.?"

"Great. I just picked up two more parks up in North Myrtle Beach. Those things are like a twenty-four-hour cash machine, man. If you have the cash money to buy them, with like no mortgage, they just keep paying you back. Ya know what I'm saying?" Bo Jr. got up and dumped a bucket of opened oyster shells over the bank and into the river. "That stake from the lost boat of pot got it all started. After the first one, it's all been gravy, and now that my parole is up, I'm free to move on."

"Free? What do you mean, buddy, you've been free?"

"Yeah, but NASCAR don't see it that way. Not if you want to buy a car franchise. They want all that arrest and parole stuff gone, dude."

Darrell Jr. was massaging Ophelia's shoulders.

"Do what? What the hell you talking about, NASCAR?" RayRay took another toke of a new dessert joint and passed it to Tina.

"NASCAR, man, that's what I'm talking about. You interested? This is the big time, brother." Bo Jr. stared into RayRay's eyes. He was no longer intimidated by anyone. He saw RayRay as family and as a business partner. Three years of working together had proven the relationship.

"How the hell you gonna afford one of those franchises, man? That's a lot of cash and a lot of recurring investment. You ain't got pockets that deep." RayRay walked over and looked at the river. He was thinking of how things in the world come around in a circle. NASCAR roots were with the old liquor runners who learned to drive country dirt roads with hot cars. Some of the greats were from around these parts. Now their descendants, who were still essentially in the same business, might have a car in the race.

"That's why I'm talking to you, brother. Oh, we got another partner in this thing too."

"Yeah, who?"

"Darrell Jr. and Ophelia." The couple smiled when Bo Jr. announced their connection.

"That's right, RayRay. You ain't the only one that's got some cash to launder." Ophelia took a long slug of her beer.

"What kind of money you talking about throwing around, Ophelia?"

"Since Darrell Jr. and I bought the Happy Snapper, we have picked up a couple of the other strip joints that Tony had. It's amazing how much cash goes through a place like that, especially when the mob ain't taking a cut. But we need to shelter a little cash, if you know what I mean, and I think you do."

"What's Darrell Sr. got to say about all that?"

Darrell Jr. finally weighed in. "We agreed to put a One-Eyed Flounder gift shop in each Happy Snapper, and he gets a cut. He's happy. We've got a whole new line of coconut tits and fluorescent dildos with "Myrtle Beach" stenciled on the side. They're big sellers. He's happy."

The partnership was developed, and the car was named for the strip joint, the only partner who cared for publicity. The Happy Snapper and One-Eyed Flounder car, number thirteen, became a well-known Southern favorite. Their pit crew was an all-girl team that dressed for each race in white sheer tutus, florescent pink thongs, matching thin, mesh tank tops, and white stiletto heels. Their pit times were slow, but few cared. They had the most popular car on the circuit. NASCAR did not object, and the crowds grew.

Tina downed her third tequila shot and turned up the Lynyrd Skynyrd tune on her boom box. She thought that all of this business talk was bringing down the party, and someone needed to change directions. She stepped up on the picnic table and started to dance, bringing hoots and shouts from the crowd. She was proud of her body and didn't mind showing off to help crank the party up. She seductively removed her top, and a party got started deep in the swamp.

Lust and pride create a perilous path

Vernon, Harley, and David sat in the prison cafeteria eating thinly sliced processed turkey, canned cranberry jell, canned string beans, and some kind of turkey helper stuffing with no gravy. David still wore sunglasses to help protect his eyes. The partial eyelids not eaten by the crabs did not allow him to blink. He took it in stride and mimicked Stevie Wonder occasionally, but he was not a singer.

Driggers limped over and asked, "Can I please sit with you guys?" He cowered and continuously scanned in all directions. He was a scared man.

"I don't know, Driggers. What have you done for us today? Why should we let you sit with us?" Vernon had not forgotten Driggers's role in his painful introduction to the mob, but Vernon was Driggers's best friend in the joint.

"Because you boys are my only hope. These convicts are going to kill me, I know it."

"What makes you so sure we're not part of the plot?" Vernon raised his hand with a plastic knife ready to jab, but only laughed and went back to his canned meal.

Driggers shielded his head with his hands to ward off the blow that never came. "Please, you gotta help me."

"No, we don't." David looked at him and raised his glasses to reveal a hideous eye.

"Yeah, dude. We ain't gonna help you. Maybe we'll help you like you helped us." All three laughed, and Driggers dropped his head and tried to eat. Other inmates just stared at him and occasionally pointed for intimidation. It had been three hard years.

The morning after Thanksgiving, the guards found Driggers dead in his cell with a meat thermometer sticking in his ear.

God's swift sword strikes with wrath
Divests the indifferent
And plows justice a path

Murph and Booney held their traditional Thanksgiving lunch for employees at the Frisky Rabbit. Frankie showed up. He had been helping clean the place during the off-hours.

"Frankie, buddy, how are you doing? Come on, let's eat some turkey," Murph offered. "A growing boy like you needs all he can eat."

"Already ate at home with my folks, but I could eat some pie."

"How's school going this year, bud?"

"Great." He gobbled a quarter of a pumpkin pie covered with whipped cream.

"What about college? Gonna be able to pull that off?"

"Yeah, no sweat. Going to Coastal Carolina in Conway. Already paid for it, a couple of years ago." He stuffed in another mouth full of pie.

"Do what? How did you do that?" Booney jumped in, amazed at this kid. "You mean you paid for your first year, right?"

"Nope, did a little deal, and it's all paid for, all four years. Even got a little pocket money." He took another bite. "I've been working two or three jobs, always got something going."

"Yeah, I know you got things going. Just don't tell us. Good for you. Just watch yourself, don't get greedy, and things will work out."

After Frankie turned eighteen, he helped manage the Frisky Rabbit. He studied marketing and finance in college and became a banker and investment manager. Frankie knew where the money went in Myrtle Beach. He knew the secrets. Soon Frankie had pieces of turf all over town.

Booney and Murph put forward the highest bid for the Blue House at state auction. They kept the Frisky Rabbit because, after all, it was the Frisky Rabbit. It was the place to be for summer workers, and it provided a respectable income. They put pool tables, foosball tables, and big-screen TVs in the gambling room of the Blue House and kept the restaurant and upscale bar. They hired a chef from a famous Charleston restaurant, and their business moved up a social notch.

As their customers aged, they moved from the Frisky Rabbit to the Blue House. They kept the private club open for members only. They still opened on Sunday for bingo. Eddie and Vera continued to bring a bus full of elderly citizens each week to the event. Booney's and Murph's new motto was "Customers for life."

Diligence and patience reap as they sow

Vera was putting the final decorative touches on the dining-room table. She looked out at two canoes floating down the river. She heard a car pull into the yard and the engine shut off. "Eddie, they're here."

"Be there in a second."

Vera wiped her hands on her apron and checked her always-perfect hair in a hall mirror. She opened the front door as Evelyn and Guido stepped on the porch.

"Oh, I'm so glad to see y'all. Come on in." They hugged Vera as Eddie stepped to the door.

"Guido, how are you?" They shared a firm handshake and pats on the back.

Vera stepped toward the car. "Edna, do you need some help, honey?"

"No, Vera. This baby seat is a little tricky. It'll just take a minute."

"Here, let me get him." McKenzie reached in from the opposite door and struggled with the safety latch. "Got it. OK, little buddy, ready to see Aunt Vera?"

Vera stepped quickly to the car. "Oh, let me see Little Mac. I've missed him so much."

"Eddie, the house looks better than ever. Looks like it's keeping you busy." Guido surveyed the improvements to the shrubbery and then noticed a new greenhouse in the side yard. Two new birdhouses sat on the edge of the side porch, ready for paint. "Been fishing lately?"

"Almost every day, Guido. Catch what I need and float the river. It's perfect. How's the best doughnut chef on the Grand Strand doing?"

"Great, thanks. We have a little news, but I'll wait and let Evelyn share it with you."

The group moved inside the yellow house on the Santee River. Vera and Eddie had sold their vacant back lot in Myrtle Beach to a hotel that needed land for a new parking lot and used the money to buy the mob's river house at a state auction. They moved to their new paradise, and Eddie had his solitude.

"Sit down, the turkey is ready. Eddie, help me bring the food in while everyone gets settled."

"I'll help," Evelyn chimed in.

Vera served a lovely Thanksgiving feast with all of the fixings.

The humble and kind have spirits that glow

"Guido, you were saying something about good news. What's up?" Eddie asked.

"I'll let Evelyn tell you."

"You all know that we have both worked at the Krispy Kreme for over three years. We've learned a lot about the business, especially since I became the manager, and we've been looking for something of our own."

She looked around with an excited look, momentarily harboring her secret for a greater impact, but she couldn't wait. McKenzie put his hand on Edna's shoulder and smiled. Little Mac pounded a spoon on his plate.

"Well, last month Mr. Ackerman told us he was going to retire and move to Boone, North Carolina. He told us he planned to sell the KK. So, Guido asked him how much, and to make a long story short...*we bought it!* We're the new owners of the Myrtle Beach Krispy Kreme."

Evelyn bounced in her seat and clapped her hands. Vera got up from her seat and gave her a hug. Guido sat back in his chair with a proud smile. Eddie patted his back and shook his hand. Edna and McKenzie smiled. Little Mac threw his pudding on the floor and waved his hands in the air. No one cared. It was a happy time.

Edna and McKenzie moved into Eddie and Vera's house, a central location at a very reasonable price. Evelyn and Guido rented the garage apartment next door. They were the next generation, with a different baseline of expectations for the beach paradise. They had learned to live with the proliferation of beach family variety stores that drew tourist customers with window advertisements for Asian-throwing knives, tattoos, Confederate flags, and camouflaged print bikinis.

Another summer season at the beach was over, and the summer workers were gone. They went back to school or back home to hourly wage jobs in department stores, grocery stores, or construction labor. None of these jobs would compare to their jobs at the beach in the summer. The excitement, the nights, the experience, and the memories were all the things that would bring them back every summer for vacation, introducing the next generation to their own interpretation of a resort paradise. The scam artists came and went, but the game was always the same: taking the money the tourists were so eager to give. The hotels changed names. The restaurants and bars changed. Putt-Putt parks were built, remodeled, and abandoned like the structures of ancient societies. But the tourists still came, with the same desires.

On most mornings Guido, Evelyn, Edna, and McKenzie met on the beach for a short walk while enjoying coffee and Krispy Kremes.

The Surf was the same, but the Turf had changed.

True love and good family temper the sins,
Bring forward the young, teach the lessons again.
Within a happy heart, envy has no hold
Greed can gain no place in the satisfied soul.

—The End—

Made in the USA
Lexington, KY
12 September 2014